G000162507

Sean McCaffery

You Are

Totally Screwed

Sean McCaffery You Are Totally Screwed

Copyright © 2016 Stephen Hunt

Published by Yellow Dot Publications

First Canadian Edition

Sean McCaffery You Are Totally Screwed

is a work of fiction. Any resemblance of characters in this novel to real people alive or dead is coincidental.

Yellow Dot Publications

3272 Randy Clark Rd.

Battersea

Ontario

Canada K0H 1H0

ISBN: 978-0-9947463-1-3

For Ned

Book One

Do not withhold discipline from a child; if you punish him with the rod, he will not die. Punish him with the rod and save his soul from death.

Proverbs 23:13 -14

The little boy on the top of the trunk gave a violent sneeze.

'Halloa, sir!' growled the schoolmaster, turning round. 'What's that, sir?'

'Nothing, please sir,' replied the little boy.

'Nothing, sir!' exclaimed Mr Squeers.

'Please sir, I sneezed,' rejoined the boy, trembling till the little trunk shook under him.

'Oh! sneezed, did you?' retorted Mr Squeers. 'Then what did you say "nothing" for, sir?'

In default of a better answer to this question, the little boy screwed a couple of knuckles into each of his eyes and began to cry, wherefore Mr Squeers knocked him off the trunk with a blow on one side of the face, and knocked him on again with a blow on the other.

'Wait till I get you down into Yorkshire, my young gentleman,' said Mr Squeers, 'and then I'll give you the rest.'

Charles Dickens, Nicholas Nickleby

Prologue

They found the frog in Cack Alley. Flint pulled it from a broken drain pipe that dripped filth into a stagnant pool. The frog was green with flecks of sewery brown, a bloated thing that filled Flint's palm. When it tried to jump away Flint caught it by the hind leg so that it stretched like a rubber toy. Flint thought this was hilarious, and he grabbed one of its front legs too, pulling out the body to its full length and then squishing it back again, making wet sounds with his lips as if playing a farting accordion.

Sean thought it funny at first, and laughed along with Flint. Toys were scarce at home, so the frog was a fascination. But Sean lacked the natural cruelty of six year olds, and something changed as he watched the frog struggling in Flint's grip. It wasn't ugly any more. It was a harmless thing. He sensed its pain and fear as it tried to escape the giant hands that wrenched and tore and twisted. A slushy stirring began in Sean's stomach.

He asked Flint to let the frog go. OK, said Flint, smiling, then he swung the frog by the back legs as hard as he could against a rock. The frog burst. Wormy entrails splashed from its belly. But it didn't

1

die right away. It limped from the rock trailing its intestines behind it as Sean watched helplessly, wanting it to be whole again, wanting his mum to come and make it better, but knowing that there was nothing anyone could do.

The frog stopped crawling, its guts caught on a stick. It opened its mouth as if to cry out, but instead its tongue uncoiled from the wreckage of its head and hung there dripping slime. At that, all the colour in Sean's world drained into a white whorl and he threw up uncontrollably as Flint laughed and laughed.

Sean hated Flint then and swore he'd never play with him again.

Never!

CHAPTER 1: Bleeding Mental

"Get down you daft bugger before you break your stupid neck!"

Flint was up the lamp post, dangling thirty feet above the pavement where Sean's grandmother stood cursing him for the stupid sod that he was. The lamp post stood outside Sean's house, its black paint pocked with rust. To Sean's eye it looked diseased, like everything else in this shitty town. The UK Clean Air Act had been passed in 1956, the year Sean was born, but thirteen years later word still hadn't reached Duggin, where factory chimneys and terraces of coal-fired slums weighted the air with lung-searing soot.

Flint was fifteen, two years Sean's senior, and right now was just one slip away from getting no older. He swung back and forth, hands gripping the narrow cross-bar that jutted at right angles from the lamp post. The bar flexed under the weight of Flint's wiry frame as he pulled monkey faces and jabbered like a chimp.

"You're not right in the bloody head you're not. Come down here now before I come up and fetch you, you stupid get."

Sean's grandmother could no more climb the lamp post than she could turn cartwheels, but Sean, looking into that brick face, could just imagine her giving it a go, hitching up her sack of a skirt and treating the neighbours to a view of her terrible behind as she

3

followed Flint up the pole. He almost laughed, but the smile died on his face as Flint dropped one hand from the bar to scratch his arse, baboon-like, as he held onto life by a single spindly arm.

Fear flared in his gran's eyes and a horrible anxiety mushroomed in Sean's guts as he thought of what might happen next – what he might be forced to see.

"Leave him be Gran. Let's go inside. It's up to him if he wants to kill himself."

Sean had meant to sound casual, but the tremor in his voice gave him away. Flint stopped his chattering and looked down at Sean, lips spreading in a malicious grin. He began to swing, higher and higher, back and forth, letting go with one hand and then the other, each sweep of his scrawny body raising the tide of nausea in Sean's belly. It was a display of agility and madness; a circus stunt without a safety net.

Flint flipped his body to bring his legs up and over the bar so that he hung upside down, the crosspiece behind his knees. He was loving this, feeding on the terror in the two faces below. Pushing it further, he released his hands from the bar and stretched both arms down toward the ground as if intent on diving head first into the pavement, cheating himself deliberately of any last-chance grasp at safety.

Sean was on the verge of panic. He didn't care if Flint died. After all, he hardly knew him. They lived just doors apart on the same street, but their worlds never touched. Sean was a Grammar School boy and Flint was this weird kid from the Secondary Modern with the slab-faced parents who seemed never to let him out of the house. If Sean were to hear second-hand that Jimmy Flint had died, even by splattering himself with a fall from this very lamp post, it would have been more a cause for curiosity than regret. But *seeing*

4

Flint die - that would be something different. Watching the life ebb from a twitching, crippled body would be more than Sean could bear.

He'd had this horror ever since Flint had killed the frog all those years ago. He'd avoided Flint after that, had never played with him again, so he'd hardly noticed as Flint's appearances on the streets became fewer and fewer.

Now that Flint was in the Secondary Modern, and Sean had entered the Grammar, there was no reason why they should ever have any contact. But Flint's influence was still there. The experience with the frog had left him with a morbid fear of violence. Watching Flint hanging from the lamp post, Sean could almost feel knee caps bursting from splintered legs, ribs shattering against the pavement, the splat of face on concrete and the snap of tooth on stone.

"Come on Gran, let's go," he pleaded.

"Alright, our Sean, maybe your right. Let's leave him be."

Sean's gran had figured it out. The mad kid up there was playing for attention. If they left, maybe he'd give it up and come down. Ignoring him might actually save the stupid bastard's life. She nudged Sean towards home. But as they stepped away from the lamp post Flint let out a scream that sent her lunging back with arms spread wide, colliding with Sean as he buried his face in the woolly expanse of her cardigan.

Flint cut short the scream and burst out laughing. He'd got them going with that alright, and now the old cow was dickering about down there like she might try catching him, the dozy bitch. Time for even more fun. He reached up, gripping the cross bar with both hands, arched his body, still upside down, and hooked his feet over the thin metal rod. Then, loosening his grip, he unfolded himself to

5

hang bat-like by the toes, his only support a single hand gripping the upright of the lamp post. It looked impossible. Sean felt his balls shrink as Flint hung there, taut and concentrated, not grinning now, knowing that with this stunt he was laying all his cards on the table. Sean's gran crossed herself as she watched Flint holding onto his life by his boots. "Jesus, Mary and Joseph," was all she said, and that in a whisper.

And then he dropped. Sean flinched away as real fear flashed in Flint's face. He buried himself against his grandmother's bulk as Flint swung sideways and grabbed desperately for the upright with his free hand. Sean cringed, waiting for the thud and splatter, but a different sound caused him to turn, to see Flint hit the pavement on his feet and sprint unharmed towards his house. He couldn't believe it, but there was Flint in full flight, clearing the gate with a running leap. He grabbed at the lip of the concrete porch above his front door, swung himself up, and within seconds was reaching for the wooden sill of his open bedroom window. Like a rat to its hole he was through to safety just as the car nosed its way around the entrance to the cul-de-sac.

Sean hadn't heard the car approaching even though it was the only one in the neighbourhood, a pale blue Ford Anglia just like the coppers used on Z-Cars. Only the Flints had a car, and Jimmy Flint's ears, tuned for survival, could detect the sound of it from miles away.

The car moved slowly down the middle of the street, passing in state before the terraces on either side as Vinny and Elsie Flint paraded their superiority: he squat and heavy in the driver's seat, she next to him, narrow and gimlet sharp. A hammer and a chisel.

The car stopped outside Flint's gate, halfway between the entrance to the street and the dead end where the pedestrian entrance to Cack Alley was the only exit. Vinny Flint opened the driver's door, letting out a cloud of smoke from a stubby cigar, aware of Sean and his Gran under the lamp post, and barely controlling a smug twist of his lips.

He went into his ritual, first opening the boot to remove two wooden ramps and placing them against the kerb in front of his chain-link fence. He detached the padlock and swung the gate out across the pavement, returned to the driver's seat and inched the car over the ramps and onto the concrete slabs that were the tombstones of a former garden. He cut the engine, got out and refixed the padlock to the gate. He opened the door for Elsie Flint, waited until she emerged, then slammed it shut to draw the attention of any neighbour who might have missed the show.

Vinny Flint paused by the car for a while, one hand on the shining chrome of the rear fins, the other cradling his cigar, a full inch thick. He looked up and down the street at nothing, then passed under the porch that his mad son had climbed just seconds before, leaving the car to obscure the entire front window of the house.

"God made 'em and the Devil paired 'em," said Sean's gran, her face a mask of contempt. "Just look at the state of 'em would you - Lord and Lady Muck, driving around town as if they own the bloody place. And cigars! Who the hell does he think he is? Wins a few quid on the Pools and acts like he's Winston Bloody Churchill."

Sean's gran rummaged in her purse and brought out a pack of Woodbines, lighting up as she leaned against the lamp post.

Sean had detached himself from her and recovered some composure, but his voice still shook. "Two thousand quid, Gran. That's more than a year's wages at the DIC."

"Maybe. But folks with brass should look after their own. Why don't they buy some proper clobber for that lad of theirs and give him a decent feed? The poor bugger looks half starved. A good plate of Irish Stew might be all it'd take to sort him out."

"Calm him or kill him, eh Gran? Especially your Irish Stew."

"Cheeky bugger," she said, cuffing Sean gently with the back of her hand.

But then she turned serious, looking hard into Sean's face. "I suppose it's no wonder the lad's the way he is with parents like that, but I'm warning you our Sean, you stay away from him. Mark my words, that young Flint will come to a bad end one of these days, and you don't want to be around when he does."

"Not much chance of that Gran," said Sean, thinking of the Grammar School, then university, and his plans to leave Duggin, and the likes of Flint, far, far behind him.

But there Sean was wrong.

Dead wrong.

CHAPTER 2: DIC-Heads

The birds woke him at dawn, the twittering of some insomniac sparrow starting off the whole damned chorus.

Bollocks! thought Sean. Why the bloody hell do the sodding sparrows have to start that bleeding racket on the first day of frigging school? And why do they sound so fucking cheerful? What does living in the eavestroughs of a Duggin slum give them anything to be sodding cheerful about?

He turned over and crunched the ratty pillow against his ears, but the birdsong had an infuriating penetration. What's wrong with the damned things, he thought, are they mental or something? Why don't they fly off to somewhere decent - they have wings don't they? They could live anywhere. Why choose Duggin? Why choose Lancashire for that matter? Do they actually like the shit and the stench? No, not even a retarded sparrow would choose to live here. My God, I'm living with the derelicts of the sparrow world, he thought, just like I'm living among the dregs of humanity.

It was a really bad way to begin the day.

He uncrunched the pillow and stared at the ceiling two feet above the top bunk bed where he lay. Where would I fly to if I were a bird? he thought..... Anywhere.....anywhere except stinking, putrid, bleeding Duggin!

Well, just a few more years to put up with it. He was almost fourteen now, and if he played his cards right just four more years and he'd be out of this shit-hole and starting at some university as far away from Duggin as he could get. Where would that be, he wondered - Southampton? Sussex? Exeter? He didn't even consider the northern universities – Leeds, Newcastle, Glasgow – God help us, not Glasgow! No, the South was the place for him. The South where he'd never been. He'd never been to Glasgow either, but his vision of the South included everything that Duggin lacked: clean air, tree-lined streets, open spaces that weren't littered with garbage and, most important, people he might actually like.

He'd seen them on *University Challenge*; cynical students with hanging hair and wire-framed glasses. They'd smirk at Bamber Gasgoigne - cool counterpoints to his shirt and tie respectability. Every week there'd be a John Lennon oozing self-confident contempt, and a Cher, or a Dusty Springfield half-dressed in colours almost vibrant enough to burst across the screen of the black and white TV. He even admired the Huberts and Wilhemina's from Oxbridge with their snotty superiority and strangled accents. At least they didn't sound like the ee-by-gumming-sheep-shagging half-wits of Duggin.

And he was just as clever as they were. He pressed his own mental buzzer each time Bamber asked a Starter for Ten, and more often than not he beat the students to the answers. His mother would sit there saying "Clever Lad", and even his father was impressed enough not to tell him to shut up. It was about the only

10

time that miserable bastard allowed him an uninvited word. After all, University Challenge was Heducational with a capital H - not like that bloody Monty Python rubbish.

And just think.....if he was brighter than all those students at thirteen, imagine what he could achieve when it was his turn to leave school? Oh my God! To leave school, and wash the dirt from his feet as he boarded the train for Liverpool, and push on from there to some university in the South where he could finally become himself.

Every hour there'd be a train leaving for Runcorn-Crewe-Birmingham and London Euston with connections in between to Peterborough and Norwich, or Taunton, Exeter, Newquay and St. Ives. There was even a boat train to Harwich and the Continent. And if you landed in London you could get absolutely anywhere..... anywhere in the whole world! The announcer at Lime Street Station promised a deliverance more compelling than anything the Catholics could ever concoct, but Sean prayed to God anyway. Just let me get the hell out of Duggin and escape at last to live among people with ideas and energy and enthusiasm for something other than the few paltry quid doled out in the weekly wage packet from the DIC.

The DIC - God, how he hated that place! The Duggin Insulated Cables. The DIC where all the Duggin DIC-Heads worked. The factory that sprawled across the town like a putrefying fungus, poisoning the air, the body and the spirit. The factory where his dad slogged away at 8 hour shifts day in and day out, and double shifts back to back when he could get the over-time. And all so that he could bring home the pittance that kept the whole teaming McCaffery clan on the brink of absolute poverty.

11

He lay there and thought of his father - Patrick McCaffery - the man who couldn't keep it in his pants. Patrick McCaffery, forty years old and already saddled with seven bloody kids. Seven of them, and still he was shameless enough to show his face in public!

It had been a terrible day when he'd first found out where all those babies came from. Roger Healey had told him, and Roger Healey was two years older and had sworn he knew all about it. He'd explained it in graphic detail. The man got on top of his wife and jammed his dick up her minge. If he left it in for five minutes she'd get a baby. If he left it in for ten she'd get twins.

Sean had been overwhelmed with disgust. The thought of his parents doing something like that shattered a vital belief in their decency. But Roger Healey had sworn on the Bible it was true. They called it shagging and he claimed he'd even seen photos. But that was clearly impossible – who would ever allow themselves to be photographed showing their privates? It was vile beyond imagining! But Roger Healey was sure of his facts, so sure that he was intent on stabbing his dad the first chance he got.

Sean had learned a little bit more about sex since then, but none of it had been good. He knew now that you didn't get a baby every time you did it, but that made things worse. That meant his dad might have forced his mum to do it ten times, or twenty times, or even a hundred times, the filthy bastard. The idea that his mum might be a willing partner never entered his head, the whole thing was so foul. His dad was the one behind it, he was certain of that.

And as time went on, and Sean paid more attention to the rumpus in his parents' bedroom at night, and as the babies kept coming, he began to feel more and more that Roger Healey had been absolutely right about his stabbing ambitions, even though those had come to nothing, and now, at sixteen, Roger Healy had a kid of his own.

Sean didn't understand it - how could people go around showing off their kids when everyone knew that kids came from doing disgusting things with your genitals? By rights, every couple pushing a pram should be crimson with shame. And as for his own father, how could he get up to stuff like that and still go to Church every Sunday like there was nothing wrong with him? Sean suspected that his friends with smaller families thought the same thing, and looked down on him and all the McCafferys from the heights of moral superiority. Thank God for his friend Bill O'Rourke who was one of nine - his dad must be the dirtiest bugger on the planet.

He heard his mother move from bedroom to toilet to bathroom and then down the stairs, creeping along so that she wouldn't wake the kids. A softness tempered his discontent before it flared back to life. She was giving herself the only time of day when she could be properly alone. In another hour there would be bedlam, as everyone fought for the toilet, the sink and a place at the table, while she nursed the baby and tried at the same time to make sure that everyone had some type of clothes on their back and at least a mouthful of breakfast before being packed off to wherever they were going.

Sean threw back the old sleeping bag from his bunk. He and his three brothers slept together in the tiny bedroom, and each morning their vapours displaced the air with a smog that stuck in Sean's throat like someone else's phlegm. He leapt out of his bunk, feet crashing to the linoleum floor, and pounded across the room to fling open the window.

Another dawn chorus began.

13

"Shut those bloody curtains!" Colin, eighteen, eldest of the kids, and by far the smelliest person in the world.

"Get rid of that light!" Fergus, sixteen, brilliant, bitter and twisted.

"Shut up, I'm trying to sleep." Keiran, twelve and irrelevant.

Sean left the curtains and window as they were, and trudged in his pajamas to the toilet. At least being first up meant he was also first to empty his bladder. Very soon the toilet would be a no-go area after a full scale onslaught by the other boys. God help the poor sod who had to follow Colin! He was amazed that the porcelain hadn't crumbled to rubble under the influence of the vile stuff that came from that filthy bugger's dick.

He went next door to the bathroom and washed his hands and face, the first to use the face cloth, the towel and the toothbrush. Last out of bed and he'd have been rinsing snot out of all three. Most of the Grammar School kids wouldn't have believed that he didn't have his own toothbrush, even if he'd been mad enough to tell them. They thought that *In My Liverpool Home* was just a folk-song – the over-privileged bastards. He descended the narrow stairs to the front room where the source of his foul temper, and his dread of the first day of a new term, was laid out neatly on the settee.

There they were – the foul fruits of his mother's labour – the symbols of shame he'd take into the new school year. There were new elbow-pads stitched to the arms of the frayed purple blazer; the holes in the seat of his grey pants had been darned with large, black, indestructible stitches, and new cardboard cut-outs had been placed in the soles of his shoes - Cornflakes in one, Rice Crispies in the other.

Marvelous. Just bloody marvelous! He was going to look just bloody marvelous in that lot.

Humiliation ate at him as he changed into his clothes. Today there'd be the usual posturing in the schoolyard, the kids showing off their leather-soled Ox-Blood Comos, wide cut pants, and Ben Sherman shirts, each trying to outdo the other while he slunk in the background with his ragged arse and his Kellog's box insoles. Thank God it was a boy's school - he'd rather cut his own throat than face girls dressed like that. He pushed open the kitchen door and sat at the table, glaring at his mother without a word.

She was standing by the stove toasting mounds of Wonderbread for breakfast. She was a handsome woman of thirty eight, and her seven kids had yet to turn her black hair grey. But Sean was working on that. He knew it wasn't her fault that he was dressed in shabby hand-me-downs, or that the table and chairs were Salvation Army Specials, but he blamed her anyway.

She smiled at him bravely. "So, the first day back at school."

"Yeah, can't you tell by the new clothes?"

A shadow crossed her face. Sean felt a stab of remorse, but his expression didn't change.

"Are the others up?" she asked.

"I don't know. They smelled like they were dead but I didn't check. If Fergus has snuffed it can I have his new shirt?"

"Don't talk like that Sean, you know it's the best I can manage." She sounded weary and apologetic, but Sean wasn't falling for that trick.

"Maybe if you started working and stopped breeding we'd all manage a bit better."

The words were out of his mouth before he could drag them back. His mother whirled on him and the back of her hand took him full across the face.

"You wouldn't dare speak to me like that if your father were home."

He took the blow in silence, ashamed of himself, but said nothing. He got up from the table and strode towards the door.

"You can't go to school with no breakfast!" she shouted after him.

He turned toward her and saw that the burst of fury had disappeared. Troubled eyes were searching for damage to his face. He wanted to turn back, but a child's pride wouldn't let him.

"See you later," he said, and walked out.

CHAPTER 3: Birds of a Feather

The school bus stop was in the town centre, a mile away from the rougher area where Sean lived. He slouched into the entrance of Cack Alley with head down and hands in pockets. Betty Fairclough, one of the neighbourhood scrubbers, was leaning against the wall. She was eighteen years old and already looked like her mother. Her hair was fresh from bed and a cigarette lolled from a mouth plastered with lipstick. Her dog was taking his morning crap, a wiry terrier squatting right in the middle of the pavement. Betty looked on as if she might have done the same herself had the occasion demanded.

When the dog had finished, she peeled herself from the wall and sauntered out of the alley leaving Sean to negotiate the stinking pile as if she'd placed it there on purpose. The entire alley was like this, a minefield of dog turds, some intact and others scuffed or trodden with a trail of furious smears beyond. God what a place! What a stinking, shitty, horrible place this was! And people like that - how he hated people like that.

Cack Alley led through a tunnel under the railway tracks, onto a rough path through derelict land where scrub and weeds colonized the exposed foundations of industrial buildings long since gone to ruin. Further along, the track was hedged in on either side by

17

hawthorn and elderberry, the rank vegetation interrupted here and there by the crumbling walls of other wrecked buildings. The path was littered with cigarette boxes, newspaper wrappings from the fish and chip shop, plastic bags full of God knows what, and the occasional relic of some encounter between people who couldn't be bothered to find a better place for a shag. Sean knew all about Johnnies, and was right behind the Pope when it came to filthy disgusting things like that.

The alley ended on the main street that ran towards the town centre, emerging through a narrow passage in a wall of small shops - the chippy, a newsagent, and the local Co-op. On the opposite side of the street was one of the entrances to the huge factory that dominated the town.

Sean turned left out of the tunnel towards the town centre, and crossed the road. He walked past the entrance to the DIC with its traffic barriers and glass-fronted sentry box, the little man inside looking important in his uniform as he pressed buttons to make the barriers go up and down. The lorries going in were loaded with copper ingots, and those going out carried massive capstans wound with cables. Beyond the entrance, the factory perimeter stretched for miles, most of it enclosed by spiked metal railings taller than a man, thousands upon thousands of upright spears to keep out the thieving bastards who kept Solly's Scrap Metals in business.

In the distance, peering through the fence, Sean could see his friend Bill O'Rourke waiting to meet him. He was early for school too, and had likely been through the same morning performance. Sean had once read in American Geographic that the best way to avoid being eaten by a bear was to go hiking with someone you could out-run. When it came to poverty, and keeping one foot off the bottom rung of the Grammar School ladder, Bill was Sean's hiking partner.

Bill ignored him as he approached. He seemed absorbed with the scene beyond the open gates of the furnace room – the spurt of orange-green flames as sweaty overalled figures laboured in front of the fires.

"A vision of Hell," he muttered. "Fire... stench..... the damned."

He turned a dirty blond head towards Sean, his big black National Health glasses reflecting the sunlight, and then resumed his scrutiny of the factory. He was a short sombre figure with a face like a welder's mask, his eyes behind the glasses blue, cold and serious.

"Bloody Shithole!" he said.

"You're not so bad yourself," replied Sean.

"The DIC, I meant. Just look at it. What a waste."

Sean gazed at the trailers loaded with logs that served as kindling for the furnace.

"Yeah, the only trees in Duggin and they throw them in the fire. Bleeding typical"

"I was talking about the labourers."

"Them..... who gives a toss about them?"

The DIC smelted copper and turned the ingots into insulated wires. Everything from the tiniest copper threads to the huge cables that carried power on the National Grid started off as the ore that rumbled into Duggin on rail cars. It was a filthy dangerous place. Sean's dad was one of fourteen thousand working there, a wire drawer who tended machines that spun the ingots into thinner and thinner strands, squeezing the metal through ever decreasing dies and then coiling the wire tight on enormous capstans. A snapped cable could slice through flesh and bone, and there were tales of

19

more than one worker who had stumbled too close to the capstans and had been sent home in a bucket.

"That's what you get for being stupid," he thought aloud. Bill gave him a sidelong glance, aware that Sean was in one of those foul moods when he hated everyone and everything.

But it was the DIC that held Sean's focus now, the DIC and its population of drones, marching back and forth at the sound of the factory buzzer. He hated the bloody DIC and everyone in it, hated his father for risking eyes and hands every second of his working day, and all for thirty quid a week. Thirty measly quid! And those morons at the Secondary Modern, aching for their sixteenth birthday and the chance to sign on for life at minimum wage.

Life! What kind of life was that?

"Hey Sean, how does a DIC-Head order four pints of bitter?" Bill's dour expression lightened briefly and he almost smiled.

"Dunno. How does a DIC-Head order four pints of bitter?"

Bill held up the back of his hand, index and little finger extended on each side, the middle two fingers bent in half like stumps.

"No, you got it wrong," said Sean. He held up his hand showing two fingers and two stumps.... then closed one eye.

Bill chuckled mirthlessly, and the two of them continued to gaze into the factory, each lost in his own thoughts.

Despite Sean's rant, he and Bill were lucky. Two years ago they'd passed the 11-Plus exam and won places in Grammar School. The 11-plus was supposed to keep the working class in their place, but a few proles managed to sneak through each year. At the richer schools the kids were taught how to deal with the multiple choice intelligence test that involved no arithmetic, no literacy, and no opportunity to explain why you chose the answer you did. Sean and Bill had figured it out on their own and avoided the failure that would have meant spending the next four years at a Secondary Modern to learn a trade, or just bide time before signing on at the DIC, Fords, or a hundred other sweat-shops where they'd earn a pittance for ever after. Stupid kids with wealthy parents seemed to find a back door into the Grammar School despite failing the exam, but Sean was too far removed from that situation to figure it out.

Meadowlands was the nearest Catholic Grammar to Duggin, three miles away in a swanky area away from the factories. It was run by the Rodriguan Brotherhood whose mission was to beat an education into their pupils with any weapon to hand. Both he and Bill were reminded constantly by their parents, aunts, uncles and every other adult Catholic in Duggin, about how fortunate they were to be going to such a school. It was never said, but the message was clear: buckle down, accept the discipline, get your O levels, and you might not have to work in factories like the DIC.

In the meantime going to the Grammar School didn't alter the fact that neither Sean nor Bill had a proper arse to their pants. Grammar School scholarships paid for their education, but didn't put Grammar School clothes on their backs. They were a shabby pair, a fact often noted by the Brothers in front of their classmates. But the two of them were sharp with an unusual intelligence, and were tolerated because of it.

"Ready for it?" said Sean, turning away from the factory fence.

"I suppose," said Bill.

"Cornflakes and Rice Crispies for me this week, what about you?"

"Coco Pops."

"Coco Pops?..........Coco Bloody Pops! You're getting a bit uppity aren't you?"

"My dad brought home a case of them. Fell off the back of a lorry. They taste like shite but they wear well."

21

"And at least yours match."

Somehow this conversation cheered Sean up.

And then there was Paula Yates to look forward to.

Chapter 4: Beauty and the Beasts

The usual crowd gathered at the bus stop outside the Hope and Anchor. The younger lads in short pants and purple blazers were trying to push each other into the diced carrots outside the front door of the pub, while the sixth formers lounged against the wall with their cigarettes and made comments about the girls walking by.

"I see that Fearon hasn't improved over the summer," said Bill nodding toward a tall sixteen year old with dark curly hair and a smug expression. He was in the centre of a group of other sixth formers showing off their new clothes.

"Just look at the tosser," said Sean "it must be eighty degrees this morning and he's buttoned up in a frigging Crombie."

"Well, he's a Suede Head, isn't he? Has to wear the uniform even if it means getting heat stroke. As if you could mistake him for anything else with that bone-headed caper."

Fearon had separated himself from the group and was performing a rhythmic dance, his Oxford shiners tapping and twirling on the pavement as he whined the words to some moronic Northern Soul ballad. He was a regular at the Wigan Casino All-Nighters where the Mods and Suedes would gather on a Saturday evening and prance about until dawn, but the sight of him cavorting on a Monday morning in his big overcoat was so ridiculous that

Sean and Bill couldn't help bursting into laughter as they approached.

Fearon stopped singing. "Hey lads look, a couple of vagrants in Meadowland blazers. Can't have that can we?"

He twirled with an outstretched foot as Sean and Bill walked by, the toe end of a size ten Oxford taking Bill just under the sternum and sending him hard against the pub wall. The dance went on without missing a beat, Fearon looking prouder than ever.

Sean helped Bill to the steps of the pub where he sat straining for breath.

"One of these days," said Sean glaring hatred. "One of these days that bullying bastard's going to get it."

"Yeah, one of these days," gasped Bill, "but until then I'm keeping out of his way. Christ that hurt!"

"Never mind, here's something that'll cheer you up." Sean nodded towards the corner of the street where a sixth former from the Girls' Grammar had just appeared. "Just look at her Bill – takes your breath away doesn't she?

"Oh, you're so bleeding funny."

But Sean wasn't kidding. He hadn't seen Paula Yates all summer, and now, at the sight of her, Duggin didn't seem such a bad place after all.

Perfection. She was absolute fucking perfection! Red-gold hair trailing down her back, intelligent blue eyes that could stop you in mid-stride, breasts beneath her open blazer pushing hard against the buttons of her blouse. She'd hitched up her skirt to show inches of street thigh before the Convent drag-down, and her long slender legs stirred something deep inside Sean's belly. The feeling had nothing to do with that disgusting business between his mum and dad – this was something as lovely as that other thing was vile. As

24

she drew nearer Sean's blood foamed in his veins and his heart hammered against his chest as if it would leap out at her feet. She was everything he could ever possibly want.

"You're gaping like a moron McCaffery."

Sean snapped his mouth shut, but passion bubbled over into words.

"She's Helen and Galadriel," said Sean. "A Pre-Raphaelite goddess."

Bill smirked. "Yeah, she's a corker all right."

"A corker! Is that all you can say, a corker? She's ....she's...... Oh, had I the heaven's embroidered cloths!"

"A catch-cloth is what you need right now more like it I'd give you a hankie if I could be sure you wouldn't give it back."

"You're disgusting O'Rourke."

"Come off it Sean, you just want to shag her like everyone else. And as for poetry, she wouldn't know W.B. Yeats from Donny Osmond. You'll be blathering on about slaying dragons next."

"And I would. Just for a smile I would. Looks at those lips Bill, wouldn't you risk everything just for a smile?"

Fearon broke the spell.

"Hey lads take a gander at that. It's Ginge the Minge. Let's have all members upstanding."

Fearon's gang burst into laughter. One of them grabbed the inside of his elbow and raised his forearm while making a fist. The others copied him, hooting and gesticulating like a bunch of imbeciles.

Fearon continued. "Have you ever seen a lass fill a uniform like that? Not many of them tits to the pound, I'll bet." He made a groping motion at his crotch. "Hey Ginge, want a soft job? Cop hold of this till it gets hard."

25

Sean watched Paula glide by, shamed as she included him in the scornful glance before continuing on her way to join the other girls at their own bus stop further down the street. He wanted Fearon dead.

"So, you want to slay dragons?" sneered Bill. "Well, go get him Galahad."

It was a joke, but Sean took it to heart. What would Paula think if he gave Fearon the thrashing of his life? Could this be his big chance? He imagined himself grabbing the ignorant prick by his lapels, nutting him hard on the nose, and then beating him to a jelly before he had a chance to react. He measured the distance between them, calculating how fast he could move. He could take him by surprise. Three quick strides and a good solid boot to the bollocks would do it. He imagined Fearon doubled over as he dragged him down the street by that mop of curly hair and flinging him at her feet to apologise.

Bill saw the calculating look on Sean's face. "Go on Sean," he said, "do it. Only the brave deserve the fair."

Adrenalin rushed to the pit of Sean's stomach. Tension built in the muscles of his arms and legs as he weighed his chances. Two seconds and that useless piece of shit could be on his back as the Corn Flakes and Rice Krispies went to work on his kidneys. A wild excitement built inside him as he imagined battering the bastard. He could do this – he could really do it!

But then Fearon gave one of his crew a playful shove that sent him sprawling, and Sean saw the length of his arm and the size of his fists. He remembered the pain of all the casual punches that Fearon had given him just for the fun of it - him and so many other younger kids. Fearon was three years older, five inches taller, and vicious. Sean imagined the thrashing he'd take if he failed, and knew that no-one would break it up or give him a hand once the fight started.

A fight was a rare treat, the best entertainment of the school day, and the more brutal the better. The boys would form a ring, pushing him towards Fearon each time he tried to back off, keeping him in range of fist and boot. There were no rules. This wasn't Tom Brown's School Days, this was Duggin in 1969, and fair play didn't come into it. The fight would continue until he was beaten to the ground and given a thorough kicking. That would be bad enough, but God help him if he shed a tear, no matter what type of battering he received. He'd be a laughing stock for days until forced into another fight to prove himself.

Sean saw all this clearly: saw his tattered blazer being ripped from his back, and his busted shoes being held up for everyone to laugh at. He saw the Corn Flakes and Rice Krispies waved about in derision, and he saw Paula Yates looking at him with scorn. His resolution crumbled. His muscles slackened and he slouched back against the wall, defeated before striking a blow.

"One of these days," he whispered. "One of these days, I'll get that bastard!"

"Yeah right," said Bill. "One of these days."

.

CHAPTER 5: Indecent Assault

"Hey boys it's the God-Mobile!   And look, here come the Priestlings."

A white van pulled into the school car park, driven by Brother Jerome. In the back were a dozen boys, from second years to sixth formers, all of them immaculate in white shirts with their school ties done up just right. Perfectly polished shoes hit the gravel as they climbed out and headed for the schoolyard. A lardy youth with blubbery lips and a pale nervous face made his way toward the group of third formers where Sean and Bill were waiting for the school bell to sound the beginning of the new term.

"Oy, watch it lads, here comes Pervert Purvis. Backs to the wall if you haven't got your chain mail undies on."

Kevin Purvis, his face flushing, swung away from the group to stroll on his own around the perimeter of the yard. He was one of the God-Squad, the Priestlings who spent their Sundays at the Seminary doing whatever they did out there in preparation for a life of the cloth. None of the boys quite knew what went on at the Seminary, but in Purvis' case most of them were prepared to guess.

"Looks like Perv got out the wrong side of the bed this morning," said Ronny Johnson.

"How's that?" asked his side-kick, Brian Rylands.

"Wearing Brother Jerome's shoes, isn't he?

The laughter was interrupted by the school bell. The mob of boys jostled their way through the entrance doors and along the corridor to the Assembly Hall, ignoring the frantic urgings of old Brother Michael who stood there yelling "Twos please! Twos please" like some geriatric Noah caught in a stampede. It was all any boy had ever heard him say, and they mimicked the words back at him, knowing him to be too old and useless to do anything about it. Even the brand new first formers recognised that the senile git could be ignored, and they pushed and shoved against him before descending the steps into the hall to take their places at the front by the elevated stage. Behind them came the second formers, and then the thirds, Sean and Bill among them, and then the upper forms took their places until the sixth formers slouched in at the tail end. As the hall filled, the boys separated into their classes row on row, and massed in two equal blocks with a central aisle between them

The air buzzed. Brother Leo, had left suddenly at the end of the summer term and a new headmaster had been appointed during the holidays. Everyone waited to see who they'd be up against.

"Bet you he's a homo like Old Campy."

"Course he's a homo, they're all bloody homos, aint that right Perv?"

"Yeah, they've got another one for you Pervy darling."

"Nah, Leo wasn't a homo, he was knocking off Sister Agnes."

"Yeah, that's all bollocks about him leaving to become a priest - he's buggered off with her."

"Sister Agnes? God help him! I'd rather go ten rounds with Muhammad Ali than shag that old sow."

"Hey, I've heard he's a Choco. One of them African missionaries."

29

"That's bollocks. It's the Africans that are black. The missionaries are all white you dick-head."

"And anyway, you can't have Chocos caning whites."

"Yeah, goes against nature don't it?"

"They say he's got a Cambridge degree."

"Then he can't be a darkie can he? They don't let coons into Cambridge"

The buzz subsided as Horse-Face Logan, the Latin Master, walked onto the stage and sat at the piano. He did this with a ridiculous air of ceremony, just like he did everything else. He stood at the piano with his nose in the air looking down flared nostrils at the boys as if trying to find out who'd farted. When he'd gained everyone's attention he sat down at the keyboard and struck a pose, hands poised above the keys as if about to tackle Rachmaninoff's 3rd. Then he launched into Hail the Conquering Hero as a cue for the teachers to make their entrance into the hall.

Horse-Face must have been out of practice over the summer because he cocked up right off the bat, hitting a fistful of bum notes and drawing attention to his mistake by scrambling for a recovery. It sounded bloody awful. The boys began to snigger as Horace's face turned as red as his coppery hair.

"Dickhead," whispered Sean to Bill. But Bert Halligan, one of Sean's classmates, was bolder and called out, "Who's that bleeding wanker on the Joanna?" The noise from the piano was drowned under hoots of laughter and whistles from the rest of the boys, and it would have gone badly for Bert if the teachers hadn't begun to file in just at that moment. As it was, Horse-Face recovered the tune, and decided he'd preserve more of his precious dignity if he carried on and pretended not to have heard. Bert became the term's first hero.

The lay teachers entered the hall through the west doors, two at a time and took their position on an elevated walkway that ran the length of the hall on the western side. The Christian Brothers entered at the same time from the east doors on the other side of the hall, and the two groups of teachers stood facing each other over the heads of the boys. At the back of the hall, the sliding doors that enclosed the small chapel had been pulled aside, as they were on Saints' Days, and candles were lit on the altar.

But today all eyes were intent on the stage where Horse-Face was crucifying *Judas Macabeus*. As he reached a murderous crescendo a door at the back of the stage opened and a figure walked swiftly forward. He stood before the boys, still and silent as if inviting inspection. There was a brief, muted exclamation that died as they gaped at the thing looking down on them.

"It can't be human," whispered Sean.

"Huggerly-Faced Bastard!" gasped Bill.

God had created Brother Loredano to scare the shit out of schoolboys. He stood perfectly erect with hands held loosely across his abdomen, skeletal fingers intertwined. Black hair was pasted against his head like a skull cap, and the grey skin of his face was stretched over a massive protruding forehead so that the eyes looked out from a cave. The ridges of cheekbone were chiseled into a deaths-head that smiled with a narrow lipless line. But it was the jaw that held them transfixed. It jutted forward like an immense counterbalance to that crag of a forehead. It was monumental. The entire school could play soccer on that chin.

Bill was right - he was one ugly looking bastard. But there was nothing comical about that face. And, while the boys stared, not so much as a snigger escaped any of them. There was strength in that chin, and strength in that slab of a forehead, and in the black eyes

31

too. The sardonic smile said *Go on - take a good look - and then laugh if you dare. Laugh just once and see what I'll do to you.* No one took the challenge. One by one their eyes dropped, moving from the face to the bony fingers, to the shoes peaking from beneath the long black robe. Anywhere away from that silent, threatening skull.

As if satisfied with the effect, the Head turned to Horse-Face on the piano and nodded briefly. Immediately, the Latin master tinkled the introductory bars of the School Hymn with a look that said *For God's sake don't let me screw up now*, and then that impossible jaw dropped open like a back-hoe and the headmaster led the assembly in song:

Saint Rodriguez, hear our voices
Followers with hearts afire,
Singing praises sweet with music,
Wisdom's Hall our one desire.
Saint Rodriguez, lead us onward,
Knowledge, faith let us acquire.

Shaughnessy, the Head Boy stood next to a curtained recess at the side of the stage, and faced the assembled boys. As the song progressed he pulled slowly on a rope that gradually lifted the curtain to reveal a statue of St. Rodriguez de Cordoba, the founder of the Rodriguan Christian Brotherhood and patron saint of the school. The story went that St. Rodriguez had had a vision centuries before that had compelled him to wear a dress while teaching kids to read and write. The idea had caught on and the Rodriguans had been interfering with children ever since.

The statue was life-size in Plaster of Paris. The eyes of the painted face were turned heavenward in what was supposed to be divine rapture, but to Sean looked more like pissed puzzlement. His arms were held straight and slightly out from his sides with open palms turned upwards. To the saint's right was the statue of a young boy reaching up to the open hand with an eager expression. An equally eager young girl stood reaching for the left hand. This was supposed to convey the divine gift of learning being channeled through the saint to the needy children.

The daily unveiling of the statue was taken very seriously by Shaughnessy who timed the raising of the curtain so that the heavenward gaze of St. Rodriguez was revealed just as the last verse of the hymn concluded. He didn't look at the statue during the song but stood at attention facing the assembly and pulled on his rope with a perfectly straight face. It took a pride in imbecility to become Head Boy, but the rugby team could be relied on every year to supply a candidate with the required intellectual disability.

The curtain was at the level of the saint's knees by the end of the first verse, and the rough country clothes of the young Spanish children were visible, the girl in a long blue dress, and the boy in baggy brown trousers. The curtain continued to rise as the second verse commenced:

Guide to all our righteous teachers
Guardian of our noble School

But there was something wrong. The composure of the Head Boy began to waver as the singing stopped in the front ranks and confused giggles broke out. The first formers had never seen the statue before, but surely this couldn't be right, even for a Dago..........

33

Ignoring them, the Head Boy kept tugging away on his rope as the boys further back sang on:

Bring us all to Wisdom's station
Bring us all to ....

But the laughter was spreading from the front of the hall to the older boys at the back as more and more of the curtain was raised. Finally only the teachers were left singing as the saint's heavenward gaze was revealed.

Saint Rodriguez, hear our pleading
Patron please we............

But this was no St. Rodriguez dispensing knowledge to a young lad and lass - this saint was handing a bottle of Newcastle Brown to the girl, while his right hand invited the boy to accept an enormous inflated condom. The eager smiles on the childrens' faces showed they could hardly wait to begin the day's lesson.

The entire school dissolved into laughter, and even one or two of the lay teachers couldn't help smirking. Feeling that somehow he was the object of the fun, the Head Boy turned to look for the first time at the statue. His response was right out of Tom and Jerry. His chin hit his chest and his eyes opened enormously wide as he gazed at the huge condom waving gently above his head. He turned to face the assembly with his gob still gaping, and the boys burst into fresh gales as they saw the look of helpless horror on his face. The stupid sod didn't have a clue what to do.

"Maybe he'll hang himself," whispered Sean.

"Noose such luck." replied Bill.

The headmaster walked to the side of the stage where he could see the statue, and the laughter subsided as the boys waited for his reaction. He looked at the statue for no more than a second, and without the slightest appearance of concern leaned across and took both the beer bottle and condom from the saint's hands and placed them on a table to the side of the stage. He turned to face the boys, and with calm deliberation brought his right hand to his forehead and began:

"In the name of the Father....."

The boys stopped laughing immediately and followed his lead, making the sign of the cross.

"....and of the Son and of the Holy Spirit, Amen."

A Credo was added to the usual Hail Mary and Our Father, then the new Headmaster addressed the boys for the first time. There were no words of welcome. He just spoke, with precise enunciation, and everyone listened.

"As you know, Brother Leo left Meadowlands Grammar School at the end of last term and I have been appointed Headmaster". No explanations, just the fact. "My name is Brother Loredano and you will address me as such, or as Brother, I don't care which. As Headmaster, I believe it is my duty to make Meadowlands the best Grammar School in the North of England, and this I intend to do."

"Shit!" whispered Bill.

"Shit's right," said Sean.

"I accept nothing less than one hundred percent effort from myself" continued the Head, "and I expect nothing less than one hundred percent effort from every student and every teacher in this school. If anyone feels unable, or unwilling, to meet these expectations it would be better if that person were to leave this school immediately."

There was a pause, and a slight shuffling of feet, but no one made a move. Poor Brother Michael looked terribly sad, but he stood his ground wondering frantically how he would ever get the boys into twos.

Brother Loredano continued. "Good. I'm pleased to see you are with me."

"If he looks pleased I'd hate to see him upset," whispered Bill.

Sean was about to reply, but the speech continued and he didn't dare.

"Each boy at this school will receive an education that cannot be provided anywhere else in this area. This education will allow those who make the best use of it to enter the university of their choice. Even scholarship boys from areas such as Smellins, Widnes and Duggin may qualify for entry into Oxford or Cambridge after their A level examinations. I expect that those boys, in particular, will appreciate the opportunity afforded them and will make every effort to raise themselves above their origins."

Sean and Bill exchanged glances at this, but were too astonished for words.

"As well as providing an unparalleled education, I will ensure that this school operates under the strictest Christian code. Therefore, if any person has reservations about the precepts of Roman Catholicism, that person may leave at once."

Again a pause, and again no one made a move.

"Good. Then I look forward to working with you towards the greater glory of Meadowlands Grammar School, the greater glory of the Catholic Church and the greater glory of God."

"Sieg frigging Heil", whispered Bill.

"And now we have some unfinished business from last year," continued the headmaster, with a slight acceleration of speech hinting at a lighter tone. "I am delighted to announce that the Meadowlands cricket team had a spectacular summer season and retained the area championship for the third consecutive year."

Shaughnessy brought his clumsy mitts together in applause that spread reluctantly through the boys. He was back on familiar ground here as chief arse-licker

"I would now like to invite the Captain of the school cricket team to accept the trophy. I also have medals for the other team members. Would the following boys please approach the stage."

He read the names of the first eleven, and the boys separated themselves from their classmates to process towards the stage. As each name was announced the Head Boy led the congregation in applause. When all medals and trophies had been distributed, leaving only the condom and beer bottle on the table, the Head's voice slowed, the tone hardened again, and the mouth lost any hint of a smile.

"I also have a less pleasant duty to perform with respect to the last school year, and one which I hope will remind you all that while you are in uniform your behaviour is my jurisdiction irrespective of whether you are within the school grounds or not."

"Oops! Someone's fucked," whispered Bill.

Sean nodded, "I'd say fucked is about right."

"While high spirits may be expected on the final day of school prior to the summer recess, this does not give occasion to disregard any school rule. Be assured that should any boy engage in behaviour to the detriment of this school's reputation, that boy will be dealt with in the most severe manner, irrespective of the time and place of his misconduct."

"Get on with it," whispered Sean, "who was it?"

"I expect every Meadowlands boy to act in an exemplary Christian manner, and this means at all times to treat teachers, fellow students and members of the community with the greatest degree of respect and courtesy. It has come to my notice, however, that a group of boys on the way home to Widnes," and here he pinched his nose as if smelling the factories, "took it upon themselves to sing a vulgar song on the school bus."

A sigh of relief sounded from most of the six hundred boys in the hall. Only twenty of them came from Widnes.

"T'was on the Good Ship Venus," said Bill with a smirk.

"My God you should have seen us," replied Sean, happy to be off the hook.

"When asked to desist by the bus conductress," continued the Head "the Widnes boys responded by abusing her in the most profane fashion."

"And if that twat Shaughnessy keeps twisting his fucking face like that," whispered Bill, "the entire Widnes crew'll be down on the suck-holing prick as soon as school's over."

"Now let me be quite clear about certain things," continued the Head. "I believe that when a boy puts aside his dignity by behaving in such a manner, that boy reduces himself to the level of a beast. As he chooses to behave like a beast, so shall he be treated like a beast. And I believe that beasts can best be disciplined by a sound thrashing. There are some who disagree with me on this, but they are wrong." His tone allowed no room for argument.

"Certain so-called progressive elements, Humanists and the like, believe that beating a boy is a humiliating and degrading experience for the victim. I agree wholeheartedly with this view. However, unlike these Humanists, I believe that such humiliation and degradation are good things. They are, in fact, the whole purpose of

38

corporal punishment. The boy feels this humiliation and degradation because he is not an animal, and therefore the punishment reminds the boy of his human condition. It reminds him of the dignity that he has set aside voluntarily, and it encourages him to regain it. I therefore consider it my moral duty to administer corporal punishment whenever I believe it to be of benefit to the recipient. I also believe that such punishment is most effective when applied publicly so that humiliation and degradation are felt to the utmost. I have ascertained the names of the boys involved in the school bus incident and I now ask that these boys approach the stage. Rodney Strong......"

As Rod Strong moved out into the aisle Bert Halligan, still flush with his success over Horse Face, couldn't restrain himself and broke into a burst of ironic applause. This was met by laughter and a few additional claps from those who dared, but the support dried up immediately when the Head turned his gaze on Halligan.

"So we have a jester," he said. "Or, as Shakespeare would have it, a fool. Do you know your Lear laddie? You'll find in Lear what happens to fools who overstep the mark. But for now, since you admire louts to such an extent you'll be happy to share the stage with them, won't you? Step out laddie, and join your friends. Glenn Lowry, Edward Small, Thomas Dean......."

The hall was silent as he called the names. As each of the boys stepped out they received reassuring pats on the shoulder as they made their way to the aisle. They might beat each other senseless in the schoolyard, but they were all comrades when one of the Brothers was laying into them.

The chosen climbed a short flight of steps to the side of the stage and formed a huddled group at the top, uncomfortably aware of being on show. Finally he turned to them with a business-like air and reached for a narrow bamboo cane that lay on the table alongside the condom and beer bottle.

"Strong, you were called first, so I'll start with you. Come here laddie and let's see if you deserve that name of yours." The Head wasn't making a joke. He sounded as if he really meant to find out.

Rod Strong swaggered to the front of the stage and stood to the side of the Head, a cane's length away, knowing what was required of him. He faced the assembly with an impudent smile, his dump-truck frame as wide as it was high.

"Left or right-handed Strong?"

"Right Brother"

"Let's have the left one then."

Strong extended his left arm with open palm upwards, his hand a lump of millstone grit. The Head extended the cane until its tip lay against Strong's fingers at the level of the first joint. He brought his arm back slowly in a wide arc so that the cane extended behind his back, all the time looking at the spot where it had lain against the boy's hand. He paused, took a breath, and brought the cane streaking back along its path to smash against Strong's fingers. The impact sounded like the crack of a whip.

Sean clenched his hand spasmodically. "Christ, that hurt," he gasped.

Strong released his breath with a hiss but kept his arm extended and didn't move the hand.

"Tough bastard,' whispered Bill with genuine admiration. Strong was a thick-headed dick most days, but right now he was everyone's hero.

The Head allowed himself the briefest glance at Strong's face and then brought the cane to rest lightly against his hand again, aligning it exactly with the bright red weal that crossed the fingers. Again he

40

brought the cane back and again there was the whistle and the crack. Again Sean clenched his fist, and again Strong kept the arm straight and the hand open. The boys maintained a fascinated silence as the challenge played itself out.

After the third stroke Strong blew out his cheeks and dropped his hand with a small look of triumph. Six strokes was the maximum, three on each hand, and his right hand was tougher. He held this out now and even allowed himself a slight smile; he wasn't going to crack.

The Head smiled also. "No, no laddie, you'll need that hand for writing. It's the left hand I want." His tone was gentle, as if offering Strong some kindly advice.

Muttering broke out in the hall but was quenched by a single glance from the Head. Everyone knew that six on the same hand was out of order, but no one was about to say so. Strong held out the left hand again, but this time gingerly, and the arm trembled ever so slightly. The Head took his time aligning the cane along the purple ridge that had swollen across the fingers, tapping gently on the spot to let Strong know exactly what was coming.

It landed right on target, and for the first time Strong let his hand fall slightly after the blow. The first formers at the front of the hall could see his teeth biting into his lips. Most of them were terrified, thinking this was to be business as usual in their new school. Strong wasn't play-acting the tough guy any more. It was useless to pretend that he wasn't in agony. But there was a look of determination on his face that grew only more fixed as the fifth blow brought the first audible grunt of pain from his lips.

Six was the maximum, there was no getting around that, and the Head looked hard at Strong as he laid the cane across the crippled hand and prepared for the final stroke. Strong looked back, his eyes

41

eloquent with hatred. Coward, they said. You vicious, bloody coward. Meet me in the schoolyard and I'd kick your bollocks right up your arse, you bullying bastard. The stick lashed against the bruises, and Strong bit down hard to stifle a cry. Sweat had broken across his face but his eyes were dry. Then in an act of defiance he lifted the hand again and invited a seventh blow. Bill O'Rourke had to stifle a cheer.

"That's quite enough for today Strong," murmured the Head. "Now what do you say?"

Strong shook his head, not understanding.

"Come on laddie; when someone does you a service without you asking for it what do you say? Surely even the rudiments of polite interaction are known in Widnes."

"Thank you'" said Strong.

"Thank you what, Strong?"

Thank you, you sadistic pervert, thought Strong. But the throbbing agony of his ruined hand got the better of him and he said "Thank you, Brother."

"My pleasure," said the Head as if with irony. No one was fooled.

Strong descended the steps of the stage, and walked slowly to the back of the hall, his left arm dangling with the palm held open and forward so that every boy could see the extent of the damage. With his back to the Head he was grinning, and the boys grinned back with admiration and solidarity.

But there were no smiles among the boys on the stage. They were grey with fear. Not only about the impending thrashings, but the lasting humiliation for anyone unable to follow Strong's example.

"Now who's next?" asked the Head turning toward the huddle. "What, no volunteers? Well then, let's have the Jester shall we? Let's see if he can find anything amusing in this."

Bert Halligan was a pasty boy of thirteen who was about as tough as a blancmange. He backed away into the group as the Head gestured him to the front of the stage, but the other boys thrust him forward to stand cringing where Rodney Strong had put on such a brave show. This was to be Halligan's first caning. In fact, it was to be his first beating of any kind. His parents enjoyed his witty impudence, knowing there wasn't a grain of harm in him. The idea of striking him with a cane for venting his humour would have disgusted them. Unfortunately for Halligan, the Head didn't have the same appreciation for comedians.

"So do you know your Lear laddie?" asked the Head for the second time.

Halligan, who had been brought up on Shakespeare, was too afraid to answer.

"Don't worry boy, you'll know it before you leave this school. Suffice for now that Lear's jester was an impertinent fellow who finished his days at the end of a rope. It's a fitting reward for fools, and you can count yourself lucky that I have to limit myself to a stick. Left or right handed?"

Halligan couldn't bring himself to say a word, but stretched out a pudgy fist opening the fingers reluctantly, joint by joint. The Head tapped the cane across the soft skin, and Halligan closed his eyes, twisting his face in pain even before the cane was raised. It would have been funny if this was just a game, but it was very far from that. After his failure with Strong, the Head needed to break someone, and a harmless weakling like Halligan would do nicely.

The cane sliced deep into the fatty fingers with a sickening splat. Halligan let out a scream and jammed the hand under his arm pit, drumming his feet on the floor of the stage in a dance of anguish, unaware of anything except the white hot agony. Until now he hadn't known that such pain could exist. The Head waited, leaning on the cane until the dance subsided. He stared at the boy impassively as if he'd had nothing to do with his writhing.

"The hand boy. Let me have the hand."

Halligan raised his arm again, but he couldn't undo the fist. He stared at it as if it held something terrible. He pleaded wordlessly for mercy, the blubbery lips trembling.

"The hand boy."

The Head's tone was gentle but insistent, and slowly the hand opened. Halligan looked once at the livid scar, and turned his face away, sickened by the sight of it. The Head placed the cane along the red track and raised it for the next blow. But Halligan couldn't take it. He pulled his hand away as the cane came down and it crashed into the Head's robe with a bony crack.

"Got the bastard!" whispered Sean, and there was a ripple of satisfaction through the ranks of boys in the hall.

But if flesh and blood existed beneath those robes it was nerveless stuff. Not one chiseled line altered in the Head's expression as the cane slammed into his leg. And, as if practiced in the movement, he immediately brought the cane up and around in a low arc to deliver a slashing blow across the back of Halligan's thighs. Halligan screamed. With his damaged right hand wedged beneath his left armpit, his feet drummed on the floor as he rubbed frantically with the other hand at the back of his legs, all the while whooping and howling. It looked like a piss-take of a Red Indian war dance from a Hollywood Western. All Halligan needed was face-paint and a head-dress.

But it wasn't funny. It wasn't funny at all.

"You get one of those each time you move your hand, laddie." said the Head calmly, "So if you want to make matters worse for yourself that's entirely up to you. Now let's have that hand again."

"I can't brother," whimpered Halligan. "I can't......I can't......"

"Yes you can laddie," said the Head. "As part of your education at this school you will learn the principles of cause and effect. Your behaviour has caused me to invoke a disciplinary measure, and now you are experiencing the effect. The effect is unpleasant, and because of that you will learn not to create any such effect in the future. So let's have that hand out again. Now."

The Head made it sound perfectly reasonable, as if he truly believed it himself, but Halligan's response was to bow his head and burst into tears, crying in the heart-broken way of children when they are asked by adults to do something that is totally beyond them. Even Fearon looked at the floor and shuffled his Oxfords as Halligan's tears dripped onto the stage.

"Get the hand out laddie," repeated the Head. But Halligan just cowered deeper, face down and shoulders shrugged up against his ears, his rounded back convulsing with sobs.

"Very well then boy. Cause and effect. Your choice."

It was said with the slightest tone of reluctance, but the hand that reached for Halligan's neck didn't waver. The Head pulled him forward by the collar, pressing down hard so that he bent double at the waist, and before the terrified boy could react brought the cane down with flailing force against his buttocks.

Something shifted in Sean's mind. He was there on the stage. The cane sliced deep into the soft tissue of his arse. Fatty globules of blancmange flew from the tip as it was swung high and brought down again and again. He dropped his head, breathing deeply as the blood rushed from his brain, but he couldn't escape the sound of screaming, or the pain of that splatter of flesh each time the cane did its business. The hall began to see-saw.

"For God's sake!" he heard himself calling, "For God's sake!"

But it wasn't him. The voice was deeper and came from the ranks of the teachers. It was Ben Gibbs, the head of English, striding towards the stage, his face contorted with a look of outrage. The Head stopped his work as Ben approached and dropped the cane to his side with the air of someone who had finished a routine job.

"Thank you Mr. Gibbs," said the Head, releasing Halligan's neck, "perhaps you would take this boy to Sick Bay and have Mrs. Smith look after him."

Halligan remained bent double, his arms crossed against his chest with hands gripping the lapels of his blazer, his knuckles white. A slow stream of spit dribbled from his mouth. Ben approached him, and without looking at the Head, laid a hand gently on the boy's back. He bent down and spoke to him slowly, easing Halligan out of shock and coaxing him towards the exit at the back of the stage.

The Head ignored them both and turned to the other boys who had clustered like terrified sheep into a silent huddle. Glenn Lowry was sobbing silently at the back. The Head raised his cane to waist height, holding the end with a bunched fist and the tip with the fingers of his other hand. He flexed it playfully. His voice was still calm and business-like, as if the brutalisation of Halligan was all in the normal course of events.

"I expect that the next fellow I cane will know exactly what is expected of him", he said, and looked at each of the cowering boys in turn, daring any one of them to hold his eye. None did. His gaze lingered on Lowry.

"Isn't that right, boy?" he asked.

Lowry opened his mouth but he couldn't get words passed his blubbering lips. He nodded his head in a desperate show of obeisance. The Head flexed the cane so that it bent almost double.

"Don't nod your head at me laddie," he said. "You may have the brains of a donkey but I expect you to have the manners of a Meadowlands student. When I ask you a question you will respond with either "Yes Brother" or "No Brother", do you understand me?"

Lowry nodded his head again, and then squeaked out a panicked "Yes Brother" in a girlish pitch that the rest of the boys would mimic back at him for months afterwards.

The Head looked at each of the boys again, stroking his cane with a loose fist along its entire length.

"As a Christian, I deplore violence of any sort," he said, "but when the means of retribution justifies its ends, I'm prepared to use corporal punishment to fullest extent allowable by law........"

"If that was legal, then so's rape," whispered Bill.

"....What I was obliged to do to those boys this morning appalls me," continued the Head, "and I hope I never to have to do it again......."

"Lying bastard," whispered Sean.

"....But let me warn you - I never forget a face, and now that I've seen each of you before me for punishment once, I will remember if I ever see you before me for that purpose again. Should that occur, I promise that I'll thrash you to within an inch of your wretched lives. Now get out of my sight."

There was a pause, then the boys scuttled off stage in a frightened mob, Lowry squeaking "Yes Brother" and "Thank you Brother" in a way that was going to get him a good kicking at lunch time.

"And now," said the Head, summoning the sembalance of a smile, "on to more pleasant things."

"...as Joey Mengele said at the seaside," whispered Bill.

"As the more intelligent of you may be aware," he began, "it takes a lot of money to run a school of this size, and with these facilities. The government provides some of this money, but the rest we have to find for ourselves. Our major expenses include the heated indoor swimming pool, maintenance of the all-weather soccer pitch....."

"...Piss-ups in the Brother's house," whispered Bill.

"....Little boys for Brother Campion," countered Sean.

".....the annual purchase of text-books, supplies for the science labs, and provision of the excellent meals that you all enjoy at lunch time."

The last item would have raised a laugh if the boys were in a laughing mood, but no one so much as sniggered.

"I'm a great believer in people paying their own way in this life......." continued the Head.

"......as opposed to in the hereafter," whispered Bill.

".....and for that reason I am going to give you all the opportunity to contribute to the fiscal health of this school. On the Saturday after next we will be holding a sponsored walk in aid of the school building fund, and I expect as many boys as possible to take part. The route of the walk has yet to be decided, but it will amount to about ten miles for the younger boys, and twenty for the upper grades - a feat you should all be capable of."

No one cracked a smile. The Head Boy would have laughed, as duty demanded, but he was too thick to get the pun.

"Over the next two weeks," continued the Head," I want every boy to gather a list of sponsors who will agree to pay a fixed sum for every mile walked. I expect all parents to contribute, even if it is only a penny or two per mile from the Widnes and Duggin households."

"I don't believe this prick!" whispered Bill, knotting his fists.

"I do," replied Sean, "and he's only saying what the rest of the bastards think."

"So talk to your parents," continued the Head, "Go and visit your grandmother, and call in on those aunts and uncles you neglect. But don't leave until they've signed your sponsor sheets." The giant chin jutted forward. "And as an incentive, there will be a prize for the boy who raises the most money."

"And I wonder who that will be," whispered Bill, nodding towards Shaughnessy who was already smirking with self-satisfaction.

"Wouldn't you just love to take a cricket bat to that face," said Sean. But his fantasy was shattered as the Head's threatening tone returned.

"And one last thing before you go to your classes," said the Head. "I will have that boy who violated the statue of our patron Saint. Mark my words – I will have him. And when I have him, that boy will wish he had never been born. Dismissed!"

The boys filed from the hall rank by rank, silent until they had passed the swing doors into the corridor, where they burst into a chorus of universal hatred.

"So what do you think?" asked Bill, as if he really didn't know. But Sean answered him anyway.

49

"I think that whoever pulled that stunt with the statue is probably filling his pants right now. And I wouldn't trade my Kellogg's boxes for that poor bastard's shoes, stitched leather soles or not."

CHAPTER 6: You Say You Want A Revolution?

The schoolyard was unusually silent at recess. No one was in the mood for soccer or cricket. Instead the boys gathered in muttering groups that wandered the yard aimlessly, falling silent only when approached by one of the supervising teachers.

-That bastard'll pay for what he did to Halligan.

-If he thinks he can scare me with that bleeding stick, he can think again.

-I'll shove it up his arse before he touches mine with it.

-Ugly twat.

-That's not a forehead, it's a bleedin' five-head.

-A friggin' six-head if you ask me.

-And did you see the chin on it?

-See it? You could see it from space!

-And what about when he bent Halligan over - I thought he was going to slip him one right there on the stage.

-Old Campo would have done, the filthy sod!

-I reckon he gets off on it like those weirdos with the spanky mags.

-What d'you mean?

-Stuck out a mile didn't it, soon as he got hold of that cane.

-Come off it.

-Didn't you see? I could have hung my blazer on it.

-I wonder why he let off Lowry and the rest of them?

-Blew his load on Halligan, didn't he.

-Eh?

-Could tell couldn't you? Jappo one minute and then spurt!, back to normal.

-You're vile, Wilson.

-I'm telling you, it's why they wear them robes. One big catch-cloth.

-Ben Gibbs looked like he was going to swing for him.

-Ben's all right.

-One of the best is Ben.

-The only decent one if you ask me.

-No, Brother Lundy's OK.

-What, because he plays a guitar? Give me a break!

-Not exactly Hendrix is he?

-I tell you, Lundy's alright.

-What are you then, one of his bum chums? Gonna join the Priestlings are you?

-Anyway, I'm not going on no sponsored bleeding walk.

-Me neither.

-Nor me.

-Delicious meals......- my arse.

-A penny or two from the Duggin households - who the fuck does he think he is?

-Even those from Widnes and Duggin can rise above their origins......Jesus Christ!

-I'd like to rise above him with a bloody big stick.

-Well maybe it's time to put the bastard straight.

-What d'you mean?

-Simple - we can either yack about it, or do something about it.

-Like what?

-Dunno yet, but I'll think of something. -

-You're all talk Johnson.

-Am I? You'll see.

-Hey! What do we call him?-

-Well if you're Lowry you call him Yes, Brother, No Brother, Thank you Brother.....gutless prick! -

-I've got it, lets call him THE HEAD!

-Bollocks!-

-Don't be bloody daft Rylands, everyone calls him the Head.

Rylands stuck out his jaw, scrunched his eyes, and brought two craggy fists to his forehead.

-Don't you get it? Not the Head. I mean, THE HEAD! He'll never know we're taking the piss out of that huge bloody chin of his.

There was a ripple of appreciative laughter, and before the end of the day, the Head had become THE HEAD!

Glenn Hardy, the Arts Master, lounged in the corner of the Teachers' Common Room, reclining in an old leather arm chair, his feet up on a battered coffee table and his head tilted towards the ceiling. He was entertaining himself by blowing smoke rings. At twenty one he was the youngest teacher in the school, an Old Boy like a few of his lay colleagues, and the most recent addition to the staff.

He'd joined Meadowlands during the last week of the previous summer term, his arrival causing a sensation among the boys. He'd shown up late on the first day, sauntering into morning assembly half way through prayers, wearing a floral shirt, no tie, and sporting a three inch pony tail tied with a thin red ribbon at the back. He'd brought the entire proceedings to a dead stop. There couldn't have been more gaping mouths if Brother Leo had taken to the stage in Sister Agnes's knickers.

Leo had soldiered on through assembly, but short of doing the knickers thing there was no way he was going to recapture his audience. Art classes had been cancelled later that morning, and when they resumed in the afternoon they were conducted by a newly shorn Mr. Hardy wearing a white shirt and his old school tie.

Still, Glen had become an instant hit with the boys. He was a good teacher too, always showing enthusiasm for whatever artistic efforts they attempted in his classes. Talent didn't matter, having a go was good enough. He looked the archetypal Poofta as he minced about giggling like a girl, and a rumour had started that he might actually be Kevin Purvis's secret father.

The boys christened him Gladys, and thought him one of those harmless arse-bandits you could actually get to like. That was until the end of school on Gladys' first day when Raquel Welch had shown up on a Norton Commando just as the boys were heading for the buses. The thigh boots, the tits bulging against the tight white tee-shirt, and the mini skirt right up to her arse had raised a forest of erections and brought all progress out of the school to a standstill. And then Gladys had come poncing out of the main doors into the car park, had planted a huge slobbery kiss on Raquel's pneumatic lips and roared off on the pillion for what every cock-hobbled boy was convinced would be hours and hours and

54

hours of rampant thrashing sex, the lucky, lucky bastard. After that there was no doubt about Gladys' sexual orientation, but his nickname stuck anyway.

Yes, a dark horse was old Gladys, and all the students liked him. He seemed so different from his colleagues. He never started class with a prayer, and at assembly he kept his head bowed during the morning mumble but was never seen to cross himself. For a while the boys called him Heathen Hardy, but it didn't last - he had only to open his mouth and it was definitely Gladys talking.

Horace Logan settled into the seat next to Gladys, flashing his horsey teeth and snickering down his nose like Mr. Ed. It was Horace's way of saying hello.

"So, how does it feel to be on the other side of the fence Glenn? Or should I call you Mister Hardy now?"

Horace chuckled as if his question were profoundly comic.

"You used to call me just Hardy when I was a pupil here," he said.

"Ah yes, and when I was a pupil at this school, many years before you studied here, my teachers called me Logan. It's one of Meadowand's traditions. It avoids familiarity between staff and students and maintains the proper student-teacher distance. That's so important, don't you think?"

Gladys ignored the question. "As a Latin teacher, Mr. Logan, I'm sure you're very much in favour of the older traditions," he said.

"Oh, no need for Mr. Logan now Glenn. As I say, you're on the other side of the fence. Horace, please call me Horace.

"Horace? We used to call you Horse-face. I bet the kids still do."

"Yes, little terrors, I'm sure of it. Ha! Ha! Ha! Where they get these names I can't imagine, but better Horse-Face than many another epithet, eh?"

"Well, we called you a few things beside Horse-Face as well."

"Yes, I'm sure you did. Ha! Ha! Ha! I'm sure you did. Boys will be boys, cheeky little devils. Mind you," he continued, drawing down his lips as if chewing on a bad carrot, "I don't hold with this modern form of pranksterism. A few jolly japes is all well and good, but interfering with our patron saint's statue in such a vulgar manner goes a bit beyond the pale, don't you think?"

Gladys looked at him with open astonishment. He'd thought, four years ago, when he'd been a student at Meadowlands, that Horse-Face's Enid Blyton routine was just an act to lighten his achingly boring lessons. But no. It seemed as if Horse-Face was the genuine article – he really was a silly, pompous, dick-head. Gladys couldn't help bursting into a peal of girlish laughter.

"Well, I'm glad to see you're settling in to the new term," said Horse-Face, standing. "We must have lunch together some time. Bye for now." And he cantered off towards the tea pot.

Gladys lit another cigarette from the dog-end of his last one, and went back to practicing smoke rings. He found they worked better if he didn't inhale. It was probably healthier too. He saw Brother Campion looking in his direction and an acquired reflex made him straighten up. He took his feet off the coffee table and almost palmed the cigarette. Shit, he thought, the old pederast is coming over.

It wasn't usual for the Deputy Head to socialize at recess in the Teachers' Common Room, but he made a point of it at the beginning of every term. He'd find other things to do at recess as the term progressed.

"So, Hardy, I'm pleased to see that you begin the new term properly attired."

There was no friendliness in the comment, and the pun was entirely unintentional. He talked as if Glenn Hardy were still in school uniform, and Gladys couldn't help responding as if that were the case.

"Yes Brother," he said, and stubbed out the cigarette before he'd hardly started on it.

"It's important to set an example, Hardy, remember that."

"Yes, Brother."

"There were some fine prospects we interviewed for Arts Master last year, so I hope we made the right choice."

"I'm sure you did, Brother."

"Being an Old Boy was your big advantage you'll understand. We like a sense of continuity here. A new teacher who already knows the ins and outs is less likely to rock the boat isn't he?"

"Quite so, Brother."

"Good. Well I hope you'll settle to the routine during your probation. A smooth transition is what we want, isn't it? We play as a team here, and we have our own style. Take my advice Hardy and watch the more experienced players. Follow their lead and you'll not go astray."

"Yes, Brother."

"Good."

Gladys thought he was going to say "Good Boy" and lay that pudgy palm on his head. Instead it fell on his shoulder. Mercifully, the touch was brief, and he fought the impulse to squirm away until the dirty fat bastard had taken it off and left. He felt soiled by the touch. He wanted to scrub the spot with disinfectant, but instead he lit another cigarette and inhaled a huge drag, spraying smoke with a sweep of his head as if to fumigate the space where Old Campy had stood.

"Not much has changed since your day has there Glenn?"

Ben Gibbs settled into the chair vacated by Horse-Face, and by the look of despondency on his face Gladys knew he was referring to the public thrashing at assembly.

"No, it would appear not Mr. Gibbs......unfortunately."

"Unfortunate? Yes, one might call it unfortunate. But then there are so many other words one could use for it aren't there? Barbaric, inhuman, cold-blooded, wanton, obscene, vicious, cowardly, and, I have to say, tragic. I had hoped that the new Headmaster might have moved beyond the methods of the Inquisition, but it seems that we live in an age, at least in this institution, where terrorism is still the first, and often the only, resort.

"So you're not impressed with Brother Squeers then?"

"Impressed!"

Gladys blushed. Ben needed to talk this out and had chosen Gladys as a person who might actually listen. He deserved better than facile comments.

"I know what you mean Mr. Gibbs," he said, choosing his words more carefully. "I was whipped often enough when I was a pupil here, and all it did was make me further inclined towards the behaviour that earned the whipping in the first place. Further inclined, but more careful not to get caught. Everyone knows that's the usual reaction, and yet the beatings continue. You have to suppose then, that the motivation behind thrashing boys is something other than the imposition of discipline. I'm afraid that if you're looking for a Headmaster with more liberal views you shouldn't look for one carrying a stick and wearing a dress."

Gladys felt he'd made quite the speech, and was proud of the punch line, but Ben didn't smile.

"Not all the Rodriguan Brothers are alike Glenn. The order has its good men as well as its parasites and predators. In that, it's like most other closed societies. Unfortunately, this school seems to have a preponderance of the wrong sort. A Head with the right qualities could have changed so much here, put a halt to the abuse and created an environment for vibrant and enthusiastic learning. Instead he begins his tenure by reinforcing the rotten foundations that have supported this institution for decades."

"And now we're stuck with him for the foreseeable future," said Gladys in a tone that might have suggested either statement or question.

"It would seem so. Nothing short of a revolution is likely to shift him, and where might that arise in a society such as this?"

"Yes," said Gladys, "Where indeed?"

Chapter 7: Suckhole!

"Bleedin' Chunks!"

Ronny Johnson looked into the aluminum container on the dinner table, his face contorted with disgust. "First day back at school and they feed us bleedin' Chunks!"

The seven other boys around the table appeared equally enthusiastic about the meal as they stood behind their seats waiting for the teachers to enter the dining hall. Bill O'Rourke peered at the lumps of gristly meat floating in the brown gravy.

"Like a dysenteric bowel movement," he said.

Sean was briefer. "Shite," he said.

"And look at the chips!" wailed Ronny Johnson. "There's hardly enough for one each. Bloody dinner ladies on the take again."

"Ladies? What ladies?" said Sean.

"Ugly fat cows," said Johnson.

He glared at a group of middle aged women standing in front of a table at the back of the dining hall, waiting to accept the dirty plates and scrape the leavings into the swill bin. Their faces looked as if the sight and smell of the pig swill never left them.

"Dare you to ask for a top-up," said Sean.

"Yeah, go on Johnson," said Rylands. "Tell them they've been short changing us and demand your rights. We pay enough don't we?"

Sean blushed. His meal came courtesy of the State.

"You go ask them Lover Boy," said Johnson, pushing the chip tray towards Rylands. "Maybe Sweaty Betty'll trade you some chips for a big French kiss."

Rylands was a handsome athletic charmer and thought himself a ladies' man. The other boys didn't let him forget it.

"Maybe she'll take you behind the bike sheds and show you her knickers."

"Ask you to stroke her hairy behind."

"You're vile Smithers," said Rylands.

"Don't want the chips any more then?"

"I've got a better idea," said Rylands." He picked up the half-empty chip container and did a quick switch with the heaped platter on the adjacent table where the teachers sat.

The other boys looked at him with admiration and fear. All of them resented the double portions of food piled up on the teachers' table, but no one had ever had the guts to pull a switch. And if the greedy bastards figured out who'd helped themselves to their chips there'd be hell to pay.

"Switch 'em back Rylands," said Molyneaux, a short, worried-looking boy.

"Yeah, I don't want to get in the shit for a few chips," said Walker, glancing around for an empty seat at another table.

"I don't care," said Rylands. "And I'd take their bleeding chunks as well if I could stomach them."

"Good man," said Johnson, and started to laugh under his breath with a wheezing chuckle.

61

"Switch 'em back quick," pleaded Molyneaux. "They're coming in and Gruntle's with them. If he sees our chips we're done for."

"I hope he does see them," said Rylands. "And if he wants them back I'll throw them in his ugly fat face."

Johnson started to laugh out loud, and Sean, Bill and Rylands couldn't help joining in. The boys at the other tables looked over and saw what they'd done. A murmur of astonishment rippled through the dining room.

The noise ceased as the teachers paraded down the center of the room to their table at the top of the hall. Gruntle, the chemistry master, was in the lead and took the sudden silence as a mark of respect. He looked very superior as he scanned the table for the seat with best command over the food. That was when he saw the chips, and the change in his expression unleashed a brief explosion of laughter at Sean's table from all except Molyneaux and Walker. There was an echoing ripple of laughter down the hall that was quenched as Gruntle cast a swift glance at the tables around him.

Johnson could hardly control himself. Tears squeezed out the corners of his eyes and his knuckles were white as he gripped the back of his chair. His lips squirmed for control, threatening to part in a raucous great belly laugh at Gruntle's expense. Rylands was no better off. A high pitched wheeze whistled out of his chest as he tried to keep his head down to avoid exploding at the look of childish resentment on Gruntle's fat ugly mug.

Gruntle saw that Sean's table had pulled a switch but couldn't say a thing about it without exposing the unfairness everyone knew existed. He wrestled for control of his expression but couldn't hide the fact that he wanted his chips back, and wanted them back very badly. Every second he stood there gawping at the heaped pile on

Sean's table he was making a bigger and bigger fool of himself. He was furious - impotent and furious.

"What are you laughing at Johnson?" he roared. "What's a streak of useless flesh like you got to laugh about? Lift you head up boy and say Grace."

Johnson straightened up, but one look at Gruntle's face was enough to push him over the edge. He looked Gruntle right in the eye and just about managed to shout "Grace!" before dissolving into hysterical laughter. After a second of stunned silence every boy in the Hall roared along with him.

Gruntle was paralyzed. His moon face went into a purple eclipse, and for a glorious moment Sean thought that he might have been provoked into the terminal stroke that every chemistry student at Meadowlands so fervently wished for him. But he was disappointed as Gruntle leapt for Johnson with an agility that belied his three hundred pounds, dragging him upright by the hair and slapping his face back and forth, his arm swinging as wide as his bulk allowed him.

Johnson didn't feel a thing. He laughed even louder as the chubby hands assaulted his cheeks, and continued to laugh as Gruntle stood there sweating in confusion.

"Get out!" he screamed. "Get out now you....you......Damned impudence! Scruffy ......Dirty.......You wait outside the Headmaster's office until I come to deal with you."

Johnson staggered away from the table. He kept laughing all the way to the door, a ripple of applause marking his passage as he threaded his way between the tables. Hands reached out to touch him as he went by to what had to be a brutal thrashing.

Gruntle choked on the defiance. These boys should have learned their lesson from the new Head's excellent example this morning.

63

And yet here they were, insolent and as bold as brass. He wasn't going to have it. He rounded on Sean's table where Rylands was bubbling over, completely out of control. Gruntle wanted to kill him. He could have picked up his fork and plunged it right into Rylands' throat.

"Rylands, stop braying like a demented donkey and say Grace," he roared.

Rylands shook himself theatrically and took a few deep breaths to gain some kind of composure, but his voice was still quivering with laughter as he began, "For what we are about to receive........."

He couldn't help it. His voice broke and he squeezed out the rest of the prayer in a fit of giggles "May the pigs eat what we leave......Ha! Ha! Ha! Ha! Ha!!!!"

The hall erupted again. Gruntle stood gaping. His hands curled into fists, and Brother Lundy, as if reading his thoughts, sprang forward and frog-marched Rylands out of the hall, hissing into his ear and telling him, no doubt, about how the headmaster was going to beat him black and blue.

The hysteria in the dining room calmed a little as Brother Lundy returned to where Gruntle was beached like a whale. He stood in front of his colleague and cast a quelling eye over the boys until the last laugh was stifled. Then he turned to Sean's table and glanced briefly into each face. If discipline was to be restored, a proper Grace had to be said by a boy from this table. And what's more it couldn't be an easy victory using the likes of Molyneaux. It had to be someone else, someone with a little more standing.

"McCaffery," he said. "You will please say Grace."

Oh God, why me? thought Sean, even though he knew. He'd been amazed by the pluck of Rylands and Johnson. He'd felt like punching the air and roaring YES! at the sight of Gruntle's apoplectic response. But now it was his turn. He looked around and found anticipation on every face. Sean was known for his cynical wit, and it was obvious that the boys were expecting him to come up with something clever and biting. They wanted a Grace laced with poison.

He looked up at Brother Lundy. He didn't like him, but then he didn't hate him either – not the way he despised most of the Brothers. And Brother Lundy had said please. He'd asked him politely. Sean knew it was a ploy, but how to respond? His allegiance should be with Rylands and Johnson, who were waiting outside the Head's office for the thrashing of their lives. They'd turned all their schoolyard mouthings about mutiny into concrete acts of courage. He had to do the same. But the vision of Halligan's agony was still raw, and Sean cringed at the thought of it. And anyway, it was Brother Lundy asking, not that fat bastard Gruntle. Asking, not demanding. Everyone should know there was a difference. Making a mockery now seemed not just disrespectful, but dishonourable as well.

He opened his mouth, and the words tripped out reluctantly. "For what we are about to receive...........\"

He looked around again. Expectations pressed in on him. He could almost hear their thoughts.

- Go on Sean, let's hear a good one!
- Let's have Grace with some Chunks in it!
- Shit on him Sean!
- Solidarity brother!

His mouth hung loose. He could taste the choices: the blasphemy so sweet; the words Brother Lundy expected like vomit in his throat. This was his big solo, but what was he going to give them - Mick Jagger or the Singing Nun? It all came down to the single phrase that would finish the lunchtime prayer. The Catholic drivel that would appease that fat bastard Gruntle, or the nasty little rhyme that would earn him the respect of every boy in the room... and a thrashing he'd never forget?

He couldn't possibly foresee what his decision would set in motion, but he knew what he ought to say with a conviction felt deep in his guts. Instead he bowed his head and muttered,

"May the Lord make us truly thankful."

His words created a vacuum - an enormous void, aching to be filled. If there can be degrees of silence, the stillness in the dining hall defined the absolute zero. There had to be something more. Sean couldn't let them down. There was a punch-line coming. He was just pausing for effect. *Come on Sean*, they urged, *let's have it. If you leave it at that the bastards have won. Come on Sean......Come on!*

But Sean kept his head down, his face crimson. There was nothing else. No Jagger. He was the Singing Nun. He was the Singing Fucking Nun!

The hiss started at the back of the hall. "sssssssssssssss......." and grew as it rolled towards Sean's table. Even the boys around him joined in; all except for Bill O'Rourke who stared fixedly at his plate as if it were the most important thing in the world.

"sssssssssSSSSSSSSSSSUUUUUUUCCCCCCCCCCKKKKKKKK......HOL E!!!!"

And then there was the slurping of spit in 300 mouths as they mimicked the sound of Sean's lips working away at Fatty Gruntle's ring-piece.

The quelling eye had no effect on them now. They were outraged. Betrayed. One of their own had switched sides after two heroes had gone to the wall. He'd humiliated them. The slurping went on and on, and behind it the word was spat out time and again.

"SSSSSSSUUUUUCCCCCKKKKK HOLE!!!!

SSSSSUUUUCCCCKKK HOLE!!!!!!!!. SUCK-HOLE!!!!!!!!!!!"

And Brother Lundy was letting it happen, as if part of him admired the two lads who'd made their stand. He'd asked for the Singing Nun, as was demanded of his position, but maybe he had a greater respect for Jagger.

And to heap shame on shame it was Fatty Gruntle who came to Sean's rescue. Seeing an opportunity to regain the authority snatched from him by Johnson and Rylands, he pushed in front of Brother Lundy roaring "Stop it! Stop it right now!"

The boys nearest to him quit the slurping first, and silence spread backwards to the edges of the hall. Gruntle's finger waved over the boys like a pound of uncooked Cumberland.

"If I hear that word one more time, I will make a public display of the person who utters it," he shouted. "When a boy like McCaffery behaves in the obedient and respectful manner that I expect of every Meadowlands pupil, I will not tolerate such an obscene and disgusting response."

The silence was worse than the hissing contempt. Sean was allied with Fatty Gruntle. Fatty Gruntle was defending him. Fatty Gruntle was his friend. Christ God Almighty!

"Now sit down," continued Gruntle, "and when you have finished your meals, you are to remain in your places until I give you permission to leave."

The hall filled with noise; angry mutterings, chairs scraping viciously against the linoleum floor, the clash of cutlery and the clatter of plates. Before he sat down, Gruntle reached over Sean's table and swapped back the platter of chips.

67

"With two missing from this table you'll not need all these," he said, and waddled to his seat looking very pleased with himself.

"Greedy fat shit," muttered Sean as Gruntle turned his back, but it wasn't loud enough for a true show of guts, and everyone knew it, especially Sean himself.

He sat down and made a grab for the chips, but another hand was there before him. He reached for the chunks but they were taken away too. He tried to pretend that this was normal, but how could it be when he was too ashamed to lift his eyes from his plate? Everyone around him was silent. Even Bill O'Rourke was tight-lipped.

The platters moved from hand to hand, but somehow they never made it to Sean. They were put back in the middle of the table where he had to reach for them himself. As he did, the boys shrank away from him as if he were diseased. Even Molyneux and Walker despised him. His appetite was gone. He ate to occupy the time.

The chunks were gristly globs of flesh, the chips limp fingers of grease, but he choked them down. He was last to finish the main course, and was about to reach for dessert when he saw that the other boys had divided the apple pie between them. He said nothing. What could he say? He couldn't even look them in the face. And he had a horrible feeling that at any minute he just might burst into tears.

The angry hum of conversation in the hall increased as the stacking of plates fell silent at the end of the meal, and the boys shifted in their seats, eager for their thirty minutes of freedom before the start of afternoon classes. Only Sean's table remained silent. Eventually Fatty Gruntle lumbered to his feet.

"I won't have prayers of thanksgiving made a mockery of," he began. "The two boys that chose to make a joke out of saying Grace will be dealt with by the Headmaster in an appropriate fashion......"

"Leather cassock and bullwhip," whispered Bill O'Rourke, forgetting for a second that Sean was in Coventry.

".....but I consider you all to be guilty for encouraging and supporting such disrespectful behaviour. And I will not tolerate that vulgar and disgusting performance when one boy elected to do his duty." He put on an unctuous smile, and spoke as if granting Sean a huge favour. "McCaffery, you may now go and enjoy recess. The rest of you will sit here in silence until I decide that you can leave. And you will use that time to consider the reasons that you are being held in detention."

Sean didn't move, praying for a bolt of lightening to strike him dead - him and Fatty Gruntle both. A minute ago he could hardly wait to get away, but now his release was just another betrayal. If he threw Gruntle's offer back in his face, if he stayed and showed just a little of the solidarity that had been expected of him, maybe he'd escape the worst consequences of his cowardice.

But Fatty Gruntle was having none of that. He could read Sean's face and smell his fear. It was a skill developed over more than twenty years of his own brand of teaching.

"Go on boy," he said. "Out you go." And his blubbery lips pulled back in a smile that turned every stomach in the hall.

Sean pushed back his chair, aching to throw a word or a fist into that pudding of a face, but he knew he didn't have the balls. Each step towards the door was a step away from self-respect. The hiss was the barest whisper, but he heard it at every table.

"SssssssssssssssuuuuuuuuuuuuucccccccccckkkkkkkkkkHOLE!"

Sly boots flashed out and hacked at his ankles. Gobs of spit flecked the front of his blazer. Even the first formers looked on him with contempt. He was a blackleg scab. Scum. He was everything he would have called some other poor bastard who'd just chickened out.

He knew that he'd have to make up for this. Knew he'd have to do something to show whose side he was really on. Something outrageous enough to get him accepted again. Something that took real guts.

But right now, with the boots flailing and the spit flying, he couldn't imagine what that might possibly be.

Chapter 8: Galahad

Sean wanted to hide in the toilets. Instead he made his way to the playing fields and trudged, head down, to Cockblock Brook, the narrow stream that separated the Meadowlands Boys' Grammar from the West Meadow Girls' Grammar on the other side. He avoided the boys from St. David's and St. Andrew's houses who had eaten lunch at the first sitting. They didn't know he was a suckhole. Not yet. But they'd find out soon enough. If he joined them now it would be all the worse when they turned on him later.

The brook was just a few yards wide and no more than a foot deep in the middle, but the steep banks sloping down to the muddy water made it an effective barrier against the type of intercourse that the boys most wanted with the girls, and that the teachers on both sides of the brook were most anxious to prevent. The West Meadow girls knew this and taunted the boys by promenading up and down the banks with skirts hitched way up their thighs, and blouses unbuttoned right down to their nipples. Their uniform was supposed to include maroon belly knickers, but it was a sport with the least modest of them to show how much they flaunted the rule.

The day was hot enough for Fearon to have discarded his Crombie, and he prowled the brook with his lackeys ranking the girls on shaggability. Sean hardly looked at them as he slumped down on the bank at a point as far as possible from the rest of the boys. It wouldn't be long now, he thought, before fatty Gruntle would let out the second sitting, and then the shit would fly.

Sure enough, just a few minutes later the rising clamour on the playing fields told him that St. George's and St. Patrick's houses had been released from detention.

They were on him immediately. Not one of them spoke, but they all started grunting for greenies and launching them at his back. He would have been covered in phlegm if it wasn't for some look-out who shouted that the Stomachs were coming - Fatty Gruntle, Snake McClatchie and HAL, patrolling the playing fields on the look-out for anyone having too much fun.

Sean turned his face away and caught sight of Bill O'Rourke walking towards him. He felt a huge wave of gratitude, and a smile spread across his face before he realized that Bill hadn't seen him yet. He was too late to wipe the smile away before Bill caught sight of him, pulled up short, made a charade of forgetting something back at the school (even striking himself on the forehead, the stupid sod), and turned back to where he'd come from. Sean couldn't blame him, but Bill turning away from him like that was harder to take than any amount of snot and saliva. He squeezed his eyes tight to hold back self-pitying tears. *You're pathetic*, he thought, *truly fucking pathetic.*

Klank clattered towards him on his leg-irons, arms swinging out left and right as he pulled himself along on his crutches. He waited for Klank to launch a greeny too, but Klank gave him a straight-forward grin from his lop-sided head and rattled past, carrying on his circuit of the soccer field where the able-bodied were doing, without a second thought, what Klank could never dream of. And yet Klank had a grin for everyone, even a scum-bag like Sean who realized, for the first time, how alone Klank must feel every minute of every lunch-break. The boys might pity him, but free time was too precious, and soccer too important, to make room for Klank's leg-irons. And anyway, he seemed happy enough, Spina Bifida notwithstanding - as he would joke at his own expense. So the poor bugger clattered along on his rounds, dispensing grins, and killing time, until he could sit in class again just like everyone else.

A soccer ball careered over Sean's head and landed with a splash in the brook on the girls' side of the water. A gang of lower sixth formers came charging up towards the spot where he was sitting, shouting abuse at each other. Fearon was in the lead, and Sean thought it wise to get out of the way. Stick around and he'd be hurled six feet into the ditch and told to go fetch. He elbowed his way through a crowd of younger boys who were gathered at what they thought was a safe distance, yelling taunts in their whiny voices. Any minute now one of them would be grabbed and sent for a swim. Sean turned to see who it might be.

And there, on the other side of the brook, was Paula Yates.

Everything else disappeared. Bill, Gruntle, Fearon, ceased to exist. She was with a group of friends, but they could have been stark naked and Sean would not have noticed. He couldn't move. A rush of fizzy blood flooded his heart, and his eyes stretched wide to take in every inch of her. She was passing the point where the ball lay at the side of the brook, and one bright spark, deciding that this was a God-given opportunity to get a good look up her skirt, made a move to go scrambling down the bank to retrieve it. But Fearon grabbed him by the collar and yanked him back. He had other ideas.

"Hey Paula," he yelled, "do us a favour and get the ball for us would you?

She gave him a withering look.

"Come on Paula, I'm sorry about this morning, it was just a bit of a joke. Not funny, I know."

He looked and sounded sincere, his voice so politely middle-class. A smile broke across his handsome face. Winsome, is how Sean would have described a smile like that, the fucking prick. Paula's friends whispered to her in girlish giggles and she looked appraisingly across the brook at Fearon. Coquettish, Sean thought to himself, and hated that cocky bastard with a murderous intensity.

Paula detached herself from the group and walked to the edge of the bank. She leaned forward to see where the ball lay on a patch of grass at the edge of the brook, her red gold hair falling forward to frame the perfect curve of her generous breasts. Sean heard the collective sigh, and was ashamed to find himself joining in. She straightened up and then squatted down at the lip of the bank with her knees pressed together. Sighs turned to groans. Paula put one hand on the grass behind her, and pointed one leg straight out and down to get a foothold amid the grassy clumps of earth on the broken slope. She was being ultra-careful, but every boy knew there'd be that microsecond chance as she stretched out the other leg to make her descent.

And there they were!!!! Oh my God, one agonising flash then gone - pale blue lace, and hardly enough cloth to cover the head of a kitten. Hands reached into pockets for loose coins and lost sweets. She was half way down the bank and the leg show was over, but all eyes were on her breasts now as the boys jostled each other on the edge of the slope to get the best view down her blouse. She shuffled to the edge of the water, and as she stooped to pick up the ball, there

74

was an unrestrained "Oooooooh!!!!!" as her blouse parted and all but the tiny part of her breasts covered by the pale blue bra was revealed to those on the grandstand.

Paula lobbed the ball with an underhand swing and sent it sailing over the heads of the boys to roll away on the grass behind them. She expected to see them scatter after it, but not one of them moved. And suddenly she understood. She was looking at a pack slobbering hounds, while her cheeks burned as bright as her hair. Sean willed himself to walk away, to show that he wasn't one of them, but the brain between his legs wouldn't let him.

She paused at the bottom of the bank considering what to do. It would be easiest to scramble back to the top by turning her back on the boys, but that would give them a triple X view of her backside, being all too well aware of the paucity of her knickers. Harder would be to shuffle up the slope facing forward, but at least that way she could attempt some preservation of modesty.

She pulled her skirt down low on her thighs, placed both hands behind her on the bank and, leaning back, began to shuffle up the slope, bending her knees as little as possible. It was slow progress, and she felt ridiculous and humiliated, but the determined look on her face, and the steady contempt in her eyes, challenged the leering mob. Sean hated himself for looking on with them, but he just couldn't look away.

She was nearly at the top, and needed just a last boost to set her bottom on the grass, when her shoes slipped on the loose soil and she fell backwards against the slope. To avoid tumbling down into the water, she abandoned the effort to keep her knees together, and in the few seconds it took for her to regain her footing one Latin scholar roared *Sanctum Sanctorum!* and the rest of the boys broke into an uproar of foul-mouthed jabbering as if they'd escaped from a madhouse for the sexually disturbed. Fearon was chief among them, making masturbatory motions with one hand and slapping the back of his neck with the other.

Paula flushed scarlet, turned her back and scrambled up the slope showing off all of her gorgeous bum. This brought a fresh round of jabbering from the boys as if the sight of her behind had robbed them of human speech. Fearon yelled above the sounds of the menagerie.

"Well, I think that settles it lads? After inspection at close quarters I think we can agree that Ginge the Minge really is a genuine redhead."

Another chorus of jungle sounds and Paula's lips quivered with sobs.

The sight of her like that unlocked something in Sean, something that had been clawing at him ever since Fearon had spouted his filthy remarks earlier that morning. Without thinking of what he was about to do, he found himself running full tilt towards Fearon's back. There was no time to talk himself out of it this time. It was a reflex of pure hatred. The flip side of hopeless love. His shoulder smashed low into Fearon's spine, Fearon's arms shot skywards, his body arched back with the force of the blow, and he was sent cartwheeling down the bank to land face down in the slimy water.

For a few seconds there was astonished silence as if the boys and girls on either side of the brook had witnessed a miracle. The impossible had happened. The most notorious bully in Meadowlands had been sent headlong into the ditch by a little weed from the third form, and was sitting there spitting sludge and looking like an absolute gob-smacked dick-head, while the weed glowered down on him as if daring him to come back for more.

They couldn't have been more stunned if Klank had pulled off his leg irons and done a tap dance.

And then one of the boys laughed. The expression on Fearon's face was priceless. The arrogant prick looked like a retard playing in the mud. Those curly locks he was so proud of were plastered across his forehead and the snide self assurance was knocked clean off his clock to leave him gaping like an imbecile as he tried to figure out what had happened. And then it came to him. Somebody had hit him. Somebody had actually hit him!

The laughter spread across both sides of the brook. Everyone, boys and girls alike, were falling about in hysterics. And these were genuine belly laughs too, not the sham stuff Fearon's buddies had choked up for the sake of humiliating Paula.

Fearon knew it. He could hear the effortless expression of people having fun at his expense - making fun of him....him! His faced burned with humiliation, and there was murder in his eyes, absolute bloody murder. Somehow that made everyone laugh all the more. Everyone except Sean. He just stood there looking down at Fearon, still sitting gob-smacked in the slime, and reveled in the marvelous cathartic glow of a job well done. Go get him Galahad, Bill O'Rourke had sneered that morning. *Well Bill bloody O'Rourke*, he thought, *what do you think of that?*

Fearon spotted him, saw his was the only face among the seeming thousands that was not contorted with laughter, and he knew, incredible as it seemed, that Sean McCaffery, that scruffy little bastard from 3X, had shoved him down the bank. A latent fear that he might have to take revenge on someone his own size gave way to an incandescent fury.

"You!" he screamed, pointing a dripping finger at Sean. "You!!!!"

Sean didn't flinch. He was looking across the brook at Paula Yates, and she was looking right back at him. He'd saved her. Only something as wild as this could have shifted the focus from her mortification, and Sean had provided it. Her eyes were still rimmed with tears, but they were shining now with a very different kind of light. He held her gaze, hopeless passion written on his face, and she smiled at him, warm and kind and lovely, so that even if he never got to kiss those lips he'd still be forever grateful for those few precious seconds. And then she retreated back into the throng of her friends and was gone.

Sean turned away too, and every eye that fell on him gleamed with satisfaction. *Right on!* they all said, though not a word was spoken. *Right on!.....And tough luck son, because you'll not live to see another lunch time.*

The bell sounded to call the boys back to class, and the crowd at Sean's back parted to let him pass. Hands reached out to touch his shoulder as he led the boys back to the school. Redemption had come with that insane act of courage, and the chicken shit suck-hole was now everyone's conquering hero. At least until the end of the day....until school finished.....and after that......well........?

Behind the departing crowd there was a frantic splashing from the bottom of the brook. The bell had brought Fearon back to what remained of his senses. He dragged himself up the bank, his new clothes coated in filth.

"You're dead McCaffery!" he screamed.

"You..... are...... fucking....... dead!!!"

CHAPTER 9: Preacher Man, Teacher Man

It was a wild afternoon in class. Sean had flung Fearon into the brook, he'd been rewarded with a smile from Paula Yates, and now he felt like he could do anything. He was dead...*Fucking Dead!*..... but there was life in him yet.

Religious Studies was taught by Brother Jerome, a pock-marked little man sagging gracelessly into middle age, though he'd barely reached thirty. He moved with the lethargy of terminal depression, and carried the same energy into his lessons. Today's class was all about Purgatory and, with an hour of it to sit through, the boys would know by the end of it what Purgatory was all about.

Brother Jerome gave them the Catholic party line, droning on about the fate of the departed as if he'd just come back from a guided tour of the hereafter. He painted absurd pictures of sinners hovering above the flames of Hell as if suspended on hooks in a rotisserie. These were not the hard core mortal sinners, he explained, the murderers and blasphemers, those were screaming below in the sulphurous pit just like they deserved. No, those in purgatory had died without absolution and were suffering for the venial sins they'd committed after their last confession.

Sean almost laughed out loud. Maybe it was the scene that had just played out at the brook, but he could just imagine it - some poor sod walking out of the confessional in a state of absolute grace, the rosary rattled off, and his soul scrubbed spotless. Next minute, he's out on the street when the wind blows Paula's skirt up around her waist, and he's so rapt in unclean thoughts that he doesn't see the truck that sends him to his final reckoning. Before he knows what's what he's standing before St. Michael who's shaking his halo with the book open on his lap.

"Tough luck," says St. Mike, "if you could have just have kept your dirty mind off Paula's parts for those last few mortal seconds, I might have let you through. But it's down into Purgatory for you old lad until the folks at home have prayed you back up to heaven."

According to Brother Jerome, the departed could only escape from Purgatory if friends and family took the time to pray them out of it. Sean imagined thousands, no billions of souls, twitching on their hooks as the Almighty held their feet to the fire. Every now and again there'd be a yank, and one of them would go shooting up a few yards as a praying relative scored a hit.

Sean had had enough of this shit.

"Excuse me Brother," he asked, "what about those sinners with no-one to pray for them? Do they hang in Purgatory forever? It seems harsh of a compassionate God to discriminate against those without a family."

A frown added another shade of ugliness to Brother Jerome's spotty face. He was groping for an answer when Sean cut him off.

"And what if your relatives didn't like you? I suppose they could keep you in Purgatory just out of spite couldn't they? And what would happen if you just needed a little push to get you over the top when the prayers stopped? Wouldn't it be even worse to be peering through the gates of Heaven without ever getting in?"

Brother Jerome was not used to questions. He liked to prattle Catholic dogma without thought or interruption. And there was a definite hint of impertinence in McCaffery's questions that he didn't like at all. But Sean had put on a straight face and looked genuinely interested in the mechanics of salvation. Brother Jerome fumbled for an explanation, not willing to admit ignorance.

"It's a very complex thing......," he muttered, trying to dredge up an answer, ".....A very complex thing....." The implication being that Sean was too stupid to understand it. Then his brow cleared as inspiration descended.

"That's why we should pray daily for all the departed whether we have known them or not, so that they may be all raised together towards the heavenly Father."

What a load of bollocks, thought Sean, imagining the entire population of Purgatory being yanked en masse towards heaven with a big grunt as the Celestial Prayer-Catcher fielded a universal petition. The whole thing was fucking ridiculous.

Limbo was next on Brother Jerome's tour of the after-life – the cheerless place where unbaptised babies go when they die. It was the ultimate guilt trip for Catholic mothers, generations of them conned into baptising their kids rather than risk the possibility of an eternity of abandonment. Brother Jerome even suggested that the boys should conduct surreptitious baptisms over the prams of heathens when the mothers weren't looking. Just flick some holy water, make a sign of the cross, say the magic words and you could save a wee child from eternity in an orphanage for the dead.

Sean thought that carrying around baptismal water might be a little impractical and was about to ask whether spit might do, but decided he'd be pushing his luck. His hand went up and Brother Jerome was stopped short in his nonsense.

"I expect Brother that there must be an awful lot of Chinese babies in Limbo," he said.

There was a ripple of laughter from the class, but Sean kept it deadpan.

"What do you mean McCaffery?"

"Well, considering that hardly any Chinese are baptized, and seeing that there's so many of them, and that the infant mortality rate in China is so high, I reckon Limbo must be chocker-block with Chinese babies. Not to mention Indians and Pakistanis."

The ugly frown returned to Brother Jerome's face. Somehow the idea of Limbo being crowded with foreign babies had never occurred to him. There seemed something wrong with the picture, but he couldn't deny the logic of it. He was about to resort to the usual reflex in such cases, and descend on Sean with a roundhouse slap in the face, when Bill O'Rourke put his hand up and didn't wait before asking his question. He kept it deadpan too.

"Do babies in Limbo grow up Brother, or do they stay babies for ever and ever?"

Brother Jerome didn't know. He'd never thought about it, the way he'd never thought through any of this garbage. A faint blush began to appear as a backdrop to his pimples. He looked besieged. He was about to mutter "It's a very complex thing..." when Sean chimed in again.

"Don't you think it's a bit unfair, Brother, that the babies should be kept away from their mothers forever just because they haven't been baptized? I mean it's not their fault is it? And what if the mother were to die and go to heaven while her baby was stuck in Limbo? You told us last class that in heaven we'd all be re-united, but wouldn't the mother be a bit cheesed off if she couldn't be with her dead baby?"

The classroom began to buzz. Religious Studies was usually a snorer, but Sean had got them thinking - mostly that Brother Jerome was a dick-head. It showed on their faces, and Brother Jerome's blush deepened to a sweaty scarlet. Bill O'Rourke butted in again.

"What do the babies do in Limbo, Brother? Do they just kind of sit there and gurgle or do they get to play with each other?"

That was enough – direct insolence! He wasn't having this in his class. He strode toward O'Rourke with an arm outstretched for a back-hander, but Horrocks got in on the game and diverted him.

"Do they ever learn to speak properly Brother, or do they just talk baby talk forever?"

He turned toward the new voice, his hand still poised for a slap, but then the rest of the class joined in, questions coming from all sides so that his head looked as if it might screw itself off as he twisted it back and forth with no time for an answer in between.

-Are they in one big nursery Brother, or do they get sorted?

-By age maybe?

-Do you get older after you're dead, Brother?

-Maybe they sort them by colour?

-Wouldn't that be discrimination?

-There'd have to be a Gozzilion cribs in Limbo.

-Do babies sleep after they're dead, Brother?

-What about feeding? Does someone have to bring them bottles?

-Who changes their nappies?

-Do you have bowel movements in Limbo Brother?

-Do any of them ever get into Heaven?

-Course they do. They Limbo dance under the gates!

Authority and credibility went out of the window with the general roar of laughter. Brother Jerome knew deep down that something was terribly lacking in his concept of the after-life, but he wasn't prepared to think about that now. He had to stop this insolence. Discipline, that's what was needed; a good solid beating to bring them to heel. An example – he needed to make an example of someone.

He reached out blindly and, as luck would have it, grabbed Kevin Purvis by the hair. Purvis looked up at him in total bewilderment. He was a good boy, from a decent Catholic family of the right sort. He was flabby, and girlish, and one of the Seminarians, and had never been beaten in his life. If there was one boy that the others thought might end up in Brothers' robes it was Perv Purvis. And now he was being pulled out of his seat and dragged to the front of the class.

Brother Jerome knew he'd made a mistake. He liked Kevin Purvis, knew him to be quiet, and modest and no trouble. But he couldn't let him go now, that would be showing the class how rattled he was. They'd have won if he did that - and what then?

"I won't have this behaviour," he shouted. "I won't have this heathen disrespect in my class."

He pushed down on Purvis's head, bending him at the waist.

"Eh up," said Horrocks in a stage whisper, "Perv's got another one of 'em at it."

The ripple of laughter only steeled Brother Jerome's resolve. "I won't have this insolence," he yelled, "not if I have to make an example out of every one of you."

He looked to the blackboard where a cane would usually hang, but there was no weapon to hand. For want of anything better he brought his hand down on Purvis's behind with a liquid slap, and then raised it again for a second blow.

"Ooooh Naughty!" whispered Horrocks. "I like that!"

Brother Jerome didn't hear, but Purvis's face burned with a humiliation that had nothing to do with the undeserved punishment. Brother Jerome slapped him on the arse four times, counting *One... Two... Three... Four...* as if that was what he had meant to do all along, and feeling more and more ashamed of himself at every stroke.

"And let that be a lesson to all of you," he cried. "I won't tolerate disrespect for the Catholic Church, and if any of you lack faith in its teachings I'll make damned sure you're thrown out of this school on your back-sides."

He'd no sooner finished his speech than the bell sounded for the next class, and he strode from the room knowing that he'd made an absolute bloody fool of himself. Hooting and laughter erupted as he slammed the door, and he trembled with rage as he made his way to the staff room - rage, shame and a darker feeling that sloshed in the pit of his stomach.

He'd thought he was through with all that, but it was still there. Christ, after ten years of self-control, it was still there! He felt like plunging the hand that had touched Purvis's bottom into a cleansing fire, but there was no denying the sick excitement that had set him shaking. Sitting in a corner of the Brothers' Common Room away from his colleagues, he replayed the Religion lesson obsessively as he chain-smoked his way through a pack of Capstan Full Strength. What had happened? How the hell had he lost control?

"McCaffery," he decided at last. "It was that scruffy little bastard McCaffery."

85

Ben Gibbs entered 3X to the usual roar of inter-class chaos. Mr. Grodon, who delivered Geography and discipline with the aid of a size 10 gym shoe, had just left, and the effect had been like popping the lid off a well-shaken bottle of Tizer. Ben's entrance had no effect whatsoever on the effervescence, but he didn't care. Kids were supposed to be rambunctious. If the events at morning assembly had in any way quelled the warm disrespect that he knew the kids felt for him, he would have counted it a terrible loss.

Ben was as bald as a pebble, his round shiny head belying the fact that he was only 45. He always wore the same tweed jacket with the leather patches on the elbows, and a woolen tie that he didn't know how to fasten. He was a quiet, gentle slob, and in all his years of teaching he'd never once used corporal punishment.

Ben had come to accept violence as natural to adolescent boys, particularly those from disturbed families, and he had interviewed enough parents at PTA meetings to understand why certain students were brutal. But he could never reconcile himself to violence in adults. It shamed him to see a child beaten or humiliated by a teacher. He'd taken Halligan to sick bay that morning and left him there with the school nurse. She had pursed her lips at the sight of the lacerated flesh on the boy's backside, but had said nothing. Silence, that was the problem with this systematic abuse, the way it was all accepted in silence.

The accelerated X-stream boys were Meadowland's brightest, selected after their first form exams. They were schooled towards academic excellence by a strict and rigorous attention to the curriculum. If an X-stream boy failed to understand a concept, at least he could parrot back the facts after writing them out a hundred times for the lousy teacher who had failed to get the message across. Passing GCE A-Levels and improving the school's statistics was what the X classes were all about. Every X class boy was expected to enter University after leaving school whether he wanted to or not. Sean and Bill were in 3X, and university was still four years away, but the prospect was all they lived for.

"All right, settle down now boys," said Ben, and the din retreated gradually as he waited.

Ben had an obligation to cover the material in the English curriculum but the direction he'd take to do it would depend on any number of ideas that might pop up a as the lesson progressed. That was the fun part - improvisation, and the ready brilliance of the boys. He really loved his job. Today he'd planned a lesson on figurative language, but he'd get around to similes and metaphors later. While hiding out in his office he'd picked up the morning paper to stop himself brooding on the Halligan affair, and had been struck by a number of the headlines. Turning a broad flabby back to the boys he wrote on the board in exquisite copperplate:

"Hiring of new fire-fighters sparks hot debate in City Council"

"British sheep farmers being fleeced by the Common Market."

He paused for a moment with the chalk poised, shrugged his shoulders and wrote:

"Choir master in assault case must face the music."

The boys were grinning when he turned to face them. There was no need to waste time on explanations, but he couldn't resist.

"Alright boys," he said, "You have left school and, filled with the spirit of Orwell and Hemingway, you must live by your wits as freelance newspaper reporters. It's a noble calling. However, if the editor doesn't read what you write you don't get to eat, so you must capture his attention with a good headline. Choose any subject you like, and over the next ten minutes I want each of you to come up with three headlines that the editor can't possibly resist.

He could almost hear a mental click as the boys registered the idea and moved into creative mode. McCaffery's eyes glassed over, O'Rourke was eating the end of his pencil, Rylands was stroking an invisible beard and Dougan's finger was excavating his nostrils as if to massage his brains from the inside. Every now and again there would be a wicked grin and a flurry of writing, and Ben would smile as if he could read the thought bubbles above the students' heads.

He walked slowly between the desks, the students leaning over their scribble as he approached, and then leaning back as he moved on. He wasn't hassling them. He walked because he preferred walking to keeping still. It was the only exercise he cared for. Squeezing his accordion at weekend ceiledhs might be good for the arms, but any physical benefit was more than offset by drinking several pints while doing it. After ten minutes he hoisted one fat buttock onto the corner of the teacher's desk and let his gaze wander over the boys, looking for an eager face. There were several.

"OK, Ashton, impress me."

Ashton cleared his throat and held his exercise book in front of him as if reciting from the Bible.

"Sheep Farmers' Meeting Convenes in Ramsbottom," he announced.

There was a ripple of laughter and a few groans. Ben smiled indulgently.

"If such a coincidence of event and location were actually to happen your headline would be a pearler," he said, "but you'd probably starve waiting for the opportunity to use it. Dougan, what do you have?"

Dougan shuffled a slimy manuscript and read:

"Sheep farmers tell government they won't have wool pulled over their eyes."

More groans and a few titters.

"Horrocks, your turn."

"Sheep Farmer's say the Common Market is Really Baaaaahd!!!"

Horrocks received an appreciative laugh.

"Ask an idiot," sighed Ned as he turned to the blackboard and erased the sheep headline.

"Now," he said "does anyone have anything less ovine to offer?"

Bill O'Rourke put his hand in the air, and after getting the nod announced;

"Physics Teacher States Pressure and Strain Accelerated Nervous Breakdown."

This was pushing it. Hamish Ferguson, the unbalanced physics master, legendary for his fits of rage over botched homework, had been replaced by HAL the previous year, and was understood to be a current inmate of Rainhill Psychiatric Hospital.

But Ben smiled saying "And you could, no doubt, add the Density of his students as contributing to his complaint. Phillipson, what do you have?"

Phillipson hesitated. He looked down at his page and then up at Ben. He turned his eyes back to the exercise book and mumbled

"Nothing Sir."

"Come on, Phillipson," said Ned. "I saw you scribbling away just now. Don't tell me it was just automatic writing. Even if it was, let's hear what the spirits have to say. I'm sure it can't be worse than the offerings we've heard already."

Phillipson looked again at his book and flushed, but he appeared more angry than embarrassed. He took a deep breath and blurted out:

89

"Spanking New Head of Grammar School Beats against Reform of Corporal Punishment."

The class was silent, all eyes flickering between Phillipson and Ben; the one defiant, the other looking into the distance, deep in thought.

"Very good, Phillipson," said Ben at last. "It seems the preface for a very sad tale, so maybe we'd better move on. Alright boys, Figurative Language. What it is, and how, when and why it is used......... and abused. Similes, metaphors and imagery."

And so the class progressed, in a more sombre atmosphere than it had started.

Things perked up again towards the end when Horrocks asked whether he could be excused to visit the toilet. Ned considered for a moment:

"Alright Horrocks, but first extemporize figuratively on your condition. Do you need to pedal on the Nitrogen Cycle? Does the flood beat against the dam? Do you wish to shake hands with the Bishop? Come on Horrocks, outdo me."

Horrocks grinned. "Actually sir, it's a tortoise head."

Ben, disgusted and delighted, burst into laughter with the rest of them.

Chapter 9: No Mercy

Bill O'Rourke was unusually quiet as he left school that afternoon with Sean. Normally, they'd exchange a cynical review of the day's lessons, each telling the other how much the teachers still had to learn. But right now Bill had no idea what to say. After all, what do you say to a condemned man?

Why didn't I think of earning myself a detention? thought Bill. Just a few words to shit-faced Shaughnessy about his shitty face and I could have been back in class right now, writing a hundred leisurely lines. Instead I'm lumbered with being the best friend of someone who's about to get the living shit kicked out of him, and there's nothing I can do about it even if I was mad enough to try.

Groups of boys stared at them as they made their way through the school gates towards the bus stop. Some followed surreptitiously, not wanting to show too much eagerness for what was about to happen. After all, this was not going to be a fight, this was going to an execution. They'd expected it at afternoon recess, but Fearon hadn't appeared in the schoolyard. Instead he was sitting outside the sick bay while the nurse dried his clothes and – get this for a lark - the only thing she'd had to cover him up with was one of the Brothers' old cassocks. The look on his face spelled murder - murder for anyone who even thought about calling him

Brother Fearon, and murder for that little shit who'd had the nerve.........the absolute fucking nerve to............Jesus, he was going to kill the bastard!

"Like being on a bleeding tumbril," thought Bill as they trudged on. "All we need is Madame Lafarge."

As if hearing his thoughts, one boy dodged in front of them and drew a finger slowly across his throat. The group around him burst into excited laughter. Some had been there to see Sean's attack on Fearon, others had just heard the story, and there were even those who pretended to have seen it because to have missed something like that was like missing your first shag. In the few short hours between then and now Sean had become a celebrity; a third year who had brought the school bully to his knees and made him the laughing stock of the Boys' and Girls' Grammar schools. But now it was payback time, and admiration for what he'd done didn't reduce the blood-lust of the boys in the slightest. First hand or second, everyone had heard Fearon's words from the bottom of the brook, and some of them mouthed them again as Bill and Sean walked by.

"You're dead McCaffery. You are fucking dead!"

Bill prayed that that didn't include him too.

Fearon wasn't at the bus stop yet, but there seemed to be a lot more boys than usual waiting for the number 97 to Duggin. There were even some who had missed their own bus and would be walking the 12 miles to Widnes just to be present for this. They weren't milling about in a jumbled queue as they usually would, vying to be first aboard when the bus pulled up, instead they were in a herding pattern, forming a rough circle around Sean and Bill, moving the two boys inexorably towards a narrow grassy verge in front of the houses that bordered the road. There'd be plenty of space there for what was about to happen, but they still jostled to be in the front row for when Fearon showed up. Some had even climbed on top of a nearby garden wall, clinging to the privet bushes to get their heads above the crowd. An elderly woman leaned from her upstairs window and roared at them to get down, but she might have been shouting at the wall itself for all the good it did.

'Bloody Collisseum," thought Bill, as he gazed anxiously up the road, hoping that the bus would come early before Fearon arrived. There was no sign of it.

A party atmosphere developed as the crowd attracted more and more boys to itself. The throat-slitter was at it again with his finger. Next to him some little prick made a gun out of his hand and pointed it at the side of his head. He cocked his thumb and threw himself sideways to the ground. This set off a mime fest of violent death, with boys choking at the end of imaginary ropes, disemboweling themselves, and acting out the intentions that Fearon was sure to have on Sean's testicles. Stage fights broke out with colossal head butts to the face and full-blooded boots to the bollocks, all of it laced with banter:

-Cor smell that?

-Bet I can guess where that's coming from.

-Don't take your bike clips off McCaffery or we'll drown in it.

-Hey, hear about the last bloke Fearon nailed?

-Hospital for a month wasn't it?

-Teeth gone, front and back.

-Nose spread all over his face.......splat!

-Balls kicked to a jelly .....ooofff!!!.

-Never walked straight again.

-Evil bastard that Fearon.

-Glad he aint after me.

-Doesn't know when to stop, that's his problem.

93

-Has to be dragged off.

-No chance of that today.

-Safest to let him get on with it.

-Play dead, that's what I say.

-Unless you're dead already.

-Hey, he's coming!

-Ooooh, now you're for it McCaffery.

-He's gonna bleeding maim you.

-Wearing his Oxfords too. Look at them toes caps.

-God, they make a right bloody mess when they go in.

-Better run it McCaffery.

-Better run it or you're bleeding dead.

But Sean wasn't about to run. The crowd wouldn't let him, and even if he did there'd always be tomorrow, or the next day. Fearon would get him eventually, so what was the point? And anyway, whatever happened in the next few minutes would have been worth it for that smile from Paula Yates. Sean was in love, and like many a poor sod before him he was going to pay dearly for it.

Fearon threw boys left and right as he pushed his way into the open space. The cassock was gone, the stylish grey pants were spattered with mud, and the white Ben Sherman shirt was skew-bald with patchy filth. He stood close to the inner circle of boys, leaving a gap between himself and Sean - enough to get in a good swing with his boot. Bill O'Rourke looked at the floor and shuffled backwards away from his friend to join the ring of boys behind him. It unmanned him, but his friendship stopped short of suicide.

Fearon took his time, pacing back and forth along the inner perimeter of the boys, eyes fixed on Sean's face, a bunched fist slapping massively into his open palm. He ground a heel as if Sean's face was underneath it. He looked Sean up and down, deliberating where to hit him first.

"I'm going to fucking murder you McCaffery,' he said without a hint of exaggeration. Sean looked back at him, full in the face. If he was going to die, he'd do it on his feet, not on his knees.

-Go on Fearon, give it to him!
-Knock his bleedin' head off!
-Right in the goolies. What you waiting for?

The same boys that had patted Sean on the back at lunchtime were screaming for his blood. But Fearon wouldn't be rushed. He was going to take his time and enjoy this.

"I'm going to cripple you," he said. "I'm going to kick you unrecognizable. I'm going to boot your balls so far up your arse you'll need a vacuum cleaner to get them out again. And when I'm done with you that Yates bitch will puke all over your ugly face."

Sean grinned at him then, guessing his secret. Fearon intended to make sure that any outside chance Sean might have with Paula Yates ended here and now. He was going to rearrange Sean's face so badly he'd be freak show material for the rest of his life.

Fearon grabbed Sean by the collar, twisting the cloth in his fist so that his knuckles ground into Sean's throat, forcing his chin up so that Sean gazed right into his eyes. He'd put the boot in later. Right now he wanted to feel flesh on flesh. He wanted the satisfaction of destroying Sean's face with his bare hands. He placed his free fist against Sean's nose, pushing on it gently, and then drew it back in a straight line, letting Sean know exactly where it would land. The

Head had done exactly the same thing while caning Rodney Strong that morning.

-Go on Fearon, mash the little bleeder!
-Smack him a good one!
-Knock his frigging teeth out!

The circle of boys swayed in and out as they fought for position while giving Fearon room to do his stuff. No one wanted to miss any of this.

Fearon grinned. He looked around at the crowd, proud to be able to give them what they wanted.

"Say your prayers McCaffery," he said, and drew his fist back an inch further.

Sean didn't believe in guardian angels, but someone must have been watching over him because the circle of boys surged suddenly around Fearon knocking him off balance as he launched the fist. It went whistling past Sean's head as Fearon stumbled forward, dragging Sean by his collar and falling on top of him as he hit the ground. The boys stumbled over them, treading hard on fist and face. Behind them came a whirlwind swinging a house brush.

"Clear off! Clear off the lot of you. Hooligans is what you are. Nothing but a bunch of bloody hooligans!"

The old lady had been shouting from her bedroom window for the louts to get off her privets when one of the little bastards had given her two fingers. Two fingers indeed – the height of abuse! That was that. Her Albert hadn't died in the War to save the likes of little shits like that, and she'd not spent all this time on her own, keeping the house and garden decent, so that a gang of bloody yobs could come along and vandalise it. She'd reached for the nearest weapon and come down on them in a fury. Right now she was pounding away at some curly-haired lout lying at her feet while the other boys fled up the street or threw themselves on the platform of the bus that had pulled up beside her. She was stabbing him in the face with the bristles as he swung his head back and forth to trying to avoid the pummeling. And, God forgive her, she was enjoying every second of it.

"'Ang on luv, don't kill the lad. No sense in goin' to Chokey at your age, is there now?"

The bus conductor gripped the handle of the brush as it came up for another thrust, allowing Fearon to scramble out of the way and dive to safety on board the 97.

"That'll teach the no good rubbish," she said.

"Aye luv, and if I have any trouble with 'em on the bus, I'll know where to come for help."

He gave her a big grin as he climbed aboard and pressed the bell. The double-decker grunted away from the kerb with its cargo of hooligans, and the conductor waved at the old lady as she stood leaning on her brush as if she'd just finished sweeping the streets. She waved back, grinning, and feeling better than she'd done in years.

Chapter 10: A Good Battering

Fearon muscled into a seat opposite Sean and Bill, his face raw from the bristles of the old lady's brush.

"Don't think you're getting away with it McCaffery," he snarled, "I haven't even started with you. You and me are getting off this bus together, and when we do, there'll be no one to get in the way, just you bloody well wait."

Sean looked at him with barely a flicker of expression, while Bill O'Rourke pretended to be invisible. Bill didn't want any part of this. It wasn't his fault that Sean had gone barmy over some West Meadow tart. He got to his feet two stops before the place he usually got off and mumbled something about having to call on his auntie Joan. Sean gave him a quizzical smile, but said nothing. Bill flushed ruby red, but it didn't stop him from leaving anyway. Fearon weighed his big fist before letting it fall heavily onto his thigh. This time there was no pleasurable anticipation in his face, just impatience to get on with the job.

Fearon lived in the posh suburbs outside of Duggin where greenery replaced the concrete, but he got to his feet at the rough end of town as soon as Sean made his move towards the exit. A group of boys got up to follow, but Fearon turned on them.

"This isn't your stop," he spat. "It's his.......and mine."

The boys saw the dangerous look on his face, and even those that usually got off at the stop decided to take a longer walk home.

The bus pulled in to the curb on the main road near a line of shops, and for a second Sean considered stalling in front of the windows. Fearon wouldn't dare attack him in the open, he'd wait until he took Cack Alley back to the cul-de-sac. Maybe he should go the long way around, skipping the alley and walking the extra mile along the roads to come into the cul-de-sac from the top end, rather than under the railway arch and through the Entry. But something drove him on. It was almost as if he wanted this showdown with Fearon, as if he were some romantic hero who really wanted to die for his woman.

Despite the bravado, Sean was still a coward. He was afraid of pain, and Fearon scared the life out of him. And yet, as he came to the break in the line of shops, with the entrance to the DIC on one side of the road, and the path towards Cack Alley on the other, he turned his steps deliberately away from safety and began to walk, towards the isolation of the winding track.

Heavy-soled Oxfords crunched on the gravel behind him. Fearon wouldn't jump him just yet, they were still too close to the road. He'd wait for the right spot. Sean looked ahead judging where it would happen. Another twenty yards and the walls of wrecked buildings on either side of the track gave way to waste ground scattered with garbage. Fifty yards further on the track turned sharply to wander amid a stand of squat elderberry bushes that blocked the view from the road. It would be the perfect place for an ambush. That was where Fearon would do it.

As Sean approached the bushes, the nerves along his back and buttocks seemed to branch into a web of anticipatory pain, shrinking again as he caught sight of the dog squatting in the center

99

of the path. It was Betty Fairclough on her evening outing, letting her animal void its seemingly endless supply of shit. The realization that Sean was glad to see her made him aware of how badly afraid he was. He side-stepped the dog and continued along the path. The Oxfords crunched behind him.

Another fifty yards and the track twisted again. There, the bushes on his left were interrupted by a stone wall that ran along the length of the path. It was the side of an old storage shed for the railway, and the name of every lout in Duggin was scrawled across it in paint, or chiseled into the brick. Opposite, on the other side of the track, the bushes grew tall and dense.

This was it. No one around, and as far as possible from help in either direction. He slowed his pace as he reached the wall, almost as an invite. He read the graffiti:

Smozzer Rules!!
Big Annie does it for a tanner.
Paddy Morgan's got VD.

He wondered if Paddy Morgan and Big Annie were acquainted.

Shit! He reached out with both hands to stop his face from crashing into a drawing of a big hairy cock. He hit the wall, spun around, and then skipped sideways to avoid the toe cap that chipped the bricks next to his hip. Jesus! - that brick dust could have been his bollocks. The impact must have hurt Fearon despite the weight of his shoes, but his face showed only a choking rage. It was swollen, streaked grey with dirt from the street and red with the bristles of the brush. He grabbed Sean by the collar and swung back his fist, but the stupid bastard couldn't learn from history. He just couldn't stop himself from running off at the mouth.

"You dirty, scruffy little bastard," he spat, saliva spraying into Sean's face. "You smelly, ill-bred piece of shit. You low-born fucking cretin." It was poetry by Fearon's usual standards.

"I'm going to spread you all over that wall. I'm going to kick ten colours of shite out of you. And when I'm done they'll be carrying you back to your slum in a coffin."

"Get on with it then. Stop your bleeding mouthing and let's see you do it."

The voice came from behind Fearon. Sean couldn't see who it was, but it wasn't an adult's voice, and it sure as hell didn't sound like Superman to the rescue. Fearon kept hold of Sean's throat, but he turned his head to look behind.

"Eff off!," he said. "Eff off NOW or you'll get it too."

Sean caught the briefest glimpse of Jimmy Flint before Fearon turned again and blotted him out. Fearon didn't know Jimmy Flint or he wouldn't have made such a stupid mistake. The fist came back for a blow that would have demolished Sean's face, but it was caught from behind by slender bone-hard fingers that dug hard into the tendons of Fearon's wrist.

Fearon looked totally bewildered. He looked back at Flint as if he'd just discovered that Popeye was a real person. He kept hold of Sean with one hand and strained against Flint with the other, but Flint forced Fearon's arm further and further back until it twisted in the shoulder socket and caused him to cry out in pain.

Fearon let go of Sean's throat and spun around, untwisting his arm and launching his free fist in a roundhouse blow at the side of Flint's head. Flint seemed hardly to move, but in less than a second he'd dodged the fist and landed three short jabs, right, left, right, into Fearon's gut. Sean stepped out of the way as the blows sent the bully reeling back against the wall. Sean thought he might have been wrong about Superman until Flint opened his mouth again.

"You don't tell me to eff off you toffee-nosed twat. And you don't swing for me neither."

Jimmy Flint was twenty pounds lighter than Fearon, and at least two inches shorter, but he carried himself as if he were twice his size.

"Eff off," Fearon gasped. "Eff off now and I'll let you go. Otherwise I'll fucking kill you."

Tough words, but they came out of a quivering mouth.

Flint laughed and spat a gob of phlegm onto Fearon's shoe. It was enough to push Fearon through the red lights of instinct. He lifted both fists and slashed back and forth at Flint's head. It was the type of blundering viciousness a bully is used to getting away with, and effective only when the victim is scared to a standstill.

Flint was neither scared nor static. He leaned easily away from the fists, then landed a flurry of punches in Fearon's gut, the skinny arms working like co-ordinated pistons, slick, precise and methodical. He finished the session with an uppercut to the chin as Fearon doubled up, hard enough to bring him upright and send him backwards so that he banged his head solidly against the wall. It was done with such grace that Sean couldn't help but admire the brutality.

Fearon was stunned by more than the blow to his head. This wasn't supposed to happen. Skinny wimps like Flint were supposed to run away when they were told to eff off, or were battered without a fight if they didn't. Flint was breaking the rules. By the feel of it, he might also have broken Fearon's jaw. It didn't seem possible.

"For a Grammar-Grub you're not very bright are you?"

"What?" said Fearon. "What?" He looked totally confused. He even glanced an appeal at Sean, as if he might translate.

"Wot?" mimicked Flint. "Wot? Aren't you supposed to say pardon? That's rude that is. Looks like I'm going to have to teach you some manners."

The pistons went to work again, one fist to the nose, the other to an eye, and as Fearon covered his face with his hands, the fists moved automatically to his unprotected gut. Fearon's hands moved back to protect his mid-section, and the fists resumed the battering of his face, right to the left cheek, left to the right cheek, right to the mouth, left to the eye, right under the chin to lift him up, left into Fearon's nose that blossomed with a spray of blood. It was the work of a few seconds to reduce Fearon from an arrogant posturing bully to a whimpering wreck. He doubled up again, tucking his elbows into his gut and covering his face with his hands. Almost immediately he pulled them away again and stared terror-stricken at the great gobs of blood on his fingers. His blood. Not somebody else's – his!

"I'll get you for this!" he screamed. "I'll get my brother on to you. I'll get the police. You just wait, I'll fix you!"

Like Flint had said, Fearon wasn't very bright. Better to have stayed down and blubbered like the victims he was so used to tormenting. After all, what would Fearon have done if some poor battered sod had been stupid enough to threaten him? – Correct - exactly what Flint is doing now.

The punches go in harder than before, and Flint takes more time to pick his spots. It's less fluid, and a lot uglier. Fearon has no idea how to defend himself as Flint opens up each weak spot, batters it and moves to the next. He keeps up a casual commentary as he goes about his work.

"Get me will you?" Whack, in the right eye, already blue and bulbous. "Now how are you going to do that?" Whack, and Sean hears teeth shatter together. "Your brother? Don't know your brother, but give him this from me." Whack, and a bright red line dribbles from the cheekbone. "The police? Going down am I? I'd best make it worth my while then. Whack, whack, whack, all of them under the ribs, and Fearon folds forward dripping blood and snot down his fancy Ben Sherman shirt. Flint grabs him by the curly mop of hair and forces his face up.

"Fix me will you? Now how are you going to do that when I ain't broke? Reckon it's you who's broke." Whack whack, whack, whack, four short jabs with the right into his face making an absolute bloody mess of it.

Fearon's crying like a baby now, a horrible gurgling wail that bubbles through his blood.

"Get off," he's screaming. "Get off. Please! Leave me alone. Please! I'll tell my mum of you. I will. I'll tell my mum."

Flint laughs. It's not a sneer, it sounds more like genuine pleasure, a disturbing sound against the backdrop of Fearon's pleading. And still the fists go about their business as if there'll never be an end to it.

Sean reacts to the blood, the snot and the tears. He's nauseated by the cringing humiliation of Fearon, crying for his mummy like a five year old. No one, not even a bullying shit, should be reduced to that. He reaches out and places a hand on Flint's arm. The pumping stops.

"I think that's enough Flinty, don't you?"

Sean was scared. He hardly knew Flint, and he wasn't sure if interrupting his fun would earn him a battering as well. But Flint grinned at him.

"Want to finish him off yourself do you? Go on then, give the bastard a good kicking. I'll make sure he doesn't touch you."

Sean wasn't even tempted. It would be like kicking a downed cripple.

"No, my mam said I had to look after my shoes. Don't want to dirty them on an ugly sod like that."

Flint laughed. A different tone now - amused. And Sean breathed a sigh of relief.

"Well I'm not so fussed about my shoes, or my bleeding mam, the old bitch. And as for you," he said, dragging Fearon away from the wall and turning him around to face back up the track, "you can eff off home to your mummy and tell her anything you bleeding well like!" And he sent Fearon sprawling forward with a full-blooded kick up the arse.

Fearon fell heavily onto his hands, but picked himself up in terror and sprinted up the path towards the main road, still crying as he ran.

Flint pointed after him, laughing as if he were watching some character maimed in a slapstick cartoon.

"Look at that," he said. "What a Wally. Picks on you regular does he?

Sean shook his head. "No, just today."

"Well you let me know if he comes it again. I'll sort him out any time you like."

"Thanks."

"No trouble. Good bit of fun that. You going home now?"

"Was going to."

"I'll come with you. Got any fags?

"No.......not on me"

Flint gave him a sidelong look and sniggered.

The two boys walked the rest of Cack Alley side by side. It was the first time thay had been together there since Flint had killed the frog. They crossed under the railway arch into the Entry, and as they came to the opening of the cul-de-sac Flint paused.

"Do us a favour mate."

Sean felt a glow of pride - Flint was two years older than he was.

"Yeah, what do you want?"

"Take a look and see if the old man's car's in front of the house. If the bastards aren't home yet I can sneak in."

"What do you mean? Why do you have to sneak in?"

"Suspended from school aren't I, so the bastards locked me in my bedroom didn't they? Then they eff off to work and expect me to stay there with a pile of bleeding books. Bollocks to that. Got to eat something haven't you? Got to get a drink don't you? So I got out through the window onto the porch then down. But there'll be bloody murder if I'm not back before they get home. Go on, take a shufty and let me know."

Sean walked a few paces out of the entry into the cul-de-sac and looked at the terraced houses to his right. There were five of them, the middle one Flint's. There was no car out front. He looked at the porch above the front door and then to the window above. It was slightly ajar.

"Looks like you're safe," he whispered out loud.

"Ta!" said Flint. "See you!" And he ran past Sean full tilt to his door, leapt for the sill of the porch, swung up, flung open the window and was through, all in a matter of seconds. Sean stood gaping until Flint's face appeared at the window grinning. He gave Sean a thumbs-up and pulled the curtains across.

Sean felt another flush of pride, then sagged with relief as he turned left to his own door. It had been a crazy day, a roller coaster ride with crashing depths and incredible highs, and at the end he'd re-made a friend and escaped what was bound to have been the worst beating of his life.

No wonder he'd forgotten his grandmother's warning.

Chapter 11: The Poster Boy

Bill O'Rourke wasn't given much to displays of emotion, the welder's mask proving a tad inflexible. Nevertheless, Sean could see he was uncomfortable as he strolled towards him on the morning after his scrape with Fearon. At two hundred yards he knew that Bill had seen him approaching. He was waiting in the usual spot by the railings, looking down on the DIC furnace. As Sean drew nearer Bill began to shuffle his feet, kicking small stones between the gaps in the fence into the factory grounds below. For Bill that was significant athletic exertion, and it showed the extent of his agitation. He kept turning his head towards Sean as he approached, trying to examine his face in a series of rapid glances without actually staring at it. Sean kept his head down deliberately. He even thought of faking a limp.

As Sean got nearer Bill stopped the sidelong glances and the soccer practice and fixed his gaze on the multi-coloured flames of the furnace.

"Alright Bill?"

Bill turned his head slowly and flicked a quick glance at Sean's face, then did a double take and stood gaping. Sean kept it dead-pan.

"How's your auntie Joan then?"

"What?"

"Your auntie Joan. How's she doing? Alright is she?"

Bill remembered, pasty face tingeing pink.

"Yeah......yeah, she's fine. Mam said she was sick and told me I should go and see her. You know, cheer her up a bit......provide a bit of company."

"I thought she had five kids."

"Yeah......yeah........she has......five of 'em........but they're a bunch of miserable bastards. Mam said I should go round. You know what me mam's like.......bloody daft......."

"Yeah, right."

They trudged towards the bus stop in silence. There was nothing unusual in that, except that today Sean could sense the periodic sidelong glances, and feel, almost like a vibration in the air, the tension of Bill's burning curiosity. Well tough shit Billy Boy, thought Sean, if you want to know what happened you're going to have to ask me about it aren't you? And you're not going to do that because you're rightly ashamed of that heroic performance of yours yesterday, just like you should be. Sick auntie my arse!

But Bill did ask. As they rounded the corner to the bus stop, Bill caught sight of Fearon standing in the middle of his cronies and stopped as if he'd walked into an invisible wall.

"What the hell happened?" he said.

Fearon's pretty face was ruined. Dark glasses failed to hide the blue-black bubbles protruding from beneath both eyes. The aquiline nose he was so fond of sneering down looked as if it had

109

been pumped full of congealed blood. His nostrils were caked with black crusts. Swollen lips were segmented by black vertical lines that gaped red when he spoke, and his voice had the spit-flecked gurgle of someone trying to work his mouth after a bad experience at the dentist. He was telling his buddies about the fight. Sean paused to listen, and Fearon cast him worried glances as he piled on the bullshit.

-Six of 'em. Bikers. Big bastards too.

-Where'd they jump you?

-Cack Alley, just by the shed. Must have been hiding in the bushes waiting.

-Did you get any of them?

-What? I sorted all of the smelly bastards once I got up again.

-What d'you mean?

-Jumped me from behind didn't they. Put the boots in and then came at me with studded belts. Lucky I had my Crombie on or I would have been cut to bits.

-Jeez!

-Could have killed you!

-You're telling me! Anyway, I roll to the wall so they can't get behind me – have to come from the front where I can get a swing at them. I get up and drag off the Crombie and roll it around my arm to shield against the belts, then I get a couple of good ones in with the Oxfords and two of them go down holding their nuts.

-Right on!

-The other four keep at it with the belts, but I grab one belt as it comes down, pull the greasy bastard towards me and nut him right in the face. Spread his nose all over.

-Just three to one now.

-Yeah, and I can handle that no sweat. I drop the Crombie and hold the guy with the broken nose in front so they can't use the belts without slicing him, then I get the toe cap of my Oxford under one of the bastard's knee cap and give it him again in the teeth as he goes down. That felt good I'm telling you.

-What about the other two?

-Bet they were shitting themselves.

-Yeah, they couldn't get me while I was holding on to their mate, but I couldn't get at them with my fists neither like I wanted to, so I fling the guy at them and run in behind him swinging. I get the first one right under the chin - smack! and he goes out like a light. The second one tries to run it but I grab him by the hair and smash his head against the wall.

-Bet you smashed the bastard's skull.

-I don't reckon so because he turns around and pulls a flick-knife on me.

-Get out!

-Yeah, one of those with the six inch blade that shoots right out of the handle. I don't mind telling you that got me worried a bit.

-Did you run it?

-Thought of it, but you know, that knife got me so pissed off I just wanted to ram it up his arse.

-What d'you do?

-Well, he makes this lunge at me doesn't he, right for the heart, so I jump backward and give an overhead kick with the Oxfords as I throw myself onto the ground. Reckon I broke his wrist with that one because the knife goes flying and he stands there screaming. I back him against the wall and knocked seven colours of shite out of him.

-Wow, did you send for the cops?

-Cops? What good are the cops? My mum and dad wanted to send for them when I got home, but I told them to forget it. I just walked to the hospital and got myself stitched up. This cracker of a nurse gave me an injection in the arse for tetanus, so while I've got the pants down I gave her an injection for nothing.

Fearon's buddies laughed like they were supposed to, and Fearon looked again at Sean as he finished. The message was plain. Truce. You keep quiet and I'll leave you alone. But the story was so ludicrous, and Fearon's cronies so gullible, that Sean couldn't resist it. Leaning against the wall behind the group he started to whistle the theme tune to Jackanory, the BBC story-time program for kiddies.

The laughter stopped. Sean looked full into Fearon's face for a second, as if to say "Yeah, right!" and then walked on towards his usual perch still whistling.

The Fearon gang were a slow bunch, but the message was obvious even to them. The biggest of them, the one who'd always wondered if Fearon really was as tough as he made himself out to be, broke into a slow grin and picked up the tune where Sean had left off. The others moved away instinctively, allowing room for what was about to happen. But Fearon had learned now what a thorough battering felt like, and was spineless when it came down to an even match.

"Piss off McCullen," he hissed through split lips. "If them bikers hadn't done my arms in I'd knock your frigging teeth out."

"Try it," said McCullen. "I'll wait for you to get better Brother Fearon, and then you just try it."

The others looked on, eyes flickering between the two boys, but when Fearon did nothing, they sidled slowly towards McCullen. Fearon turned away as his friends of just seconds before burst into

112

laughter and chanted Jackanory! Jackanory! Jackanory! His reign as the Meadowlands hard man was over.

"Guess you got lucky with those bikers," said Bill as he hoisted his butt onto the wall. It was more a question than a statement.

"Yeah, it seems they kept James Bond up there a bit too busy to deal with me. Looks a treat doesn't he? I like him like that."

"Yeah, just dandy. In fact, I think he looks even better than Paula Yates over there."

Sean turned his head so fast he almost dislocated his neck. He'd been desperate to see her again. He'd even gone to bed early so that he could close his eyes and see her smiling that heart-stopping smile at him until he had fallen asleep. And now here she was.... Oh Sweet Jesus Christ!

She walked towards the boys, keeping to the other side of the street, eyes forward with that air of disdainful superiority which everyone acknowledged was hers by right.

A cat-call from one of Fearon's ex-friends was cut short by a boot to the shin from McCullen. He was going to run the pack his way from now on. Fearon didn't want to be seen, but Paula's side-long glance towards the group slowed to a gaze of wide-eyed wonder as she caught a glimpse of his battered mug. She scanned quickly along the line of boys until her eyes fell on Sean. The battering ram in his chest felt as if it would break his ribs as her eyes lingered on his. They were filled with questions.

He answered her with the smallest of shrugs, and twisted his lips into a tortured smile. She smiled back at him, the force of it almost knocking him off the wall.

"Reckon you're in there Sean," said Bill as he watched her sway towards the girls' bus stop.

"You reckon?" asked Sean, blinding himself to the O'Rourke satire.

"Course you are. Just cure yourself of that drooling habit, and she's yours."

The remarks rolled off Sean's back. She'd noticed him. Deliberately. She'd sought him out and smiled at him again. He felt as if he could achieve anything.

***

Even the Head's Frankenstein features couldn't re-awaken Sean to the ugliness of the world. He actually wasted some compassion on the poor celibate sod. Just imagine going through life denying yourself even the vaguest chance of a shag with Paula Yates? And all to impress some mythological God who'd probably tell you at the final reckoning that you were a bleeding idiot. No wonder the Brothers were all so fucked up.

The Head drew assembly to a close with a rant against the Abortion Bill in which females were variously described as harlots, tramps and murdering sluts. The Abortion Bill had been an ongoing theme at assemblies for the two years since it had become legal for women to terminate pregnancies in hospitals. Every week it had been Abortion Bill this and Abortion Bill that, and the boys had been deluged with Catholic propaganda about the evils of every procedure for the surgical removal of fetuses – all except the hag-and-stick method that was one of the few recourses before.

Today the boys were directed to exit the Assembly Hall through the school foyer so that they could view a poster display of murdered children. A wave of anticipatory nausea washed through Sean's guts as he made for the door, but he decided he'd look at the

114

floor and think of Paula rather than subject himself to the images of macerated babies.

The first-years exited first, gratifying the Head with high pitched whinnies of disgust as they passed through the display. But when the second-years filed out, those remaining in the Hall were surprised by the sound of laughter punctuating the groans. By the time Sean's class left the Assembly Hall the laughter had drowned out everything else.

The foyer was crowded with boys all pushing their way towards the focus of the comedy, as if Morecambe and Wise had dropped in to perform an Abortion Special. Fresh eruptions washed through the foyer each time one group advanced and another retreated from whatever was causing the fuss, and the corridors and stair wells rang with laughter and excited conversation as the boys made their way to the classrooms.

One poster stood out from the rest, hand-made, and definitely not part of the original display. Sean and Bill stared in disbelief for the time it took them to drink it in, then doubled up in hysterics. It was priceless. Absolutely, bloody priceless! Whoever had done it was a fucking genius.

There was the Head standing in the middle of a circus ring. The huge slab of forehead, the monstrous mandible, the lipless gash of a mouth, the cadaverous flesh, the skeletal frame, all of it perfectly, unmistakably The Head. But this Head wasn't wearing the regulation Brother's habit. No, his cassock was resplendent with gold braid down the front and gold epaulettes on the shoulders, and this Head was wearing a flashy Ring-Master's hat. He had arms raised, wielding a cane in each hand. Spotlights lit him from both sides, picking out the craggy outlines of his monstrous face and lighting a fire in each deep set eye. He looked as if he were about to

115

deliver a severe two-handed thrashing to someone just out of view, and the expression on his face, and the barest hint of an erection straining against his robes, showed that he was raring to go at it.

But it was the caption that caused Sean to crack up. Arched over the top of the poster in vibrant gay lettering it read:

Tonight in the Meadowlands Assembly Hall
By Special Arrangement with the Rodriguan Brothers
Barnum and Bailey Present:

ABORTION BILL AND HIS DANCING SEALS

Sean was creased. His gut hurt him from laughing. Even Bill O'Rourke was scarlet from hysterics. This was perfect, just perfect - ten times better than the stunt with the statue.

Someone shoved Sean aside, and he stumbled with Bill towards the staircase, almost helpless with laughter. They were half way up the stairs when the uproar in the foyer died suddenly. Looking over the banister they saw the Head pushing through the crowd of boys, lashing out left and right with his cane to clear the way. His expression was almost the same as that in the poster. Sean ached to see how it would change as he came face to face with himself, but all he could see was the Head's rigid back, stiff as a plank. He waited for the bony hands to claw at the poster and tear it into pieces, but instead the Head removed the drawing pins from the corners, rolled the poster calmly and carefully, tucked it under his arm and moved through the crowd of boys towards his office. The boys scuttled aside to let him pass. Somehow, the Head's quiet composure was infinitely more threatening than an explosion of rage.

116

Chapter 13: The Great Butt-Hole Rebellion

The Head said nothing about the poster during assembly the following morning, but it was the only thing the boys wanted to talk about. Who the hell could have done it?

-Betcha it's Rodney Strong getting his own back

-No, he'd never come up with that, he's thick as pig shit

-Couldn't hold a pen anyway after that caning. Fingers like bleeding bananas

-It's got to be one of the sixth formers

-Why

-Dunno.......it's just....

-Just what? Just because they're sixth formers? There's more bleeding suck-holers in the sixth form than there is in the first year.

-Hey, you didn't do it did you Halligan?

-No, but I wished I had.............. the stinking, skull-faced, shitty-arsed twat.

-I guess you're not a Loredano fan, then?

-Fuck off!

-Great drawing. Got to be an A1 artist whoever it was.

-Who's good at art and hates the Brothers.

-I dunno..... and almost everyone.......in that order.

-Betcha the Sponsored Walk Competition's just a trick to catch him.

-What competition?

-Haven't you heard? Everyone's supposed to design a poster for the Sponsored Walk as an art project. Winner gets a prize.

-What, a prayer book and a string of Rosary beads? No thanks.

-Well it won't be a subscription to Penthouse, that's for sure.

-I reckon they'll just check the style and nab whoever does one like Abortion Bill.

-Don't be bleeding daft. If the Poster Boy's smart enough to pull off an Abortion Bill, he's smart enough not to fall for that malarkey.

-Anyone claiming they did it yet?

-What? Like the IRA claiming responsibility. You must be bloody joking.

-Whoever did it wouldn't last five seconds in Meadowlands if he owned up.

-Oh, I don't know. I reckon he'd last long enough for the Head to flay him alive.

-Sadistic bastard.

-Friggin' weirdo if you ask me.

-As bent as Old Campy.

-Worse. Campy's just a Paedo, the Head's as twisted as a bleeding corkscrew.

-Campy still hanging around the showers after games?

-Yeah, habit of a life time.

-And he's still collecting lost kit in his office.

-Yeah, you have to go and dress up for him if you leave your games togs at home.

-While he wanks off under his desk.

-And he's the bleeding history master! Got nothing to do with sports.

-Dirty filthy sod.

"Well I'm sick to death of the bleeding pervert," said Sean. "Why do we let him get away with it?"

-What the hell can we do about it

-Can't kick him out of the shower block can we?

"But the brass balls of the bastard! Hanging around the changing rooms so that he can scope out your bare arse in the stalls."

-Selecting the form isn't he

-Like...... He's gotta nice bum - I'll invite him to my office at lunch time.

-Offer him a taste of my sausage

-That's the way it goes isn't it Purvis?

Purvis flushed bright red and strode away from the group, looking as if he might burst into tears.

-Prancing bleeding pooftah!

-Even walks like a tart.

-You'd walk funny too if you'd spent as much time as him in Campy's office.

Sean remembered sitting in isolation on the side of the brook just two days before. They were against the Brothers, not their own classmates. "Come on guys, Purv's pretty harmless," he said.

-Ooh, fancy him yerself do you McCaffery

-Throw down a sixpence and you might get him to bend over.

- Ben Doon and Phil McCrackin

-Aye laddie, and Phillup McCavity.

"So funny aren't you," said Sean. "But I'm telling you, Campy's not going to be scoping my butt-hole after games this morning."

-Oh no? So what are you going to do about it?

"Listen up," said Sean, "and I'll tell you........."

Chuck Bones, the games master, was one of the lay teachers at Meadowlands. Actually, describing him as a teacher was pushing it a bit. He knew how to organize a game of soccer, or cricket, and when it came to rugby he was a dab hand at encouraging students to beat the crap out of each other on the playing fields. But actually teaching anything? Well, academics weren't really his strong suit. Still, he wasn't a bad guy as teachers went, and only laid his hands on the boys when demonstrating the art of the tackle. He was a tall hefty chap of twenty five, a prop forward with Smellins Rugby Football Club owning a sparsed-tooth grin that he wore like a medal.

But he did have a cruel streak, and he exercised it on any boy that tried to dodge the games period. He hated slackers and he despised wimps. If you forgot your kit you were sent to Brother Campion's office to try on whatever he might have in his cupboard. If Chuck guessed what else might be tried on there he regarded it as part of the punishment for skiving off. He discouraged boys from bringing excuse notes by reading them out publicly in the changing rooms as the rest of the boys got into their kit. Today Georgie Colbourne was the victim.

Georgie was so piss-poor he made even Sean feel rich. He was under-nourished, grey-skinned and clad every day in the same threadbare hand-me-downs. His sports shirt had more holes than a string vest, and his shorts looked like a baby's nappy. Chuck held Georgie's note at arm's length by the tip of his fingers as if he might catch something from it. It was scrawled on cardboard ripped from the back of a Typhoo Tea Box.

"What's this Colbourne?" asked Chuck, "Something for my sports card collection?"

As luck would have it, the front of the cardboard scrap showed a picture of Alan Ball nodding one in for Everton FC, no doubt under the influence of a stimulating cuppa.

"It's written on the back sir," mumbled Georgie.

"And in pencil too," said Chuck with a sneer. "Blue pencil, or is it eye-liner? Not yours Colbourne, I hope?"

"No sir, me mam's."

"Your mam's eh? And what does your mam have to say for you? Let's take a look."

Chuck composed himself, and still holding the scrap at arm's length read it out loud.

"Dear Mr. Bones, please excuse our Georgie games as he's gotta boil on his arse."

The changing room exploded with laughter as Georgie stood there melting with shame. Chuck let the laughter roll before tossing the scrap into the rubbish bin and sending Georgie off to Old Campy's. No doubt Campy would investigate Georgie's arse for the truth of the matter. Yes, Chuck could be a real bastard at times, just like the rest of them.

When they were all kitted up and outside, Chuck stood in front of the boys as they lined up on the edge of the playing fields.

"Soccer today gentlemen," he said, "and the two Captains will be......... Pickering........and.......McCaffery. Pickering, heads or tails?"

"Tails Sir."

The coin spun and Chuck caught it with a practiced flourish.

"Heads it is. McCaffery, you get the first choice."

Sean and Ralph Pickering came forward to stand on either side of Chuck, and scanned the boys lined up in front of them. Rylands was blowing out his cheeks and flexing his knees in a rapid bicycling motion as if he were bursting for a shit. He was a magician with a soccer ball, the brains in his feet making up for what he lacked in his head. He was so confident about being picked first that he actually started moving towards Sean, his lover-boy face plastered with a self-confident grin.

"Hand on, hang on," said Sean. "I'm still thinking."

Rylands paused where he was, the grin undiminished, certain that Sean would pick him anyway. Any other day that might have been the case, but today his smarmy expression rubbed Sean the wrong way. He scanned the boys again. Klank stood at the end of the line, leaning on his crutches and gazing out across the field towards the brook. He paid no attention to the team selection. He'd be picked last as usual. He could have been excused games without a fuss, but his parents made him join in. They liked to boast that he wouldn't let his disability stop him doing anything. His mother had even bought him a tennis racquet once, the stupid cow. Still, he could be handy on the rugby field where he was allowed to trip up the opposition with his crutches, and if a soccer match had to be decided on penalties he could swing his leg-irons to reasonable effect (though God help the goalie who let one in from Klank!) But for the most part he was a liability, and spent the game rattling up and down the sidelines while pretending to have a good time.

Sean shifted his gaze between the calm resignation of Klank and the smug self-assurance of Rylands. "Alright Rylands....," he said, and Rylands walked forward with an I-told-you-so smirk plastered on his kipper. "...you can go back to your place. I choose Kla.......Mike Dennis."

The gob-smocked expression on Rylands' mug was easily worth the thrashing Sean's team was about to get. As for the look on Klank's face, that was pure gold.

"Well done McCaffery," whispered Chuck, and Sean felt for the first time that Chuck was not so bad after all.

The game went as predicted, Sean's team getting slaughtered despite a spectacular defensive effort by Klank, who used his crutches to bring down attackers with some spectacular fouls. He was even handed a yellow card, earning a round of applause from the team. Rylands played for vengeance, hammering in five himself, and assisting with all the others. With victory in his pocket, he even cannoned a few directly at Klank, trying to knock him over just for fun. But as the boys left the field all that was put aside. A group gathered around Sean to check on the plan.

-So, you going to do it then?

"Sure, aren't you?"

-I will if you will.

"It'll only work if we all do it."

-You're going first though, aren't you McCaffery?

"Yeah, I'll finish my shower and then you lot follow. Is everyone in?"

-Yeah, they're dead keen.

"-The Great Butt Hole Rebellion, eh?"

-Yeah, I can hardly wait to see the look on old Campy's ugly mug."

A tiled wall ran down the centre of the shower block dividing the showers on one side from the drying area on the other. A long towel rack was fixed to the front of the wall, and at each end were openings into the showers themselves. The boys entered through one of the openings and shuffled through the spray to the other, or got pushed along if they spent too much time lathering their parts. Once out, they dried off and then went back into the changing room to dress.

To Brother Campion the sound of splashing water was like shit to a fly. He entered the changing room bang on schedule and took up a position at the head of the shower block where the boys emerged all wet and steamy. Today he actually dragged a chair in with him and sat there shamelss like a filthy old sod. As if to excuse the inexcusable, he shouted to the boys behind the wall.

"Every boy must take a proper shower. I'll have no dirty boys in this school. You'll file by me as you come out. Any dirt on you and I'll send you back."

And then he waited, with hands tucked into his cassock, bold as brass.

Sean was first out as planned.

"Here boy, come here and let me take a look at you."

Sean made a quick grab for his towel and held it tight in front of his crotch as he stood before Campy for inspection.

Campy looked him up and down, his eyes bugging behind thick-rimmed spectacles.

"Come on laddie, get that towel out of the way."

"Why Brother, what do you want to see?"

It was asked in such a polite manner that Old Campy was stunned into silence. He was so surprised that it didn't occur to him to react with the customary back-hander. His doughy cheeks turned pink, and he stuttered as he tried to think of something to say. There was nothing. He was caught. Suddenly, the dirty boy excuse seemed pathetic, but he had to go through with it now he'd started.

Backing off would only reveal him for the nasty pervert he really was.

"Put that towel down boy," he shouted. "I'll not have you hiding dirt from me."

"But I didn't get dirty there Brother, I was wearing shorts."

There was a titter from the other boys as they emerged from the showers. The colour of Campy's face deepened to a blood red, and a tic twitched at the corner of his mouth.

"Don't you answer back to me, boy. Turn yourself around and let me see there's no filth on you. I'll not have filthy boys in this school."

Sean turned around, and deliberately placed the towel across his buttocks.

"What do you think you're doing boy? Drop that towel at once don't you hear. Drop it at once."

"But I'm not dirty there either Brother, my shorts covered me front and back. What do you want to look at down there?"

There was no answer. How could there be? Campy shook like he was having a fit, guilt plastered all over his face. The titters had grown to outright laughter now, and Campy lifted his gaze from Sean to look down the line of boys. Every one of them was holding a towel tight against his crotch – not a pubic hair in sight. And, God bless him, there was Klank at the back, starkers except for his leg irons, hiding his dick and grinning away with the best of them.

Everything about Old Campy was swollen except the sad little member that dangled under his cassock.

"Mr. Bones!" he yelled. "Mr. Bones, come here immediately!"

Chuck came jogging into the shower block expecting to break up some fist fight, but his face registered a dull puzzlement as he looked at the line of boys standing there quietly. To him, the fact that there wasn't a cock in sight didn't seem to be in any way strange. But then, he wasn't a willy-watcher.

"Yes Brother Campion, what's the trouble?"

"These boys are being insolent," he spat. "These boys are.......are.........." he stumbled over his tongue, searching for some excuse. Foam flecked the corners of his lips as he stuttered. "These boys need to be disciplined Mr. Bones. They are a dirty rabble. They won't.....they won't......"

"Show me their dongs!" whispered Dougie Horrocks so that everyone heard, and fresh laughter rocked through the boys.

Somehow Old Campy stumbled to his feet. He'd been caught alright, like a teenager found wanking off by his mother. He just wanted to get out of there, dig a hole for himself and disappear down it for ever. He couldn't face the boys so he turned on Chuck.

"These boys need to be disciplined Mr. Bones," he roared. "They are your class. A rabble. A dirty, disobedient rabble." He dragged his chair to the exit. "Discipline, Mr. Bones. I must have discipline. And I won't have........any dirty..........boys in this.......school. I won't have ....dirty boys!" And then he was gone.

"Not today you won't," said Horrocks, and the boys laughed so loud that Campy could hear them all the way back to his office. Now that he'd gone, the boys were unashamedly starkers again and were flicking towels at each other's arses.

Chuck was utterly confused, but it seemed that whatever had happened was something to do with McCaffery. "Now then McCaffery'" he said towering over Sean and looking down on him with hands on hips "what have you been up to?"

Sean looked up at him, the picture of innocence. "I don't know sir. I just held my towel like this," he put it in front of his crotch, "and Brother Campion didn't seem to like it."

"Couldn't see his knob," said Horrocks in his echoing undertone.

Both Chuck and Sean pretended not to hear, but Chuck found it harder to keep a straight face than Sean did. He was disgusted at Campion's incursions into the shower room, but as a junior lay teacher at Meadowlands he didn't dare question the Brothers, especially the Deputy Head. It seemed that this boy had somehow done what he had been unable to do. A low murmur of respectful laughter spread through the boys as they saw the look on his face.

"Alright," said Chuck, trying to inject a stern note into his voice, "whatever you did, make sure it doesn't happen again. Now all of you get dressed."

He strode out of the shower block to a round of applause, half for Sean, and half for himself.

Brother Campion slammed the door of his office and fumbled at the latch of a cupboard. It was next to the one where he kept the lost gym gear. He was tempted to up-end the bottle of Scotch and suck it straight down his throat, but he mastered himself enough to pour a tumblerfull before throwing it back. He poured another, then lit a Hamlet and drew on it ferociously. The alcohol and nicotine numbed the obsessive urge that had sent him down to the shower block and, as the shaking subsided, rationalization began working on his self-respect.

By God, he'd not have any dirty boys in this school! And by God, any insolent puppy who tried to thwart him would pay for it. Who was that hard-faced little swine from 3X? He knew most of them in their school uniforms, and many them starkers, but he couldn't place this naked boy. Not yet. He was trouble obviously. A ringleader. The type that must be dealt with before he got out of hand.

He could ask Mr. Bones to identify him, but he was reluctant to bring up the incident in the shower block. And he had a bad feeling about Mr. Bones. Him and that Harvey fellow. Young teachers with their misguidedly Liberal opinions.

No, he'd have to find out from one of the boys. One of his special friends. Who? Who could he trust in 3X? Purvis! Yes, Kevin Purvis was in 3X. A nice boy.....a very nice boy. The second tumbler of Scotch kicked in, and he realized that he'd missed Kevin over the summer recess. He was overcome with a wave of fondness for the boy. There were so few of them these days that he genuinely liked. So few of the right kind. But Kevin was one; a quiet, understanding, boy. A discreet boy. He'd invite Kevin to his office at lunchtime for a chat. That would be nice. Yes, chatting with Kevin would be very, very nice.

Chapter 14: Summoned

Sean strutted the playing fields at lunch time. Wherever he went there were grins of solidarity. Even a few boys from the lower sixth punched his shoulder as he went by and said "Right on!" He felt as if he could jump the brook, walk right up to Paula Yates and ask for a date.......almost.

Everyone had heard about the Great Butt Hole Rebellion. Other boys gathered round Sean him telling their own tales of defiance as if he were some great rebel leader. Right now, Eddie Lowry from 3C was telling the crowd how they'd pulled a stunt on Horseface in Latin class.

-Larry Flanagan did it. Sneaked a piece of folded up paper round the class. Told everyone to pass it on to Wanky Wallace.

-What was in it?

- HorseFace thought he knew and made one of his daft bloody speeches about it.

-What, you mean he got hold of it?

-Yeah, caught Sproggers passing it on.

-Might have known it'd be Sproggers.

-So what happened?

-Made this speech didn't he. Made up with himself he was for catching us. Anyone would think he was Sherlock Bleeding Holmes. We almost died laughing when he opened the paper.

-What did it say?

-He didn't open it right away. Went prattling on in that stupid accent about when he was boy.

-Malcolm bleeding Muggeridge.

-Yeah, and grinning all over his cheesy face, chuffed to death.

-WHAT DID IT SAY?

-Told us he used to do EXACTLY the same thing when he was a lad in this very same class. God, I almost pissed my pants when he said that. "You can't fool me boys, I've seen it all before. Done it all before too. Nothing new here you know. I used to do exactly the same thing when I was your age and sitting right where you are sitting now."

-WHAT DID IT SAY YOU BASTARD!!

-On and on about his school days like he was one of the Famous Five. "Yes, I used to send little packages like this to my chums. A cheeky message to make them laugh, or some sweets we'd sneak into our mouths during class."

-Ooooh wasn't he the rebel!

-What a tearaway!

-"So, who's this addressed to," he says. "Wallace eh? One of your pals sending you a little tidbit? Something to pop into your mouth when I'm not looking hmmm? But I am looking aren't I Wallace? I've seen it all and done it all. You can't fool an old hand like me Wallace. Maybe I'll eat your little tidbit myself."

-And then he opens the paper and that filthy bastard Flanagan had blown a phelgmy green yocker right in the middle of it. You should have seen HorseFace. Turned as green as the snot. Thought

130

he was going to puke. "Bon Appetit!" roars Flanagan and we all collapsed howling. God it was hilarious. Never laughed so much in my life.

Sean thought it was marvelous. Insubordination everywhere. He almost believed he really was that great rebel leader.

Silly sod, it lasted until half-way through Biology class that afternoon.

Old Stooley taught Biology – Old Stooley with no goolies. The story went they'd been blown off in the war, though why his testicles had been such a strategic enemy target, and how they'd been destroyed without taking the rest of Stooley with them, was a mystery no one seemed to care about. It was just an accepted fact that Stooley was sans balls. Which might have explained why he approached today's class on human reproduction with such obvious reluctance.

He hated talking about sex. Every time he had to mention reproduction or genitalia he'd start with the same appeal......"Now let's not be silly about this, boys....." including himself in the directive as if he just might pull out his knob and play the drums with it.

Today poor Stooley was in despair. Even in a Catholic school, the O-level curriculum demanded that boys be taught how babies were made. That meant he had to mention penises right from the get-go. There were a few giggles as he mumbled the name of the offending member, but when he started on the subject of testicles the class fell about as if he were a stand-up comedian. Some of the boys actually had heads down on their desks crying hysterically with laughter, while others kept the show going by tormenting Stooley with a barrage of questions.

-What's a Eunuch sir?

-Is Eunuch Powell one - the racialist?

-He's got balls enough.

-Wants to cut them off the blacks though. Stop them breeding.

-What happens if they get blow.....I mean cut off sir? Do you die?

-No, but I bet you wished you had.

-Why are they so hairy sir?

-Why do they hurt so much when you whack 'em?

-Why do they have to hang down like that?

-Hanging down is asking for trouble isn't it? I mean, they're just asking to get blow......cut off, aren't they?

Poor Stooley hardly knew where to turn. He realized that there was some great joke going on, but he couldn't for the life of him understand it. Why were they acting so silly when he'd asked them especially not to? And why did they react with such rude laughter when he stated that both testicles could be removed, and quite often were, in domesticated animals, without causing any long term injury. These boys were a complete mystery to him.

He was about to dig an even deeper hole for himself on the subject of vaginas when the school secretary walked into the class. She was Stooley's wife, and her sudden appearance brought on a new round of hysterics.

"Oh no!" whispered Horrocks. "He's got her in for a demo."

"Think of Grandma! Think of Grandma!" whittered Johnson.

"No need to", replied Horrocks, "my sac's already gone raisin bag."

132

His wife whispered something into Stooley's ear and then left, glaring daggers at the boys for making her husband's life such a misery. Stooley held up his hand, and there was a slight reduction in the hilarity.

"McCaffery," he shouted over the noise, "the Headmaster would like to see you in his office immediately."

It was like magic. One second the biology lab sounded like the Chimp House at Whipsnade, the next it was as silent as a church. Every eye turned on Sean. You didn't get called down to the Head's office, especially after something like the Great Butthole Rebellion, unless you were in for a trashing. There were smiles all round in anticipation.

Sean got to his feet, heart pounding, and sauntered to the door trying to look like Rodney Strong heading for the stage. He might as well act the tough guy in public, because in a few minutes he'd probably be howling in private. It had to be a thrashing - what else could it be? His guts turned over at the thought of it. There were a few sniggers as he moved between the desks, but no one said a word. The message was all in their looks – I wouldn't be in your shoes for a million quid!

His mind hit replay as he made his way to the Head's office. What was it? Had Fearon's parents complained? Was it Brother Jerome and all that crap about Purgatory? Campy! I bet it was Old Campy! The old wanker was getting his revenge for missing the arse parade after games. And what would that be worth? Two strokes? He could handle two....maybe. But Sweet Jesus, the way the bastard had laid into Rodney Strong! Four? Could he take four without doing a Halligan? Six? His nails dug into his palms as he thought of six. As for getting any at all across the backside, just the idea turned him sick.

He stopped outside the Head's door. It was varnished oak with a black sign at eye level that read HEADMASTER in white letters. Room 101, he thought, behind that door.......

Idiot! he told himself as he raised his fist to knock. Why did he have to be such an idiot? Why couldn't he have kept his head down, let the teachers get on with their crap, and kept his stupid mouth shut? But no, he had to be a smart-arse. And just look where it had got him?

He looked at the two lights above the door: Red for PLEASE WAIT and Green for COME IN. Red was lit.

Moron! What the hell had he been trying to prove? The bastards always won in the end. He'd get a thrashing here, and then another at home when his father found out. "Ad-'ere.......Had'ere..... ....ADHERE!.... yourself to discipline!" his father would shout, as he adhered Sean to the wall. Always on their side he was. They were always right. He should always to be grateful to the damned Brothers no matter what the bastards did with him.

He looked up at the lights again. Jesus, it was on Green! How long had he been standing there daydreaming? He left the door handle slippy with sweat as he stepped inside, the worms in his gut slithering towards his bowels.

Sean had been in the Headmaster's office only once before, last year when Brother Leo had been in charge. Leo had lectured him on being respectful to his teachers and had tapped his hand with the cane as if it were a ritual required of him. There'd be no such luck with the current psycho.

In Leo's time the room had stunk of cigarettes, the walls painted with nicotine. Now the walls were a clinical white and caged in aluminum book cases. Ranks of file folders filled the shelves, and the desk was piled with more of them, stacked neatly in groups as if to display the enormous amount of work it took to be a headmaster.

The Head was hard at it right now, writing on a piece of foolscap, his eyes invisible under the crag of forehead as he looked down at the paper. He continued to write for several minutes, until Sean began to believe that the green light had been a stress-induced hallucination. Any second the Head would look up and ask him what the hell he was doing in his office, and give him an extra thrashing for impertinence. What should he do? Cough? Sneak out again? One thing was certain – he would never dare interrupt the flow of that pen.

Eventually the hand stopped, the pen placed neatly in its stainless steel rack alongside its matching propelling pencil, the foolscap gathered together, tapped square along the edges and placed in a folder to the Head's left – done! Only then did the black eyes fix themselves on Sean's face. The Head said nothing. His eyes said nothing. The expression on that Cubist face said nothing. But somehow the walls of the room rang with accusation. Sean was scared half to death.

"McCaffery Brother, 3X," he blurted. "You sent for me."

The Head continued to look at him for several seconds, as if to take a mental photograph of his face.

"Yes.....McCaffery......3X," he said, "One of the Assembly Hall whisperers . You and that unsightly fellow." His voice was neutral. "Do you know why I sent for you?"

By now Sean could have listed half a dozen reasons, all of them worth at least six of the best, but he wasn't going to fall for that trick no matter how terrified he felt.

"No Brother," he replied, and tried to sound as if it were true.

"I've sent for you because there are certain teachers at this school who have brought your name to my attention. Do you know why?"

So it was Campion! Oh sweet Jesus, he was really in for it now.

"I'm sorry Brother," he croaked, and then realized it sounded like an admission. "No, I don't know why Brother."

The Head's face creased slowly into hard lines.

"I will not have rebels at this school McCaffery," he said. "I will not abide those who defy authority. Boys like that are a cancer – a malignance that gives rise to greater malignancy. I will cut out that malignancy McCaffery. Cut it out before it spreads, and eradicate it from this school. Do you understand me?"

Sean's mouth was dust. He tried to swallow but there was no spit. He was going to be thrown out – expelled! The consequences crowded in on him - his father foaming at the mouth, his mother in tears, a classroom at the Secondary Modern with all the half-wit factory fodder, his friends off to the Uni and him stuck in Duggin forever. My God, he'd end up in the DIC. The DIC! His entire future was crumbling.

The Head continued. "I will not tolerate boys who find it amusing to desecrate the symbols of our faith, or those who work their wits to produce obscene articles such as this."

Still looking directly at Sean, he reached down and picked up a roll of paper that he opened slowly to reveal the poster of Abortion Bill. How could Sean have ever thought it funny? The Head was right, it was obscene, sick, the work of some nutcase; he wanted nothing to do with it. Nothing!

"But I didn't do that Brother........ I know nothing about it............ it wasn't me Brother." He was almost yelling his denial. Right now he'd accept responsibility for absolutely anything else, but to be associated with that poster was fatal. He was white with fear.

"Nothing about it McCaffery, are you sure?"

"No Brother! I mean yes Brother – I didn't do it honestly, I can't even draw Brother."

"I know you didn't do it boy. I asked you what you know about it."

The face had morphed again, the hard lines softening.

"I'm asking you McCaffery because I know you are one of the right sort. You are a boy who cares about this school. You appreciate its traditions and its values."

Sean was gob-smacked. What the hell was he talking about? Was he dragging him up only to slam him down harder? And what was that expression on his face – that unctuous look? What in the name of Sweet Jesus was going on?

"I'm correct in this aren't I McCaffery?"

Oh you're correct alright Brother. If it means I'm off the hook, and I'm not going to get expelled and am not even going to get a thrashing, you're absolutely one hundred percent correct Brother. I'm anything you say I am.

"Yes, Brother, of course Brother."

"I thought so. I'm rarely mistaken in a boy. Mr. Gruntle mentioned your exemplary behaviour in the Dining Hall on Monday when other boys chose to display their insolence. I also heard from Mr. Bones that you showed a particular kindness to a rather unfortunate boy in your games class. It is for these reasons that I've singled you out to assist me."

"To assist you Brother?" Fatty Gruntle, you bastard, what have you gotten me into?

"Yes McCaffery, to assist me." The Head brought his hands together on the table in front of him, finger tip to finger tip. He leaned forward across the desk.

"This is our school McCaffery – yours and mine. Its purpose is to educate, not just in the scholastic sense but to instill within its students the proper values, moral and religious, by which they will regulate their future lives. As Head of this school it is my duty to ensure that its purpose is met. However, I can best achieve my goals if my staff, the prefects, and the ordinary students are willing to assist me. Do you understand?"

Sean stood to attention. Blank-faced and tight-lipped he gave the slightest of nods.

"Good, now tell me what you know about the boys responsible for this poster and the desecration of the school statue."

The tips of the fingers slid past each other and the hands came together in a clasp. It was time for brass tacks, but Sean had no idea what to say. He wanted desperately to get out of there. If he'd known anything at all about the poster boy he would have blabbed. Blabbed and sold out, just to escape. But he was as much in the dark as everyone else.

"There's no need to hesitate boy. I'm well aware of the code that binds schoolboys together, but you and I subscribe to a greater code don't we? And you need not fear about reprisals – whatever you tell me will be held in strictest confidence."

"But I don't know anything Brother."

The intertwined fingers clenched at each other so that the knuckles stood white against the skin. The Head's pally expression gave way to impatience and then morphed again into persuasion.

"Come now McCaffery, you must have heard something. The boys responsible for this are show-offs. They are braggarts. They do it to show how clever they are. They boast about getting one better on the rest of us. Tell me McCaffery, who's been bragging? Who's been swaggering around the schoolyard?"

"Honestly Brother, no one's heard anything. We've all been trying to guess who it might be but so far we haven't a clue."

The Head looked hard at Sean for several seconds, not just at his face, but at his shoes, his trousers, the cut of his uniform. All amity vanished.

"Where are you from McCaffery?"

"Duggin Brother."

"Duggin......."

"Yes, Brother."

"You are aware, I hope, of the opportunities opened to you by attending Meadowlands?"

"Yes Brother, of course Brother."

The Head pulled a sheath of papers from one of the file folders on his desk – Students K – N. He glanced through the papers briefly.

"You are a clever student, McCaffery. At the top of your class in most subjects."

It was a statement, not praise, and Sean said nothing.

"If you continue to do this well you may even be Oxbridge material - Durham at least. Things are changing these days." He looked, briefly, as if he didn't approve. "That would be quite an elevation for a Duggin boy."

Again Sean said nothing, though his mind filled with what he'd like to say to the snotty twat.

"Of course, whether you attend university or not, any university at all that is, will depend not only on your academic performance but also on a recommendation written by me. I hope that my recommendation will be greatly in your favour. Do you understand me McCaffery?"

"Yes Brother." Oh yes Brother, I understand you perfectly, you blackmailing bastard.

"Excellent! So when these boys reveal themselves, as they must do eventually, you will report to me immediately."

"Yes Brother."

"I'll be waiting then. But don't keep me waiting too long."

He reached for his fountain pen and a fresh piece of foolscap. The crag descended, and as he began to write he said, "You will not, of course, mention this conversation to anyone."

"No Brother."

"Dismissed."

Sean was mobbed during afternoon recess. Everyone wanted to know what had happened. He'd returned to class with hands that could use a pen, he was walking normally, there were no signs of physical or sexual violence. His classmates were both disappointed and bewildered.

-What did he want you for?

-Had Old Campy been onto him?

-Did you actually speak to the ugly bastard?

-What does it look like up close?

Sean had known what was coming, and he'd spent the remainder of Stooley's Biology class trying to come up with some feasible story. The bigger the lie, the more people are inclined to believe it. That's what Doc had said in Cannery Row. He'd give it a shot.

"He wants me to write something for the Brothers' Newsletter doesn't he?"

"What's that?" asked Bill.

"Some bullshit the Rodriguans publish every month. Some kind of magazine."

That set them off.

-What – like Monks Only?

-Choir-boy centerfold and all that?

-Exclusive Feature: Masturbation - Does it really stunt your growth? – The Midget Monk tells all.

-Hands-on Instructions for Celibate Sex.

-Bad Habits: Confessions of an Arse-Bandit Brother.

Bill cut through the crap. "So why'd he pick on you anyway?" he asked.

"Can you believe it? He wants an article on how the Rodriguans are educating kids from depressed areas like Duggin."

Yeah, so why'd he pick on you?" Bill persisted.

"Because I'm from Duggin aren't I, you idiot. And I can write. At least that's what Brother Ambrose had told him. He'd read the story they put in the school newspaper last year, the one Ben took from my English homework."

Bill smirked. "What the rip–off of Walter Mitty? Talk about plagiarism!"

"It was supposed to be a rip-off you tosser. We all wrote one. It was one of Ben's exercises."

"So what are you going to write: A Day in the Life of a DIC-Head?"

"Dunno what I'm going to write yet. He says he wants something to show how under-privileged types are being dragged into respectability by the efforts of the Brothers. Some rags to riches type bollocks."

"But you aren't rich."

"No, but unlike you I'm not intellectually impoverished either, and it seems like the Head wants to take the credit for that. He wants me to write how grateful I am for the chance he's giving me."

141

"He didn't say that did he?"

"No, not to my face, but that's what he meant. He even said if I made it to Oxbridge one of these days I could do a follow up story. Had the bleeding nerve to call it The Great Escape."

Sean knew he was pushing it with than one, but so far Doc's thesis about lying seemed to be holding water.

"You aren't going to do it are you?" asked Bill.

I would have spat in the bastard's eye," said Horrocks.

"Oh yeah, well there he is," said Sean. You go right ahead."

Horrocks looked towards the Head as he stood at the school entrance sweeping his black-eyed gaze across the boys. He looked away again quickly.

"Easier said than done isn't it?" said Sean, walking away from the mob while Horrocks was still on the spot.

Sean felt pleased with himself - the lie had been believed. But what was he going to do about the truth?

After school finished, Fearon sat opposite Sean on the bus. There was no need for words. It was pay-back time. Everyone called him Brother Fearon now, even kids he knew he could beat to a jelly. Or thought he knew. That was the problem. That skinny sod in the alley had looked like a push-over, but then..........Anyway, it was all McCaffery's fault, and he knew for sure that he could take McCaffery. And today was the day.

Bill was sitting next to Sean, crossing and recrossing his legs like he was about to piss himself. It wasn't far from the truth. The story about his aunt Joan wouldn't work twice, and Fearon might not content himself with just the single victim.

Fearon got to his feet when the two boys rose to get off. He was a menacing shadow as they walked towards home. But as they

142

approached Cack Alley the shadow dropped further and further back, and then disappeared entirely.

Jimmy Flint was leaning against the wall by the entrance.

"See you tomorrow Bill,' said Sean casually.

"Yeah, see you tomorrow Sean," said Bill, looking quizzically at Flint, then at Fearon's departing back.

Sean walked into the alley, followed by his minder.

Chapter 15: Sponsored What?

Gladys Hardy fluttered about the classroom waving his hands in girlish delight at the creations coming to life under the paint-brushes. Today everyone had to design a poster for the Sponsored Walk and the best poster would go on display in the school. They would even use it on the sponsor forms – it was just sooooo exciting!!!!

Only Gladys had any real enthusiasm for the poster competition. Most of the boys couldn't give a shit. After all, who cared if your poster was chosen to hang in the school gallery? Not to mention that the winner would get a good kicking for being a suck-hole. But Gladys flitted from boy to boy ooohing and aaahing and letting out little squeals as if they were all Andy Warhols. Sean remarked that most of the designs appeared rather pedestrian, but only Bill got the joke.

"Looks like the Dole queue," Sean muttered, waving a hand at a depiction of grey figures shuffling toward the horizon in a dreary line.

Johnson's poster was the exception, but then Johnson was exceptional. His poster was alive with action. At the bottom left corner, the boys were a mass of purple splashes emerging from the gates of Meadowlands which were marked by a pair of crossed

144

canes. The splashes meandered, becoming smaller and further apart, toward the top right of the poster where a stylised Ferris Wheel and Roller Coaster identified Sandcaster's Joyland Funfair, even though the fairground was to be strictly off-limits to the walkers.

On the route between Meadowlands and Sandcaster some of the splashes were making detours. A group was gathered under a sign that might have read The Fox and Hounds, and another group were camped out in a wood from which smoke was billowing as if they'd set it on firet. In the center of the wood a group of splashes encircled a gyrating blob of pink topped off with a streak of navy blue, which, for some reason, just had to be a naked West Meadow girl waving a pair knickers over her head.

The boys actually on the path between the school and Sandcaster were being herded along by jagged figures in black carrying long sticks. And scattered throughout the poster were hundreds of tiny flecks blowing in the air, like leaves caught in a windstorm, all of them being wafted towards the school where they changed into pound notes that entered a funnel on top of the building. Three red arrows emerged from the bottom of the funnel: a thin one ending at the school playing fields, a thicker one ending at the Brother's mini-bus, and the thickest ending at the Brother's House where cases of beer were stacked to the window frames.

Gladys was delighted, giggling like a girl and clapping his hands. It was the reason everyone liked Gladys. He was by far the biggest kid in the class.

"Brilliant Johnson!" he cried. "Just brilliant, I love it! Just look at those devils in the pub, now that's where I'd be for sure - thirsty work a walk to Sandcaster. Or in the woods, the woods eh? Looks like there's lots of fun going on in the woods, my goodness! And just look at those cheeky beggars riding on the bus. Now that's what I call using your head – get someone to sponsor your fare, that's the ticket, and who'd be the wiser? Excellent! Well done! All you need now is a title. There's plenty of space along the top. Come on, let's take a look at your penmanship."

Everyone gathered around Johnson's poster. The fact that Gladys seemed to be encouraging him in sedition had them in uproar. If one of the Brothers was to come in now Gladys wouldn't have lasted another five seconds at Meadowlands. But he didn't seem to care.

"Come on Johnson, spell out Sponsored Walk over the top and you're done."

Johnson was a dab-hand at calligraphy. He wrote deftly with a thick paintbrush daubed in heavy purple paint, inventing a sprawling font on the spot, the letters crawling across the top of the poster like a line of shagged-out boys. When he'd finished there was another burst of laughter and he looked up with a self-satisfied smirk on his face.

"Hey Johnson, what's a Sponcered Walk then?" Halligan pronounced the Sponk with a hard K, and the whole class burst out laughing again.

Johnson's smirk caved in. "What do you mean........?"

"A Sponkered Walk – what the hell's that? Is it anything like a Sponsored Walk? You know, with an S in the middle - like S for Stupid."

Johnson looked down on his spelling. Shit! The whole thing was ruined. Sponcered Walk.....how could he have?......Fuck! What an idiot! There was no way to change it. Bollocks! And he'd made a damned fool of himself as well. He picked up the paint brush and obliterated the entire poster in a scribble of purple scrawl.

"No! No! No!" wailed Gladys. "It's lovely......perfect......it encapsulates the whole thing so beautifully, even the spelling. Half the boys on the walk won't know what sponsored means, never mind how to spell it. Oh please don't do that, I was going to put it in the gallery!"

And lucky for you that you didn't, thought Sean – your feet wouldn't have touched the ground.

By the end of the day a new verb was born in Meadowlands. Even Ben Gibbs acknowledged it as he handed back the homework assignments. "Two out of ten," he said, spinning Dougie's exercise book over the heads of the boys to land on Dougan's desk. "You really sponckered that essay!"

The Poster Boy struck again on Thursday morning.

The winning poster for the Sponsored Walk competition had been put on display near the entrance doors to the Assembly Hall. It was an arse-crawling effort from Jeffery Bates in the Lower Sixth, and showed a group of sweaty-faced boys, all with the same pious expression, filing past a collection basket into which they dropped wads of bank notes. The basket was emblazoned with a cross and a sign reading *For Our School*. Standing next to the basket was a Rodriguan, modeled after the statue of St. Rodriguez, smiling down on the foot-sore students. The caption at the head of the poster read Come One, Come All to the Meadowlands Sponsored Walk 1969. It was total shite, and only the fact that Master Bates was one of the Priestlings saved him from a thorough kicking.

But now the Bates poster had vanished. In its place was something done in a deliberately similar style, but advertising what appeared to be a very different event. The header read exactly the same, word for word, except for the replacement of a single letter. That letter made all the difference. The sweaty-faced boys were there alright, but they definitely lacked any appearance of piety. Instead, their faces were contorted in expressions of frenzied self-abuse, tongues lolling, eyes rolled skyward, lips drawn back from clenched teeth. St. Rodriguez was there as well, looking on with an expression that seemed to exhort the boys to even greater efforts, as his own fist tortured something monstrous. The basket was there too, and the sign that still read For Our School, but the offerings and the presence of the cross made it all the more blasphemous and obscene. As a parody of the original poster it was brilliant. Brilliant, sick, hilarious and depraved.

The First Years on the way to assembly scampered past it with blood-red faces. After all, just looking at something like that might be a mortal sin. The Second Years were split between shock and hilarity, while the boys in the upper years fought to get the best view of it just like they'd done with Abortion Bill. Most were hysterical with laughter. Others, like Sean, were stunned into silence. This was suicide. When he was caught, and the Head would make damned sure he was caught, whoever had done this would last just long enough at Meadowlands to get the thrashing of his life. Fooling around with the school statue was one thing, but depicting the founding father in the participation of something so foul was vastly different.

The poster wasn't a cartoon. The expressions on those faces had taken meticulous work. Superficially, the effect was comic, but looking deeper there was a sordid intensity to the thing that disturbed Sean deeply. The eyes of the boys rolled not just with passion, but with guilt and fear. And the saint's expression was laden with wanton violence. The thing was vile. Subversive, repulsive, and very, very clever

Brother Michael approached the mob in his usual attitude of despair. The First Years had been moving into the assembly hall nicely in twos and then something had happened. First there was a traffic jam and now pandemonium. He yelled Twos Please! Twos Please! at the top of his voice, but the boys just surged around and past him to join the melee. He was almost knocked off his feet. It was too bad, just too bad, the insolence of this new breed of schoolboy. What had happened in the last sixty years to create such a foul-mannered rabble?

Suddenly he had had enough. He slapped the head of the boy nearest to him, a full blooded slap that hurt his hand and pushed the boy aside. He slapped out again, right and left, using the back of his hand in one direction and the front in the other, lashing at heads and faces as he cleared a path towards notice board. And then he stopped, staring at the thing that had given rise to all the excitement.

The laughter died around him as the boys shuffled backwards to give him space. He looked at the poster for several seconds, his old face slowly draining of colour, the hostility of his expression seeping away to be replaced by a look of infinite sadness. His rheumy were moist as he removed the drawing pins from the corners of the poster, slowly, carefully, then he rolled it into a tight tube and turned to face the boys. Those closest to him looked down at their feet, and those at the back dispersed quickly into the assembly hall. Brother Michael looked at them, hardly comprehending how such a thing could come to exist.

"Move along boys," he muttered finally. "Twos please," and then went to deliver his horrible burden to the Head.

Chapter 16: Summoned Again

The call came half-way through Maths class. Waiting outside the Head's office Sean searched desperately for a possible culprit. Who the hell could it be? Who was mad enough? Talented enough? Who had the balls? Speculation had been the sole schoolyard occupation all day, and Sean had flitted from group to group hoping desperately to find someone he could finger. No one. There had been absolutely no one.

The Head didn't believe him. And the Head was in no mood for games. This wasn't the unflappable Head who'd removed the condom from St. Rodriguez's palm on Monday morning, and it wasn't the unctuous Head who'd offered Sean a role in some righteous moral conspiracy on Wednesday. This Head was a seething fury of determined vengeance. There was no farting around with fountain pens and foolscap this time - as soon as Sean entered the office he thrust the poster into his face and demanded to know right then and there who was responsible for such filth. Sean must know! Some boy in this school must know. Somewhere in this school there lurked a sewer-minded filthy braggart, and Sean would tell him who it was and would tell him right now!

-But I don't know who it is Brother!

-I will have it out of you boy.

-But I can't tell you anything Brother!

-Can't or won't?

-I can't Brother.

-You can't tell me, but you know who it is.

-No Brother, I can't tell you because I don't know.

-Who has been talking?

-Everyone Brother.

-Who has been boasting?

-No one Brother.

-Don't lie to me McCaffery. The person who did this did it for personal and public gratification, to show off in front of his obscene friends. Now who is he?

-I don't know Brother. Honestly, I don't know!

The Head had been standing, jutting his face into Sean's, using it like a weapon. Now he sat down, and the energy of his fury contracted into a cold hardness.

-I won't be trifled with, McCaffery.

-No Brother.

-Shut up and listen.

-Yes Brother.

-I asked for your assistance in this matter because I was led to believe that you respected the Christian values on which this school is built.

-I do Brother.

-I'm seldom wrong in assessing the character of a boy, but I'm beginning to suspect that I have made a mistake with you. I don't like making mistakes McCaffery, and I won't have boys trying to make a fool out of me.

-I'm not Brother.

-Shut up!

A cane appeared in the Head's fist as if out of nowhere, and he punctuated his outburst by slamming it down on the desk. Sean was shocked into a terrified silence.

-I will not tolerate dissent in this school. I will uncover any faction that seeks to undermine the order that I impose, and I will weed it out root and branch before it grows to bear the seeds of rebellion. I will not tolerate willfulness or disobedience from any boy. I will not allow the expression of any opinion within this school that conflicts with the policies and doctrines that I promulgate. Any boy that disagrees with my position may leave. Any boy who voices his disagreement will be thrown out. Do you understand me?

-Yes Brother.

-Then understand that your views are irrelevant. Any expression of doubt and dissent on your part is insolence and will be punished as such. Your teachers are your superiors, and you do not question what they teach, be it a matter of fact or of faith, and you neither question nor impede their actions under any circumstance. Do you understand me?

-Yes Brother.

-Good, now hold out your left hand.

-What?......I'm sorry Brother.........What have I done?

-You have just questioned me, that's what you've done, now hold out your hand.

Sean held out a palm slick with sweat. The Head rose and in the same motion brought the cane whistling down on Sean's finger tips. It was as if Sean had grasped a rod of white hot iron. He yelped with the agony of it and thrust the hand under his armpit, crushing it against himself.

"Let me have it again McCaffery".

Every instinct told Sean to keep the hand where it was, but then he remembered Halligan howling in anguish as the cane lacerated his buttocks. He held out the hand, fingers already swelling crimson and purple. He tried to flex them, ever so gently, and met a hard resistance at the joints. They felt permanently damaged. The second stroke almost brought him to his knees. He bent double as the pain speared up through his arm and into the back of his head, bursting against his skull. He ground his teeth to prevent himself from crying out, and he knew that never, never, never could he hold out that hand again; not for anything, not even if meant immediate expulsion, the pain was so terrible.

"Let that be a small taste of what to expect should you offer any further impudence to your superiors, McCaffery. And I expect you will have the information I require from you in the very near future. Now get out."

Sean staggered straight to the bathroom and plunged his hand under the cold water tap, his fingers engorged with blood, agony throbbing with each pulse. He tried again to form a fist, but the hand was useless, swollen into a rigid mass, the skin shiny and blue-black.

Jesus! Rodney Strong had taken six of those. Six! And never uttered a word. His own weakness shamed him; not just the response to the pain, but the certainty that he would shop the Poster Boy in a second rather than face the Head again. But what could he do? How could he deliver the Poster Boy when he had absolutely no clue who he was? The situation was impossible.

That evening Flint met him again at the entrance to Cack Alley. He seemed disappointed that Fearon was nowhere in sight.

"Not bothering you any more is he?"

153

"No".

"Well just tell me when he needs another kicking and I'll sort him out for you."

"Thanks", said Sean, "I'll let you know".

They walked together towards the Entry, Flint quite comfortable to saunter along in silence, Sean feeling obliged to find something to talk about.

"You're at Duggin Secondary Modern aren't you?"

"Yeah. Borstal Billy's. Well I was before they suspended me.

"What did they suspend you for?

"Fighting mostly.

"Mostly?

"Yeah, fighting and stealing and stuff. Nicked someone's pen and the little bastard clatted on me to the teachers. Got six off Billy Bollox the Deputy Head, so I got hold of the little bastard after school and twatted him. Took a file down Billy Bollox's car too. Fair's fair eh?"

He laughed a high whinnying laugh and spat a gob of phlegm into the nettles.

"How long's the suspension?

"Don't know really. Going to the School Board isn't it? Might get expelled.

"Bet your mum and dad are pissed off."

Flint's face changed. The sudden hatred was so intense that Sean pulled away as if expecting a blow. Flint walked on for a few more paces then seemed to shrug himself back into his former spirits.

"Hey, I put the shits up you and your Gran the other day didn't I?"

Sean flushed, remembering how Flint's antics up the lamp post had scared him half to death. He kicked a stone into the nettles and turned his face away. He let his shoulders droop and slid his hands into his pockets, slouching along.

"My Gran thought you were going to break your bleeding neck."

"Why'd she care – She's not my bleeding Gran is she? And even if she was......." The blazing hatred was back.

"Why'd you do it? Climb the lamp post, I mean."

"Don't know. Something to do.....Bit of a lark."

"But one slip......."

"So – my neck isn't? What do you care?"

Flint looked like he really wanted to know. Sean shrugged - Mr. Tough Guy.

"Would have made a right mess outside our house. My mam might've made me clean it up."

Flint gave a short laugh. He punched Sean gently in the upper arm (it hurt) and the boys walked on in silence. They'd passed the wall where Fearon had taken his beating and were close to the railway viaduct when Flint spoke next.

"What's it like going to that poncey grammar school with all them divvies?

"Alright, I suppose. Teachers are mostly wankers, but the Brothers are worse."

Sean felt guilty about Ben Gibbs and Gladys Hardy, but he wasn't going to make any exceptions in front of Flint.

"Head a hard bastard like ours is he?"

"What do you think.......?"

Sean held out his left hand. The swelling had subsided, but evidence of his thrashing was still there in the livid bruises that marked the tracks of the cane. Flint whistled and looked at him with a new respect.

"Beauty!" he said, and Sean expanded with pride.

"What you get that for then?"

Sean told Flint all about the statue, Abortion Bill, the Sponsored Wank and the Head's demand that Sean tell him who was behind it all.

"You're not going to clat are you?" asked Flint

"How can I? I don't know who it is."

Flint thought for a few seconds and then started laughing.

"You're not too smart for a Grammar Grub are you?"

"What d'you mean?"

"You let yourself get caned when you could've stuck it to some other bastard."

"I don't get you."

"Look, who at school do you really hate?"

"I don't know. Fearon maybe, but he's just a tosser. I should feel sorry for him really."

"Come off it, you must hate somebody. I hate everyone."

"So what's your point?"

"Well you just blame them don't you? That way they get nailed and you don't."

"What? You mean set someone up?"

"Not just anyone. Pick some poxy bastard you really hate and drop them in the shit. Stands to reason doesn't it? Logical like."

Flint grinned. He gave Sean another playful punch on the arm, the knuckles like stones, and Sean began to appreciate what Fearon must have gone through.

They'd reached the end of the Entry now, and Flint asked Sean to check if his dad's car was parked up. It wasn't, and Flint was gone in a flash, over the gate, up on the porch, through the bedroom window, and back to his cell.

As he watched him disappear, Sean wondered if the world might not be a better place without the likes of Jimmy Flint.

Chapter 17: Sound Advice

Although the boys still mouthed about bringing down the Brotherhood, most of them had decided that it was OK to take part in the Sponsored Walk.

If the destination had been the new Roman Catholic Cathedral in Liverpool, there would have been no takers. But there was nothing religious about Sandcaster. It was on the coast, and there were penny arcades, bingo stalls, dirty postcards, sticks of rock, candy floss, and of course, Joyland – one of the biggest funfairs in England. So it wasn't really a sponsored walk for the school's benefit, they were going to do it for fun. In fact, their intent was to drag the reputation of Meadowlands in the dust behind them.

The Brothers wanted them to walk in uniform to showcase school spirit. Well, there'd be high spirits all right. They'd rampage through Rainford, lay waste to Ormskirk, run riot through Maghull and descend on Sandcaster like a purple plague. If there was any trouble to be had on the way they'd find it. If there wasn't, they'd make it. It would be a lark, make no mistake about that – a right bloody lark. So Sean, all earnest and innocent, did a tour of his relatives to justify the campaign.

His Gran's face lit up when he called at her house on Saturday afternoon. Sunday was his usual visiting day, so seeing any of her twenty grandkids was a happy surprise on a Saturday. His daft uncle Albert who lived with his Gran was off on one of his shopping trips to Liverpool buying some bloody suit he'll never wear to please some girl he'll never meet, said his Gran, and she was celebrating her freedom by chain-smoking in every room of the house, and letting the ash lie wherever it fell. She sat Sean down in the front parlour with a mug of tea and a slice of fruit cake and told him not to worry about the crumbs – sour-face would clean up when he got home. Actually she loved her son just as much as her grandson, but the fact that uncle Albert was a whining wimp of an unmarried virgin made her playacting all the more believable.

Aunt Winnie and aunt Theresa showed up when Sean was on his second mug of tea. They were his grandmother's sisters, and shared her slabby plainness, but their widows' black was the only dour thing about them. Like Sean's Gran they'd outlived hard working husbands, and had carried on afterwards as if the fun at the wake had never ended. Their husbands had probably died of exhaustion.

Winnie and Theresa squeezed onto Albert's new sofa, their arses parked on the plastic wrap that Albert refused to remove. The other furniture was older than the great-aunts themselves: a huge chest of drawers against one wall with a speckled mirror above it; a slab of table under a window that looked out onto the mossy garden; a glass-fronted cabinet in one corner containing family photos; and an ancient gramophone hidden inside a hinged cabinet as big as an armchair. Everything made of mahogany and brought to a glossy finish by Albert's daily grind.

As soon as Winnie and Theresa were settled, Sean's Gran went to the chest of drawers and pulled out a bottle of Jameson's from among a jumble of linen. She brought three tumblers from the kitchen and set them down next to the bottle. Winnie and Theresa lit up their Woodbines, and within a minute the tiny room was a blue fog, the afternoon sunlight slicing the air into parallel blocks like one of HAL's Physics experiment at school.

His Gran passed the Jameson's to Winnie who unscrewed the cap and passed it on to Theresa to pour, as if each were accepting joint responsibility.

Winnie: Come on, let's have a proper measure, that little splash is no good to anyone.

Theresa: Alright, alright. Hold your bloody horses. I'm coming around again.

Gran: Pour it all at once you daft beggar. It's not like tea. It doesn't get stronger at the bottom.

Theresa: Don't tell me how to pour whisky, I've been doing it all my life.

Gran: Weaned on the stuff.

Theresa: You and me both. Cheers!

-Cheers!

-Aaahhh!

-Nice drop of Irish never hurt anyone.

-Oh, I don't know about that.

-What about Paddy Farrell? Didn't do him much good.

-Him what had the big lorry?

-Aye.

-That weren't a drop, that were a bloody barrel-load.

-Amazing no one else were killed.

-Crashed it right through the wall of Duggin Labour Club.

-Lucky it were after hours.

-Lucky! If the bugger had crashed that lorry an hour earlier he would have taken half the riff-raff in Duggin with him. That would have been lucky.

-Can't win 'em all, I suppose.

-Always late, Paddy Farrell.

-I reckon he were trying to break in for a pint.

-A pint? Paddy Farrell never touched a pint. It were always a gill of the hard stuff for Paddy.

-Went up in a blue flame when they cremated him.

-Whoosh! Gone.....

-And that new Labour Club's no better.

-New? It's been up twenty years.

-Aye and filled with the old bloody rubbish from Day One.

-Labour Club? Now there's a joke. A day's labour'd kill the bloody lot of them what sup in there.

-Something wrong with your arm Theresa?

-No, why?

-My glass is empty.

-Aye, and what did your last servant die of?

-Albert out is he Agnes?

-No, he's in the kitchen cooking us a roast - what do you think you daft beggar?

-Liverpool?

-Aye, and more bloody suits. Closet full of them upstairs. None of 'em ever worn.

-Round the bend that lad.

-Lad? He's thirty bloody five.

-Aye and daft as a brush. What happened to that girl at the Co-op?

-All in his mind I reckon.

-Where was he going then, all them Sunday afternoons reekin' of after-shave?

-Dunno, the graveyard most likely.

161

-Graveyard – what the hell for?

-Buggered if I know. Molly Burton said she saw him sittin' by his dad's grave blubbering.

-What, your Samuel? But he's been dead fifteen years.

-Aye, and never much of a father before that.

-A damned shame at Albert's age, him with no lass.

-Eeeeeh, by thirty five I'd had me fill of men.

-Aye, me an' all.

"And what are you bloody smirking at our Sean?" said Steve's gran.

Sean couldn't help it. It was ridiculous to think that three old hags like that could have ever been attractive to men.

Theresa seemed to guess his thoughts. "I were a raven-haired beauty in my day," she said, and took a huge gulp of whisky as if to toast her past.

"True enough," said Winnie. "We were all good-looking lasses. I had more offers than I knew what to do with."

"Offers for what?" asked Sean.

"You mind your cheek," said his Gran.

"Aye, I had a fair following meself," said Theresa, "though Alfie Scoggs were the one I really wanted. Broke my heart over him I did. Lovely lad he were."

"Alfie Scoggs!" said Winnie. "You could have had Alfie Scoggs any time you liked, you know that. Alfie Scoggs was always mooning around after you."

"Oh aye, I knew that alright, but the daft beggar could never shape himself to ask me, could he? Stood there gawping every time I went by and never said a word. Looked like he'd had all the stuffing knocked out of him, the silly sod."

"Them shy 'uns are no bloody good to you," said Sean's Gran. "You need a feller with a bit of nouse. If he can't stand up for himself, how's he going to stand up for you?"

"Aye, but Alfie Scoggs weren't shy with no one else - just me. I reckon it were because I were three years older than him, so he reckoned I wouldn't be interested. Dozy bugger, I would have taken him in a second."

"And made a man of him in a minute," said Winnie.

"Aye, that and all," said Theresa, and the three of them burst into girlish giggles as the whisky bottle made its third round.

The lesson of Alfie Scoggs hadn't been lost on Sean. He tried to sound casual, but his voice squeaked as if his pants were too tight.

"Did you really fancy someone three years younger than you Aunt Theresa?"

Another round of giggles erupted. There was no fooling them.

-Eeeeh, you've got yourself a lass have you?

-Who is it then, our Sean?

-Not some trollop I hope.

Sean blushed scarlet. "Don't be daft," he said, "I was just curious."

-Aye, I bet you were

-And you want to watch that curiosity of yours when it comes to the lasses.

-Specially the ones older than you.

-Aye, curiosity has gotten many a feller a damned sight more than he bargained for.

They laughed again, lit new Woodbines, hoisted the whisky, and looked like they were having a fine old time at Sean's expense. He got up as if to leave.

163

"Come on now pet, you keep your arse parked there, and take no notice of them two," said his Gran, as though she hadn't been laughing as hard as her sisters. "If you've got yourself a lass, good luck to you."

"But I haven't Gran," said Sean.

"No," Theresa interrupted, "but you've got the hankering for one haven't you, and she's a few years older than you isn't she cock? Happens all the time at your age."

"I keep telling you......." complained Sean.

"Well you can tell it to the Marines," said Theresa, "I know better. And I'll tell you a few other things an' all. You're a good looking lad, and you'll have no trouble getting your fair share. But don't be a bloody Alfie Scoggs, that's all. Mooning about'll never get you nowhere, whether it's with a lass or 'owt else. Stand bold and you'll do alright. If you take a fancy to a lass, you just go up and tell her. If she's got any sense she'll take you on, a strapping lad like you. If not, then you're better off without her. Either way, you've lost nowt. I'm telling you, take my advice and you'll do alright. Mope around like a wet rag and you'll go wanting."

"No ask, no get," said Winnie.

"And I'm asking for another measure," said Theresa, tapping her glass.

"And after that speech," said Sean, "I'm asking all three of you to sponsor me for two bob in the Meadowlands Sponsored Walk."

"Two bob! Cheeky little beggar," said Winnie, laughing.

"Aye, and we walked right into that one, didn't we?" said Theresa.

The lad learns fast," said his Gran with genuine pride.

Sean left a little later with the promise of six shillings in sponsorship from his Gran and her sisters. Not bad.....not bad at all. And maybe they were right – maybe all you had to do was ask.

He walked home in a daze, his mind fixed on Paula Yates. Stand bold, he told himself. Faint heart never won fair maiden. No ask, no get. By the time he reached his door he was almost believing in himself.

How was he going to pull it off? Now was the time to do it; none better. Right now he had the advantage. He'd flung Fearon at her feet, shown his mettle, and proved he wasn't one of those namby-pamby fellows who Theresa despised. But where did he go from here? None of it was any good unless he got to speak with her. The unwritten rules hadn't allowed Theresa to make the first moves on Alfie Scoggs, and Alfie had lost his big chance to great uncle Syd, dead for almost twenty years. But how had uncle Syd pulled it off when Theresa had been in love with Jimmy? He should have asked her about that.

Hi Paula, how's it going? That's what he'd say to her all casual.

Fine thanks, how are you? she'd say, smiling.

Oh I'm fine. I was just wondering whether you'd like to come to the pictures with me on Saturday. To the matinee. Butch Cassidy and The Sundance Kid is playing. Supposed to be good. No pressure, just an invite, no sweat if she said no. *But, I'd love to!,* she'd say, and he'd say *Great! I'll meet you outside at two thirty* and she'd say *Great, thanks!*

And then he'd hold her hand during the show, and she'd turn to him in the dark, and he'd put an arm around her shoulder, and she'd lean against him, and he'd stroke her hair, and she'd look up at him and move her face close to his, and he'd bend his head to hers, and he'd kiss those perfect lips, and she'd cling to him, and he'd kiss her again and again.

Bollocks! It was all a load of fucking bollocks

He didn't have any money for the pictures and she probably wouldn't want to see Butch Cassidy and it probably wasn't the right thing to ask her to meet him outside the picture house and he didn't have a car or a motorbike or the guts to pick her up at home and his clothes were all shitty hand-me-downs and she was taller than he was and he'd look ridiculous walking next to her and he was just thirteen and she was sixteen and if he said Hi to her she'd probably just keep on walking by without even a look and he'd die of embarrassment and all his dreams would be destroyed in that one terrible moment and he'd never be able to hope again and never again be able to imagine that one day he'd be more to her than just this scruffy little kid who'd pushed some prick into the brook on her behalf.

How could he risk that? It wasn't fair!

Oh God, what was he going to do?

CHAPTER 18: More Posters

It was on the Thursday before the Sponsored Walk that the Poster Boy struck again.

All week Sean had lived in terror of another call to the Headmaster's office. Every morning he'd walked through the school gates with a sensation of suffocating dread, and had left in the afternoon with a huge inhalation of relief. He hadn't been able to concentrate on lessons, and at lunch and recess he'd abandoned his usual friends and wandered between groups of boys to spy, saying nothing, listening for clues, and then drifting off when he was noticed.

And every day he'd waited for another poster to appear. The mystery obsessed him. Who could the Poster Boy be? How could he find out? Would he really shop him if he knew who it was? Yes, yes, yes, and live with the secret – anything to escape the threats of that black-robed bastard. He'd even considered Flint's idea of blaming someone innocent, Fearon maybe, but the idea of Fearon having the mental wherewithall to produce the posters like those was ridiculous. Blaming some smarter kid would only lead to an investigation that might get him deeper into the shit.

He could see no way out.

The third poster showed up in the morning. It was taped to the screen of the television set in the Language Lab. Horse-Face Logan jumped two feet backwards when pulled off the TV cover and found himself staring at a caricature of Head. It was head and shoulders, the features distorted even beyond their natural ugliness. Tattooed onto the massive forehead were the words **Big Brother**. Underneath the drawing was written: **Is Watching You!** There were a few titters at Horse-Face's reaction, but the poster didn't raise any laughs. When the boys of 4X spread the word to the rest of the school at morning recess, they didn't joke about it. Some even suggested the Head had done the poster himself.

The fourth poster appeared just before lunch break, tacked to a notice board in the sixth form block. A set of iron gates dominated the picture, with Meadowlands as a hulking mass in the background. Behind the gates, black-robed figures stood in attitudes of threatening authority over huddles of purple-blazered boys. With just a few splashes of paint, the artist had managed to inject brooding violence into one group and cringing fear into the other. Looking closer, it could be seen that on the arm of each black robe was a white band, and on the band an ambiguous emblem. The sign at the top of the gate read Work Means Freedom.

One of the Priestlings spotted it first and took it into the Sixth Form Common Room to give it to Shit-face Shaughnessy, but it was snatched from his hands and moved from fist to grasping fist as each boy examined it in and passed it on. No one wanted ownership for more than a few seconds. When it came to Shit-Face, he glared around at the other sixth formers as if he'd already achieved his ambition of returning to Meadowlands as a teacher, and then stalked with the poster out of the room. Everyone knew that within a minute he'd have his tongue firmly lodged up the backside of the nearest Brother.

Poster number five was hung in the toilets next to the school entrance doors. It was spotted at afternoon recess. Fatty Gruntle, waddling around on supervisory duty, noticed that the toilets seemed to be attracting an unusual crowd, suggesting that either the school lunch was having a disastrous effect or there was a fight going on behind the doors.

As luck would have it, Sean was standing in front of the poster when Gruntle bellied his way to the front of the mob. The fact that Sean was the only boy not in a state of wild excitement registered in Gruntle's mind as he took in the details. Two words were scrawled in red across the centre in an animated script that urged the boys to action - **Fight Back!** Surrounding the words were scenes showing how the boys might take their revenge on the teachers in Meadowlands. Some of them were quite funny: Chuck Bones sprinting up the rugby field in borrowed kit that failed to cover his privates as the kids laughed him on; Horse-Face Logan peeking out in terror from the inside of a grand piano as boys beat on it with hammers. Other scenes were brutal. Brother Campion bent over his desk, hands nailed to the woodwork as a purple-clad figure rams a stake into his anus; the Head beset by a circle of cane-wielding boys, flaying him to bloody ribbons; Gruntle strapped to a table as boys tip a cauldron of scalding offal into his screaming throat.

Sean recognised Bosch, but Gruntle wouldn't have had a clue. And even if he'd seen a Bosch painting, Gruntle would have called it filth. That's what he called the poster now. Filth. Absolute filth. He tore it down and landed a back-hander full in Sean's face. He roared at the boys to get out, landing more blows on those closest to

169

him. When the toilet was clear he hurried with all the speed his bulk allowed towards the Head's office.

The summons came just before the end of classes. Sean wanted desperately to run for the temporary safety of home, but he knew that was pointless. He needed Meadowlands. He had no choice.

The Head was standing outside his office, waiting for him. He couldn't recall later if he had come to a standstill and was dragged the last few steps, but he did remember being hurled bodily into the office. That's when he saw the other two posters for the first time. He gaped at them stupidly while his mind went into frantic overdrive in search of something to say.

Nothing! Absolutely nothing! He could think of absolutely nothing!

"Who is it McCaffery? Tell me who it is McCaffery. I want to know right now!" The Head's voice had an edge of madness to it. Dangerous, dangerous madness.

"I've given you all week McCaffery. Now tell me who is responsible. TELL ME!"

And then for the second time that afternoon the back of a hand slapped him hard across the face. The blow unlocked something, the blow and those two words scrawled across the poster in the toilets. He almost screamed back at the Head.

"How can I tell you what I don't know, you..........you......?" He stopped himself before calling the Head a bloody fascist, but the injustice and hopelessness of his situation drove him onwards. "Can't you understand? I don't have a clue. Nobody does. You can beat me all day and night and it won't make a damned bit of difference. I DON'T KNOW!!"

The Head leapt at him, caught him by the arm and forced his hand out in front. The cane appeared out of nowhere and came slashing down on Sean's palm. The Head kept his grip on the arm, not allowing Sean to withdraw it and the cane came down again.

"Don't you dare talk to me like that McCaffery. Never, ever speak to me like that again or I'll make you wish you'd never set foot in this school. I will have that boy's name from you. I will have it by one means or another. I will not be trifled with." The cane came down a third time. "I report to the Board of Governors at the end of next week. By that time you will have brought me this boy's name or I promise you will face the consequences." The cane made its last descent . Do you hear me?"

Sean buckled as his arm was released. Spikes of agony radiated through his hand and arm. He couldn't answer. The pain was everything. He bowed his head, reeling with nausea. The Head took this as a yes.

"One more week McCaffery, you have one more week!" and he thrust him out of the office.

Sean staggered to the toilets, making his way across a floor that tilted and swayed. Everything was spinning, turning white. The only fixed point in his world was the pain that burned and burned and burned. God, how could he stop the pain? He used his good hand to turn on the cold water, and then plunged the other hand into it, hanging on to the edge of the sink to stop himself from collapsing onto the piss-drenched floor. He bent forward over the sink, breathing the cold spray.

The school bell rang for the end of classes. In just a few minutes the toilets would be flooded with boys. He caught sight of himself in the mirror, tear-streaked eyes and hair matted against the sweat of his forehead. He couldn't be caught like this. There'd be questions he wouldn't dare answer. He backed into a stall and sat on the toilet with his head between his knees, the crippled hand tucked under his armpit. It had been just a few days since he'd sworn that he could never take another thrashing from the Head, and yet here he was again, only this time everything, absolutely everything was much worse.

Where could he go from here? Why had he been singled out for such an impossible task? How could he escape the violence of that maniac? Bastard! he thought. You lousy stinking bastard!

He crept from the toilets when he was sure the rest of the boys had gone home, returning to his empty classroom to pick up his bag. On the way out he met Ben Gibbs in the corridor. Instinctively he hid his damaged hand and tried to give his favourite teacher a friendly smile. But Ben looked concerned.

"Are you alright McCaffery?" he asked. "You don't look well at all."

"I'm alright sir," said Sean. "I just felt a bit faint at the end of classes and had to go to the bathroom. Probably some bug."

Ben looked unconvinced.

"Are you sure? I've noticed you haven't been quite yourself lately - down in the dumps – and now this. Is there something bothering you? Anything I can do to help? Everything alright at home, I hope."

Sean could have cried. It was just like Ben to sniff him out. He looked just like a big Saint Bernard dog. All he needed was a brandy keg and a lot more hair.

"I'm alright sir, honest. Just a bit queasy that's all."

As Ben looked down on him Sean had the urge to tell him everything, to show him the battered hand, and to beg for his help. But what could Ben do? If Ben took his part against the Head, the

Head would fire him and there'd be one less decent teacher at the school. It was hopeless. Absolutely hopeless.

Ben patted him on the shoulder. "OK then McCaffery, get yourself home lad, he said. "And remember you can always have a chat with me if you need to."

"Yes sir," said Sean. "Thanks sir. I will sir."

But Sean knew he wouldn't.

Chapter 19: The Perfect Plan

Sean missed his usual bus and was glad of it. How could he have explained the obvious thrashing to Bill O'Rourke when his visits to the Head's office were supposed to be oh so very pally? The excuse that he was writing something for the Rodriguan Gazette would wear thin in a hurry if it looked like the Head had been beating the story out of him.

He was surprised when he saw Flint lounging at the entrance to Cack Alley.

"You're a bit late tonight aren't you?" said Flint, as he turned with Sean along the shit-strewn track.

"Yeah, I got delayed while the frigging Head did this to me." He turned his left hand palm-upward, the flesh cross-hatched and the fingers a bulbous blue-black. Flint whistled appreciation.

"Really laying into you isn't he? What was it for this time then?"

Sean told him the story of the three latest posters, not mentioning Orwell, Auschwitz or Bosch, guessing that Flint wouldn't have a clue what he was talking about. At first Flint called Sean a stupid bleeding dickhead for not taking his advice about shopping some other prick, but then he laughed.

"I still like that wanky one best," he said. "Tell me about that wanky poster again."

Sean described the second poster to him in graphic detail, making it funnier than it really was. Flint howled, tears in his eyes, and Sean glowed with pride in his performance. When he'd calmed down, Flint asked why the Poster Boy had called it a sponsored wank. What kind of wank was that? Was it like when you all did it together for a lark? Sean almost rolled his eyes until he remembered who he was dealing with. Instead, he explained the whole concept of the sponsored walk and how the Poster Boy had twisted the idea to come up with his artwork.

Flint still looked bewildered. "What? You mean half the bleeding school is going to waste a Saturday slogging it to Sandcaster and then give the money to the bleeding teachers? Are they bleeding mental or something?"

"It might be a bit of a lark," said Sean. "There'll be a lot of stuff to get into on the way."

"Bollocks to that," said Flint. "I'd hop on a bus and head straight for the fairground."

"We're not allowed to go the fairground," said Sean. "There's going to be a big picnic in Victoria Park and then we're all going back to Smellins in mini-buses."

Flint looked at him as if he couldn't believe what he was hearing. "No bleeding fairground?...... We? What do you mean WE?....... Don't tell me you're going to do it too?"

Sean flushed with embarrassment. "Yeah........ well......... everyone else is doing it."

They'd stopped by the wall where Fearon had got his pasting, and the look on Flint's face suggested that he might like to beat some sense into Sean as well.

"Are you fucking mad? Just look at your hand. Just think about what that bastard has just done to you. And you're going to half

175

knacker yourself for him. What have you got in there, pig-shit?"
And he rapped a hard knuckle on the top of Sean's head. It hurt like
bloody hell, but Sean didn't dare say a word.

"Well I've signed up now," he whined.

"So bleeding well unsign yourself. You said it was voluntary
didn't you? So unvolunteer, that's what I'd do. Especially if some
bastard had laid into me like what he's done to you. You'd have to
be a right bleeding tosser to go arse-kissing after that."

Sean explained that he couldn't get out of it. He'd already got his
grandparents and his sixteen aunts and uncles to sponsor him to the
tune of five quid. They were all dead keen for him to do the walk.
They seemed proud of him for some stupid reason. He couldn't tell
them he'd changed his mind because he'd gotten a caning. They
didn't know what went on in Meadowlands - they all thought you
only got caned when you deserved it, and serve you bloody well
right. His dad would give him another thrashing if he found out
what the Head had done to him.

Flint looked thoughtful. It was an expression Sean hadn't seen
before.

"Five quid eh? That's a lotta dosh. Too much dosh to be wasting
on a bleeding dump like Meadowlands."

"Well I don't have a choice now do I?" said Sean, "So what's the
point of going on about it?"

Flint looked like he was going to rap him on the head again, but
he stopped himself.

"You really aren't all that smart are you?" he laughed. "Can't see
what's obvious can you? Can't even see how to make yourself five
quid for doing nothing can you?"

"What do you mean?"

"Does anyone at school know how much money's been promised if you go through with it like one of them wankers?"

"No, not yet."

"Is anyone going to check on how much you pull in?"

"They haven't said anything about that. We just do the walk and give in the money."

"No forms then?"

"No."

Flint laughed. "What a bunch of dickheads! They're just asking for it aren't they?"

"What do you mean?"

"Obvious isn't it? What happens if you get sick on the day of the walk and you can't go?"

"Nothing. I wouldn't go and that would be that."

"But what if you weren't sick, and you still didn't go, and no one knew about it except me an you?"

"You mean pretend to go and........."

Flint beamed like a proud teacher. "That's right! Now you're getting it. You tell the family you did the walk. You tell the school you were sick and couldn't make it. The family cough up and you get to keep the dosh. And you don't have to walk a step to get it neither. Perfect isn't it?"

"But that's......thieving.........fraud. I mean it's stealing isn't it? I couldn't steal from my own family – they don't have all that much to begin with."

Flint looked disappointed again, like a teacher landing back at square one with a dunderhead.

"You're not thinking straight are you? Look, if you do the walk, your relatives are out of pocket, the dosh goes to the school, and them wanky Brothers get to spend it on beer and fags. If you don't do the walk, like I said, your relatives are still out of pocket, but the dosh goes to you. Either way the five quid gets paid. Depends who gets it doesn't it? Makes sense to me that it comes to you rather than them tossers. Almost like keeping it in the family isn't?"

Sean started to walk towards the Entry. He didn't want to hear this. It was wrong – dead wrong – and yet there was a terrible logic to what Flint was saying. He wanted to get home, away from Flint's influence. Sean tried to walk on quickly but Flint slowed him down, setting the pace. He felt as if he was pulling against some invisible force. Flint smiled.

"Come on mate, you have to admit it makes sense doesn't it?"

Sean didn't want to answer, but Flint wouldn't let him go.

"Come on admit it. You'd rather have five quid in your pocket than let it go to the bastard who's just given you a good hiding, wouldn't you? Come on, wouldn't you?"

Sean felt sick, as if breathing bad air. Flint was a lot smarter than he'd thought. He had him cornered.

"Of course I don't want that bastard to get it," he blurted, "but it's not as simple as that."

Flint smiled, putting his foot into the open door.

"But that's where you're wrong mate aren't you? It is that simple. Simplest thing in the world." He took Sean by both shoulders, so they came to a halt, and leaned in close.

"Listen - my mam and dad are buggering off in the car this weekend and keeping me locked up. Stupid gits have put a bolt on the bedroom door. Cunts haven't figured I get out through the window yet. They just leave me a loaf, a jug of water and a piss-pot and reckon 'llI stay where I'm told. Some chance of that old son, eh? So what do you say me and you get together this Saturday and have a right old time while your mates are doing the old arse-crawling routine. Be a lark eh?"

Sean shrugged away. He wanted to shout NO!!! But how would Flint respond? Would Sean end up getting the Fearon treatment?

Flint could see him wavering. He put a hand on Sean's elbow as they walked on.

"Come on Sean mate. I've got no one else to hang about with on Saturday, and it'll be fun just you and me. I haven't got any other friends except you. Come on mate, do us a favour. I give that tosser a good punching for you didn't I? I look after you don't I?"

Sean sought desperately for an excuse. He had to find some way to convince Flint that it wouldn't work.

"But what would we do?" he said. "Where could we hide out? I'm supposed to be in Sandcaster all day. If anyone was to see me in Duggin I'd be in real shit. No........."

Flint slapped him on the back before he could say another word.

"Great! I knew you'd do it. I knew you weren't one of those tossers. Fantastic! And don't worry mate I've got a plan all worked out. Me and you are going to have a great time."

Sean saw too late that a direct NO! should have been his only response.

"What plan? I don't think......."

"Listen, you're going to love this. It's perfect. What do you say me and you go to Sandcaster on Saturday, only we'll go on the train, and we'll go to the funfair, and we'll have a lark, and you can tell your mam and dad that you really did go to Sandcaster with no word of a lie. Brilliant eh?"

Flint looked really proud of himself. Sean was horrified.

"Sandcaster, are you mad? What if the other kids see me? What if the teachers see me, or the Brothers?"

"But they won't will they? We'll go there in style while they're sweating their bollocks off on the road. And we'll be at the funfair while they're at some poncey bloody picnic in the park. You told me yourself the funfair's off limits."

Sean grabbed at a chance. "Anyway, it won't work. I don't get the money till the walk's over, and I haven't got any for the train, or for the funfair. I only get a shilling a week pocket money, and that'll never get us as far as Sandcaster."

But Flint was ready for him. When it came to this type of thing Flint was way ahead of suckers like Sean.

"Look Sean, just you trust your uncle Flinty. I've got a bob or two stashed; plenty to get both of us to Sandcaster with enough left over for the funfair. You come along with me and I'll see you alright, don't you worry."

"But I couldn't pay you back."

It was as if Flint had put the words in his mouth. He wasn't just clever at this, he had a real genius for it.

"Sure you could. Here's the deal. I pay for everything on Saturday, train fare to Sandcaster and back, all the funfair stuff, and when you get the five quid we split it fifty-fifty down the middle. Can't say fairer than that can you?"

They'd reached the end of the Entry where it opened out into the cul-de-sac, yet Sean felt as if walls were closing in around him.

"Now you're not going to let me down are you," said Flint. "You're not a bleeding chicken are you?"

It was his last chance, but he could see no way out. If he went against Flint he'd certainly get a battering, and he'd been brutalized enough for one day. He tried to inject a sneer into his voice as he turned towards home

180

"No, I won't let you down," he said. And I'm not a bleeding chicken."

But as he walked away from Flint he remembered saying Grace in the dining room the last time he'd chickened out.

And just look where that had gotten him.

PART TWO

"Go at once, this very minute, stand at the cross-roads, bow down, first kiss the earth which you have defiled, and then bow down to all the world and say to all men aloud, 'I am a murderer!' Then God will send you life again."

-Fyodor Dostoevsky, *Crime and Punishment*

Chapter 20: So What Did You Expect?

Sean's mum shook his shoulder gently and whispered so she wouldn't wake the others.

"Time to get up love."

She tip-toed from the bedroom and left Sean to stumble thick-eyed to his feet. He made a small gap in the curtains and poked his head through. It was a gorgeous, sun-splashed morning, perfect for the sponsored walk. God, how he wished he was going

He'd spent a restless night thinking of the fix he was in. What if he got caught? What if someone he knew spotted him in Sandcaster away from the rest of the walkers? What if Flint pulled some stupid stunt and got them arrested? It would be just like that crazy bastard. Just imagine the shame as the police car arrived at the door. Imagine the contempt of his family when they discovered that he'd conned them out of money they could barely afford. How could he ever look any of them in the face? And then there were Ben and Gladys. How would they react? But maybe he wouldn't even see them again. The Head would expel him first, and all hopes of escaping Duggin would go down the toilet.

It got worse over breakfast.

"They've picked a perfect day for it," said his mum as he sat down at the table. He could tell by her smiling bustle that she was feeling pleased with him. Up at 7.00 a.m. on a weekend to do a good turn for his school. If she only knew!

She took the frying pan out of the cupboard and placed three thick slabs of bacon into it.

"You'll be needing a good breakfast with twenty miles of walking in front of you," she said, as if she needed the excuse. Bacon was a luxury in the McCaffery household.

"I'll make your sandwiches while that cooks."

She took a tin of Princess sockeye salmon from the cupboard. What the hell was she up to? His dad sweated his balls off in the DIC six days a week on a diet of corned beef and cornflakes. If he found out that she'd been feeding him bacon for breakfast and salmon for lunch there'd be bloody murder.

But his mum's happiness found vent in generosity. She spooned the salmon onto slices of heavily buttered bread, and when he wasn't looking, reached into the porage box, took a chocolate-covered wafer from its hiding place and wrapped it up with the sandwiches. She put the package in his blazer pocket and looked down on him with a big smile. This would have been marvelous if he really was going on the walk, but the way he felt right now she might as well have plastered his sandwiches with shit.

She served him the bacon, and then pressed a crust into the fatty suspension on the bottom of the pan – bread and dripping for her breakfast. He wanted to push his plate toward her and say "You have this mam, I'm not hungry." But he knew it was hopeless. She'd worry he was sick, and she'd keep the bacon for his father's dinner rather than eat it herself. No doubt the miserable sod would want to know why it was bacon instead of Shepherd's Pie on a Saturday evening, and if she was daft enough to tell him there'd be a right bloody palaver. Christ, the cheap pettiness of it all!

But was he really trapped? Was there no way out of this? Couldn't he just explain everything that had happened with Flint?

But that would mean bringing the Brothers into it too, and the thrashings, and she'd never believe he didn't deserve them, especially after he'd admitted he'd been about to rob her blind. And then she'd be around to Flint's house, and her and Elsie Flint would be going at in the street. Sean's mum might be as mild as the Virgin Mary, but she'd fight like a docker's whore if anyone messed around with her kids. And then what would happen to Flint? He'd be locked in his bedroom after his parents got through with him, but God help Sean when he finally got out again.

"Come on Sean, eat it before it gets cold."

Go on! his conscience urged - own up you bloody coward - tell her everything and start afresh. He looked into her eyes and she smiled at him. He couldn't do it. It would be like punching her in the face. He forced the bacon down his throat hoping it would choke him.

During the school week Sean thought nothing of wearing the purple blazer of Meadowlands Grammar through the streets of Duggin. But at seven thirty on a Saturday morning he felt as much out of place as a clown at a funeral. There were few people about as he walked past the shops opposite the entrance to the DIC, and he avoided the curious eyes of those that stared at him.

Old Ottie Ward, the newsagent, was taking down the metal shutters that protected his windows from the Duggin yobs.

"Saturday morning detention is it?" he said. Behave your bloody self and you could have stayed in bed."

Sean would have walked by without a word, but today he needed an alibi.

187

"Sponsored walk," he grunted.

"Eh?"

"Sponsored walk. Raising money for the school."

"Bugger me! On a Saturday?" Suddenly, Ottie was all gruff smiles and curiosity. "Where are you walking to lad?"

"Sandcaster."

"Sandcaster! That's nigh on twenty mile. You'll be bloody knackered. How long's that going to take you then?"

"Dunno. All day I reckon."

"Aye, and all bloody night if it were me. Come in here a second."

Sean followed the old man into the dingy shop. He felt trapped. People who bought a paper from Ottie often left the shop knowing the contents front to back without ever turning a page. But today Ottie was inclined to be brief.

"Sandcaster eh? Not been there for bloody donkey's years. Well if you're going to be hoofing it that far you'll be needing something for the road."

He reached into the glass case that kept chocolate bars away from sticky fingers and handed Sean a sixpenny Mars Bar.

"There lad, that'll keep you going a mile or two."

Sean didn't know what to say. He'd never seen Ottie like this. He took the gift, but felt as if he were thieving it from behind Ottie's back. He stood there dumbstruck, but the old man saved him with crusty kindness.

"You'll not get to Sandcaster if you stand there bloody gawping all day. Now bugger off! Some of us have work to do."

Sean buggered off miserable and humiliated. Just a few days ago the walk had seemed like a mug's game. Now he'd be glad to do it on his knees.

"Idiot!" he told himself. "You stupid fucking idiot!"

Duggin railway station was on a side street not far from the school bus stop. Sean cast a wary glance along the road before darting through the entrance doors. A neighbour seeing him taking a train to Liverpool early on a Saturday morning in his school uniform would definitely tell his parents. No one's life was their own in Duggin.

Flint was in the waiting room as planned. So, this was it. He was committed now.

Sean had a few seconds to observe Flint before he was spotted. What a verminous-looking parasite, he thought, lolling there with his ragged arse on one seat and his filthy shoes propped on another, the butt end of a slimy cigarette smoldering between his lips. He embodied everything Sean despised in the worst of the Dugginites, and yet here he was, linking himself by choice to the essence of everything he hated.

Flint looked up as Sean entered, his expression hardening as he saw the school blazer.

"What you're wearing your bleeding uniform for you prick?"

"I've got to. I'm supposed to be on the sponsored walk aren't I, remember?"

"But look at you. You're going to stand out a fucking mile!

"What the hell has that got to do with anything?"

Flint looked at Sean like he'd said the most incredibly stupid thing. Then, seeing the anger in Sean's face he gave him a tight-lipped smile. No good having the witless bugger backing out of the deal now.

"OK, not to worry. I've got the tickets like I said, so we're off to Sandcaster changing at Liverpool. I'll look after them so we have to stick together, right?"

189

Sean was still glaring.

"Right?" he repeated with a dangerous edge.

"Right," said Sean, though he knew there was absolutely nothing right about it.

Flint was busy during the train journey to Liverpool. By the time they reached Lime Street Station the mirror in the toilet was smashed, there was piss and worse on the floor, toilet rolls had been unraveled along the tracks from Huyton to Edge Hill, and FLINT was scrawled in big black letters on the doors and walls. As he was about to leave the carriage, Flint doubled back to his seat and took a Stanley knife to the uphostelry, ripping out the innards. "There," he said to himself, "Perfect!" And just one last thing. He took out his felt tip pen and wrote **Sean McCaffery was Here September 20th 1969** on the back of the seat.

Sean had joined the crowd of people queing to leave the platform. A guard was checking tickets at a turnstile that let the passengers into the station. Next to the turnstile was a metal gate, about four feet high. The gate was closed.

Flint dragged Sean out of the queue and said "OK, now follow me." He started to run toward the gate, pulling Sean alongside him for the first few yards until they were both sprinting, hidden from the ticket collector by the line of people. Sean had no time to argue, but he knew immediately what was happening. That bastard Flint hadn't bought the fucking tickets!

He weighed his options and found he didn't have any. If Flint leapt the barrier and escaped, Sean would be left on the platform with no money and no ticket. The guard would call one of the coppers lolling about the station, and they'd drive him home in a Panda car to face his parents. That possibility didn't bear thinking about. If he leapt the barrier with Flint, at least there was a chance

190

he'd get away with it. So when Flint vaulted the gate Sean was just behind him. The ticket collector saw the streak of purple, let out a roar, and was off in pursuit. Bugger taking tickets, he thought, this was his real job, catching thieving yobos.

Lime Street Station was teeming on a Saturday morning, but Flint moved like a rat in a familiar maze, zigzagging through gaps and barely touching the wall of people. Sean was having a harder time of it. He tried to keep close behind, but the dodging and weaving threw him off just like it was meant to throw off pursuers. As people avoided Flint they'd stagger into Sean's path, and each time he'd blunder into someone Sean would turn around to see the ticket collector gaining ground. Flint was smarter - never let them see your face, keep your head down, and run! Up-end geriatrics, topple baby carriages, bring down cripples if need be, but never turn around until you have to fight. There'd be plenty of face-time in court.

The crowd had seen it all before. Lime Street Station was a magnet for every pick-pocket, shoplifter and shirt-lifter in Liverpool. If a couple of kids were making off with someone's gear, that someone should have kept a better look out shouldn't they? And if some prat in a uniform were after them, the prat could expect no help whatsoever. The kids could bounce off whoever they liked, but if Mr. Uniform so much as jogged an elbow, God help him.

That's what saved Sean. The hand of the guard was almost on his collar when Sean dodged behind three hundred pounds of Cunard docker. The guard's shoulder hit the docker somewhere in the ribs and brought him to a stand still. Then he made the mistake of grabbing Cunard's arm and attempting to shift him aside. He might as well have tried shifting the QE2. Cunard looked down at the hand on his arm, and then looked into the guard's face as if asking him whether he really wanted to do that. The guard decided that he didn't, and removed his hand very carefully.

"Thieving little bastards," he said, as if to explain himself. Cunard kept looking at him, silent, until the guard turned and shuffled back to his booth.

Sean's legs were rubber as he darted out of the station onto Lime Street. Flint, hiding in an empty shop doorway, grabbed him as he fled past and dragged him inside. Sean sagged down against him, gasping. Flint burst into hysterical laughter and Sean's rage exploded.

"You stupid bloody bastard Flint", he yelled. "That guard almost had me, and then where would we have been? You said you'd bought the bloody tickets, you lying twat!"

Flint laughed even more at Sean's panic-stricken face, and sat down in the doorway doubled up, tears streaming down his cheeks.

"Well screw you Flint," said Sean, aiming a kick. "I can do without fucking shits like you!"

Next moment he was flat on his back with the last of his breath knocked out of him. Flint, reacting with long practice, had caught his foot and lifted it high into the air to send Sean crashing to the concrete floor. He might easily have smashed Sean's skull. Now he knelt with one knee on Sean's chest, leaning hard into the point where his ribs met, keeping the breath from coming back.

"Now you just listen to me Sonny Jim," he said. "You and me are going to have us a nice day out in Sandcaster, just as we planned. And while you're with me, you do what I say, understand?"

Sean couldn't find breath to answer, and Flint knew it.

"Understand?" he asked again, and put all of his weight onto the knee.

Sean managed to nod, his eyes pleading with Flint to let him breathe.

"Good lad," said Flint, holding Sean's chin with one hand and patting his cheek with the other. "Now you stick with me like I said and we'll get along just fine."

Flint released the pressure on Sean's chest and pulled him to his feet. He walked off towards Commercial Street Station where they'd catch the train to Sandcaster, while Sean leaned against the wall sucking in huge lungfuls of air.

"God help me," thought Sean as he weighed his options and decided to follow Flint.

God wasn't listening.

Chapter 21: Water Sports

Flint bought return tickets to Sandcaster with a note pulled from a wad in his pocket. Where he might have got the money Sean didn't want to know, but obviously, not paying for the Duggin to Liverpool leg had been done just for the hell of it.

They left Sandcaster Station and headed directly for Joyland, the sprawling funfair that was Sandcaster's main attraction. To get to the main entrance, visitors had to cross a series of wooden bridges that crossed sections of the artificial lake that ran along the perimeter fence. There was no charge to get into Joyland, but once over the last bridge every type of shyster was waiting to empty your pockets.

The lake was peppered with boats that could be hired by the hour. A few were rowing boats and the rest were motor boats with a seat for the person in charge of the wheel, and another for a passenger, often as not in charge of a bottle.

Flint stood on the first bridge looking at the action on the water, and then, with a curt "Come on," motioned Sean to a dock where the boats were moored. A spectacularly fat lady dressed in a marquee lounged on a sun chair at the entrance to the dock. She turned piggy eyes on Flint.

"How much for half an hour?" asked Flint.

"Half an hour of what?" said the Fat Lady.

Flint leered but decided not to push his luck.

"Half an hour on the motor boats."

"That'll be a quid, and two bob for every five minutes if you don't come in when you're called. I start the clock when you get on, and you pay when you get off. And if you want to fart around all day I'll have none of your bloody lip when its time to cough up."

"Well you're a real charmer aren't you?" said Flint. "OK, we'll take that blue one, number seven, my lucky number."

"Let's see your brass first," insisted the Fat Lady, not moving an ounce of flesh.

Flint shrugged, pulled out his stash and riffled a wad of pound notes under her nose.

"There you go," he smirked. "Just imagine all the pork pies you could buy with that lot."

The Fat Lady looked as if she could have made short work of this skinny little bastard, but that would have meant getting up. She shifted the marquee aside and let the boys through.

"It's ten thirty now," she grunted, "that'll be a quid at eleven, and half a crown for every extra five minutes."

"Hey, that's not what you said a minute ago," snarled Flint.

"Well it's what I'm saying now," said the Fat Lady, "and if you don't like it you can piss off."

Flint didn't bother to reply. He strolled along the dock to boat number seven and climbed into the driver's seat. Sean got in beside him and unhitched the mooring rope as Flint started the motor. The boat picked up speed as Flint put his foot down hard on the pedal, and though they were going no more than ten miles an hour there was a satisfying wake from the prow as they moved out into the lake. Sean felt a slight easing of anxiety. At least for thirty minutes of this horrible day Flint couldn't do much but cruise around on the water. And what damage could he do there?

But on the lake Flint was unreachable, and therefore invincible. He could do whatever he liked out there and no one could do anything about it; at least not immediately. The fact that he would have to come ashore at some point wouldn't deter him in the least.

Two little girls, no more than ten years old, were sitting in their boat throwing bread to a flotilla of ducks that had gathered around them. At first, Sean didn't realise what Flint intended, but as he drew nearer to the girls without slowing down Sean yelled and made a grab for the wheel.

"Watch out Flint you're going to hit those kids."

"Yeah'" said Flint, shoving Sean's arm away. "Let's scare the shit out of them."

The ducks took off in a squawking flurry as Flint ploughed through them, and the two girls screamed as they saw Flint's boat heading for a direct hit. Flint's boat smashed into theirs dead centre and sent it rocking violently. If it wasn't for the old car tire nailed to the prow, the collision would have splintered the boat and sent it to the bottom. Without life-jackets, the girls would have gone to the bottom too. They started howling for daddy.

Daddy was in another boat with his wife just a few yards away. He'd watched Flint's approach in mute disbelief, but now he exploded in a fury.

"I saw that you little bastard!" he yelled. "Just wait till I get my hands on you."

He turned his boat towards Flint's and jammed his foot down on the accelerator. He looked big enough to snap Flint in half, but Flint just laughed in his face and veered away as a huge paw passed within inches of his face.

"Got to catch me first, haven't you, arsehole," taunted Flint, and actually turned his boat back towards him. This time Sean was closest to the flailing fists, and he cringed out of their path as they threatened to send him unconscious over the side.

Flint was carrying less than half the weight of the other boat and could manoeuvre around it with ease. He kept just a hand's breadth out of reach, driving the girls' father wild with frustration.

"No one touches my lasses and gets away with it," he roared. "I'll tear your bloody bollocks off when I get my hands on you."

"Come on then," laughed Flint, steering towards him again and then veering away. "Here's my bollocks for you."

He stood up in the boat, unzipped his pants and pulled out his cock. The proximity of it turned Sean sick. The two girls set up a new round of screaming as they caught sight of the thing, and were joined by their mother who outdid them both. The father had sheer bloody murder in his eyes, but now he was less concerned about ripping Flint's genitals off than sheltering his family from the sight of them.

"I'll have the bloody law onto you, you dirty little get, just see if I don't," he yelled. "You get away from my kids with that filthy thing."

Sean grabbed the wheel of the boat and turned it away from the other two. The sudden movement caused Flint to lose his balance and he fell backwards, almost pitching into the lake. But he was laughing hysterically now, just like he'd done in the shop doorway outside Lime Street Station. He recovered his seat, lounging backwards, his gob gaping wide and his dick still hanging out.

Sean steered towards the bridge, intent on getting past it to the clear water beyond. The crowd milling towards Joyland slowed as the boat approached, and a knot gathered directly above them.

Sean, intent on the wheel, hadn't realized that Flint was still exposing himself, but looking down at Flint's crotch he could see that his cock was more prominent than ever. Flint was bellowing with laughter, having the time of his life. The boat emerged on the other side of the bridge, but the spectators above had shifted across, like rubber-neckers at a road accident.

Sean kept his head down as gobs of spit, burning cigarettes and a half eaten toffee apple rained down on them. A thunderbolt wouldn't have been out of place to put paid to that foul erection. Once out of this boat, thought Sean, that's it -I'm off! He'd hitch-hike home, or find the sponsored walkers and pretend he'd arrived late and had been trying to catch them up. Anything to get away from this madman.

With the audience behind him, Flint zipped up and pushed Sean's hands off the steering wheel. He headed towards the next bridge where a muscle-head was floundering about in a rowing boat. His girlfriend was sitting in the bow, soaked and silent, as the oars flailed and scooped and the boat angled left and right without making an inch of headway. Thirty feet above them, a group of old-timers were shouting directions and having a whale of a time.

-Left hand down son.

-Now both together. There you go, you've got her straight.

-Hang on, don't dip.

-Aw shit, he's gone and soaked the lass again!

There was a burst of good-natured laughter from the group as muscle head's girlfriend shook the water out of her hair. She gave him an encouraging smile while he glowered and sweated and tried to ignore both her and the chorus above.

-Lift the oars man - don't scoop.

-You're rowing, not stirring your bloody tea.

-Watch it on the right, you're going to brain her!

-Ooh, that were close!

-You'd better get yerself a crash helmet lass.

More laughter as the lummox waltzed about on the water, his vest soaked with sweat and his big biceps doing more harm than good.

Flint couldn't resist the sight of someone in distress. He put his foot down and went at full speed towards the boat, almost clipping an oar as he sped by. His wake hit the rowing boat side on causing it to pitch and roll. The woman in the bow grabbed for the gunwhales, shifting her weight with the boat and making it rock even more. The crowd on the bridge Oooohed and Aaahhed, expecting to see both Muscle-Head and his missus going for a dip, but with a frantic feathering of oars he managed to get the boat under control.

"You bloody maniac," he roared. "Keep your bloody distance."

Flint turned the boat around and headed back. He wore a feigned expression of concern on his face and passed the boat even closer than before. "I'm sorry sir, I didn't quite hear you," he called as Muscle-Head lifted an oar and lunged at him as he went by. His girlfriend was in tears.

"Stay away for God's sake," he screamed. "You're going to have us over!"

With his back to the rowing boat, Flint howled with laughter, but as he turned to approach it again, he wiped the grin off his face and replaced it with that same look of genuine concern. He steered straight for the boat as the crowd on the bridge motioned him away, shouting and waving arms to the right and to the left as if to deflect Flint's boat by force of will. Flint pretended they weren't even there. He stood at the wheel and bore down on the boat calling out with that mockingly polite accent.

"You'll have to speak a little louder sir. I'm afraid that my motor is rather noisy. What is it you said?"

The crowd on the bridge took it on themselves to answer.

-Keep away you dozy get, you're goin' to have him in.

-Are you bloody deaf? He wants you to stay back!

-No common sense these snobby little bastards.

Flint turned his gaze to the spectators after setting a course that would ram the boat from behind. He seemed oblivious of the impending crash as he put a cupped hand behind his ear and called to them.

"What's that? I can't hear what you're saying when you all speak at once."

Sean grabbed for the steering wheel and diverted the boat just inches from collision. Muscle-Head launched a roundhouse at Flint as he went by, and Flint ducked it with the ease of long practice. He was about to launch a roundhouse of his own at Sean when a megaphone sounded from the lakeshore.

"Number 7 return to the dock immediately. Number 7, come in now!"

The Fat Lady had finally roused herself and was bellowing. Beside her, two small girls were clinging to their mother, and all three seemed to be in tears. The father was pointing towards Flint's boat and cursing. He didn't need a megaphone to be heard.

"Exposed himself he did, the dirty little get. Flashed his member right in my lasses' faces. Just wait till I get hold of the bastard, I'll rip it off and make him eat it."

Flint forgot about battering Sean and turned the boat towards the commotion. Just a few feet from landing he swung the boat around to move parallel with the dock. The father ran alongside the boat waving his fists and hollering threats. The Fat Lady waddled alongside him for a few steps before giving up.

"Come out of there you filthy little bastard," he roared, "while I knock you into the middle of next week."

Flint had enjoyed his success with the Old Etonian act, and tried it on again.

"Now that would be rather foolish of me, wouldn't it" he said. "So I think I'll stay here......on a Saturday."

"I'll 'ave you yet, you hard-faced little twat," said the father, "and then just see what I won't do with you. I'll teach you to whip it out in front of my wife."

Flint smirked. "Oh would you really?" he said. "That's terribly kind of you. I'll just turn the boat to face her and then you can show me how it's done."

Flint turned the boat, and with a theatrical flourish began to fumble with his fly. At the end of the dock the Fat Lady had put aside her megaphone and was speaking hurriedly into a two-way radio that crackled responses.

Sean's world began to crumble. She was calling the cops. The police would find some way to get them to shore, and then it would be handcuffs, helping with enquiries, a court appearance and Borstal. No university, no escape from Duggin. Just the doors of the DIC swinging open for one more Duggin DIC-Head. Tears welled in his eyes as he gave in to utter despair.

Flint wasn't concerned in the slightest. He waved a non-Etonian salute at the Fat Lady and turned the boat back towards the lake. Muscles had moved on, and the crowd on the bridge had gone too. Flint drew the boat up against one of the stone pillars supporting the bridge and held on to a vine that wound its way up to the railing above. He gave it a quick tug, and then bent down and pulled the drainage plug from the bottom of the boat. He grinned at Sean's horrified face and then threw the plug as far as he could towards the middle of the lake. Water started gushing in as Flint swung himself onto the vine and started to scale towards the railing thirty feet above.

Sean almost shit his pants. He had a phobic terror of heights. He watched Flint make short work of the thirty feet to swing a leg over the railing and onto the bridge. With the water lapping at his ankles, he could think of no alternative but to do the same. If he clung to the vine and called for help, help would come in uniform, and he'd rather die than face that.

Flint leaned over the railing and grinned down at him.

"Come on Tarzan," he called, "Your feet are getting wet."

The crowd crossing the bridge didn't seem to be paying any attention. The boat was hidden beneath the walkway so that no one above could see it going to the bottom. And there was no novelty in boys clambering about and risking their necks. This was Joyland, home of roller coasters, speedways and waltzers, so some idiot monkeying about on the bridge was neither here nor there.

Sean fought against panic and forced himself to grip the vine. It felt flimsy and treacherous, and the thirty feet above seemed to extend into the clouds. His hands were slick as he set them on the vine and pulled himself out of the boat. His feet fought for purchase on the thin stem, scrambling for a toe hold but moving too fast to find one. His arms gave out and he dropped back into the boat with a splash, the water shin deep.

"Get a bleeding move on Tarzan," called Flint from above. There's a couple of pigs on the dock and they're getting into a boat. They'll have you if you don't stop buggering about, and I'm not waiting around to get caught."

The idea of two cops just minutes away was all the encouragement Sean needed. He launched himself at the vine using arms rather than feet to drag himself upwards. He forced himself to look at the masonry just inches from his face as he reached above for the next hand hold and searched with feet for a toe-hold below. His heart hammered as he edged up the vine, every inch adding to the damage if he were to slip. The sinking boat was a solid wooden mass directly below him. It would shatter his spine if he fell. And the lake would drown him in seconds. Would Flint jump to the rescue? Not a chance!

The stem of the vine grew narrower as it spread and thinned towards the top of the concrete support. Sean was nauseous with fear as he tried to slow the short rapid breathing that was making his head swim. Each time he moved a hand or foot a charge of anxiety burned along the nerves of his fingers and toes as he grasped desperately for support.

He was near to complete panic when he looked up and saw Flint's face leering down at him, pure malice in his smile as he leaned both elbows on the railing and enjoyed Sean's terror. He was little more than an arm's reach away, but he didn't offer a hand. Sean would have to let go of the vine and find a grip on the walkway of the bridge. Then he would have to haul himself up so that he stood to the outside of the railing and swing his body across to safety..........It was impossible!

He couldn't let go of the vine. He clung to it with steel-banded fingers. Perhaps he could scramble down again and swim to shore. Better wet than dead. He made the mistake of looking down for the first time. He couldn't believe that he had climbed so high; couldn't believe that he'd placed himself in such horrible danger. Every instinct screamed against the idea of climbing any further, and yet descent was impossible. He was stuck. The safe limits of his world had shrunk to the few inches of vine in his hands and at his feet. To move from there would be fatal. Every effort of nerve and sinew went into the task of keeping his body in place. He became as immobile as the bridge itself.

Flint had enjoyed the show, but now he'd become impatient. He climbed back over the railing and, holding onto it, he squatted down directly above Sean as if to shit on his head. Then he let go with one hand and reached down to where Sean was clinging.

"Come on Tarzan," he said with an effort at friendliness. "Grab my hand and I'll pull you up."

Sean, locked in panic, didn't even hear him.

"It's alright Tarzan," said Flint reassuringly. "Just reach up a few inches and I'll have you safe as houses."

He wasn't getting through. Sean was immobile. Flint tried a different tactic. He crouched down as far as he could, bringing himself as close as possible to Sean. He reached down and brushed Sean's fingertips with his own, his voice quiet but urgent.

"Listen mate," he said, "The pigs have spotted us. They're heading for the bridge. We'll both be going down if you don't get a move on."

The touch of flesh seemed to bring Sean to life again, and he looked up at Flint perched less than two feet above him.

"Come on Sean," said Flint, "Just put out your mitt and I'll grab it. You're almost there."

Flint extended his hand so that the open palm was just inches from where Sean's knuckles bunched white on the vine. With a massive effort of will Sean tore one hand from the vine and thrust it upward. Flint, unable to resist, drew his hand away just as their fingers touched.

Sean screamed and clawed, desperate to regain a grip on the vine. But Flint reached out again and grabbed his wrist, hauling him upward so that Sean could grip the railing and swing his feet onto the edge of the walkway. Flint flipped himself over the railing, caught Sean in a bear-hug, and pulled him to safety.

The two boys clung together, one in tears and the other laughing. It lasted for just a moment and then Sean broke away as he remembered the police pursuing them across the lake. He risked a brief glimpse backwards, and then took a longer look. There was no sign of the cops, just the usual puttering of holiday-makers in the boats, and the Fat Lady in the distance still prancing about on the dock. He turned back to Flint with a look of wild-eyed hatred.

"Come on Tarzan," said Flint coaxingly. "I had to get you moving didn't I? And you're alright now aren't you?"

Flint was ready for an attack. If it came he'd heave Sean back over the railing to cool him off. He didn't think of consequences beyond that.

"So, it was a bad joke, but I'm not joking now", he said. That fat cow's called the cops and she's pointing right at us."

Sean felt like a fool turning around again to look, but when he did there was the Fat Lady just 200 yards away with two coppers and she was firing a finger right at him. At a run the cops could be on the bridge in less than a minute.

"I don't know about you," said Flint, "but I'm buggering off."

He turned his back on Sean and fled towards the entrance to Joyland. Sean glanced at the cops advancing at a trot towards the bridge, and then at Flint disappearing into the crowd. It took less than a second to make the wrong choice.

He ran after Flint.

Chapter 22: All the Fun of the Fair

They fled into the chaos of Joyland. People were everywhere: jostling for rides on the bumper cars, the speedway and Ferris wheel; pumping coins into one-armed bandits and pin ball machines; queuing for toffee apples and hot-dogs and sickly masses of candy floss. They waited in line to spend sixpences on the darts, the air rifles, the coconuts shies and a hundred games they could never win. They dropped empty cartons of cockles and mussels, and newspaper greased with the remnants of fish and chips that filled the air with their stink. And the air throbbed with the clamour of pop music blaring from every stall and the excited babble of a mob detemined to experience every square inch of this awful, thundering Bedlam.

Flint threw himself into the crowd and Sean followed. He felt again that terrible fear of a hand on the shoulder that had been part of his day ever since he'd arrived at Duggin Station. Finally, Flint halted in front of a huge warehouse painted with stripes of purple and pink. Two enormous theatre masks hung above the entrance, one grinning, the other with lips curled down in misery. Just like me and Flint, thought Sean. Alongside the masks a row of crooked letters, each a different colour, spelled **FUNHOUSE**.

Flint threw two shilling pieces at an attendant, the door to the Funhouse rumbled open, and the boys walked into a blaring pandemonium. The noise battered at them: screams and shrieks, the thunder of machines, the Stones playing Jumping Jack Flash, a voice screaming Do you want to go FASTER? and overlaying it all a deafening mechanical laughter.

They were standing on a metal walkway six feet above a riot of people who were being spun, swung, tossed, shaken, twisted, dropped, and all but dismembered. Sean walked towards a stair that would take him down into the chaos, but as he approached a barrier showing the smiley-mask swung down to bar his way. If he had been moving any faster it could have brained him. He turned around, but a second barrier showing the misery face fell to block his exit. A blast of cold air shot up his trouser legs from a grill beneath his feet, and laughter cackled from a speaker overhead. A crowd of teenage boys watched him from the floor below. The fan and the laughter stopped as the barrier lifted to let him through. Flint ran through with him and they both descended into the funhouse.

Sean moved towards a wooden disk set flush with the floor. A crowd of people sat on it grinning with anticipation of what would happen next.

"'Hang on a minute Tarzan," said Flint, "let's have a gander at it first."

Gimme Shelter started up on the speakers and the disc began to spin faster and faster. The people sitting at the edge were flung off in seconds to roll into a padded barrier around the perimeter. Those closer to the middle clung desperately to the slick wood as the disc picked up speed, scrambling with nails and feet for a grip before sliding to the edge and being flung violently into the heap of bodies at the barrier. Do you want to go FASTER? screamed the voice, and everyone, including those that had been flung off, yelled YES!

Eventually just one person was left in the centre of the disc, smirking at the crowd. As the disc slowed there was a rush to get on board again and the person in the middle was shoved to the edge to be flung off with the others as the disc picked up speed once again.

"Looks like fun," said Sean, hoping that Flint might find about five hours entertainment in it before heading home.

"No, " said Flint, "this looks like more fun to me."

He was gazing up at the walkway where a girl of about sixteen had just entered with a group of friends. She was a real beauty. Peaches and cream, dangling blonde ringlets, blue eyes and skinny legs disappearing into a flouncy summer skirt that was only just long enough. Peaches squealed as the barrier came crashing down to block her way. The crowd of boys jostled each other to get the best view. Flint was ogling openly, his mouth slightly ajar, a thin string of saliva bridging his lips. And then it happened, a blast of air, the flouncy skirt lifted high above her waist, a scream, peachy cheeks glowing, lacy white knickers, long legs buckled at the knees, arms flailing to control the flying fabric and hoots from the boys mixed with the cackle from the speakers. Sean was transfixed, blood hammering in heart and crotch, his eyes pulled wide.

"Not bad eh, Tarzan? Imagine swinging on that."

"She's lovely," muttered Sean, not meaning Flint to hear.

"Lovely? Jesus Christ, who cares about lovely? Anyway, you wouldn't know what to do with it, so you might as well stop gawking. The show's over - unless you want a blimp of her mates – Robber's dogs the lot of them."

Flint grabbed Sean by the arm and for the next half hour they went from machine to machine, to be spun and twisted and churned in a sea of sweaty bodies. Sean was nauseous, blood swirling in his head, but he was willing to endure it if it kept Flint away from the outside world.

But the excitement of the Funhouse was wearing thin. Time to head out, said Flint, the chase would be off now so they would be safe. He prodded Sean to the exit and then hesitated just as they were about to leave.

"'Hang on a minute," he said "let's have one last go in the Barrel."

Sean wasn't keen on this. The barrel was an open-ended cylinder about thirty feet long and six feet high lying on its side and rotating at a brisk walking pace. You entered from one side and shuffled through the barrel sideways matching your pace with the rotation. Too fast and you'd be climbing the wall in front. Too slow and you be carried up the wall behind.

A pug-faced woman let the kids on one at a time and her pug-faced brother at the exit shouted directions to keep the crowd moving through. It had been a claustrophobic horror when Sean had first tried it, but he'd been forced through by Flint and had emerged without making the stumble that would have sent bodies crashing down around him. Now Flint was telling him he had to do it again.

They made their way to the queue, but instead of joining it at the end, Flint forced his way in front of a tall skinny kid with buck teeth so that they stood right behind Peaches and the Robber's Dogs.

"'Hey mate, there's a bleeding line you know!" complained the kid.

Flint looked him up and down.

"You're no mate of mine, Rabbit-face, and if you talk to me like that again you'll be picking up those teeth of yours with a broken arm. Understand?"

Rabbit-face understood and kept quiet.

The Robber's Dogs got into the barrel and Peaches followed them, the girls clinging to each other and giggling as they struggled to match their pace with the rotation. Sean climbed in behind Peaches, and his body thrilled as she jostled against him, smiling as she caught on to his arm. He became bold and held her elbow when she stumbled. He shuffled sideways confidently, but then Flint, standing on his other side, kicked him hard in the ankle so that he tripped over his own heel and went tumbling to the slippery surface. On his way down he let go of Peaches, but clutched at Flint who folded all too easily to crash down on top of him.

Within seconds the barrel was a sprawl of tumbling bodies. Sean could hear Peaches somewhere in the chaos, screaming and giggling in the girlish way she had done when the air had lifted her dress. The Robber's Dogs were screaming too, revelling in the naughty sensation of tumbling around with strangers.

But then something changed.

"Get out!" screamed Peaches. "Get out! Get out!"

It was impossible to get out. No one could make any headway while the barrel was turning, and the pug-faces were quite happy to keep it going provided there was no obvious chance of a fatality. After all, the fun of falling was the reason people rode the barrel in the first place. But Peaches was screaming hysterically, repeating over and over "Get out! Get out!" The other girls in the barrel caught the panic and began to thrash and flail. And then, thank God, the pug-faces figured out that something had gone badly wrong, and one of them pushed the emergency stop.

210

Those nearest the exit untangled themselves and spilled out giggling now they were safe, but Peaches kept up the keening wail as she fled to a bench along the wall where she bent double at the waist, knees clenched and hands covering her face, shaking and howling hysterically. Male-pug approached her. He'd seen claustrophobics lose their nerve in the barrel before, but this looked a lot worse.

"You alright love?" he asked her, and touched her gently on the shoulder.

Peaches screamed. He leapt back, and his sister rushed forward to see what was the matter. As she approached, Peaches threw herself at the woman and clung to her, sobbing through tears and snot.

"Come on Tarzan, let's get out of here," said Flint. He dragged at Sean's arm, and Sean allowed himself to be hustled out into the sunlight. Flint threw himself onto a bench and grinned.

"Now that was fun eh Tarzan?" Have a good time rolling around with them lasses did you?

Sean said nothing, thinking of Peaches and the chaos. What had happened to make her scream like that?

"Alright, if you're not going to talk, I'm going to eat. So what did your Ma put in your butties then?"

Flint reached into the blazer pocket that bulged with Sean's lunch as if he had every right, and took the plastic bag containing the sandwiches. The crush in the barrel had flattened them and the juicy red salmon had soaked through the bread. Flint separated the slices and looked at the thick layer of mashed fish.

"Cor, your mam doesn't half treat you alright doesn't she," he said.

He threw the top slice of bread onto the ground and began to lap at the salmon on the other slice dog-like, scooping it up with his tongue and swallowing it with great gobs of spit.

Sean thought of his mother in the kitchen that morning and his revulsion congealed into a ball of pure hatred. What would be his chances right now if he were to have a go at Flint? A solid hook as he opened his mouth would shatter his jaw. Or what about his eyes? Two fingers jabbed hard and Flint would be helpless. Then he could take his money and be away. "Do it!" he screamed at himself. "Blind the vicious bastard. Stamp the fucker to death. Go on Sean, do it!"

But Flint had an animal intelligence that sensed the tremor of intent. He paused, leering at Sean. "Come on," his eyes said, "you just bloody well try it and see what you get."

Sean turned away and Flint grinned, red flecks of salmon showing against the yellow of his teeth. He crammed his mouth with the last of the sandwich, biting into the centre and throwing the crusts to the floor. He wiped sticky fingers across his mouth, and then rubbed them back and forth under his nose. A thought struck him and he began to laugh, a high pitched wheeze crackling through phlegm. He spat a pink mass onto the ground and began to laugh again, his eyes moist and his breath coming in short gulps. He looked at Sean and controlled himself enough to share the joke. He wafted his fingers under his nose again, inhaling deeply.

"I do like a bit of fish," he said. "Yes, I'm very partial to a bit of fish."

And he cracked up again into hysterical laughter.

Chapter 23: Off to the Races

Sean followed Flint through the maze of stalls.

"Three darts for sixpence gents an' win a prize for yer muvver. Come on gents, try yer 'and. What about you likely lads? Just a tanner lads and bring 'ome a prize."

Flint stopped in front of a stall run by a boney teenager not much older than himself.

"Come on lads, spare a sixpence and make my day."

A row of playing cards was stuck to a board behind Boney, each spaced about a half inch apart. The cards and the board were pock-marked with holes.

"'Ere yer go lad, three darts for a tanner. You can't miss."

Flint handed over sixpence and Boney gave him three darts - snub-nosed things with warped plastic flights.

"What the hell am I supposed to do with these bleeding things?" snarled Flint.

"Stick any three cards cock and yer a winner."

"With these? They'd bounce right off."

"Best watch yer eyes than 'adn't yer," said Boney, pocketing the sixpence.

A dangerous look flashed across Flint's face, but Boney stared him down. He was even thinner than Flint, but there was the same toughness about him, as if he was put together with steel rods and wires. Flint spat on the ground, brought his arm back and threw the dart as hard as he could. He hit the Queen of Spades full in the face the dart going deep into her eye. He smiled and launched the other two darts, throwing them hard enough to penetrate the cards and the wood beneath.

"There you go son, wot did I tell yer? Easy ain't it? That wins you a goldfish."

"A goldfish? What do I want with a bleeding goldfish?"

"'Ow the 'ell would I know, but that's wot yev won."

A school of goldfish floated in the rank waters of an aquarium on the bottom shelf of the prize table. Next to them was a menagerie of stuffed animals, bags of mouldy Licorice Allsorts and a collection of other prizes, none of them worth sixpence.

"What about that picture?"

Flint pointed to a framed picture of Marilyn Monroe on the top shelf, all legs and tits and teeth.

"Five wins for that lad. Cost yer 'alf a dollar."

"What! It isn't worth more than a bob."

"Suit yerself. An' anyway, it's not for a wanker like you. Stunt yer growth wouldn't it?"

Boney rocked gently on the balls of his feet and brought his long arms to the front of his body, bent at the elbows with hands curled into half fists. He looked mean and very, very fast. He'd dealt with Flint's type every day since he'd started this racket and knew he could put him away in no time. Flint knew it too.

"Let's have my bleeding goldfish then."

Boney dipped a net into the goldfish stew and pulled one out of the murk. He inverted the net over a plastic bag full of water, and the goldfish flipped and gulped as if it were washing the slime from its gills. The bag had a draw string around the top that formed a carrying handle. Flint hooked a finger around the string, spat on the ground again by way of thanks and walked away from the stall with Sean in tow.

They zig-zagged through the crowds, the only two people for miles who were not having the time of their lives. Flint swung the bag around on the tip of his finger, then without a change of expression he let it fall to the ground and sauntered on.

Sean stopped. Ever since Flint had won the damned fish he'd been wondering what he would do with it. Flint couldn't take it home with him, that was obvious. The best that Sean could hope was that he'd throw it in the boating lake. At least the water there looked cleaner than in the aquarium. But now there it was, on the ground, flipping spasmodically as its world leaked out onto the tarmac. Sean crouched down to rescue it.

"Leave it!"

"I'll have if you don't want it Flinty."

"I said leave it!"

Flint stood over him, the toe of his boot just inches from Sean's face. But there was something so horrible about the frantic gasping of the fish that Sean couldn't let it be. He remembered the frog in Cack Alley and his guts heaved.

"If you didn't want it why did you take it?"

"I won it didn't I? And I'll do with it what I want, won't I?"

Sean risked the boot by picking up the bag, the fish flapping in the remaining dribbles of water.

"Look Flinty," he whined, "I'll just take it back to the guy. It'll only take a minute."

Flint grabbed hold of Sean's wrist and squeezed.

"Drop," he said.

Sean clung on to the bag and Flint squeezed tighter, the fingers biting into bone.

"Drop....Now!" he said.

Sean resisted, though he felt the pressure would shatter his wrist. Flint looked into his face and curled his finger tips to dig the nails deep into Sean's veins. The pain was horrible.

"Drop," said Flint, "NOW!"

The pain was beyond bearing. Sean let the bag drop to the ground. Flint didn't release the wrist, but squeezed even harder as he brought his foot down repeatedly on the bag, turning the fish into a pink-orange slurry. When he'd finished he let Sean go.

"Now, if you want to take it back you can go right ahead," he said.

Sean couldn't bring himself to look at the mess, but his mind reeled with the image of a massive boot descending again and again to smear him across the tarmac. He couldn't block it out. His stomach lurched as he turned away and staggered through a white mist as the crowd jostled him left and right. The colours of the stalls melded into a slur of pastel, and his legs buckled as the funfare racket receded behind the rush of blood in his ears. He collapsed against a hot-dog stand, and the smell of rancid grease, and ketchup, and fried onions, and burned offal, and the image of that fish being pounded to a froth were more than his stomach could take. The bile rose to his throat, he bent double and launched a fountain of puke.

"Oy, bugger off with that you dirty, filthy bastard!"

The hot-dog vendor roared at Sean as the queue in front of his stand tap-danced sideways to avoid the river of vomit. Sean, lost in wretchedness, supported himself with one hand on the stall and kept ralphing even when there was nothing left to bring up.

Flint was loving it. He stood over Sean's hunched body and patted him vigorously on the back.

"That's it Tarzan," he said, "better out than in, eh? I told you not to eat that crap but you wouldn't listen would you?"

"Hey you, get that dirty pig away from my stall or I'll bloody well skin you."

The hot-dog vendor gestured at Flint with a meat-slathered knife as if he'd just butchered the last person who'd pissed him off.

"Give us our money back and we'll go," said Flint, more to the crowd than to the hot-dog man, "it's your fault he's heaving up."

"You've 'ad nowt from me, you lying little bastard," roared the hot dog man. "Now just you bugger of out of it."

"Nowt? We've had more than enough thanks. And if you can't keep your fingers out of your arse you'd better keep them off your fucking sausages."

The hot-dog man raised his knife as if he were ready to gut Flint on the spot, but then Sean recovered enough to stagger back into the crowd. The people who'd seen him hurl parted like the Red Sea. Flint followed him, one hand on his shoulder.

"Make way," he shouted. "After eating that shite he'll be starting at the other end any second."

Sean sank onto a seat in front of a stall. Other seats were occupied by players, each sitting in front of a sloping board with numbered holes in it. An atmosphere of intense excitement was whipped up by a commentator as each player threw a heavy plastic ball up the slope in an attempt to land it in one of the holes.

The game was called the Kentucky Derby. Attached to the wall behind the commentator were a series of pulleys that dragged eight wooden horses from a starting line to the finish. A painted backdrop hinted vaguely at a race track. A horse moved forward each time its

217

player sunk a ball in the hole. If a ball went into the hole at the top of the board, the horse would move forward several lengths. But to do this the easier holes had to be avoided. If the ball wasn't sunk at all it would roll back to the player with agonising slowness as the horse remained motionless. The players arms moved frantically, launching the balls, waving in excitement as a ball was sunk, or pounding the board in frustration as they waited for a missed ball to return.

The commentator put his heart into his job, working himself up into a fever of excitement as the lead horses approached the finish line. A buzzer sounded and there was a scream of excitement as some player came in first. The commentator's assistant fished about in an aquarium, and Sean looked away as the bile rose to his throat again. Meanwhile the horses were wound back to the starting line and the commentator started to drum up new business.

The assistant stopped in front of Sean's seat. He was a kindly old man who saw at a glance that Sean was not feeling well. But he had a business to run.

"Sorry, but if you want to sit there cock it'll cost you a tanner. People waiting you see." He smiled an apology, and Sean was grateful for a rare glimpse of decency.

He shifted to get up, but Flint squeezed onto the seat beside him, leaving him perched on the edge.

"'Here's a tanner mate, and I hope the bleeding donkey's worth it."

Flint flicked sixpence at the old man who caught it, and with a hard glance released a lever that allowed Flint's ball to roll down from a trap at the top of the board. It was made of dense, heavy plastic. Flint picked it up, and hefted it in his palm, a calculating look on his face.

"The jockey's are all in position Ladies and Gentlemen; and we're under Starter's Orders......." The commentator paused for effect as each player leaned forward, hands making nervous feints....."And they're off!"

Flint flicked his wrist, sending the ball skimming across the lower holes, aiming for the big numbers. Too hard! The ball crashed into the barrier at the top of the board, and rolled back, catching the edges of the holes but not sinking, returning slowly to Flint's outstretched fist, scoring nothing. He tried again, throwing the ball even harder, with the same result. Again and again he threw with still no score. He flung the ball viciously up the slope with no thought for technique. It hit the barrier, bounced upwards, crashed back on the board and zig-zagged from hole to hole on the way back to Flint. Still his horse sat at the starting line.

Meanwhile, the other horses were half way down the track. The commentator saw that Flint was a novice and couldn't resist rubbing it in.

"And it's Juicy Lucy and Sally Brown neck and neck at the halfway mark, with Hairy Mary just a half length behind. Then it's Susie Cute, Betty Blue and Dirty Dotty in a bunch with Lucy Lastick gaining ground. And the back marker is Dolly's Pratt stuck in the starting gate as the jockey tries to mount. Wait, is he up? No, he's still trying to find the hole."

The crowd watching the players burst into laughter. Sean wanted to offer advice - take it easy, roll the ball slowly - but he knew that look on Flint's face. The commentator carried on, unaware that right now he had the most dangerous job in Sandcaster.

"....And Hairy Mary makes a five length dash to pass the leaders and it's anybody's race now..... except for Dolly's Pratt at the starting gate. Sally Brown takes the lead again and Betty Blue joins the front runners with just three lengths to go. It's Sally Brown by a neck, now Hairy Mary by a head. Sally Brown, Hairy Mary....." the bell rings ".. and it's Hairy Mary the winner by a short neck in a seven horse race with Dolly's Pratt still not mounted."

Another round of laughter while Flint kept his face to the front, scarlet and furious. When the old man did his rounds for the next race, Flint almost flung the sixpence at him. The old man smiled, having seen it all before.

"Take it easy lad. Just take it easy and you'll do a lot better."

They were off again, but Flint could never take anything easy. He flung the ball up the slope and reached for it desperately as it came rolling back, everything done in a blind rage. It was only when Flint fumbled and sent the ball rolling slowly into a hole that the art of the game came to him. Even then, it took several tries before he could control his anger enough to roll the ball gently up the slope. He finished the race dead last, but he was hooked now, and paid sixpence after sixpence, determined to win just to stop the mouthings of that bleeding commentator. Sean blessed every minute that passed. If they could only stay here all day - just let Flint move up bit by bit, but don't let him win. Just fix the race so that we don't have to move away from this haven.

But it wasn't a day for that kind of luck. Once Flint got the knack he was right up there with the best of them, and it was only a matter of time before he came in first. When it happened he turned a defiant glance at the audience and then glared up at the commentator.

"Dolly's Pratt wins one at last..... and about bloody time," said the commentator without even a glance at Flint. Then the horses were wound back to the starting line as he began the spiel for the next race.

The old man came over to Flint.

"Goldfish or free game? Two wins gets you a box of Licorice Allsorts."

Flint looked sideways at Sean.

"Give us a goldfish....."

He grinned at Sean, then paused.

"No hang on a minute, I'll try another win for one of those rag dolls. Might come in handy as a catch-cloth."

The old man flicked him a card with "One Win" printed on it and moved on to collect sixpences from the other players. After they were off again, Flint went through the motions for a few throws then turned to Sean when the commentator was fully absorbed in the race.

"Come on Tarzan," he said, "I've had enough of this."

He got up abruptly and moved quickly between the adjacent stalls, losing himself in the crowd with Sean scampering behind him. They mounted the steps to The Speedway and Flint dragged Sean onto the platform just as it began to revolve. It was a roundabout for big kids, the riders sitting on wooden animals fixed to the platform that rotated at increasing speed as the operator played rock music to drown out the screams. When they were hurtling around, Flint leaned over the neck of his giraffe and grinned at Sean who was clutching the ears of his elephant. Flint pulled the heavy ball from his pocket and flicked it over to Sean. Sean reacted without thinking and caught it, turning it over in his palm.

"Looks like Dolly's Pratt isn't going anywhere for a while is she?" yelled Flint, and burst out laughing as House of the Rising Sun blazed from the speakers.

Sean wanted to fling the ball into Flint's smirking mug, but instead, he flicked it back, glad to be rid of it, and Flint snatched it out of the air before putting it once again in his pocket. The Speedway slowed to a halt and the DJ turned down the music to warn everyone to stay on board until the ride stopped. Flint got to his feet and jumped off, landing at a trot and keeping pace with the ride until Sean got off too.

They wandered Joyland aimlessly and found themselves in a quiet part of the fairground near the perimeter wall where most of the stalls had been closed down. Wind-blown newspapers with the stink of last week's fish and chips were scattered about, and the ground was sticky with dried rivulets of Coca Cola and melted ice cream. The hoardings of a Freak Show advertised the World's Fattest Woman, a four-legged duck, a two-headed sheep, and a real live Elephant Man. Should they be Allowed to Live? yelled a sign, as if being fat was a capital offence.

You've got it wrong, thought Sean, it's the freaks like Flint that should be put down, the nutters and the psychos, not the poor buggers who just happen to look different from the rest of us. The question was moot anyway, given that the entrance to the Freak Show was boarded up. Maybe the guy on the Winchester Rifle Range next door had decided on the question and taken the initiative.

Flint sidled up to the stall and eyed the rifles, each attached to the counter top by a short chain. They were no more than glorified BB guns modified to take .22 shells. Not exactly how the West was won, but the tiny bullets would make a bang for wankers. Flint

222

brought one of them to his shoulder and squinted along the barrel. The rifleman eyed him from the corner of the stall. He was a squat and heavy with a prize-fighter look. He might have been fifty, or maybe just thirty with a few bad bouts behind him.

"How much?" asked Flint.

"Three bullets a shilling."

"What do you win?"

"Nowt."

"What's the point then?"

Knuckles shrugged as if to say suit yourself, and opened the Sun at page 3.

"Alright then, here's a shilling."

Knuckles unfolded from his seat and dug into a leather pouch at his waist. Standing, he looked leaner, with a massive chest tapering down to narrow hips. He took out three small shells and placed them on the counter next to Flint's rifle. Flint reached for them.

"Hands off!"

Knuckles aimed a short jab at the outstretched arm, and the force knocked Flint sideways. Knuckles was fast, and very, very handy. Flint knew better than to say anything. Knuckles loaded the three shells into the breach of the rifle, then took a paper target and attached it to a pulley at the front of the stall. He turned a handle, and the target moved away from the counter to a metal wall at the back. Then he walked backwards to his corner and nodded at Flint to get on with it.

Flint sneered at the target as if he'd expected to have a go at killing a few Indians like the painted cowboy on the hoarding, but he picked up the rifle and set the stock to his shoulder. Sean watched yellow teeth bite into the bottom lip as Flint squinted down the barrel. He squeezed the trigger, the hammer fell with a crack and there was a metallic ping as the bullet hit the back wall of the stall. From thirty feet it was impossible to see where the bullet had penetrated the target. Flint fired off the remaining two rounds and then Knuckles got off his seat to wind the target back to the front of the stall. It was perfectly intact. Knuckles said nothing, but looked at Flint as if asking for an explanation. Sean looked away as if he hadn't seen, but he'd caught the spasm of anger in Flint's eye and the flush in his cheeks.

"Load of bollocks!" said Flint. "Barrel's as bent as a dog's dick."

Knuckles said nothing, but he wound the target back to the wall again and loaded a single shell in the rifle. He picked it up and fired it off without seeming to aim at all, and then wound the target back to the front. There was a neat hole just off centre. He looked at Flint again with a hint of derision.

Flint laid down another shilling and three more shells were loaded into the Winchester. The target went back, Flint took a deep breath, the teeth sank hard into the lip, and neither he nor Sean breathed again until the three shots were fired. As Knuckles inched the target forward, Sean found himself praying that there'd be four holes around the bullseye. God wasn't listening. Flint glared at the target like it had been dodging the bullets. Knuckles still said nothing, but the derision was plain and open.

Another shilling came out and another three shells were loaded. The target was wound back for the third time. Knuckles settled into his corner and turned to page three again. Flint shouldered the rifle with that look of cold fury he'd shown at the Kentucky Derby.

Sean realized, too late, what was about to happen.

Chapter 24: Helter Skelter

Flint swung the rifle away from the target and pointed the barrel at Knuckles' head. Sean was paralysed with fear. A scream formed deep in his chest, but he'd lost the ability to breathe. Piss leaked into his underpants. Every detail of the scene sprang into sharp focus: the bubbly spit gathered at the corner of Flint's lips; the white crease in his finger where it cradled the trigger; the look of hatred in every line of his face. He was certain that Knuckles was about to die.

"Maybe I missed that bit of paper," said Flint, "but I can't miss a big ugly bastard like you."

Knuckles didn't reply. His face set, and he locked eyes with Flint as he put down his newspaper, every movement in slow motion. Sean moved his lips in a plea to Flint but the words wouldn't come. Flint's voice was low and calculating.

"Now where should I put it? Left eye? Right eye? Maybe I'll put it right between your stinking rotten teeth..."

As he spoke, Flint moved the barrel an inch to the left, an inch to the right, an inch down. Still Knuckles stared at him, not moving at all now, but with every muscle coiled.

Flint caressed the trigger, squeezing it gently then easing off, enjoying the foreplay.

"You think you're so bloody funny don't you, taking my money and then taking the piss? Well, you're not so bloody funny now are you, you ugly cunt."

Knuckles shifted himself slowly in his seat, moving his right leg out to the side, but Flint barked at him.

"Stay still! You move when I tell you to move. Now take off that money belt and put it on the counter."

Sean let out a long slow breath, ludicrously relieved that Flint might only be intent on armed robbery. Armed robbery - Ha! - what was that compared to murder?

He found his voice at last and begged Flint to give it up, trying to make it all sound like a kid's game.

"Come on mate, a laugh's a laugh. You've made him shit his pants but don't be a mad bastard, just put down the gun and let's run it."

Flint didn't take his eyes off Knuckles. Spit flew out of the side of his mouth as he snarled at Sean.

"Shut it Tarzan, and do what I tell you. When he puts the money belt on the counter you pick it up and bring it to me. Then I'll decide what to do next."

Knuckles moved his hands slowly to his belt and began to unfasten the pouch, never once taking his eyes from Flint's. He placed the pouch on the counter, and Flint raised his head from the rifle's sights for just an instant to take a sidelong glance.

Knuckles threw himself sideways, the rifle was shoved upwards and an arm was wrapped around Flint's neck. Whoever it was must have been waiting for a safe chance to make his move, and now he had one of Flint's arms jammed up his back while he throttled him in a choke-hold.

Knuckles blew out his cheeks in a slow breath and got to his feet. He vaulted the counter and walked with deliberate steps to where Flint was being held.

"Alarm worked then, Sam?" he asked.

"Aye," replied Sam, "Knew you'd need it one day, stuck back here. Reckon I got to you just in time."

"Happen," said Knuckles.

He was a man of few words, but his fists spoke volumes. He stood in front of Flint and looked him straight in the face.

"I've got a wife and three kids," he said, "and it's lucky for you I don't like the Police."

His right fist slammed into Flint's gut, high up between the ribs. Sam was knocked backwards by the blow, and the reflex to double up almost snapped Flint's spine. A left landed in the same spot and Flint's face blackened with the effort to breathe. The next two were back-handed swipes across one side of Flint's face and then the other. Knuckles gave a brief nod to Sam, and Flint was allowed to fold to the floor, straining to suck air through a mouthful of bloody spit.

Knuckles turned to Sean cringing against the counter, but looked away again in disgust. He stood over Flint for a moment, but he wasn't a violent man, and turned back to his stall as if that was that. Sam, though, was less forgiving. He stood behind Flint for just a second before slamming the toe end of his boot directly between Flint's buttocks, sending him sprawling onto the tarmac. Flint screamed with what tiny amount of breath was left in him.

Sean hoped that Sam would carry on pounding Flint into the ground, but instead he grabbed Sean by the collar and hauled him to within inches of his mouth. The stench of his breath almost made Sean retch, but he burrowed his head even closer to Sam's, terrified of a head butt that would ruin his face. But Sam was only giving him a warning.

"Now you drag your friend out of here, and tell him that if I ever see him again I'll do more than kick his bollocks into touch. Understand?"

Sean could only wince and nod before being flung backwards to fall across Flint's heaving body. He got to his feet, and with a hand on Flint's back urged him to stumble away towards the main throng of the funfair.

They found a bench where Flint dragged himself into a sitting position, groaning as his arse and nuts touched the wood. They stayed there for half an hour as Flint sat with his head between his knees, dragging air through dripping snot, and moaning with pain.

When Flint finally straightened up, Sean pleaded with him.

"Let's go home Flinty," he said, "there's too many people after us to stick around here."

"You can go home if you like, chickenshit, but I'm not done yet."

Sean was overwhelmed with relief.

"OK Flinty, give me my train ticket."

"No."

"Lend me some cash then."

"No."

"Then what am I supposed to do?" He was almost in tears as he said it.

Flint rounded on him, his face twisted.

"You watch my back, that's what you do. And if you let anyone take me from behind like that again I'll fucking kill you."

Flint lurched to his feet, and shouldered his way into the crowd, sending a young woman sprawling. Her boyfriend spun around to fight, but changed his mind when he saw the look on Flint's face.

"Watchit mate," was all he dared, and Flint leered back at him through blood-stained teeth.

For the next hour Flint dragged Sean onto the most bone-jarring rides in all of Joyland, as if intent on showing that he could take whatever the world could deal him. And the look on his face never changed. It never wavered from that mask of cold hatred. Far more than the rides, that look scared Sean half to death.

They moved back towards the Joyland entrance. Sean's hopes rose as he saw the painted bridges and the multi-coloured arch in the distance. He wouldn't care now if the Fat Lady chased them all the way to the railway station, just to get this day over with. Let him get back to Duggin safely and he'd never complain again about its stinking factories and its lumpen labourers. He'd take his Gran's advice and never hang about with Flint again. And he'd work like a dog at school and do everything the Brothers told him. If only he could get back without anything else happening. Please God, please!

But Flint wasn't going home without one last ride.

The Tornado. Half a mile of steel track on a wooden trellis that rose and plunged and twisted and turned. A train of flimsy cars climbing and falling and hurtling around bends at impossible speed as the passengers screamed bloody murder. It was Joyland's showpiece, the thrill of a lifetime, and made to feel like it could be your last. If the chain that dragged the cars up that first slope were to slip, if the cars were to come hurtling backwards, they'd be trying to match body parts for months.

And Flint was heading straight for it.

Sean watched the cars being dragged up the first rise and realised how high it was, how open, how horribly dangerous. At the top, a section of track was just long enough for the cars to level off

229

before the first vertical drop. He felt a wave of anticipatory panic as he saw the first car edging over the lip and dragging the others behind it.

Sean couldn't do it. He just couldn't. As Flint walked towards the entrance ramp, phobic terror sloshed in his guts. Being up there, exposed, in that tiny car, with no escape except.......he just couldn't do it!

Flint was at the ticket booth.

"Half a dollar each Flinty!" said Sean, squeaking through a parched throat. "That's a bit steep isn't it? I'll just wait here while you go."

Flint had heard that squeak before, weeks earlier, as Sean had watched him swinging on the lamp post and had clung to his Granny like a fucking sissy.

"Two!" he bawled at the low-brow behind the counter, flinging two half-crowns at him. Low Brow scooped up the coins and pressed a lever that opened a turnstile. Sean couldn't move. He stood there gaping. The queue jostled behind him and a young girl prodded him in the back, urging him forward. But he couldn't move. Low Brow leaned over the counter and stared at him.

"Move along," he said. "People waiting."

Sean didn't hear. There was no way he was going through that turnstile. But Flint had other ideas. He turned to Low Brow and said "Sorry mate, he's a bit slow. Aren't you Tarzan...you're a...bit....slow!" He placed a hand gently on Sean's shoulder, but out of sight he kicked Sean's shin hard and fast with the toe end of his boot, at the same time pulling him forward in a stumbling dance. The pain over-rode the paralysing terror, and almost before he knew it, Sean was bundled into the rear car of the train on the far side from the platform where others were scurrying to their places. Flint

230

pressed his shoulder hard against him, preventing any chance of escape.

'We'll get the whip sitting here'" said Flint. "The last car always takes off when it goes over the top. It'll scare you shitless if you haven't shit your pants already."

The pain in Sean's shin gave him an excuse to blubber as he huddled into the corner of the car, but he held back tears as two girls climbed into the car in front of him. The girls were chubby teenagers, obviously sisters, and were giggling hysterically. They looked behind to share their excitement, but even Sean's terrified face and Flint's hard expression couldn't dampen their spirits. They burst into fresh gales of laughter and elbowed each other's bellies as they shuffled into their seats. They were no sooner settled than one of them stood up again and started waving her arms and shouting "Hi Gramps! Hi Gramps! Here we are Gramps!"

A bald-headed man leaned on the fence by the turnstile. His old face was split with a boyish grin as if he'd love to be on the ride himself, but his pudgy wife standing next to him had a troubled look, her fingers fluttering at her mouth.

Low Brow had left his booth and was moving along the line of cars, pulling down the safety bars so that they lay close to the riders' laps. When he had finished, he hauled on a long metal lever by the side of the track, yanking it hard towards his shoulder. There was a metallic clunk as the cars were hooked onto the chain that would pull them to the top of the first rise. The whole train creaked forward with a rumble of wheels that bounced the riders in their seats.

Sean was trapped. His safety was entrusted to a half-wit in charge of a contraption that rattled as if it had been thrown together with Meccano. Low Brow stood at the base of the rise watching the

231

cars pass by as they began their ascent. Sean and Flint were last, and as they drew level with him Flint pushed up the safety bar and spread his arms across the back of the seat grinning defiance.

Sean moved spasmodically to bring the bar back down again, but Flint chopped at his outstretched arms with the side of his hands.

"Leave it chicken," he spat, and Sean fell back into the seat, turning to look behind at Low Brow, eyes pleading for him to do something. Surely he'd throw that lever again and stop the damned train before Flint got them both killed? But Low Brow just stood there with the dull expression that Sean mistook for stupidity. Low Brow dealt with pricks like Flint every day of the week, and it was almost a regret to him that they'd all survived the ride.

Without the bar against his lap, the space between Sean and the back of the car in front widened to an enormous gulf. Without that bar in place he'd be catapulted out over Joyland at the first big drop, he was sure of it. He knew now that Flint had a death wish. That beating he'd taken from Knuckles had unhinged him completely, and he intended to take Sean with him when he went. And there was nothing he could do about it. They were already fifty feet into the climb, and even if he could clamber out of the car he'd be stuck there on the track.

There was nothing to do but breathe..... just breathe. He forced himself to drag in slow gulps of air, willing himself to outface the panic. One hand gripped the edge of his seat with the same desperate strength he'd found while climbing the bridge. With the other hand he felt in his pockets for some distraction, coins to count, a scrap of paper to read, anything to draw his mind away from the whispering voice urging him to..... jump.... Jump... JUMP!........

The Chubbys' Granddad was walking on a track that skirted the perimeter of the Tornado, leading his wife to a bench just under the first big drop where they could watch their granddaughters plummet into the dip. The old man pointed at the train and they both started to wave. The Chubbys waved back, the one on the far side leaning across the other to see her Granddad better. They were having a great time.

Sean focused on the old man, as if trying to get into his head. It's not fear, it's excitement, he told himself. You'll be old too one of these days, so do it now! Live! Have fun! He tried to copy the smile on the old man's face. He leaned across Flint, watching Granddad drop further and further away as they climbed. Flint elbowed him and pushed against Sean's arm on the back of the seat, trying to break his grip. But Sean wouldn't shift. He fixed his eyes on the old man as if he were the only object in the universe.

"Get back you weedy little twat!' yelled Flint, and rammed a shoulder into Sean's chest. But fear had made Sean immovable. The train crested the rise and began to move more smoothly as the chain disengaged. The cars coasted slowly towards the first big drop. Almost directly below, the old man was shielding his eyes with one hand, and waving slowly with the other, but his granddaughters were sitting silently now, intent on the drop just a few feet away that would send them hurtling around the track.

Sean loosened his grip on the side of the car and twisted away from Flint's shoulder so that he could lean right across to wave back at the Chubbys' granddad below. To Flint it seemed as if he hadn't a care in the world.

Flint squinted down to where Sean was waving and spotted the elderly couple for the first time. He slammed a bony elbow into Sean's guts, and as he fell back into the seat, Flint stood upright in the car and dug a hand deep into his pocket. The train was just inches from the drop. The elderly couple were a hundred feet below Flint's upraised arm. A hundred feet from the heavy plastic ball in his fist.

"Baldy headed old bastard!' yelled Flint as Sean launched himself to grab at the outstretched arm.

The first car dipped over the drop. Scream upon scream sounded as each car plummeted over the edge. But the scream from the last car was horribly different as Flint's arm descended and the ball flew towards its target.

Chapter 25: A Change of Identity

Sean crashed back into the seat as the car plummeted over the drop. Flint collapsed on top of him as the force of the descent knocked him off his feet. Sean punched and kicked, trying to push him from the car if he could, terrified now of being connected in any way with this fucking maniac. If he could have clambered into the car with the Chubbys he would have done it. If he could have leapt onto the track and climbed down the trellis he would have tried it. But as the train hurtled through each rise and fall the two boys were flung against each other in an inseparable tangle of limbs.

Flint fought back viciously, warding off Sean's fists and punching out hard whenever he had the space. As the train slowed on a long climb both boys were standing in the car, lashing out at each other in a frenzy of feet and fists. Below, Low Brow looked up ashen-faced, expecting at any moment to see one or both of them pitching to the ground. But as the train dropped again, they were flung back into the seat to grapple and kick and gouge their way through the rest of the ride until it came to a screeching halt and the passengers made their hysterical exit onto the platform.

Low Brow was at their car before the train had stopped, dragging Flint out by his hair.

"You bloody fool," he was screaming, "You could have been killed.

Sean was crying now, pointing a finger at Flint and shouting over and over again "It was him. I had nothing to do with it. It was him. It was him."

Flint shook free and hauled Sean out of the car by his blazer, wrapping his hand around his mouth and dragging him towards the exit ramp.

"Sorry mate," he said to Low Brow. "Tarzan here took one of his turns didn't he? Panicked when we got to the top and tried to jump out. Had to give him a few knocks to stop him."

"And I'll give you both a few knocks if I ever see you near here again," roared Low Brow. "I can't be doing with scraping daft young buggers like you two off the bleeding tarmac."

Sean caught sight of the Chubbys shrieking as they made their way towards the exit. He bit his way past Flint's hand and screamed again, "It was him! I had nothing to do with it. It was him, not me. It was him!"

But he was just another noise in the chaos of Joyland, and the two girls didn't even look back. They pushed their way into the crowd and ran off, still shrieking with excitement, to find Granddad.

A hundred yards away, under the first big drop of the Tornado, another crowd was gathering. The two girls ran to the place where they had last seen their Granddad waving to them, and fought their way through the rubber-neckers. Their laughter choked as they reached the centre of the fuss. There was a second of confused silence, another of disbelief and then .....

Oh Sweet Jesus! Sean had been listening for it, dreading it. The sound brought him limp to his knees. Flint dragged him to his feet and hauled him behind a tangle of shrubs that grew against the

236

trellis of the Tornado. Out of sight, he took Sean's chin with his free hand and smashed his head backwards against the woodwork.

"Now listen here you little shit," he snarled. "You and me are in this together, and if you open your stupid mouth one more time we'll both be going down. Understand?"

Sean understood alright and he threw himself at Flint screaming again.

"It was you, you murdering bastard. I had nothing to do with it. It was you!"

He continued to scream until Flint punched him hard in the throat and forced him back against the trellis. Flint could have killed him, and Sean knew it. His eyes bulged with the strain of trying to breathe but they focused hard on Flint, knowing that this maniac had nothing to lose by finishing him off. Flint understood and smiled, squeezing Sean's throat until his tongue lolled out of his mouth. He whispered at Sean as if they were enjoying a chat.

"No one knows I threw the ball at old baldy," he said, "and your prints are on it as well as mine."

Sean choked against the lie, hope flaring that the fingerprints would show it was Flint who'd thrown the ball. But then he remembered the Speedway, Flint launching something at him; remembered catching it, examining it, turning it in his fingers as he identified the ball from the Kentucky Derby, and then throwing it back to Flint in disgust. He remembered the smug look on Flint's face as he'd pocketed the ball again. Smug because he'd stolen it, or smug because he had a plan? Was it possible? Could Flint have set him up deliberately?

Flint grinned. "So Tarzan, like I said, we're in this together. And if I go down I'll make bloody well sure that you go down with me.

Because I like being with you don't I? You and me are best friends forever, aren't we Tarzan?"

He tightened the grip on Sean's throat as if he'd choke him to death if he didn't get the right answer. Sean, almost black in the face, managed an inclination of the head. Flint's grip loosened, just enough to let Sean gasp a single breath, and then he clamped hard on the throat again.

"Good boy," he whispered, and brought his face close. "Now when I let go of you," he continued, "you and me are going to walk out of here all nice and casual-like, and we're going to walk nice and easy to the train station, and when we get home we're going to say nothing to anyone, aren't we?"

Sean managed a nod, and was rewarded with another breath before the pressure was back on his throat. Black clouds were coalescing to blind him. His bowels loosened. Flint carried on.

"But if you try running it, or do any more bleeding squawking, I'll kill you stone dead. Get it?"

Sean could only blink a yes. Flint took his hand away and Sean collapsed, clawing at the grass in a blind panic when the breath wouldn't come. Flint waited until Sean dragged himself to his knees, and then pulled him to his feet before he could recover completely.

"Now you're going to walk in front," he said, pushing Sean through the bushes and onto the path, "and I'm going to be just behind. If anyone asks, you don't look too good because you've been eating fairground shite all afternoon, and I'm looking after you in case you start throwing up. I'll be just like your mam, eh? Old Flint's just like your mam, OK?"

238

Sean stumbled along the path towards the exit, moving against a flow of people heading towards the spot where granddad was.........was.........was what?

"It must have hit," he thought. "Oh Christ, with all that bloody screaming it must have hit really bad."

Far away, rising above the other sounds of the fairground, he heard the wail of a siren, getting louder as it approached them. My God that was quick! Only a few minutes had passed since Flint had let fly with the ball and already the ambulance was on its way.

Ambulance or Police?

"Please God, let it be the ambulance," Sean prayed. "Please don't let him be dead. Don't let the ball have hit his head. A broken arm. A shattered shoulder, but please God, not his head."

He turned around. He'd tell the whole story to the police, take all the consequences of his lies and his fraud, but he'd place all the blame for that truly terrible thing solely on Flint's head.

Flint was ready for him. He drove a fist hard into his gut, grabbing him by the collar and kicking him forward again. There was no escape that way. And if he tried to run forward and double back, Flint was faster. He was trapped, just like he'd been trapped all day.

They crossed the bridge across the boating lake without a thought for the Fat Lady or the scuttled boat lying at the bottom, and joined the crowd of people on their way home. Happy people. People who had enjoyed a day of innocent fun. People who had spent hard-earned cash on cheap thrills, trinkets and garbage and had been glad to part with every penny of it. Normal people.

Sean felt an unbearable sense of loss. Yesterday he had been normal too. Now he could never be normal again. There was a barrier between him and the rest of the world.   And his only companion in this isolation was the one person he hated most.

Flint.

CHAPTER 26: The Six O'Clock News

The acceleration due to gravity is 32 feet per second per second, so a ball dropped from 100 feet would be traveling at what speed when it hit the ground? About 100 feet per second, right? That's over 6000 feet per minute, or just under a mile and half per minute - about 90 miles per hour give or take. Add to that the effect of throwing the ball rather than just dropping it, and maybe the speed would double. This train is going about 80 miles per hour. If I were to stick my head out of the window and it hit the side of the tunnel........Game Over. It would be Game Over.

Sean prayed: Please God, anywhere but his head.

They got off at Duggin and tramped towards home, Sean in front, Flint a few paces behind. It was dangerous to be seen together because Sean was supposed to be returning from the sponsored walk, but Flint shadowed him all the way to Cack Alley. As they reached a gap in the bushes Flint grabbed Sean by the collar and dragged him down a bank into the ditch. He threw him on his face among the garbage and clamped a hand over his mouth.

"Now listen here, twat," he whispered, "you remember what I told you. You're an accessory now, and if you don't know what that means I'll tell you. You were with me, and you saw what happened, and you walked away. That means you're as guilty as I am.

Whatever happens to me happens to you, and if we both get sent down you can be bloody certain I'll keep you really happy in that cell, understand?"

Sean nodded.

"Now you bugger off home and tell them all what a great day you had with all your poncey grammar school friends on their bleeding sponsored walk. You haven't seen me, and you haven't been anywhere near the fair, get it?"

Sean nodded again, and Flint dragged him to his feet.

"And one more thing. You get that money from all them suckers you conned, and you get it to me pronto, alright?

Again Sean nodded, and Flint released the hand from his mouth and pushed him towards the bank.

"Now fuck off."

Sean scrambled up the slope and broke into a staggering run. Now he was free he fled towards home, blubbering with head down as he approached the Entry. Then he remembered Flint's warning and slowed his pace, wiping his eyes on the sleeve of his blazer and trying to control the sobs that ballooned from his chest into his throat. He had to appear normal.

Normal! How the hell could he appear normal ever again?

He reached the side door of his house and leaned against it, his hand on the door knob, his forehead pressed against the flaky woodwork. He didn't know how to face his family. He knew what they expected of him - the arrogant know-it-all returning in triumph with a display of superior conceit. How could he do that? The person who would have acted like that was gone.

"Are you alright Sean?"

Mary, his 8 year old sister, had rounded the corner of the house. She stood there staring at him.

242

"Yeah", he croaked through the pain in his throat, ashamed at her concern for a shit like him. He had to go inside to escape her. Somehow the act had to begin.

His mother was slogging away in the kitchen. A pan was spitting boiling lard, a can of spaghetti bolognese was burning in a saucepan, and she was at the kitchen sink peeling spuds for the next batch of chips. A pile of dirty nappies was soaking in a bucket at her feet. She looked tired and harassed, but as she caught sight of him her face lit with a smile.

"How did it go love, did you make it all the way?"

"Yeah," croaked Sean, and gave a fake cough to disguise his voice.

"Well you look tired love, so why don't you get changed out of your school stuff and I'll have your dinner ready when you come down."

"Yeah.....right," was all he could manage.

He climbed the stairs to his bedroom and sat down on Colin's bunk. He let his head sink into his hands and almost gave way to hysteria, but a thunder of feet on the stairs dragged him back as his two sisters fought to be first to the toilet. He rose and turned his back to the door in case they came into the room. He took off his blazer, changed into jeans and a tee-shirt and went down to the kitchen where his mum placed a huge plate of chips and spaghetti bolognese in front of him, the strings of pasta like worms coiled in a puddle of blood-speckled shit. Kieran gawped at the stacked plate as if Sean were getting his share as well as his own.

Sean picked up a fork and found that his hand was shaking. He'd taken a beating. His throat and ribs were bruised where Flint's hands and feet had done their work. But under this was a deeper hurt that sent a constant tremor through him. *You've got my*

243

nerves shattered! was one of his mother's favourite expressions when she was more than usually harassed by her kids. Now he knew what she meant.

He clenched the fork hard to stop the trembling and pushed the chips around on his plate. He speared one and dipped it into the blood-red sauce. He had a sudden urge to vomit and turned his head abruptly from the plate.

"Are you alright love, you look pale?"

His mother wiped the suds from her arms and scuttled over from the sink, laying a hand on his forehead to check for fever. He moved away, but she'd noticed the clammy sweat and looked at him worried.

"Are you not hungry love? You must be after all that walking.

"No, not really," said Sean pushing away his plate.

"Can I have it mam, can I have it?" Kieran shouted, springing forward to grab the plate. His mother pushed the food towards him and turned back to Sean.

"Did you eat the butties I made you and......." She didn't want Keiran to know about the chocolate biscuit......."the other things?"

"Yeah," said Sean, "and we had toffee apples and candy floss at the fairground. Maybe they've put me off."

"The fairground?" Sean's mum looked surprised. "I didn't think you were going to the fairground, I though it was just to Victoria Park."

"I....I meant the park..." he said, after what seemed far too long. "There was a small fairground set up there, and they were selling toffee apples and candy floss and all that kind of crap."

"Watch your language in front of these children," said his mother, her attention diverted from the lie. "If you've been eating that rubbish no wonder you've no appetite for good food. Why don't you go into the front room while I give the others their dinner."

Sean was shaken by his stupid mistake about the fairground. And how could he have bought all that crap when he had no money. His mother had missed that one, but from now on he'd have to watch everything he said. He slouched out of the kitchen, playing the Old Soldier, and dropped into a chair by the television. He picked up the Sun and turned automatically to page 3. It was Nina Carter again, standing there in just her knickers. It might as well have been Hattie Jacques for all the effect it had on him.

His mother poked her head around the door.

"If you're up to it love, Confession's open till six. You've got time if you nip out to the Church now."

He panicked again. Confession? How could she know? Then he remembered. Confession was a part of his normal life. Already he was forgetting it. Confession was a weekly ritual. A Brillo pad for the soul. Fine for scrubbing away dirty thoughts, foul language and the odd bit of shop-lifting, but there was no way he could confess to what he'd done today. Not in a million years.

He played the Old Soldier again.

"I'm too shattered now mam," he said. "I'll do double penance next week."

She looked him over, seeing that there really was something not quite right.

"That's alright love," she said, and went back to her drudgery.

Confession. He hadn't thought of confession. He might get away with not going this week, but what would he do next week, and the week after that? How could he kneel in that wooden cell and tell the priest behind the screen about all the lying and cheating and stealing and...and....... He couldn't do it!

He gazed blankly at the newspaper, his thoughts fixed on the impossibility of his situation. Wanking was one thing - but murder? Did the confidentiality of the confessional apply to crimes like that? No, he couldn't risk it. He could never go to confession again. But that meant he couldn't take Communion, and his mother would see that he didn't and would want to know why. And it wasn't just tomorrow's mass that he had to worry about, but next week and all the weeks after that.

What was that moralizing bullshit of Walter Scott's? – *Oh what a tangled web we weave when first we practise to deceive.* But it wasn't bullshit, was it? Sean had to spin the web and, somehow, he had to remember the position of every single thread.

Fergus entered the room. He gave Nina's tits the once over and snarled at Sean.

"If you're not reading that, give it here!"

He snatched the newspaper out of Sean's hands without waiting for a reply.

Desperate for distraction, Sean clicked on the television, and the big grey screen came slowly to life, black and white images of the Addams Family scrolling round and round and round. He got up and twiddled with the Vertical Hold button, sending the picture scrolling in the opposite direction until he'd got it right. Fergus glared over the top of the paper but said nothing. He'd never admit that he found Gomez and Morticia, or anything else, in the slightest bit humorous.

Sean leaned an elbow on the arm of his chair and cupped the side of his face in his hand. It hid his expression as the rest of the family came in after each shift finished dinner. Keiran and Colin crammed themselves next to Fergus on the couch, while Mary and Moira sat

246

on the floor next to their dad's chair. No one would even think of sitting there, even when it was empty.

Sean's dad was always last to eat at the weekend, sitting alone at the table as his wife waited on him. He said nothing as the plate was placed between his knife and fork, the tea poured and the bread buttered. There was no conversation as he ate, and even the kids were hushed as if their father's dinner was as sacred as Sunday mass. When he was done he'd leave the plate where it lay and move to his chair in the front room where he'd spend the evening roasting his feet by the fire and lighting up a series of Woodbines, moving only to spit on the coals. By bed time the air would be thick with the stench of tobacco, old feet and roasted phlegm. It didn't matter if Sean's mother had a baby at the tit, or if four year old Moira were clambering all over her father's lap - always the cigarettes smouldered, the feet baked, and his father's every breath was an exhalation of poisonous gas.

Sean's dad entered the room and let rip as he stepped over Mary and Moira to change the channel to the six o clock news. There was a groan from the girls as the Addams Family disappeared, but the boys knew better than to say a word. Sean's mother came in from the kitchen wiping her hands on a towel and stood behind her husband's chair. Reginald Bosanquet shuffled a few papers and looked out of the screen as if talking directly to everyone in the room.

"In the news this evening," he began "the Black September Crisis deepens as the truce between Jordanian and Palestinian forces is broken once again; Cambodian government forces break the siege of Kompong Tho after three months; and Elvis Presley is set to embark on his first concert tour since 1958. He allowed himself the subtlest of smiles as he read the last announcement, but then his expression

247

became sombre and his voice darkened. "But first, news of a brutal act of violence in the northern seaside town of Sandcaster that has left an elderly person dead."

Sean's dad pulled the cigarette out of his mouth and leaned forward in his seat.

"Shhhh!" he hissed, "let's listen to this."

The room was totally silent. Fergus let the paper drop to his lap, the girls stopped hitting each other with their dolls, Sean's mother stopped wiping her hands, and Sean stopped breathing.

Reginald Bosanquet looked right at him. "Police are interviewing visitors and staff at Sandcaster's Joyland funfair this evening in the search for two youths suspected in the murder of an elderly woman earlier this afternoon."

Woman?..... but.......but........Oh Christ! It wasn't the old man after all, it was.....it was.........Oh my God no!"

He'd never thought the day could get any worse, but now? Oh Sweet Jesus, why did it have to be the old woman? And Murder. It was Murder!!!! He'd whispered the word only to himself, hoping that it couldn't possibly be true. But now, coming from Reginald Bosanquet, there was no escaping it. Murder. The same crime as Ian Brady with those little kids on the Yorkshire Moors. The same crime that had James Hanratty dancing at the end of a rope.

It wasn't the DIC for Sean, it was prison.... with Flint.

Reginald Bosanquet went on. "Mrs. Avril James, a 70 year old pensioner from Wigan, and a veteran of two world wars, was visiting Sandcaster in the company of her husband and two granddaughters. Having placed the two girls aboard Joyland's Tornado roller coaster, the elderly couple were watching the ride from below when a heavy object was thrown from one of the cars, striking Mrs. James on the head and killing her instantly."

248

Reginald Bosanquet paused, and Sean's dad stubbed his cigarette viciously into the ashtray.

"Hooligans!" he roared. "Murdering bloody hooligans." And he looked round at his own sons as if to lump them all into the same category.

"Shhh! Patrick," his wife said. "Language!"

"Mr. Stanley James, husband of the victim for 50 years, and his two grandchildren, are being treated in Sandcaster General Hospital for shock. Meanwhile police have identified the thrown object as a heavy plastic ball stolen earlier from a fairground stall. The proprietor of the stall has provided a description of two youths which matches the description of the suspects provided by the operator of the Tornado."

Reginald Bosanquet disappeared, and to Sean's amazement he was looking at Low Brow standing in front of the Tornado with a microphone thrust into his face, his eyes downcast to avoid the camera.

"The two of 'em were trouble," he was saying, "I could see that but what can you do? One were about 13, a mangey little Herbert in a purple blazer. His mate called him Tarzan. T'other one were older, 16 or so, and weasley like. They were messin' about at the back during the ride, but I thought they were just acting the goat. I gave 'em both a right bol.....telling off when they got off but I 'ad no idea they'd been 'eavin' hobjects."

Reginald Bosanquet was a true professional. There was the slightest crease in the corner of his eye, but the delivery continued even and sombre.

"Evidence suggests that the murder of the old woman was the last in a series of crimes committed by the youths throughout the course of the day. The two are also sought in connection with an attempted armed robbery at the funfair. The proprietor of a rifle range stated that the older youth paid to use the range and then turned the rifle on him and demanded money. A fellow stall holder intervened to disarm the youth, but the two then fled on foot. Earlier the youths had sabotaged and sunk a motor boat on Sandcaster's boating lake, had been involved in an incident of indecent exposure, and are suspected in the sexual assault of a minor that took place in Joyland's Funhouse.

"Must have been a weedy little miner if he let that happen to him," muttered Fergus.

"Shut up you!" roared his father. "It's attitudes like yours that encourage louts and bloody hooligans. Beating up pensioners, vandalizing other folkses property. They ought to lock up the bloody lot of them and throw away the key. If I had my way I'd birch the little bastards then string them up." Spit had gathered at the corners of his mouth and his fists were bunched as if to lay Fergus out.

Fergus smirked. He'd hardly spoken a direct word to his father in years, but was always satisfied when some remark riled him into behaving like the Nazi he always accused him of being.

"Shhhhh Patrick," said his mother. "And you Fergus, either keep quiet or go and read a book."

Sean had almost called out *That's not true!* as he'd heard about the sexual assault, but had bitten back the words just in time. And then came a terrible understanding as he recalled Peaches bawling her eyes out, and Flint wafting his fingers under his nose after cramming down Sean's lunch. He was overcome with disgust. Disgust and a raw hatred. Yes, bring back the rope, he thought. And the birch and the rack. Bring back the branding irons and the garrote. Bring them all back and make that bastard scream. Break him, hang him and burn him. Hammer a stake through his heart. And after you've flung his carcass into a pit, sow the ground with salt.

But then, in the instant it took for the scene on the television screen to change, rage gave way to terror as Sean saw his own destruction in the image that his entire family were now gaping it. He couldn't move a muscle or choke out a word. He was looking at a picture of himself.

"......Five feet six inches tall, 120 pounds, brown eyes, dark hair cut short and wearing what appeared to be a purple school blazer with a crest on the front pocket."

The identikit picture put together by Sandcaster Police was definitely him. Next to him was a picture of Flint.

"Five feet nine inches tall, 140 pounds, grey or blue eyes, military crew cut, dressed in blue jeans and grey tee-shirt. If anyone has information about the identity or whereabouts of the two youths they are urged to contact Sandcaster police or their local police force immediately."

On the floor Mary and Moira were whispering to each other and giggling.

A colossal weight anchored Sean to his seat. He was unable to tear his eyes from his own image. He started to breathe in rapid shallow bursts as the bubble of panic mushroomed, but the smoke-filled air wasn't getting beyond the lump in his throat. He was drowning. The room was folding in on him. The walls were pressing against his face. He had to get out – he had to breathe.

Mary and Moira were laughing out loud now, sharing their little joke. Sean was in a blind panic. He clawed his way out of his seat, lungs bursting. He staggered to the kitchen door almost trampling the girls who rolled at his feet. He heard them as he fled from the house....

"That's our Sean" cried Moira, giggling uncontrollably.

"And that's Jimmy Flint," roared Mary, tickled pink.

CHAPTER 27: Myopia

Sean sat on the doorstep soaked to the skin, head between his legs, dragging in desperate breaths. The panic attack was fading, but his heart still pounded as if he'd been running for his life. His mother's hand rested on his shoulder as she squatted down beside him. The panic surged again as he turned towards her, knowing he was found out.

"It wasn't me...." he began to whimper, but stopped short as his mother lifted his chin, cupping it gently in her hand as she scanned his face with troubled eyes.

"Are you all right love?" she asked. "Why did you run out like that – have you been sick? You look as white as a sheet and you're dripping with sweat."

She placed the palm of her hand on his forehead and let it rest there for a few seconds. It gave him time to think.

Was it possible that she hadn't clued in? Could she be so blind? He bit back the truth trembling on his lips. He'd wanted to spit it out and get it over with – but did he have to? If his mother couldn't see the obvious was anyone else likely to point the finger at him?

He allowed himself to sag and played the Old Soldier for all it was worth.

"I just felt nauseous," he said. "Thought I might throw up so I came out here. I'm alright now, just a bit shaky."

"Well come in and sit down and I'll make you a cup of tea. I expect that walk today took it out of you."

Sean shuffled behind his mother to the kitchen and flopped down into a chair, leaning his elbows on the table and covering his face with his hands. His father came into the room just as his mother was putting the kettle on the stove.

"What's up with him?" he asked, as if Sean wasn't there.

"He's alright," answered Sean's mother. "Just a bit worn out after the walk."

His father leaned over the sink and cleaned his nose into it, flicking snot from the end of his fingers. It was another of his endearing habits. He turned the tap on briefly and ran his fingertips under it, but Sean knew that the revolting jelly would be stuck to the porcelain until his mother cleaned it up later. His stomach rolled as he imagined the phlegmy lump with its flecks of green and red. What could his mother possibly see in the man?

"Bit of a walk and he's knocked up? What's the lad made of."

"Go easy on him Patrick," coaxed his mother. "He's not well."

"Not well! If he spent less time in bed maybe he'd shape up a bit."

Sean ignored them. If he interrupted he'd be told to give less of his bloody cheek. Telling him to keep quiet was one of the few things his father actually said to him directly. Not that he cared; they had nothing to talk about anyway.

"Do you want sugar in your tea Sean?"

"No mum, just a bit of milk."

His dad was off again. "Bit of milk! Let him get his own bloody milk. Fetch me bloody carry me. No wonder a bit of a walk's knocked him up."

"Oh forget it," said Sean, getting up and opening the door to the front room.

"And less of your bloody cheek," said his father as the door slammed behind him.

"Murderer! Murderer!" laughed his sisters as he entered the room. "Our Sean's a murderer!"

A fresh bolt of panic almost floored him, but the fact that Fergus hardly acknowledged his return gave him a tremendous surge of hope. Maybe, just maybe, he could get away with it after all.

He laboured up the stairs towards bed, flung his clothes in a heap at the foot of the bunk and scrambled between the sheets without a thought of washing himself first. After all, what would be the point?

The replay started as he closed his eyes. If only......he repeated to himself....If only............

Somehow he slept, his mind closing down until his mother woke him the next morning, shaking the bunk.

"Come on Sean," she said. "It's time for mass. You've got half an hour so don't hang about. Your good clothes are on the dresser." She rushed out of the room to make sure everyone else was up, fed and dressed.

For a few seconds he lay there troubled by a fleeting nightmare. Then he was vividly awake to an infinitely worse reality. He buried his face in the pillow and curled into the blanket, trying to believe that yesterday could not possibly have happened.

But there was no avoiding the present. A pounding on the bedroom floor told him that his mother was below in the kitchen hammering on the ceiling with a brush handle. If he didn't get up soon she'd be howling at the bottom of the stairs, and then his father would begin shouting curses at his lazy bloody sons. It was a typical Sabbath in the McCaffery household.

His "good clothes" were a blue shirt and a pair of long grey trousers that had been good clothes to Colin and Fergus before him. He dragged them on and forced himself to descend the stairs. He pushed through the door to the front room, hoping to escape into the kitchen and out through the back door without saying a word. But he stopped short, rigid with fright.

His father stood in the middle of the room, blocking his way, his face florid with fury. His arms were stretched out in front of him. He thrust The News of the World in Sean's face. Taking up half the front page were the identikit pictures of him and Flint under the single-word headline. MURDERERS!

"But I didn't mean to!" shrieked Sean. He stood gaping, searching for excuses that wouldn't come.

His father dropped his arms and glared over the top of the paper.

"Have you been monkeying about with my glasses?" he demanded.

Sean looked at him, bewildered.

"One of you buggers has shifted my bloody specs off the sideboard. I can't read a damned thing without them."

His mum came in from the kitchen and handed his father his glasses.

"Here they are Patrick," she said. "You left them by the sink after your shave. And cut out that swearing on a Sunday." She turned to

Sean. "And what's up with you, standing there gawping. Grab a piece of toast and get off to mass."

"And pray that we've won the bloody Pools," said his dad with a rare touch of humor as he studied the back page of the paper for the football results.

Sean staggered out of the house and sat shaking on the back doorstep until his heart returned to his chest. It was another reprieve, but any more like that would kill him.

CHAPTER 28: No Sanctuary

The concrete cross on the roof of St. Peter's Parish Church was the only thing that distinguished it from a rundown warehouse. The windows had to be replaced too frequently for stained glass. The Catholics blamed this on Protestant yobos, but any kid in Duggin with access to a rock and a window couldn't resist bringing the two together, no matter his persuasion.

Inside the church, every door was flanked by collection boxes labeled For the Poor (as if that didn't include most of the parishioners); For the Missions; St.Vincent de Paul; and Building Fund. And that was just on the way in. There were other boxes on the way out too, so that they got you both coming and going. Maybe that was why Sean's dad stayed in the entrance hall during the Sunday service. It took a sharp man to hang onto his brass at St. Peter's, and with nine mouths to feed Sean's dad had to keep himself honed like a razor.

Within the sacristy, a main aisle led up to the altar and two side aisles ended in tiny chapels; the one on the left with a statue of the Virgin Mary clad in blue, and the one on the right with a statue of the Sacred Heart of Jesus. The Sacred Heart was exposed under a scarlet cloak as if Christ was in for a transplant. Each chapel had a collection box where it cost sixpence to light a candle if you wanted the statues to have a word with God on your behalf. At other times Sean had thought it would be as much use praying to Mini Mouse and Donald Duck, but right now he'd be willing to risk a shilling on the off chance it might do some good.

He entered the Sacristy and dipped his fingers in the bowl of holy water by the door, making an automatic sign of the cross while bending a knee in the direction of the altar. He scanned the pews to pick out family members, and headed for one as far away from them as possible.

Father Wyche paraded in wearing ornate green vestments, preceded by two tiny altar boys in pure white. The boys had the choreography down pat, doing full knee-to-the-ground genuflections in front of the altar with sweeping signs of the cross, before separating to the right and left while the priest put on his own show with his back to the audience. Father Wyche finished the Introit, left the altar and climbed the steps of the pulpit to deliver his Sunday sermon. From up there he could see every person in the church.

Father Wyche was a big man with farmer's hands that gripped the wooden rail of the pulpit so that it creaked under his weight. He was square-jawed, grey-eyed and grey-headed, and there was nothing old about his seventy years. When he delivered a lighter sermon there would be a play of gentle humour about his face, but today his lips were a black line, ruler straight. He stood in silence for almost a minute as he scanned the pews row on row, as if making an inventory of absentees. His gaze paused on Sean. Father Wyche pointed a finger directly at him, and in a voice shaking with outrage and condemnation bawled out "THOU SHALT NOT KILL!"

259

Sean almost shit himself. He half rose from his seat as if to run, but then the voice boomed out again.

"Thou shalt not kill!" repeated Father Wyche, and the outstretched finger swept across the entire congregation to include them all in the commandment. Sean dared to breathe again, but his breath was short, shallow and not enough.

"Yesterday, a foul murder was committed not far from this place." The priest's voice was gentler now, deep and sombre. "An elderly woman, enjoying a happy excursion with her husband and grandchildren fell victim to louts and hooligans who smashed her skull and left her to die."

The wild panic begin to build again. The people around Sean seemed to swell as if sucking all the air out of the church. He was caught in the middle of them, fighting the urge to run.

"We've all seen today's headlines," continued the priest, "and we've all been sickened by the senseless violence that ended an old woman's life." He paused and let his head fall to his chest in an attitude of mourning. But then he reared up and flung out both arms as if to grab the entire congregation and shake them.

"But what about the others?" he roared. "What about the thousands who are murdered daily without so much as a word in the press? Why don't the headlines shriek bloody murder day after day and week after week? Why do we feel so much horror at the death of one old woman while others perish with equal violence and with greater premeditation every minute of every day?"

The congregation didn't have a clue what he was ranting about. Father Wyche had expected shock and outrage on every face, but all he got were looks of morbid curiosity. Sean's thoughts skipped from Vietnam to Biafra, and even to the good Catholics of Sicily, before the priest got to the point.

"…..And all these victims, these murdered innocents, are done to death without ever seeing the light of day……." Sean had a momentary image of carnage at schools for the blind. "…..and without ever feeling the light of the Holy Spirit bringing life to their souls."

So that was it – the frigging Abortion Bill again. The congregation lapsed into vacancy and went back to thinking about Sunday roasts and soccer results. But Sean was drawn by the priest's words.

"The elderly woman who was killed so brutally yesterday had had seventy years on this earth to enjoy God's blessings, to raise a family, and to leave behind a legacy of her presence. We pray that she shall meet the Lord in a state of grace and enter the Kingdom of Heaven to enjoy His eternal reward. But what of those unborn children? They are sucked from the womb to die gasping in a bucket without ever seeing the faces of their wanton mothers. All the great things that the Almighty had ordained they might do remain undone, and Satan laughs in triumph. Their souls, tainted with the stain of original sin, languish forever in Limbo, never to rejoice in the presence of Our Saviour."

"And their murderers, what about them? What is their reward for this vilest of crimes? I'll tell you what it is. For the doctors it is an extravagant salary - wealth beyond the dreams of you here present. For the sluts who crave the carnal pleasures it is bed and board in a hospital that should be set aside for the sick. Yes, hotel service while they have their unborn children ripped from them. That is the current notion of justice in today's society. And who pays for all of this? I'll tell you who pays for it. You do! You pay for it with taxes taken from you by a government that condones and encourages murder with its humanist philosophy, its sex education, and its continued reinforcement of the Welfare State."

The congregation sat with heads bowed or eyes averted as Father Wyche rattled on. Abortion meant sex, and sex wasn't something that was spoken of in public. Only Mr. McGuinness from the Chemist shop had a keen eye on the pulpit. There'd be fewer abortions if Catholics were allowed to use those all those Johnnies he sold to the Protestants.

Father Wyche kept it up for twenty five minutes, raining curses on whores and harlots, berating parents for allowing their daughters unchaperoned dates with boys, and slating a school system that taught, actually taught, boys the proper use of condoms. How could there possibly be a proper use for such a vile and improper object? Here, half the men in the congregation examined their shoes while their wives flushed scarlet. Sex! There was far too much sex in the world. Father Wyche wasn't allowed any, and he was intent on spoiling it for everyone else.

For a brief period the sermon lightened Sean's load. Compared to the abortionists his sin was negligible – the priest had almost said so. The old woman had had a bloody good innings, and if she got bowled out before batting a century, well, you couldn't expect to live for ever, could you?

But the rationalization was short-lived. An abortionist, believing in his work, could meet his maker with a clear conscience, whereas Sean had done something evil, and had done it willingly and knowingly. That damned him to Hell. Hadn't he argued with Brother Jerome that there could be no such sin as murder in a society where murder was the norm? And hadn't he defined the nature of sin in his exercise book as the abnegation of one's own beliefs for personal gain? He'd been proud of the word abnegation, knowing that Brother Jerome would have to look it up in a dictionary. But he was condemned by his own words. One day he would have to pay for what he had done.

So, when the gong sounded during the transubstantiation, and the host was raised on high, Sean bowed his head with the rest of the congregation, not daring to look on the body of Christ, and in terror of the mortal sin on his soul.

Chapter 29: Family Matters

After mass, the family gathered at Sean's Gran's house. Great Aunt Winnie and Great Aunt Theresa sat perched on Uncle Albert's new sofa dressed in their Sunday black and smoking Woodbines like a pair of soot-encrusted chimneys. Albert stood behind them, watching the ash grow on the end of each cigarette, ready to wail and thrash about should a single flake fall on the plastic cover of his precious furniture. It was one of the many ways he had of making his life wretched.

Two battered armchairs stood on either side of the fireplace, making the new sofa look all the more ridiculous. Sean's mum sat in one and aunt Rita in the other. Uncle Den held himself squarely erect in front of the fireplace, drinking tea while Sean's dad and Sean's uncle Gerry were enjoying a pint at the Labour Club across the road. Uncle Den was a gaunt, pinch-faced piece of misery who passed around the collection plate at mass and laid it at the altar rail as if he'd contributed every penny himself. Uncle Gerry, who had not crossed the church threshold in donkey's years, put it about that the opposite was true - that Uncle Den supplemented his income by deft handiwork with the donations. There was no denying that Den seemed to have more cash than the other family members, and his suit was cut from a finer cloth.

Den called himself a miner, but he had a cushy job topside at the colliery and never soiled himself with a lump of coal at work or at home. Rita did all the hauling and carrying in his household, and the strain of it told in her face. She was barely forty, but looked as haggard as a pit pony. She perched on the edge of her armchair as if she had no right to be sitting, and her eyes darted nervously from face to face as she pecked at her biscuit like a sparrow. She was a slight, nervous wreck of a woman with dark shadows beneath her eyes that were due only partly to weariness.

Sean's gran bustled in and out of the room ferrying tea and biscuits as Albert watched for dribbles and crumbs. She laughed and joked with Winnie and Theresa as she hefted the huge tea pot, and smiled warmly on Sean's mum. She filled Den's cup in silence, and encouraged Rita to take more tea as if she were still the little girl who had played in her lap. Then she squeezed onto the sofa between her sisters and added a third chimney to the twin stacks.

Sean's brothers had been and gone by the time he arrived at his gran's house, and his sisters were playing in the garden. He wished he could just flash everyone a fake smile and leave, but his gran and her sisters were waiting for him, more than ready to part with their sponsorship money, and proud of him for taking it from them. He hated the thought of robbing them, but there was no other choice. If he refused the money there'd be questions he couldn't answer.

He slid into the house and paused in the kitchen to gather his courage. Winnie was talking about an earthquake she'd heard about on the radio.

"Thank God for the coal mines," she said.

"What's the mines got t'do with it?" asked Winnie.

"Let the pressure out don't they?" she replied. "That's why we don't get none of them earthquakes round here."

265

"Don't talk so bloody daft," said Theresa.

"And watch that fag!" wailed in Albert.

"Stands to reason, doesn't it?" continued Winnie. "All that stuff boiling down there in them volcanoes has to go some place doesn't it?"

"Aye, like that Mount Edna what's wiping out the Eyeties," said Sean's Gran.

"And serve 'em bloody well right if you ask me," said Theresa. "Bring it on themselves that Mafia. Thieving bunch of murdering hooligans."

"Should put them to work in the slaughterhouse," said Sean's gran. "That'd learn them."

"Our Jimmy used to work there," said Winnie.

"You're slopping that tea!" whined Albert.

"Used to come home in a right state," continued Winnie. "How they let him on the bus stinking of blood an' sheep-shit I'll never know."

"Language!" cried Uncle Den. "Let's not have that on the Sabbath."

Winnie pretended he wasn't there. "He brought home some lovely meat," she said, "and we needed it just then, right after the war. Condemned it were, but it did no harm."

"Stealing's stealing!" preached Den, wasting his breath.

"They used to paint it green, the condemned stuff" said Winnie, "but nowt that a good scrubbing couldn't fix. Boiled long enough it made a lovely Irish Stew."

"Them Irish would have been thankful for it in my great-grandad's time," said Sean's gran, and the conversation shifted to the Potato Famine.

Sean gathered his guts and slipped into the room. He did it shyly, standing next to Albert behind the sofa. But his gran had seen him, and her face cracked into a wicked smile.

"Don't stand back there cock," she said. Come here where I can take a look at you."

Winnie and Theresa turned to look at him too, three gorgons grinning through smoke stained dentures. It might have been a terrible sight if he didn't love them so much. How could he steal from women like that? He sloped around the sofa and stood in front of them with his back to Uncle Den. Winnie leaned forward, resting forearms on massive thighs.

"So you made it did you?" she asked. "All twenty mile?"

"Course he made it," said Theresa, saving him from the lie. "Nowt to it eh, cock?"

Sean shook his head, feeling like a shit.

"Used to walk half way to Sandcaster meself a few years back," said his gran. "...For the bean-picking. Hard graft for a shilling a day but there were nowt else. Buggered if I could do it now."

"Language mother," chimed Albert, pre-empting Uncle Den.

"Never did it then neither," said Winnie.

"Tell you 'owt, that one," said Theresa, winking.

"Bloody right I did," said Sean's gran. "Traipsed up to Ormskirk while it were still dark and came back home at night with the beans in the back of the wagon."

"With the beans and with Charley Endle too," grinned Winnie.

"Aye, and he were full of beans and all," laughed Theresa.

They cackled like schoolgirls.

"Enough of that kind of talk in front of the boy," snapped Uncle Den. He might as well have been talking to the grandfather clock.

"So what's the damage then cock?" asked Theresa, looking at Sean and reaching for her handbag.

"Two bob each weren't it?" asked Winnie, rummaging in her purse. Her fingers clinked through a pile of coins. "Let's see, all them's florins, but look here – there's half a crown! Here cock, you can keep the extra sixpence for yourself."

Not to be out done, Theresa and his gran gave him half crowns too. That meant one and six for himself. He hardly got that much on his birthday! He took the coins with his best look of gratitude, but it was a bleak effort at best. They could barely afford the two shillings, and the extra sixpences would be a hardship. He was on the point of babbling some refusal when Uncle Den came to the rescue.

"Mind that money goes where it should," he said to Sean's back, "and share the extra with your brothers and sisters."

The self righteous bleating twisted something in Sean's belly and he turned to spit a response into Uncle Den's sanctimonious face, but he was beaten to it by Theresa, who'd had more than enough of the prat for one morning. Only fear of Den's revenge on Rita had been holding her back.

"And what's it go to do with you?" she snarled. "I don't see you reaching for any brass. Got a bad arm again have you?"

As usual, Winnie was with her shoulder to shoulder. "Aye, short arms and long pockets is always your problem isn't it? You should be across the road with the boys right now, only you'd have to buy a round, you bloody skinflint."

Sean's gran saw Rita's face twist with anxiety, and she bit back her own attack. Sean's mother lowered her head in disgust, knowing that Uncle Den wouldn't have dared open his mouth if Uncle Gerry or Sean's dad had been there.

"I don't hold with drinking after taking the Sacrament," he said. "And I give my brass to the Church."

"Aye, and it's all bloody brass and precious little silver isn't it?" fired Theresa, twitching her fist like a mallet.

"And you're not one to go short are you?" said Winnie, keeping up the double-act, "not while there's others to take up the slack."

Sean retreated to the back of the sofa to give them clear shots. He'd back Winnie and Theresa against Cassius Clay, never mind a streak of piss like Uncle Den. He was aching to see him taken down.

"I serve the Church every Sunday," spat Den, flecks of red growing in the hollow of his cheeks.

"Serve your bloody self more likely," said Winnie. "There's never 'owt on the plate when you begin."

"And lighter than it should be when you've done," chorused Theresa, still weighing her fist. She was a heavy woman, but Sean felt she could be out of her chair like lightning if Uncle Den was fool enough to take her on.

Den slammed his cup down on the mantelpiece and Rita shot a desperate look at her aunts.

"And what do you mean by that?" he roared, "I've never touched a penny that wasn't mine."

"No, you never bother with anything less than a florin do you?"

This came from Uncle Gerry who exploded into the room bringing his wife Ruby and an atmosphere of beer and belly laughs with him. Uncle Den picked up his empty tea cup and sucked at it, his hand shaking. Gerry bent down to give Rita a kiss, scanned her face briefly and turned murderous eyes on Den. Den sucked harder at the empty cup, but Gerry turned his back on him and broke into a big grin as he looked at Sean.

269

"And how are you cock?" he asked. "Didn't knacker yourself up too much yesterday did you?"

Gerry was Sean's favourite uncle. How he could be his dad's brother was a mystery. Gerry would never stand up when he could sit down, and never sit down when he could lie down. He worked at the DIC when he worked at all, but spent most of the year on Workers' Comp. His experience of workplace accidents was long and comprehensive, but there wasn't one of them that could keep him out of the betting shop or the pub. His house was full of stuff that had fallen off the backs of lorries, and he could get a deal on anything from a sack of spuds to a colour TV. He had twin sons, though how he could have managed the required ten minutes with aunt Ruby Sean couldn't imagine.

Ruby hadn't said a word to anyone. She had cast a half-pissed smile around the room, and all but Den and Albert had smiled back. She leaned against the mantelpiece close to Den, who twitched himself more erect as he turned flared nostrils away from the smell of booze. Ruby laughed in his face. She was a stout woman of thirty five who barely came up to Den's shoulders, but it was obvious Den was afraid of her. Now she looked at Sean and said, "So how much do we owe you luv– half a crown was it?" She poked Gerry in the back and roared at him as if he were two streets away. "Go on then, you daft bugger, give the lad his money."

"A'right, a'right," Gerry shouted back. He dug his hand into the pocket of his suit and flicked a coin over the sofa towards Sean.

"Watch that mirror!" screamed Albert, clawing for the coin as if it were a grenade. He thrust it at Sean as if he wished it would blow him to smithereens.

"Thieving little sod," said Ruby. "I bet that'll never make it to the school."

Gerry burst out laughing. "Just look at the cherry on him!" he roared. "I reckon he's taking us all for a bloody ride. Sponsored walk my arse. Sponsored day at the bloody funfair more like it."

Sean couldn't find his tongue. Everyone expected him to make some smart response, but his wits had slowed to a standstill.

His mother came to his rescue. "Well I'm glad he wasn't at the fairground yesterday, not with that terrible business going on."

"Little swines," said Theresa. "Ought to be birched.

"Aye, them Manx'd make them think twice," said Winnie.

"Bugger the Manx," said Sean's gran. "Those Ay-rabs have the right idea. Chop their bloody hands off and let them fend for themselves. That'd cure 'em. People here are too soft."

"That's the problem with kids today," said Ruby, as if her twins weren't the living evidence of original sin, "there's just no detergent."

There was a ripple of laughter, and in the pause Sean's mother cast a troubled glance towards him. He wasn't even smiling.

"You're mental, you are," said Gerry. "Daft as a bloody brush."

"Me?" roared Ruby. "And what about yourself - sitting on the toilet for hours with the newspaper."

"What the bloody hell's that got to do with anything?" roared Gerry.

"Not natural is it?" said Ruby. "When you can't go to the toilet without making a meal of it."

Sean's mum decided enough was enough. "You might as well get along home now Sean and get your homework done while the house is quiet," she said. Sean stumbled gratefully out of the room.

In the kitchen his hands shook as he got himself a glass of water. The last minute had been hell – all of them talking about him without knowing it, wishing him flogged and dismembered. How

271

could he ever tell them what he'd done? He overheard the conversation from the living room as he drank.

"Something's not right with that lad of yours Lizzie," said Winnie.

"Never said a word," observed Theresa. "Not like him."

"No, not like our Sean to stand there gawking," said his gran.

"'Happen there was a rum do on that walk of his."

"I'm telling you," chimed in Gerry laughing again, "the little bugger's swindling the lot of us. He had a face like a well-slapped arse when I collared him about it."

"He wasn't well when he got back from the walk yesterday," said his mother. "I expect he's still a bit off colour." She sounded as if she were making excuses.

"I noticed that he didn't take the Sacrament this morning......" said Uncle Den, looking towards the ceiling as if talking directly to God.

"And what's that supposed to mean?" asked Sean's mum with a hard edge to her voice.

"Oh, I don't know," said Den, still with his chin in the air. "Just an observation, that's all."

"Aye, and any more of them observations," said Gerry, "and you'll be observing my fist...." He waved it under Den's nose. "....At bloody close quarters."

"Knock it off Gerry," said Ruby.

"Aye, I'll knock it off alright. I'll knock his head right off his bleeding shoulders."

"Come on Rita," snapped Ted. "I won't take any more of this on the Sabbath. I can only turn the other cheek for so long. We best be on our way." He made it sound like he was restraining himself, and

Sean heard Gerry snort "My arse...." as Den and Rita got ready to leave.

Sean gulped down the rest of the water and fled.

Chapter 30: Tarzan

Ottie Ward was standing in the street looking for someone to talk to. Sean stopped when he saw him and turned around as if to retrieve some item he'd left behind at his Gran's house. But Ottie had spotted him – and Ottie wanted something back for that chocolate bar.

"'Here he is!'" He called out, "Marco Bloody Polo. How was the walk to Sandcaster then? Got any shoe leather left?"

Sean sidled up. "It was alright," was all he could manage.

"Twenty bloody mile," marvelled Ottie, "and all of it on Shank's Pony. Maybe you're not as nesh as you look."

Sean just stood there. He could think of nothing to say. Ottie didn't mind. He enjoyed monologues.

"So did you go Ormskirk way by Old Milly Dam, or did you go by Scrape's Hill passed Johnny Ape's pig farm?"

Sean's heart convulsed. He didn't know the route the walk had taken to Sandcaster and hadn't anticipated being quizzed about it. What could he say? All those threads. He was about to take a guess, but Ottie rambled on.

"That pig farm stinks to high heaven," he said. "You can smell it from Eccleston to Ormskirk – like smokey bacon mixed with shite. God knows how folk round about put up with it."

Sean nodded his head and wrinkled his nose as if he'd had first hand experience. Brother Lundy would have had some category for that type of lie, but Sean didn't care as long as he could get away with it.

"Country air?" laughed Ottie, "Give me the DIC chimneys any day against that lot. I don't mind breathing smoke, but I draw the line at pig shit."

As if reinforcing the point he pulled out a pack of Woodbines and lit up. He eyed Sean quizzically.

"So you don't mind a bit of walking, do you lad?"

"No," mumbled Sean, relieved to say something with a grain of truth in it.

"Well, I might have a job for someone who doesn't mind hard graft. Ever had a paper round?"

Sean's eyes widened. Delivering newspapers earned good money, at least ten bob a week. That meant sweets .....clothes ......even girlfriends! With a paper round he could even afford to take Paula to the pictures. The jobs were like heirlooms, passed from brother to brother as each was swallowed up by the DIC. They were never advertised. If Ottie had put a sign up in his window advertising for a paper boy there would have been mayhem outside as the local lads fought for the door. Was Ottie going to offer him a round?

"Rob Hall's for the DIC at month's end," continued Ottie as if announcing a death sentence. "His round'll free then. I were thinking of his cousin Harry Wilkinson, but I've noticed things in the shop tend to stick to that little bugger's fingers. Never caught him at it mind, but when I do I'll cure the thieving little bastard, you can be sure o' that. Can't stomach a thief," he continued with the

275

pig shit look back on his face. "Lie to your face on Christmas Day they would."

He gave Sean a hard look, then smiled as if he were his granddad. "So, are you interested cock?"

It was like asking a Biafran if he fancied a bag of chips, yet Sean had to fight to bring a light to his eyes.

"Right then cock," said Ottie. "You go and soak your dogs and come and see me at month's end."

Sean murmured some thanks and tried to put a spring in his step as he walked away, but the coins in his pocket beat a constant reminder that he was nothing but a thieving, lousy scumbag.

He walked with head down, his feet moving automatically towards home as he relived the day at Sandcaster time and time again, and every missed opportunity to change that worst of all possible endings.

A hand grabbed him from behind. Another clamped down hard on his mouth as he woke from his daydream to find himself in Cack Alley. He was dragged off the path, hauled through a thicket of brambles, and had his legs kicked from under him so that he crashed to the ground face down on a patch of grass. One hand stayed clamped to his mouth as a knee dug into his spine so hard he thought it might snap. He tried desperately to throw off the attacker, but his arms and legs were spread-eagled and useless. Whoever had got him could do what they liked. His buttocks clenched against what might happen next. He bucked wildly and bit at the hand on his mouth, ready to chew through the fingers to get free.

"Keep still, and keep bleeding quiet," snarled Flint, "or I'll break your fucking neck."

Flint pulled back on Sean's hair, dragging his face out of the grass but keeping his hand over his mouth so that he gasped for air. Sean stopped struggling, but was rigid with fear.

"Good," said Flint, pulling Sean up into a sitting position and crouching down next to him. "Now how much have you got?"

Sean's face spat hatred. Flint lashed out. The fist hit Sean just below the ribs and he doubled up in agony. Flint pulled his head up again and slapped him lightly on each cheek.

"Now Tarzan," he began, and grinned as he saw Sean turn white at the name. "Now TARZAN," he repeated, "are you going to hand it over, or do I have to beat it out of you?"

"What do you mean Flint? What do you want?" Sean really didn't know. The panic had robbed him of reason.

"Now don't try it on with me Tarzan. And don't give me any of that La-Di-Da Grammar School lip either, because you and me are partners aren't we. We do everything together don't we? I take you for rides on the big dipper don't I, and you throw stuff down on little old biddies that snuff it, don't you?"

"You lying bastard Flint," screamed Sean, "It was you that did it, not me."

Flint shut him up with another poke in the solar plexus and continued all calm and matter of fact as Sean doubled over again.

"Your word against mine that is isn't it? Cops'll have the ball won't they? With your prints all over it remember? Anyway, it doesn't matter who killed the old girl does it, because were partners now aren't we? Flint and Tarzan – Murderers! Just like it says in the paper."

He pulled a crumpled piece of the News of the World from his pocket and waved it under Sean's nose. Sean recoiled just as he had that morning when his father had thrust the paper into his face.

There they were again. The two identikit pictures. Him and Flint. Side by side. Just like Flint said. Partners!

"Not bad eh?" said Flint. "Not many from Duggin get in the papers."

Sean couldn't believe it. Flint's face glowing. He was admiring his picture as if he were featured for some great achievement. The stupid bastard was actually proud of himself.

A new twist of fear turned in Sean's belly. Flint was a dim-wit and a braggart. He'd carry that clipping with him everywhere, and sooner or later he'd get caught gawping at it. Someone was bound to make the connection. Worse still, Flint might start boasting. He wasn't just some petty crook anymore, but someone much more important. Just about as important as you can get as far as the cops are concerned, hint, hint. Someone that half the country is looking for, eh? Bet you can't guess what I did can you? And if you tell anyone else I'll do for you too...

It was hopeless. Sean could invent the most perfect alibi, and it would all come undone with one misplaced word from that grinning moron squatting next to him. No matter how smart Sean was, no matter how much of his mental energy he put into the concealment of his guilt, his fate was totally dependent on the actions of a fool.

He made a wild grab for the clipping.

"Get rid of that picture Flint. If someone sees you with it we're done for."

Flint smiled wider as he whipped the picture away from Sean's hand. He pushed him flat on his back and laid a bony knee on his chest, folding the picture carefully before slipping it into his pocket.

"Mustn't snatch, Tarzan. It's not polite."

"And don't call me Tarzan for Christ's sake. They're looking for someone called Tarzan. Don't you understand? For God's sake Flint, you can't be that fucking stupid."

Flint slapped him across the face. Superior. Just like one of the teachers at Meadowlands.

"You're getting very cheeky," he said in his calm, dangerous voice, "and that's not nice. Me and you have got to stay friends haven't we, because me and you've got a big secret. You wouldn't want to go upsetting me now would you, because I might just go spilling the beans mightn't I?"

Sean couldn't believe it. It was as if Flint didn't understand the enormity of their situation. He pleaded with him, almost in tears.

"Please Flint, get rid of that picture, and don't tell anyone about yesterday, or we'll both go down. It won't be Borstal either, that'd be just for starters. They'd have us in Dartmoor with Ian Brady and the other psychos."

Flint had never heard of Ian Brady, and wouldn't have known Myra Hindley from the Queen Mother. But he knew about Dartmoor. He'd been told often enough that that was where he was heading, and it didn't bother him in the slightest. He spat back in Sean's face.

"Dartmoor? Who gives a shit about bleeding Dartmoor? You get fed in there don't you? The screws have only got two fists haven't they? Don't talk to me about bleeding Dartmoor. It's a frigging holiday camp. Now hand over the cash."

Sean took the coins from his pocket. Flint caught the fist before it flung the coins into his face. He pressed his fingers tips hard against the nails of Sean's bunched hand, threatening to break the top joints. The agony was excruciating. Flint squeezed then eased off, drinking in the look on Sean's face as he pressed and released, pressed and released. When he'd had enough, he allowed Sean to open his fist and scooped up the coins. He grinned as Sean clamped his hands together, protecting them from more of that horrible the torture.

"A quid," said Flint, turning over the four half crowns on his palm. "And plenty more where that came from, eh? That's ten bob for me and ten bob for you."

He pocketed half of the money and held out the rest to Sean. Sean shook his head at the coins.

"You take it," he said. "I don't want it."

"Oh no sonny Jim. We're partners remember?" Flint was smirking. "We share everything half and half. Whatever I get, you get. Ten bob. Ten quid. Ten years."

He laughed at his own wit as he jingled the coins in his hand, then slipped them into his pocket.

"Tell you what," said Flint, "I reckon you're right. Seems to me like you still owe me a quid or two from Sandcaster, so I'll take these till you've paid up your half. Now, you just keep collecting the cash Tarzan, because that's your job, and I'll keep taking it off you, because that's mine."

He laughed again, genuinely happy, and sauntered off between the bushes into Cack Alley.

When he was gone, Sean sat with his head in his hands, alone and in private for the first time since the old woman had died.

He cried and cried and cried.

Chapter 31: Helping with Enquiries

The boys were like old campaigners back home from the wars, trying to outdo each other with tales of adventure.

-Blisters? Where've you got blisters Smith?

-On his arse most likely.

-Yeah, we had to drag him half way to Sandcaster.

-And carry him the other half.

-Bollocks, I could have walked it both ways, no problem.

-That why you flaked out in Victoria Park?

-Missed all the grub.

-And the beer.

-Beer my arse, there was no beer.

-Brothers had cases of it in the van.

-Rod Strong nicked half a dozen cans and got rat-arsed.

-Half the Brothers were pissed up too.

-Old Campy must have downed at least ten.

-In the bushes all afternoon he was.

-Aye, and I bet he wasn't just pulling it out for a leak either, eh Purvis?

- Purvis, take a hold this for me Laddy. Oooh that's the ticket!

-Oops, you've gone and upset him. He's ponced off to tell on you.

-Rag-arsing poofter.

-Don't know why he's hanging around us anyway.

-Hey, did you hear about Duckworth?

-Yeah, stupid sod sneaked off to Joyland and won a big furry toy on the darts.

-Too bloody stupid to dump it and Brother Jerome caught him with it on the bus back to school. What a giveaway.

-He'll be in for it today.

-Six for sure.

-And Old Campy took his fluffy toy off him.

-Bet I know where that ended up.

-Looked a bit like Purvis come to think of it.

-Yeah, you missed a good lark on Saturday McCaffery.

-Cracking day.

-Why couldn't you make it anyway?

-Thought you were all signed up.

-Hey, what's wrong with him? Ran right into the bogs.

-Dunno. Maybe he was caught short.

-No....it looked like he was going to start squawking or something.

-Hey, his mam hasn't kicked it has she?

-Dunno. But he looked like somebody had.

Sean sat on the toilet with his head between his knees, taking deep breaths of the pissy stench. He'd thought he was in control, but exclusion from all the post-walk banter had turned him into a blubbering mess. Outside he could hear the first years swarming past Brother Michael on their way to the assembly hall. That meant

282

he had about two minutes to get himself back into shape before his class filed in. He stood up and began to open the door of the cubicle, but then remembered to flush the toilet first just in case anyone was out there. It made him feel better - his brain was still working.

Assembly followed the usual routine. The Head Boy yanked on his rope, the boys mouthed the words to the school hymn, and St. Rodriguez was revealed by degrees with his two charges. Prayers were said, the Head lauded the sports teams whether they had won or not, and then rattled on about the generosity of those boys who had shown such wonderful support for their school by marching en masse to Sandcaster. It had been a glorious day. The sun had shone on the righteous. Good clean fun had been had by all in the healthy open air. Every boy who took part should feel proud of himself for sacrificing his recreation time on behalf of the school. Every boy but one.......

"Just one boy disobeyed my expressed edict against visiting the Sandcaster funfair," said the Head, "and I'll deal with that one boy in due course."

Everyone knew what that meant, and there was a sympathetic murmur from the boys.

"Silence!" The Head, who never had to shout to make his point, now roared as if barely containing his fury.

"That one boy who visited the funfair has brought what I believe to be undue attention to this school from an *Authority* which, I believe, has no place in an institution such as ours." *Authority* was uttered with an exaggerated contempt as if calling it by name would give it more credit than it deserved. The Head continued, silencing the murmered speculations of the boys. "This *Authority* must now do its duty, and we must all suffer the disruption that this will cause to our usual activities. I will leave it to this *Authority* to explain."

The Head took a few steps away from the center of the stage, and the silence gave way to a rising tide of voices as the boys goggled at the figure who emerged from the wings.

"Christ Sean, you've gone as white as a sheet," said Bill O'Rourke looked from Sean's face to the uniformed police officer.

Sean managed to croak "Wild-shites", in an agonized voice that made it sound all the more convincing.

"Bad luck," said Bill, and took a step to the side.

The police officer looked like an over-grown prefect. He wore a flat hat instead of a bobby's helmet, and there were stripes on the arm of his uniform. That made him a detective-sergeant or something, thought Sean, guessing. And that meant something serious. Dead serious. My God, it had to be.........what else could it be?

The officer attempted a reassuring smile at the boys and turned towards the Head as if for permission to begin. The Head's expression knocked the smile right off his face. He shuffled and cleared his throat, revving up for a speech. As he opened his mouth, Rylands squawked "'Ello, 'ello, 'ello," and there was a ripple of laughter throughout the hall.

"Silence!" roared the Head.

The police officer went into a cough and shuffle routine as if he'd swallowed the tip of his pencil and didn't know whether to hack it up or shit it out. This type of thing wasn't his usual beat.

"As most of you will know (cough, cough), an incident occurred at 3.45 pm on Saturday at Sandcaster's Joyland Funfair in which an elderly woman was killed (shuffle, cough, swivvle the neck). We, the police that is, are treating this incident as murder. Two youths are being sought for questioning, one in a purple blazer (ominous pause).

"Won't they question him if he takes it off?" whispered Bill. Sean's lips didn't even twitch.

"Since boys from this school were in the vicinity of Sandcaster's Joyland Funfair on Saturday (pause as if waiting for denials), and since they were all wearing purple blazers (another pause for dramatic effect)...

"You all did it!!!!" whispered Bill.

"It's a fair cop!" murmered Rylands.

".....we need to interview all those boys to establish their exact whereabouts at the time of the murder (cough, shuffle, grunt, and a look at the Head for assistance).

The Head stepped forward again, and the police officer fell back. When the Head spoke he had regained his usual composure, and though he addressed the boys there was the slightest inclination of his body towards the police officer, so that it was obvious where his words were really directed.

"These interviews in no way imply that a boy from this school was involved in the barbarous actions of despicable louts. That, of course, is unthinkable. The one boy who visited the funfair despite my prohibition has already been interviewed and has been excluded from further investigation by the police. The interviews that will take place today are formalities to demonstrate to the public, should the need arise, that the police force has probed all possible avenues of investigation however remote those avenues might be. For this reason the interviews will be brief, and will deal only with the activities of the boys in Victoria Park at the time of the murder."

"Could be awkward for the queer fellahs, that one eh?" whispered Bill. He dug an elbow into Sean's side and nodded his head towards

Purvis. He'd expected some smart response, but his grin froze as he saw the expression on Sean's face. "Jesus, you're not going to keel over are you?" he said.

"Fine......I'm fine.......Just wild-shites........Bad guts." Sean could hardly speak. He was trying desperately to contain the fit of trembling that seemed to be shaking him to pieces. The Head carried on.

"Each boy will be interviewed separately in a room set aside for the purpose. The interviews will be ordered year by year and class by class, with the first year classes being interviewed first. Brother Jerome will escort each boy to the interview room and will accompany him back to class when the interview is finished."

The Head's tone grew even darker.

"Any boy who treats these interviews flippantly, or who, for his own amusement, elaborates any testimony with a view to creating suspicion or confusion, will be dealt with by me in the severest manner. I warn you...." And here he inclined even further toward the police officer, "...I will not have the reputation of this school impugned in any way, either actual or implied. Also, this matter is, and will remain, internal. Any boy communicating these events to the press, or to any other public media, will face immediate expulsion. You are dismissed."

The police officer made as if to march off the stage as if dismissed with the rest of the boys, but remembered himself in time and held his ground. The Head, rather than preside over the exodus of boys as was usual, walked with swift purpose from the stage leaving the police officer looking, and feeling, like an idiot.

Chapter 31: Sacrificial Lamb

The Head sat at his desk, eyes fixed in a distant stare as if lost in prayer. But he was looking through, rather than at, the crucifix on the wall in front of him.

This Headship was something he had sought throughout his entire teaching career. At various schools he'd been Junior Physics master, Head of Physics, Head of Science, Deputy Headmaster, all the time taking direction from people with less drive and less talent than himself. Now he had his own school to run, and he'd be damned if he was going to allow discipline to slip below the standards he aimed to maintain.

Discipline would be on Friday's agenda, of course, as it always was when the Board of Governors met to assess the performance of a new Head – how were the boys reacting to the change, and how discipline was being enforced? Well, he couldn't hide the fact that one boy had been inciting rebellion. After all, his Deputy, Brother Campion, would be at the meeting, and to withold that information from the Board would make him appear disingenuous. Disingenuous and weak. And he wasn't weak.

No, he certainly wasn't weak. A weaker man might have ignored the situation, hoping that the perpetrator might get bored and go away. But not him. He'd met this situation head on. He was here to enforce discipline and he wouldn't shirk his duty. It was vital that the boys see him as a man who wouldn't be trifled with. Let one of them get away with this type of insubordination and the entire school might slip from his grasp. A demonstration was needed, a demonstration of power. Before the Board convened on Friday he'd demonstrate that he was in absolute control of the situation.

McCaffery had disappointed him. He'd been sure of his strategy in catching the producer of those vile posters. He had been certain that he could cajole or frighten McCaffery into betraying the culprit. But you could never tell with the working classes. They were always apt to bite the hand that fed them. He felt something approaching shame as he thought of his behaviour towards McCaffery. He had lost control the last time that boy had been in his office, and had shown the extent to which those posters had affected him. In doing so he had exposed the fact that whoever was responsible for producing them had achieved his purpose. McCaffery now knew this, and if McCaffery knew, others would know also. He couldn't accept that. Let them know that one act of defiance had struck home and the doors would be open for full scale rebellion.

McCaffery would have to go. For the good of the school, McCaffery would have to go. The posters were no trivial act of revolt, and it was crucial that they be met with no trivial punishment. A boy would be expelled for producing those posters, and if the actual perpetrator did not come forward, that boy would be McCaffery. Clearly, McCaffery's silence implicated him in the crime. His continued silence, even after a beating, showed that he was in fear of an even greater punishment should the real culprit be revealed. It could mean only one thing – McCaffery knew who it was. Knew and refused to tell.

Yes, McCaffery would have to go, and in going any tales of the Head's outburst would go with him. Justice would have been done and, most importantly, discipline would have been restored. Of course, the boy's parents might object, might even raise a fuss, but he'd deal with that as it arose.

He'd considered McCaffery's background carefully– father a factory worker in Duggin, mother a housewife with a total of seven children, all accommodated in a rental unit on a housing estate. Expulsion may have been more difficult if the culprit had had greater social status, but as it was, McCaffery would merely be returning to the station most appropriate for one of his class. His presence in Meadowlands was, after all, an anomaly. Occasionally the working classes would produce a gifted individual, and for some misguided reason, probably based on the philosophy of that Labour Party oaf Harold Wilson, schools like Meadowlands were obliged to allow them in. But there was no denying that a student like McCaffery was an aberration, and in the natural order of things aberrations had a way of correcting themselves. This was a case in point.

Yes, that was the way out of this mess, McCaffery would have to go. The Head relaxed back into his chair, comfortable now that a decision had been made. It was the sensible, logical way to proceed. Order would have been restored, and he would have demonstrated to the boys, and to the Board of Governors, that he would brook no dissent under his leadership. It would be good for the school, and, in the long run, it may even be good for McCaffery himself. After all, hadn't the boy shown an unwillingness, or inability, to conduct himself properly in more privileged society?

The Head's eyes swam back into focus. He'd call a staff meeting and announce his decision. He turned his gaze from the wall to a

289

sheaf of papers on his desk. The crucifix looked down on him, ignored.

The teachers faced each other across the long table in the Conference Room, the Brothers on one side, the lay teachers on the other. They said nothing as they waited for the Head. Only the smokers had anything to say, and that just the reciprocal offer of cigarettes and lights. Something was up, they all knew that, and they were tense with anticipation of it. Each one of them, in his own way, was still a schoolboy in the presence of this headmaster.

The Head entered the room, brisk and determined, and took his place, standing at the head of the table. He glanced briefly down the seated ranks and made a sign of the cross. Chairs scraped back, coffee cups teetered, cigarettes were jammed into ash trays, and plumes of rapidly exhaled smoke blew across the table as the teachers scrambled to their feet. He had them all at an immediate disadvantage. The prayer over, he said "Sit!" and they sat like children attending their first class in the Big School.

"Gentlemen, Fellow Brothers," he began, "I have called this meeting to inform you of my decision concerning the boy who has been making the blasphemous and obscene graphic displays we have all witnessed over the past several days.

"The boy?" said Fatty Gruntle, his piggy face breaking into a malicious grin. "You mean you've found him?"

The Head ignored him. "This boy represents the very worst in the nature of adolescence. He is a cancer. His influence spreads and multiplies among the impressionable students of this school. He sows seeds of rebellion that if allowed to flourish threaten to undermine the very Christian values on which our community is based. His poison threatens to infect not only the body of our society but its soul. And like a cancer, he must be cut from the body he seeks to destroy – cut from it, isolated, and expelled."

"Excuse me Brother, have you identified the boy in question?" Brother Campion was trying not to look like Fatty Gruntle, but couldn't stop himself from gloating.

"I have identified the boy largely responsible for the continuation of these acts."

"And may we know who it is?"

"It is a Duggin boy. That, I think you will agree is hardly surprising. That it is a boy from the X-Stream is both surprising and regrettable."

"And his name?"

"His name is Sean McCaffery."

"Impossible!"

The Head looked hard at Ben Gibbs.

"It is not impossible Mr. Gibbs, nor, if you leave behind your proletarian prejudices, is it improbable.

"But I know McCaffery, Brother."

"And I know him too!" spat Brother Campion. "A dirty little boy. A very dirty little boy."

"A sacrilegious heathen," shouted Brother Jerome. "I might have guessed it was him. He's been nothing but trouble in my classes – questioning everything I have to say."

Gladys Hardy rolled his eyes, but there was a smirk on his face that grew as Fatty Gruntle waded back into the fray.

"A Duggin Boy! I knew it had to be one of those louts. And now I think of it, I saw McCaffery in front of the poster I took from the toilets. The other boys were laughing at it, but McCaffery wasn't and now we know why. Poison! You are right Brother Loredano, the whole lot of that Duggin rabble are poison. It was a bad day when we opened our doors to that rabble."

"We must be careful here, Mr. Gruntle," said the Head in a tone that managed to be both admonitory and supportive. "We must not tar all the Duggin boys with the same brush. Some may do well despite the limitations of their upbringing."

Ben Gibbs almost pounded the table. "Do well? What do you mean do well? I can tell you that McCaffery is streets ahead of his peers in my subject, and the school records show that he performs equally well across the board. That boy is the best Oxbridge material we have and I cannot accept that he might have anything to do with this matter. I'm familiar with his style, and those posters do not conform with it in the slightest."

"I agree entirely with Mr. Gibbs," said Gladys, still smirking.

The Head leaned forward across the table, glaring at Ben and Gladys.

"There may be Oxbridge candidates in Duggin, Mr. Gibbs, but we both know that Oxbridge scholars require more than just a sound academic background, do we not? Social considerations are at least as important. McCaffery may have brains, but he lacks entirely the other attributes necessary to an Oxbridge scholar. Yes the boy is clever, but that is precisely the reason he must be removed from this school. His actions cannot be considered mere schoolboy pranks. They have been carefully executed acts of sedition. The sacrilegious displays, and his impertinent questioning of Brother Jerome's statements of faith, are not just the exhibitionist rants of a juvenile poseur, they go much deeper. They strike at our fundamental beliefs and mock our Christian code. So, Mr. Gibbs, I would advise that if you choose to champion heretics, and seek to elevate the slum-dwellers of Duggin above their natural plane, you might also consider furthering your career in the penal training camps that masquerade as schools in that vicinity."

Ben was shocked into silence. Shocked at the naked bigotry of the man. Shocked that for a second he was almost moved to violence – to slap that man hard in the face. And shocked, also, that the threat of dismissal should fill him with such unexpected fear. He looked with disgust at the Head and then averted his gaze. The Head counted this a victory.

But Gladys wasn't letting it go at that. "What evidence do you have that McCaffery is responsible?" he asked.

The smirk on his boyish face touched a raw nerve in the Head, and he almost reached for his cane.

"Enough to satisfy me, Mr. Hardy," was all he said.

"And me also," said Brother Campion. "We don't want any dirty boys in this school. I will not have any dirty boys in this school."

Brother Jerome nodded, and the other Brothers put on their monk's faces, unreadable. Only Brother Lundy looked distinctly troubled.

"I must admit surprise that it might be McCaffery," he said. "He always seemed a rather timid child – not really the stuff of which rebels are made. Just last week he refused to join his fellows in an act of defiance in the Dining Hall. More from cowardice, I believe, than anything else. Frankly, I'm surprised he'd have the nerve to do what has been done."

The Head tried to keep irritation out of his voice, but there was an edge to his words that promised a hard time for Brother Lundy later on in the privacy of the Brothers' House. He was not prepared to brook any dissention in the ranks - there would be solidarity among the Brothers while he was telling them what to think.

"It would seem you have fallen for a ploy, Brother Lundy. You forget that McCaffery is clever. Clever, artful and sly. If he wished to hide the fact that he was responsible for the greater crimes of desecration, blasphemy and sedition, he would be unlikely to draw attention to himself by participating in some minor revolt concerning the saying of Grace. Rather, McCaffery's display of obedience was a pantomime to dissuade us of his culpability with respect to his acts of vandalism and his manufacture of obscenities."

Brother Lundy looked surprised, but the Head just smirked at him, the slash in his face opening and lifting at the corners.

"I am, of course, familiar with the nature of the Dining Hall revolt, Brother Lundy. Mr. Gruntle informed me of McCaffery's apparent refusal to participate in it. That is why I chose McCaffery to assist me in discovering the rebel among us."

Gladys Hardy couldn't help thinking that the more elaborate the Head's mode of speech the less he believed anything he had to say.

"Assist you?" he asked. "Assist you how?"

"Yes, assist me Mr. Hardy. As you should be aware from your own very recent experiences as a schoolboy, all schoolboys are braggarts, and they brag most vociferously about flaunting authority. I asked McCaffery to tell me who had been boasting about the posters and he has steadfastly refused to do so. That in itself is enough to implicate him in the matter."

"Nonsense!" cried Gladys, forgetting entirely his place on the lower rungs of the ladder. "Schoolboys protect each other from authority, and if they don't their peers make sure they live to regret it. I'm not surprised that McCaffery told you nothing."

"Hold your tongue Mr. Hardy!" spat the Head, looking as if he might swipe his hand the arts master's face. "McCaffery may be clever enough to deceive you, but he is no match for me."

But Gladys wasn't ready to back down. "McCaffery did not make those posters," he insisted. "Work of that quality is far beyond him."

"Work? Quality? What are you talking about Mr. Hardy? Filth you mean. Perversion." The Head was almost shouting into Gladys's face, but then he dropped his voice to a tone of cynical contempt. "And have you not considered that McCaffery might have had an accomplice - someone outside of this school? Someone with the talents that you seem so inclined to admire?"

Gladys could say nothing to this.

"No, Mr. Hardy, I see you haven't considered that possibility – that certainty, as I believe it is. I am convinced that McCaffery is responsible for these actions, even if he never touched brush to paper. At worst he is entirely responsible for these acts of rebellion; at best he is an accessory. Either way the law requires his expulsion."

Ben Gibbs couldn't hold himself back any longer. "The Law?" he said. "What Law? This isn't a criminal investigation. Good Christ Brother, one investigation of that type is quite enough right now! This is about boys playing pranks; childish adolescent pranks. What's this talk about the Law?"

The Head turned the full force of his contempt against Ben. His voice was calm, but spiked with malice.

"While in this school, Mr.Gibbs, you will refrain from taking the name of our Lord God in vain. And since you seem to have forgotten the Commandments, I will remind you of the Fifth - Thou shalt honour thy father and thy mother. God's Law, Mr.Gibbs, that's the Law I am talking about, the code by which we regulate our lives. And while the boys are in my school I stand in the place of their fathers, even for those who may not know, or may not care, who their real fathers are."

Fatty Gruntle snorted in a sycophantic piggy way, and his lips broke in a blubbery grin, but the Head was not joking, and a single glance knocked the smirk clean off his face.

"Clever boys like McCaffery, Mr.Gibbs, begin to feel themselves above the law. They believe that the maintenance of a certain academic standing gives them the right to adopt behaviours, and to disseminate ideas, that are contrary to our catechism. They bend the rules Mr.Gibbs. They push against our resistance believing, in their arrogance, that it is they who are resisting. Corporal punishment is often effective in beating a recalcitrant individual back into line, but when that individual pushes beyond the limits of our tolerance, there is no alternative but to eject him from our society. McCaffery may believe that his university prospects protect him against expulsion, but it is my view that this school can do with one less student on its Honour Role if the longer term result is to maintain and strengthen the Christian principles on which Meadowlands is founded."

"Hear, hear," spouted Fatty Gruntle in an attempt to re-ingratiate himself.

Ben Gibbs looked deeply sad. Gladys Hardy wore an enigmatic smile.

"I intend to make an example of McCaffery," continued the Head.

"A sacrifice," muttered Ben.

"I will prove to the boys of this school, and to their parents, that when I set out to enforce discipline I will use the strongest measures available to achieve my goal. No boy will be above the law. McCaffery's expulsion will make that quite clear."

"When and how do you intend to effect this expulsion, Brother?" asked Gladys.

"Is the boy to be given no chance at making amends?" asked Ben, pleading now rather than protesting.

After a few seconds the Head spoke directly to Ben, ignoring Gladys entirely.

"I am not an unreasonable man Mr. Gibbs. Nor am I uncharitable. Charity, as you know, is both the imperative and mainstay of my order."

The enigmatic smile on Gladys's face almost twisted into a full-blown grin. Ben, on the other hand, sensing some potential breach in intransigence, tried hard to swallow his disgust.

The Head continued. "At tomorrow's assembly I will ask that the boy responsible for the desecration of our patrons' statue, and the production of the posters, step forward. I will ask him to admit his guilt, make a public apology to me, his teachers, and his fellow students, and face the disciplinary measures that I will then enact. If he does not step forward immediately, I will give the boy until the end of the week to make his confession. If McCaffery comes to me before Friday he will face corporal punishment immediately, followed by a period of suspension. When he returns to school he will undergo weekend detentions until his lost time is made up. If McCaffery fails to come forward by Friday, I will call a special assembly at which I will call him out to face me and the school. I will subject him to a public thrashing after which his expulsion from Meadowlands will be immediate and irrevocable. In the meantime, no member of this staff will give any indication to McCaffery of his position, do I make myself clear."

"Very well," sighed Ben, using one of those curious phrases that mean just the opposite of what is said.

"Very well," said Gladys, allowing himself to smile out loud.

Chapter 32: Bondage

Sean dripped with fear. It chiseled the lines of his face. It clouded his eyes. He looked sick and drawn and weary. His friends treated him with a distant sympathy, but stayed well away. They believed he had the wild shites, and no one was going to risk catching a dose of the trots. At morning break, he sat on his own in a corner of the school-yard and fed his anxiety with the snippets of conversation that drifted past him.

-Got to be one of us hasn't it. I mean what other school wears such a poxy-coloured blazer?

-Maybe the murderer nicked the blazer.

-Oh yeah? Know anyone missing one do you Sherlock?

-Cops'll have covered that idea anyway.

-Yeah, they're looking for a psycho with really bad taste.

-No, they're too bloody stupid.

-And you're not?

-No I'm not. If I were a cop, I wouldn't be interviewing all the kids on the walk, I'd be interviewing everyone else.

-Oooooh Brilliant! You'd interview everyone who wasn't in Sandcaster on Saturday? Genius!

-Yeah. You'd do well in the force. Chief Inspector in no time.

-Chief Inspector Mong.

-Your Honour, I present evidence that the accused bumped off the old biddy in Sandcaster while he was out shopping with his mam in Smellins.

-You don't get it do you?

-Obviously not. Enlighten us, dickhead.

-Think about it. Who's to say that the Meadowlands boys on the walk were the only Meadowlands boys in Sandcaster on Saturday?

...........Silence.

Sean let his head fall into his hands.

It was the same at lunch-time. Sean couldn't face the dining hall, and no-one blamed him. Eating school dinners when you had bad guts was just asking for it. He sloped away to the corner of the school-yard and listened in again on his class mates.

-They've started with the Upper Sixth.

-I thought the Head told them to start with first years.

-Both brilliant ideas. The killer's supposed to be about fourteen so get everyone else out of the way first.

-Logical isn't it?

-Yeah, process of elimination.

-I'm surprised they didn't start with Chuck Bones, he was wearing a purple sweater on the walk.

-Yeah, and a hundred foot up on the Tornado you could easy mistake him for a teenager.

-Course you could. Lot's of fourteen year olds are six foot five.

-With beards.

-Anyway, they'll get round to us soon enough.

-Got anything to tell them?

-Yeah. Shit-faced Shaughnessy did it.

-Be great if he actually did do it wouldn't it?

-Bring the school down a peg or two?

-The place for Catholic values.

-Maybe the old girl was a Protestant. Killing Proddie-Dogs isn't a sin is it?

-The IRA don't think so, and they're all good Catholics.

-There you go then.

Sean walked a tightrope for the rest of the day. Had anyone seen him in Sandcaster? Would anyone identify him from the indentikit picture? It seemed impossible that they wouldn't. He almost sagged against the school gates as he put the first day of police interviews behind him. But relief was short-lived. As he rounded the curve of Cack Alley, there, lounging against the wall where he'd thrashed Fearon (oh, if only he hadn't!) was Flint.

"Ahhhh, me old mate Tarzan," he said, as he stood in the centre of the path, blocking Sean's way.

"Now what have you got for me today then?"

"For God's sake don't call me that!" hissed Sean. "Don't you understand what's going on? Can't you see how serious this is? The Police have been at Meadowlands all day looking for me. They know one of us did it. If you go mouthing off I've had it."

Flint smiled.

"And what's that got to do with me Tarzan? I don't go to Meadowlands do I? They aren't looking for me are they? They're looking for one of you poxy grammar grubs aren't they? Makes a change that, doesn't it?" He seemed taken by this observation, and the grin changed from malice to real pleasure. "Yeah, makes a real change that does. About time you clever bastards got to see what we've got to put up with from the pigs."

He made it sound like police investigations were a daily fixture at the Secondary Modern, and Sean realized for the first time that he really didn't know what went on at Long Lane, or Borstal Bundy's, or even at the Saint Lawrence Comp where his oldest brother had limped through his teenaged schooling.

"Anyway,' continued Flint, "I don't give a monkey's about the pigs, I just want the rest of the money you owe me, so hand it over Tarzan. Two pound fifty's my share, so you still owe me a sheet and a half."

He took a packet of cigarettes from his pocket, extracted one and threw the empty carton to the ground. He struck a match, sucked a mouthful of smoke and blew it into Sean's face.

"I don't have any money," choked Sean. "I gave you all I had yesterday. The others haven't paid up yet."

Flint took another lungful of smoke, leaned forward and cupped Sean's chin in his hand, bringing his face just inches from Sean's. His grip tightened as Sean tried to shake him off.

"Now you listen here Tarzan," he said, and the smoke spewed from his mouth and into Sean's so that he almost retched with the filth of it. "I'm just having my last smoke here, and when this is done there's none left. I don't like that Tarzan. I don't like that one bit. I like my smokes, so you better make sure you hand over the lolly you owe me because I get very nasty if I don't get my smokes. Understand?"

He took another long drag at the cigarette so that its tip glowed red. He brought it towards Sean's eye, fingers digging into his face

301

so that he couldn't move his head. Sean felt the burning heat less than an inch from his closed eyelid.

"I haven't got the money," wailed Sean. "I won't get it till the weekend when I go to my other gran's house in Liverpool. You'll have to wait."

The cigarette stayed where it was.

"Well if you can't get me the dosh, you're going to have to get me the smokes aren't you Tarzan? Your dad likes his cigs doesn't he? So I reckon he must have a stash somewhere in your house. You bring me some cigs here tomorrow Tarzan, or I'm warning you, I won't turn a blind eye to it, understand?"

Flint touched Sean's forehead with the end of his cigarette just above the eyebrow. Sean screamed. Christ, that could have been his eye! Tomorrow it would be. He knew that Flint was capable of carrying out his threat. He'd have to find the cigarettes or this fucking psycho would blind him.

Flint dropped the butt and ground it with his shoe. He still held Sean's face in one hand, but more gently now. He tapped his cheek lightly with his other hand. "Now you run along home and get Flinty's smokes from daddy. I'll see you tomorrow, same time same place. OK Tarzan?"

Sean nodded, unable to speak through the welter of fear. He turned towards home, more afraid than he'd ever been. The threat of violence terrified him, but worse was the realization that from now on he would have to do whatever Flint told him to do. He was under the control of a complete maniac.

Stealing the cigs wasn't going to be easy. The tiny house was packed with bodies; nine people crammed into the kitchen and living room so that the chances of being alone to do a bit of thieving were going to be few, and the periods brief.

He tried to keep an eye on his dad without drawing attention to himself, looking for some opportunity to filch from his packet of Woodbines when he laid it down. But his dad was a chain-smoker, and wherever he went he took his smokes with him. Going to the kitchen for a cup of tea, climbing the stairs to take a piss, walking the few steps from chair to window to gaze into the street, always the packet of cigarettes went with him as if they were necessary to his survival rather than promoting the opposite.

It drove Sean half mad to watch the obsessive behaviour. He'd seen it every day of his life without thinking about it, but now, when he needed to take notice, it shredded his nerves and raised his anxiety to an almost unbearable level. "Put the damned things down!" he wanted to yell. "What's wrong with you? Do you think they're going to walk away on their own? Do you think in a stinking pit this small you're going to lose them? What's up with you, you stupid bastard, do you think someone's going to steal them.........?"

"Something wrong with you?"

His dad glared at him, smoke billowing from his mouth and nostrils.

"I'm alright."

"Then keep your bloody head still."

"Language Patrick," said his mum.

"Well he's sitting there wagging his head like a bloody great dog."

"Language Patrick!"

"Wagging his head like a bloody great dog and following me around. I tell you, there's something not right with that lad."

"Sean, keep you head still."

"I'm off to do my homework."

303

And he went upstairs to his bedroom carrying a load of books. The stairs ended on a small landing. To the right was the girls' bedroom with the bathroom facing it. To the left was the boys' bedroom, with the parents' room opposite.

Sean went into his bedroom and ranged the books on the floor. He was about to take his English homework up to his top bunk when he paused. Downstairs, the first bars of the Coronation Street theme tune were sounding from the television. That meant everyone would be in the front room for at least the next ten minutes, transfixed with the doings of Ena Sharples, Albert Tatlock and Ken Barlow. Damn it, he thought, the kitchen will be empty and the old bastard might have left some smokes in there.

He was on the point of going downstairs again, pretending to get a pencil from the kitchen, when he paused in front of his parents' room. The door was closed. None of the boys ever went in there. It was a dark place, with a dark adult muskiness about it. A place of dark doings in the night that Sean tried to shut from his ears. But right now it might be the only place he'd find what he needed.

He stood tense outside the door, straining his ears, listening for the vaguest hint that any of his family might be doing something other than giving their full attention to the working class lives unfolding in black and white on the television screen. All he could hear was Albert Tatlock whining to Stan Ogden in the Rover's Return.

He cracked open the bedroom door.....

Bed to the left, mattress waist high, almost filling the small room, wardrobe to the right with doors closed. Window in front hung with netting, casting the room in shadow. That musky, smoky stink in the air, the adult stink he finds so repellent. Beyond the bed a squat dresser. He skips backward, heart battering as he catches

304

sight of himself in the mirror, believing in the half light that there's someone else present. He stands by the door hardly daring to go further, but the thought of that cigarette, so close to his eye, drives him on. The wardrobe is nearest, just one step away, and he pulls at the door handle.

So many times he's heard that squeak! So many times that it has become just another of the myriad sounds he filters every minute from his perceptions of the house. But now it's like a siren. He's frozen, still clutching the handle, waiting to be caught. He sees himself in the mirror again – the image of guilt-stricken terror. But no one comes. He listens. The rocky romance between Elsie Tanner and Len Fairclough has them rapt.

Guilt deepens as he peers into the wardrobe. There's his father's one *good* suit, an overcoat and an old sports jacket he's never seen him wear. On his mother's side hangs a dress she's worn just once, at Christmas and two other limp frocks looking all the more drab beside it. He pauses an instant then plunges his hands into the overcoat pocket. Nothing! He tries the other pocket. Nothing! Then the suit and the sports jacket.....nothing!

He leaves the door ajar and moves to the dresser. The first draw is full of his mother's underwear and he recoils from it, shocked and disgusted. The other drawers are full of socks, vests, old trousers and skirts, but no damned cigarettes. That leaves the long narrow drawer in the middle. It's hard to open. He tugs on it, jiggling it from side to side, getting it stuck as he pulls it out. He tugs harder, and for an instant of near disaster it slips free of its track, almost landing in his lap. He thrusts it back into place, frantic at the thought of the terrible, terrible consequences if he were to leave behind any sign of his intrusion. He edges it back into place, slowly, carefully, all the while scanning the contents:

-a hair-net.

-a tangled coil of imitation gold necklace.

-a Ronson lighter.

-a collection of plastic pens.

- a white prayer book with a picture of the Virgin Mary on the front.

- And next to it - next to the prayer book for God's sake – a packet of Johnnies!

His father uses Johnnies. He uses Johnnies and yet he's still got seven bloody kids. My God, he must be at it every fucking night! Everything becomes horribly clear. No wonder he always stands outside the sacristy doors on Sunday. No wonder he never takes communion – he'd be struck by lightning if he did. How can he even think of entering the church when he's doing it every night? Doing it, wearing Johnnies, for Christ's sake. Sean is horror-struck.

-And there's still no cigarettes!

Wohnk, wohnk, wohnk, wonhk, WOHHHHHHHNNNNNKK!!!!

The five tone theme marks the Coronation Street commercial break - the commercial break and the rush to the toilet - Jesus! He leaps from the dresser, slams shut the door of the wardrobe, and is opening the door of his bedroom just as Colin, first in line, leaps up the stairs.

Sean tries to breathe normally, but he's labouring after a sprint. He opens a book, not knowing if it's right side up, and stares through it at a kaleidoscopic vision of misery – shifting images of Johnny bags, women's knickers, his father's hands cradling his cigarettes, cradling his.......Oh God the thought of it!!.....And his mother's face so innocent...... so innocent and yet....

And most of all there's Flint.

306

Flint laughing.

Flint laughing and making all this happen.

Just because he can.

Chapter 33: Midnight Rambler

He'd gone through hell to steal the Woodbines. He'd lain awake for half the night waiting for the noises of the house to subside. Waiting for the absolute certainty that his creeping downstairs would not be heard by anyone. His brothers had come into the bedroom one by one, silent except for the tossing aside of clothes and the gathering of bedsheets around them. And one by one they'd descended into the sleep. Relaxed. Unworried. Sean had hated them for that.

His mother had done her usual check on the girls, and the light in her bedroom had stayed on until the heavier tread on the stairs had told him that his father, last to retire, was on his way. A piss and a fart in the toilet, the yank on the chain careless of who might be sleeping, and then muttered words before the light goes off. Muttered words seeping into Sean's room as he strains his ears for the sound of silence. Muttered words then the sound of a drawer sliding open. It's a familiar sound now. He knows what's going on. He sees him reaching for the packet, imagines him rolling on that disgusting thing, and then...... But he's forced to listen to the noises – to hear them snuffling and grunting like a pair of pigs, hearing it right up to the final visit to the toilet and the last thundering piss that marks the end of the whole dirty business. And he lies there for two more hours, sickened and furious and terribly afraid, until the fragile silence solidifies at last.

He'd sneaked down the stairs in darkness, on tip-toe, hands pressed against the walls of the stairway to lift his weight off the steps, counting them to avoid stepping on those two creaking boards that might give him away, every brush of toe sounding in his ears like the crash of cymbals. He'd opened the door to the living room, pushing and pulling at the same time, easing the catch free millimeter by millimeter, never thinking in his guilt that he could easily have made up a reasonable excuse for wandering the house like this in the early hours of the morning.

He'd searched the front room in darkness, feeling the greasy arms of his father's chair – nothing! Running fingertips across the smooth surface of the sideboard – nothing! Tapping gingerly between the brass and porcelain ornaments on the mantelpiece – still nothing!

That left the kitchen, and if there were none there he was done for. He touched the burn on his forehead, remembered the white hot tip of the cigarette, and imagined how much worse the agony if it had been stubbed in his eye. And he knew Flint would do it. If anyone was capable of such a thing, it was Flint. He had to find those cigarettes!

He turned on the light in the kitchen, realizing at last that if he were caught, the darkness would only call attention to his guilt. There were no cigarettes in the kitchen. None on the table, none on the countertop next to the sink, none in any of the places where his father might have put them down. He started looking in stupid places – in the cutlery draw, under the sink next to the bucket of stinking nappies, in the cupboard with the dishes, in the pantry.....

Thank you God! Oh thank you God - they were in the pantry! In the bloody pantry for Christ's sake, tucked away on the top shelf. A week's supply of Woodbines - over a hundred of them - stacked in packets of twenty, each one in its shiny plastic wrapper. Each one unopened.

Shit! The flush of relief gave way to a new wave of fear. How could he steal a few cigs from an unopened packet? They were stored there because they were unopened. If he broke the seal it would be obvious he'd been thieving. But could he risk taking a whole packet? Did his dad keep count? There were seven of them. Would he miss one? He stood there reaching out, touching the boxes, drawing back, reaching out again, unable to decide. Three times he picked up a packet, and three times he put it back again. But did he have any choice? There never seemed to be any choices! He reached out again, hearing Flint roaring Tarzan! down the length of Cack Alley.

He grabbed a box, jammed it into his underpants, and crept back to bed knowing, just knowing that this could only lead to disaster. But what else could he do?

He hadn't slept. All night the sharp edges of the box had gouged the flesh of his groin, but he hadn't dared to hide them anywhere else. It was the only secure place he could think of. Probing hands might find something hidden under his pillow; his mother might move his clothes and find the cigarettes in his pocket; she might shake him from bed in the morning and find them among the bedsheets - there was a whole world of disastrous possibilities. But no hands, none but his own, would ever venture near his crotch.

He'd arisen early, just after his dad had left for the 7.00 am shift at the DIC. He'd washed and dressed and eaten breakfast with the packet still stowed in his underpants, praying that any tell tale

310

bump might be mistaken by his mother for something unmentionable. His heart had stopped as she'd gone to the pantry for his cornflakes, and he'd eaten them dry-mouthed, pretending, as he'd done every hour since that moment of insanity on the Tornado, that this was just a normal day.

He'd made some weak excuse to leave the house early, anxious to be away from the to-ing and fro-ing between pantry and table as the rest of the kids dragged themselves downstairs. He'd been almost at the entry to Cack Alley when the shout stopped his blood.

"Sean!!"

His mother's voice. Shrill with an edge of panic. Something wrong. Something very, very wrong.

"Sean!!!!!!!"

Chapter 34: Into the DIC

Sean!!!

It could be about only one thing. Suddenly, that small carton in his crotch swelled to the size of a suitcase. She'd see right away that he'd pinched the Woodbines. She'd reach right in and wave them in his face. He was caught! Christ, what an idiot! How could he have thought he'd get away with it? He wanted to ignore her, to keep on going like he'd never heard, but already he'd responded – the broken step, the split second of hesitation that's impossible to hide. If he turned into Cack Alley now it would be to admit his guilt. He'd spend all day at school just delaying the inevitable. It was no use. He turned around, miserable, defeated and suddenly weary from the long hours of sleeplessness.

His mother was out in the street, still wearing her dressing gown, face drawn in a mixture of desperation and defiance, casting glances between the neighbours' windows and the safety of her front door. One hand was on the privet bush as if to wrap it around herself, the other was waving a package above her head.

"Sean!" she called "Sean, come here right now!"

He turned back, dragging himself along, his mind looking for excuses that couldn't be found.

"I'm sorry love," she began, "I know you've got that physics thing with your friends before school this morning, but your dad's gone without his lunch and I've not the time to take it to him, what with getting the girls ready and everything. Would you drop it at the gates for him when you go by the DIC? It shouldn't take you a minute. Just tell the man it's for Patrick McCaffery. And here's sixpence for yourself love. And now I've got to get in before the neighbours see me. Tara love, and thanks."

And then she was gone, leaving Sean shaking with relief. Relief and hatred for that stinking piece of shit who had brought him to this. Every step towards the DIC he imagined the ways he'd like to torture Flint to death.

The main entrance to the DIC was guarded by a little man in a black uniform who pressed buttons to raise and lower a barrier as lorries passed in and out of the factory. The little man spent his days inside a small brick hut with large windows on all sides so that he could keep an eye on the lorries and on the workers as they clocked on and off their shifts. Solly's Scrap Metals paid good money for refined copper and never asked any questions, so the little man had his work cut out for him.

The little man scowled at Sean as he tapped on the window that fronted the main street. He was used to kids pressing their faces on the glass, leaving trails of spit and snot, and then running off after giving him the V-sign. Only when Sean stood his ground and waved the package of sandwiches did the man indicate that he should come to the door on the other side of the barrier.

"So, what can I do for you then cock?" he asked, and Sean was surprised to see him smile. It was as if he wore a different face when approached on his own terms. Sean explained his errand, and the little man swelled with importance as he went back into his hut and used the telephone with slow deliberation.

"Foreman'll be out in a tick old cock," said the little man after putting down the phone. "He'll sort you out. Meadowlands lad are you?"

Sean nodded. He could tell that the little man wanted to chat, but he was in no mood for it himself. His silence didn't deter the little man at all.

"Meadowlands eh? Thought so by the purple blazer. Must be a bright one then, eh? Not like the yobs from the Secondary Modern. Bunch of hooligans that lot. Yobos and hooligans. Bring back the birch, that's what I say. The birch and a couple of years of National Service, that'd cure 'em. Wouldn't be so keen on spitting on my windows if it meant getting the skin flayed from their arses."

Sean nodded, saying nothing. He'd heard it all before - the instant solution for Duggin's delinquency - beat the shit out of the hooligans and put them in the army. If that meant they'd think twice about spitting on windows, who cared what other effects it might have?

The little man rabbited on while Sean gazed out over the vast space of the DIC, nodding politely as he watched the lorries unloading the copper bars onto a conveyor that fed them into the gaping mouth of the factory. The factory swallowed them up, and somewhere in its guts his dad slogged away to fashion the wire that was shit out the other end.

"Ah, here's Harry Marshall, your dad's foreman," said the little man. "Hey Harry, yon one's Patrick McCaffery's lad from the Grammar School. Patrick went out without his butties this morning and yon one's brought them from his mam."

Harry Marshall was a thickset man with a broad face fringed all around by a short ginger beard below and curly ginger hair on top. He looked tough, right down to the ginger hairs sprouting from the backs of his fingers. It was as if the factory had got into his blood and he was sprouting copper. His white foreman's coat was streaked with oil, and thick clumps of oil clung to the steel toe-caps of his boots. He looked the type of man you wouldn't want to mess around with – the type the management needed to take charge of equally tough characters who didn't like being told what to do. The grim face split into the approximation of a smile, and Sean was almost surprised to see that his teeth weren't chiseled from copper ingots.

"Brought Paddy's butties have you? Well he'll be glad of them the way your dad works - not like most of the idle bastards in here. Come on then, I'll take you to him."

Sean was about to protest, but Harry Marshall had turned his back and was striding into the yard. Sean had no choice but to follow him, skirting the mud and the oil-drenched puddles that Harry ploughed through on his way to the factory entrance. How could he tell him that this was a huge mistake, that this was going to be mortifying for both of them? Harry Marshall probably thought that Sean came from a normal family where father and son might actually speak to each other occasionally. But he didn't dare open his mouth as Harry threw wide the steel door and ushered him inside.

The noise split his head. The air tasted as if he were chewing on his father's overalls. His breath stopped. And when he gasped again he felt the dirt coating his mouth and his throat and his lungs. He wanted to spit with every breath, to rid himself of the filth. He followed Harry Marshall in the half-light down a narrow aisle

315

between the labourers at work. They glanced briefly at the strange sight of a blazer-clad schoolboy in this hell for men before focusing back on the machines that with a moment's inattention might sever a hand or an arm.

Harry led him to a glass cubicle in the middle of the chaos, and shut the door behind him. It made hardly any difference to the noise.

"You wait here my lad," shouted Harry, "and I'll go and get your dad."

He left Sean standing by a beaten up metal desk. Business documents on DIC letterhead were scattered beneath copies of the Sun and Daily Mirror open at the sports pages. From the cubicle, Sean could see line upon line of machines, radiating in all directions, as if spinning copper threads for Harry the spider.

The thought that one day he might get caught in that web terrified him, and Sean looked away from the machines towards the factory roof, as if seeking sunlight. Higher up, the windows of the cubicle were plastered with photos cut from magazines. It took a few seconds to register what he was looking at, and then Sean's faced flamed crimson.

Girls. An exhibition of naked girls. Girls with ballooning breasts. Girls with nipples popping. Girls with legs spread wide. Girls with gashed groins, faces twisted, mouths howling, begging eyes looking deep into his .....begging for what? His heart thundered. He'd never seen anything like this. Playboy, yes, sneaked into school for a gathering in the toilets, boys hollering and hooting at the vaguest hint of pubic hair. But this was something horribly different. What type of girl could allow herself being photographed doing that? How could anyone possibly force them?

And is that what it really looked like - that gaping wound? Is that what Paula Yates would look like? It wasn't possible.

He felt dizzy and repulsed. Yet somehow he couldn't tear his eyes away. He drank them in, image after image, his head turning back and forth, scanning the naked parade, his cock lifting reflexively, pushing aside the cigarettes in his underpants despite his disgust.

"What the bloody hell is going on here?"

He dropped his eyes to see his father standing in the doorway with Harry Marshall. On top of everything, on top of trespassing in his father's place, he been caught goggling at the pornographic display with a huge lump burgeoning in his trousers. If he could have been cleaved in two, right there and then, he'd rather have met a blunt axe than the look on his father's face.

"Told you I had a surprise for you Paddy. Forgot your sarnies today didn't you? Well your lad's brought them in for you. Thought he might as well see the place at the same time."

"Thought he might what!!!!?..... Are you totally bloody stupid Marshall?"

Sean had never seen his father like this. He'd seen him furious, but never with another adult. And he could hardly believe he was talking like that to his boss. There was something about his dad right now that remembered from early childhood; some fascinating power he'd all but forgotten. Next to him, big Harry Marshall began to look trifling.

"Come on Paddy. Thought you'd be pleased. You never know, the lad might fancy working here some day."

"Fancy working?..........Here?............" It was as if Harry Marshall had suggested Sean might consider a future shoveling shit.

317

Sean had never guessed his dad might despise the DIC as much as he did himself.

"You get him out of her right now Marshall! Bringing a lad into a place like this – what's inside your stupid bloody head? He's got no boots, no gloves, no helmet, no glasses - just like the rest of us, you stupid get. What if a coil broke? What if the lifter dropped a bloody ingot? You get him out of here right now, and never let me see him in here again, understand? And while you're at it you can get that filth off your walls."

And then he was gone, without a word to Sean, and leaving Harry Marshall's face looking like a slapped arse. The foreman gazed after Sean's dad, fists bunched and chest heaving as if he were about to jump him from behind. But then his stance slackened as he thought better of it.

"Come on then son," said Harry. "Let's get you off to school. Your dad's in a bit of a temper today. I reckon it's more than butties your mam's not giving him."

For once, Sean was on his dad's side. He took a deep breath and said, "I'll let him know."

Harry's face dropped. "Just joking old son," he said. "Just a joke. No need to tell your dad. Don't want to get him even more riled up do we? Got a lot of respect for your dad, I have."

He placed a hand on Sean's shoulder and steered him through the factory, tapping on him as they went as if stroking a good little dog. It made Sean's flesh crawl. The funny little man came out of the gatehouse as they approached

"All done then?" he asked. "Dad got his butties and everyone happy?"

"Fuck off Pinkerton," said Harry, and stomped back towards the factory.

318

The little man looked after the retreating back, and spat on the floor. "And what's gotten into him all of a sudden?" he asked. "Line stopped has it? Someone snapped their coil? That's what happens when they put a white coat on one of those buggers - they get to be right bullying bastards."

Sean walked towards the bus stop, unable to suppress an uncomfortable respect for his father. No wonder he was forever hacking and spitting after spending his days in a shit-hole like that. And he wasn't afraid to put bullies like Harry Marshall firmly in their place. As he thought of this, and of the stolen cigarettes gouging away at his groin, he swore to God that he'd kill that bastard Flint the first chance that he got.

Chapter 35: Biting the Hand

"Woodbines! Bleeding Woodbines! I hate bleeding Woodbines!"

"But it's all my dad smokes.

"Well he's a bleeding tosser then isn't he? No bleeding filters. Gob full of baccy every drag. I'm not smoking that shite."

Flint clenched a hand across Sean's face and pushed him up against the wall of Cack Alley.

"Now you get me twenty Benson and Hedges by tomorrow Tarzan. Twenty B and H filter-tipped or I'll rip your face off. Understand?"

Sean twisted free of the grip.

"But how am I supposed to do that? My dad doesn't smoke B and H. No one does. How can I get you B and H when no one smokes them?"

"Gonna have to buy them aren't you? Buy them or nick them. I don't give a monkey's, but just make sure your here with them tomorrow Tarzan, or I'll mark you for life."

And then Flint strode away, leaving Sean shaking with fear and anger and the despair of someone faced with an impossible task. Why was all this happening? Why were so many impossible demands being made on him? How the hell could he steal Benson and Hedges from someone who smoked Woodbines? And how could he find the Poster Boy when no one, absolutely no one in the school, knew who he was? The Head had given him a week, and now almost half of that week had gone.

At assembly that morning the Head had demanded that the culprit step forward, had announced that he knew who it was, had said that the boy would be expelled if he didn't own up. Did that mean he really knew, or was he relying on Sean to find out for him? The Head had given the boy till Friday to make a confession. To confess, take a thrashing and a suspension from the school. If he didn't come forward he'd be booted out. But was all that a bluff? Would he call for Sean tomorrow, or the next day, and try to beat the name out of him before the Friday deadline? How could he beat something out of him that wasn't there? Impossible!

Sean hesitated at the door of his house. There was a commotion going on inside, his dad's voice shouting, and someone else shouting back. That wasn't unusual, but this was louder than normal, and fiercer. He hung onto the door handle, listening anxiously. Was it his visit to the factory with the sandwiches, or was it the cigarettes? Either way, he was dead.

"Don't tell bloody lies to me." Whack! His dad.

"I'm not telling lies!" His brother Fergus.

"I'm not stupid. It's got to be you."

"You are bloody stupid because it's not!"

"Don't you swear at me you thieving bloody bastard." Whack! Whack! Whack!

The cigs then, and Fergus getting the blame. The blame, and one of the rare thrashings administered by his dad.

"Leave him alone Patrick, you've got the girls scared to death." His mum, trying to stop the beating, using the rest of the family as a shield.

"I won't have thieving in this house. I won't have thieving, and I won't have any bloody lying either. I won't have any bloody lying thieves." Whack!

"Then bloody well piss of out of it." Slam!!! Fergus having the last word and putting a door between him and his dad.

"What, you bloody little swine I'll………"

"Patrick! Leave it. I'll talk to him later. Calm down and get your dinner. Maybe we didn't count them right."

"We? What do you mean we? It's your job to do the shopping and keep your eye on things, like it's your job to make sure I have my lunch. Sending that other bugger into the factory like that, what the hell did you think you were up to? Don't you think I've got enough on my plate as it is?"

The newfound respect for this father evaporated, the miserable bastard. He was never wrong. It was always his mother's fault. His dad worked his shifts and after that everything else was fetch me carry me. Even forgetting his sandwiches was somehow his mother's fault.

Sean knew what would happen next. His mother would talk with Fergus and let him use all the foul language he liked about his dad until he got it out of his system. Then she'd stand between the two of them, literally if need be, as they inhabited the same tiny hovel, until the tempers on each side cooled. That might take days or weeks, but no matter how long it took, there'd be another coil of tension in the house that would never disappear.

And it was his fault. The battering his brother had just received was his fault. Fergus was the only one beside his father who smoked. It was a secret habit that everyone knew about, Fergus sneaking off to Cack Alley for a few draws of Park Drive - lungbullets sold in packs of five to the teenage smoker. He fooled no one,

322

coming back stinking of rough tobacco. And when his father was in a rare good mood he might even make a joke about it. But there'd be no more joking from now on. His dad thought that Fergus was a thief, and Sean wasn't going to own up. How could he? He had no excuse for the thieving. He didn't smoke. So there'd be questions. Questions he couldn't answer.

"Stuck to the handle are you?" Colin had come up behind him, home from his job as apprentice plumber. "I can fix that you know," he said, reaching for a chisel in his tool belt

"Dad's in on of his tempers. He's just been having a go at Fergus."

"So, what's new? Now get out of my way, I'm starving.

They went in together, his mum smiling at both of them and saying hello as if nothing had just happened, his dad sitting down to a plate of sausage and mash and looking as if he'd been served dog shit. He glanced at Sean with even deeper disgust as he entered the kitchen. Sean didn't wait for any trouble, passing through without a word to join Keiran and the girls watching the Flintstones on TV.

His mum followed, allowing the weight of her worries to fall into her face as she left her husband to his meal. She gestured with a finger, calling Sean silently away from the other kids. She bent down to whisper, worry straining the lines around her eyes.

"Listen love," she said, "your dad's had a bad day at work and it's best if we keep the house quiet tonight. I know you're hungry and you want your tea, but it'd be better if you stayed out from under his feet for a while. Would you mind going to your gran's for your dinner? She'll give you a buttie to get you along. Your dad's going back into the DIC for a split shift in a couple of hours, so you can come back then. Is that all right love?"

His breath, held in expectation of the worst, sighed through clenched teeth. His mum began to plead with him.

"I'm sorry love it's just that..........."

"It's OK......OK....." he said "I'll go out the front door. See you later."

She leaned forward to kiss him on the cheek, but he backed away. Either way he was Judas.

Sean's gran led him into the parlour, her rough hand gentle on his shoulder.

"So your dad's in one of his tempers is he? Been giving you a hard time has he?"

"He's always in one of his tempers. And he always gives everyone a hard time, the bastard."

Sean's gran eased herself into the ragged armchair by the fireplace as Sean flopped onto daft Albert's couch. She gave him a stony look as she lit up a Woodbine and sucked in a lungful of smoke.

"I don't want to hear you talking about your father like that, understand?"

"But he is like that Gran. He's the most miserable bloody bastard alive."

"One more word out of you like that my lad, and I'll come over there and give you a thick ear."

"But Gran......"

"Don't *But Gran* me. That man's your father and you should show him the respect he deserves."

"I do show him the respect he deserves," sneered Sean.

"You think you're so damned clever don't you?" said his Gran, her face like granite. "You think that just because you're smart enough to get into that Grammar School everyone else is bloody stupid. Well let me tell you this, our Sean, you don't get your brains from nowhere. Your father might not be able to do your damned logarithms or whatever it is you call them, and he might not know anything about them books you've forever got your nose into, but he's never had the time for any of that has he? No, he's too damn busy slogging away at the DIC so that you can have a shirt on your back. At your age he was pitched out of school right into the factory like everyone else around here. No chance of the Grammar for him. And he was good at school too. Top of his class. But did that make a difference? Not a bloody h'aporth of difference. The factory needed workers right after the war, and you went to the factory like it or not. And he's been there ever since, doing for you and your brothers and your sisters, and forever hoping that you don't ever have to do the same. So you just think on when you start criticizing your father. If he treated you like half the lazy good for nothing parents around here treat their kids, you'd be trading that nice purple blazer for a pair of overalls in short order my lad, make no mistake about it."

Sean knew he deserved the rough end of her tongue. Just that morning he'd seen what his father had to endure to bring home the pittance that kept the McCafferys afloat. The colour crept to his cheeks and he couldn't meet his gran's eye.

"I know it's hard for a lad of your age to get along with his dad," said his gran, her tone softening. "And it's hard for a man like your dad to show how much he loves his kids. But he doesn't piss away his wages in the pub, and he doesn't try to get the better of the bookies like some stupid buggers. That shows how much he cares. He's steady is your dad. Steady and honest. And you can't say much better about someone than that."

325

Steady and honest, thought Sean. Steady and honest and he comes home to a slum. That's what steady and honest gets you.

"And another thing," continued his gran. "Your dad'll always be there to back you up, no matter what. You might not think it, but God help anyone who tried to put you down if your dad were there to hear them. He's proud of you is your dad, proud as Punch, and it's up to you to give him good reason for it."

Proud, thought Sean. How can he be proud of someone he doesn't know? He's proud that I'm at the Grammar and that's about it. Me being at the Grammar makes him someone special. But what happens to that pride when Flint fucks everything up?

"No need to look like that cock," said his gran. "You look ready to start blubbing. I'm only telling you this for your own good. It never does to be too hard on your own folk."

"Even when they're hard on you Gran? When I left, my dad was laying into Fergus like he was ready to kill him."

"Well he must have had a reason for it. Fergus has given him enough cause for heartbreak before now. What new trouble's the lad been up to?"

"Dad accused him of pinching his cigs," said Sean, picking his words.

"Well your dad won't tolerate a thief. Like I said, steady and honest is your dad, and he's got no time for anyone who isn't the same. If Fergus is getting sticky fingers your dad'll try to cure him of it before it gets out of hand."

"By breaking his arms?"

"You know he won't go that far. But a solid leathering sometimes does a lot more good than harm to a lad that's going astray. You ought to know that from them Christian Brothers. They know how to put a lad straight."

326

Yes, thought Sean, all it takes is a team of bent Brothers to put a lad straight. The Head and his crew had shown that well enough.

"Come on Sean, cheer up cock," said his gran, determined to get some pleasure from his visit. "I'll go and make you a buttie. Albert's bought some ham off the bone for his dinner but he won't miss a slice or two. And if he does who's to worry, eh?"

His gran bustled into the kitchen. There was the creak of a tap and the sound of water splashing into the kettle. His gran always made enough tea for a legion even when it was just for herself. A match was struck and the gas stove popped alight. Cutlery rattled in the drawer and plates clattered. When his gran went to make a sandwich there was no messing about.

Sean's eyes swept the room, the tops of the mantelpiece, the sideboard, the gramophone. He was looking for something but he didn't dare admit to himself what it was. He couldn't allow the enormity of his sudden intention to stop him from what he was planning to do.

There it was! On the floor by her chair. The fat leather purse with its big brass clasp. Old, brown and battered, just like his gran herself. It had been the source of so many sixpences over the course of his childhood. Could he do it? Could he steal from his own grandmother. Could he rob a widow and a pensioner?

"Would you like some cheese with your ham?"

"No thanks.......actually yeah.......yes please gran!"

Cutting the cheese would give him more time. He heard the fridge door open and was on his feet in a second. His fingers shook as he clicked open the clasps. Jesus, she could walk in any second!

"Are you making tea gran?"

Stupid bloody question, but if he kept her talking he'd know where she was.

"No cock, I thought we'd have hot chocolate instead. You know, like the Queen. What the hell do you think?"

Stupid bloody answer, but it served his purpose. Christ, there were a thousand pockets in this thing. Where the hell did she keep her damned money?

"Have you got any Hovis gran? My dad has started eating Hovis and my mum won't let me have any?"

His voice was shaking almost as much as his hands – what the hell did she keep in there? – hair-clips, matches, lipstick (when had his gran ever worn lipstick?), pension book, ration book. Ration Book? Rationing had been over for almost twenty years for God's sake. Come on.......where did the stupid cow keep her fucking money?

"No, I don't have any bloody Hovis, and your dad won't get any bloody Hovis either while he's round here. Hovis, for crying out loud. What's he eating bloody Hovis for?"

"Dunno gran."

And I don't know where your damned money is either. Christ! Why the hell do you keep a set of rollers in there when your hair's like barbed wire?

Sean was getting reckless in his anxiety, tipping things onto the floor. She'd be back in the room any second now.....any second and she'd catch him on his knees red-handed.

"I don't suppose you've got any pie left from Sunday have you gran?" Time........give me time............

"Cheeky bugger. I'll have a look. Albert's normally pigged it by now, but I'll check the pantry for some anyhow."

A zipper! The money's in the bloody zipper. Thank you God!

Sean reached in and came out with a hand full of coins - sixpences, threepenny bits, big brass pennies, a few florins and two

328

half crowns. How much were twenty Benson and Hedges? He had no idea. Was half a crown enough? What if it wasn't? What if he left himself short? Stupid, stupid, stupid...why hadn't he checked? He heard the pantry door close, stuffed the two half crowns into his pocket, zipped the other coins away again, and bundled the rest of his gran's junk back into her purse. His head swam as he got to his feet. The shaking seemed to have possessed his entire body as he swayed back to the couch. Breathe....breathe....breathe...... he told himself. Be normal. It's done now.....so.......so just act normal.

He closed his eyes, trying to calm himself, attempting to find justification for what he'd done. His gran seemed to be taking her time now. He'd had all the time in the world! Why had he stuffed all that junk back in there like that? Should he try and put it back the way it was? Could he remember where everything had been? Or was her purse just the big bag of garbage that it seemed to be? He had to check.

He was on his feet and half way to her chair when his gran came back into the room carrying two plates weighed down with food.

"What, aren't you staying then?"

His face burned scarlet as he saw himself in the mirror above the mantelpiece, looking every inch the guilty thief.

"And what's the cherry on for? Caught you admiring yourself did I?"

He forced a grin, saw in his reflection how fake it was. But she'd given him an out.

"I ......er........I was just wondering gran how.........how I could..........how I could make myself look a bit older."

His gran laughed that wicked, lovely laugh of hers.

"My God, it never changes does it? Even with them you thought had more sense. And how old do you want to look cock? Old

329

enough for that lass you're after? Old enough to go and watch them dirty films they have on at the Jacey? Take my advice cock and slow down. You'll be my age soon enough and then you'll not be so keen on either the lasses or the dirty pictures. Aye, and not so keen on looking any older either. Here, get that lot down you. After all, a proper plateful's the best thing I know for putting hairs on your chest."

Sean sat down and took the plate on his knees. The sandwiches were his gran's usual doorstoppers, and there was a slice of apple pie almost as big as his head.

"Go on, I didn't make them so you could look at them. Get them down you before Albert gets back and finds his ham gone. I wouldn't put it past the miserable sod to take it right out of your mouth. No need to look so scared of it - you're the one supposed to be doing the biting. Go on and get it down you."

Sean dug his teeth into the enormous sandwich, more to hide the tremors than from hunger. His life had become far too complicated for hunger. If he were starving to death it would hardly distract him from the all-absorbing problem of Flint.

He soldiered through the sandwiches with his head down, chewing and chewing with a dry mouth, reducing each bite to a lump of grease-laden dough that he washed down on a stream of sugary tea. He said nothing, acting the trencherman to his gran's enormous satisfaction as she slumped in her chair by the fire with a Woodbine in her fist and an approving smile on her kippered lips. Christ, if she could only see what he'd been doing just minutes before? What if she were to look in her bag right now and realize? The thought made him bolt the pie and prepare to escape.

"God love you son, you were hungry after all weren't you? Don't they feed you a proper lunch at that school of yours? Here let me get you another slice of pie."

She made to get up from her seat, but Sean was on his feet before she could stir.

"It's alright gran. That was great. Just what I needed. But I've got a stack of homework tonight. English essay, maths, physics. Ton of work. I'd better get back."

His gran looked disappointed. Disappointed and curious. He kept blathering on.

"Physics is tough. New stuff this week. Thermodynamics. Got to get it done though. Better get on with it. Great sandwich gran. Thanks. Best get going now."

"Well if you're in so much of a rush to get back to your dad, I suppose I shouldn't be stopping you."

"I'll stay out of his way. Up in my room. Do my homework there anyway. Best be off then."

"So you keep saying. Alright then cock. If you've got your schooling to do you'd best be doing it I suppose. Here, I'll come with you to the gate."

She reached down to pick up her purse. It was the traditional start to her farewell. She'd walk the few steps outside to the garden gate and park herself there, leaning those hammy forearms on the woodwork as she watched him disappear up the street. But first, as she ushered him through, she'd click open the purse and slip him a sixpence. It was a sure thing. So sure that sometimes his visits were for the sixpence alone. But not tonight. Tonight he didn't want any sixpences. Tonight he didn't want his gran going anywhere near her purse. Not while he was still there.

"That's alright gran," he said, "I'm in a bit of a hurry. That homework's going to be a killer."

There was no mistaking the stunned surprise on her face. And was that just a flicker of suspicion?

"Don't bother getting up gran, I've got to run."

And then he did what he never did. He leaned over and kissed her on her cheek. He didn't know why he did it. It was always up to his gran to kiss him, to gather him in her arms before pushing him out through the gate. And it was always his role to humour her with an upturned cheek before moving away. The kiss felt all wrong. He pulled himself away and was through the door without looking back.

His gran settled herself slowly back into her chair. Now what the bloody hell was all that about? That lad had been acting strange for days, and now this. Something was up, that was for sure. Of all her grandkids, he was the one most keen on the few coppers she handed out, so why did he go rushing out like that?

A nasty thought crept into her mind. He'd said his dad had been beating on Fergus for stealing cigarettes, but what if it wasn't Fergus? What if it were Sean, and what if.......? She reached onto the mantelpiece and flipped open the pack of Woodbines. It was almost full. Thank God for that. If he'd been been filching in there after that lecture on thieving she'd skin the bugger alive. She loved Sean just like she loved the rest of her grandkids, but she knew there was something lacking in him despite him being so bright. He needed guiding that lad.

I'll just have to keep my eye on him, she thought. And then she delved into her purse for her matches.

Chapter 36: Scum

Bugger! Stupid, stupid bugger! Why did you go and act like such a stupid bugger?

Defrauding his gran and his aunts out of the sponsorship money was one thing, but outright robbery – thieving from his gran while she was in the kitchen getting him food - that was....that was....sheer filth! And then that kiss. What the hell had he been thinking? Christ knows, but it certainly didn't have anything to do with love. And she knew it too. She knew it straight away you stupid bloody sod! Bugger, bugger, bugger and bastard!

And now he had to buy the cigs. There wouldn't be time in the morning, and there wouldn't be the opportunity before meeting with Flint after school, so it had to be now. The walk home took him past Ottie Ward's shop, and before giving it any real thought he'd opened the door and was inside.

"Well, if it isn't Marco Polo! What can I do for you tonight?"

Ottie was slumped on the counter in his usual position, the Liverpool Echo open in front of him. He gave Sean the briefest of smiles before going back to the racing results. Sean realised he'd made a mistake, but it was too late now. He didn't want to ask Ottie for the cigarettes, but he had to have a reason for coming into the shop; he couldn't just turn around and walk out again. He had to buy those fucking cigs - it was as simple, and as complicated, as that.

"Twenty Benson and Hedges please Ottie."

He tried to sound casual about it, as if he were asking for a lollipop, but his voice squeaked with anxiety. Ottie looked up slowly, his expression quizzical.

"Benson and Hedges? Who wants Benson and Hedges then?"

Sean wasn't prepared for this. He looked into Ottie's face and could find nothing to say. He flushed scarlet.

"Your dad doesn't smoke Benson and Hedges and neither does your Grandmother. Your aunt Winnie and your aunt Theresa don't smoke Benson and Hedges neither. And your uncle Gerry is a Capstan Full Strength man isn't he?"

Sean buckled under the weight of unspoken accusation. How could he explain? And how come Ottie knew so much about his dad and his gran and his aunts and his uncle Gerry? But then of course he would know about them wouldn't he? He'd been serving them for over twenty years. He'd been serving them before Sean was born. Ottie knew everyone on the estate: what they smoked, what they read, what they ate, even what they thought. And right now he looked as if he knew exactly what Sean was thinking too.

"They're......they're for some boys."

It sounded ridiculous as soon as the words left his mouth. But they'd been spoken now and couldn't be unsaid. He'd dug himself into a hole, and Ottie wasn't going to let him out of it.

"Some boys eh? What boys?"

"Some boys up the street asked me to buy them. Said they'd give me threepence from the change."

"Oh aye, and why don't they come and buy them themselves? Why pay you threepence?   Men of leisure are they? Flush enough for servants, these boys of yours?

"Look, I don't know do I? I just thought it'd be an easy way to make threepence that's all."

"And what do these boys look like? Are they from round here?"

"I don't know what they look like, they're just boys. And no I haven't seen them before."

Ottie looked full into Sean's face, his eyes hard as marbles. He spoke slowly, taking his time.

"So, let's get this straight. Some boys who you've never seen before, who don't live around here, ask you to buy them expensive cigs from my shop because they're so bloody rich they can afford a bloody servant. How much did these boys give you?"

Ottie's eyes held him fast.

"Two.....Two half crowns. Half a quid," he croaked.

"Two half crowns? Half a quid for a pack of Benson and Hedges? Half a bloody quid!"   Ottie's voice swelled with contempt as he looked at Sean. "Well let me tell you something my lad, those boys of yours must be as rich as bloody Croesus if they trust you with half a quid just for a pack of B and H. One of those bloody half crowns would have been enough, with change back."

Ottie's face was menacing now – a grim melding of anger and disappointment.

"Look Ottie, are you going to sell me the cigs or aren't you. I can't keep them waiting. I told them I'd be back in a minute."

"Don't you bloody well Ottie me Sonny Jim. It's Mr. Ward to you and don't you bloody well forget it. And no, I'm not going to sell you the bloody cigs. I only take honest money in this shop. Honest money from honest folk. So you go and tell that to your bloody boys, whoever the hell they are. Or whoever the hell they're not."

Liar, thought Sean. Liar, liar, liar, liar, thief and bloody liar, and he knows it. He knows it and he's going to tell my dad, and my gran, and Winnie and Theresa and my uncle Gerry, and then everything's going to come out and I'm dead – Dead! Oh sweet mother of God how the hell am I ever going to get out of this?

"Look, Mr. Ward......"

He didn't know what he was going to say, but Ottie cut him off anyway.

"That's enough from you. You take yourself off to those funny friends of yours and tell them they'll get nothing out of me with their dodgey half quids. And since you're so well off with your new business, you'll not be needing that paper round we talked about will you? I'll give it to someone who doesn't mind working for their money."

And with that he shook his paper as if to waft the stink of Sean out of his shop.

Sean went to bed early, unable to sit in the living room pretending that it was just a normal evening. Ottie had bitten deep, but there was worse to come. As soon as he entered the bedroom Fergus grabbed him by the neck. Sean tried to force him off, but his older brother was bigger and wrestled him silently to the floor.

"Bastard!" he hissed as he pressed a hand down on Sean's mouth. "Thieving fucking bastard! Why did you steal those cigs? Why didn't you say something when the old man was beating the shit out of me? I'm black and bloody blue because of you."

He loosened his hand on Sean's mouth to let him speak, keeping it close about his lips in case he should call for help.

336

"I didn't," spluttered Sean. "It wasn't me."

Fergus clamped the hand down again and raised his other fist as if to smash it down on his face.

"Lying bloody bastard, of course it was you. I heard you poking around downstairs last night. I saw you getting up and sneaking out for Christ's sake. And don't try telling me you were going for a shit and didn't want to wake anyone - when have you ever given a damn about anyone but yourself? You're a lying, thieving, chickenshit bastard."

Sean could only look up into his face. Even with the hand removed he had nothing to say. What could he say? How could he tell Fergus about Flint? Fergus was the type who'd go straight around to Flint's house and drag him into the street for a good hiding. And where would that get him? Flint was mad enough to let out their secret just for revenge. He'd threatened it often enough.

"If you knew it was me why didn't you tell him yourself?"

Fergus looked hard at him, anger melting into disgust. He unclenched the upraised fist as if it were too good to use on a little shit like Sean

"You make me fucking sick," he hissed as he flung himself on his bunk and turned his face to the wall.

Sean curled into his own bunk. First Ottie and now his brother. He might despise Fergus most of the time for the anger and gloom he brought with him everywhere, but he had a secret jealousy of him too. Fergus was the truly bright one in the family. Everything he did had a creative ring to it, and Sean yearned to talk him about books and Woodstock and Hippies and Vietnam and LSD, and all the other things that teenage brothers exclude from their parents. But tonight had put paid to that. Tonight Fergus had taken a beating on

Sean's behalf, and Sean had shown he'd not been worth the sacrifice.

Next morning Sean retrieved the two half crowns he'd hidden under the broken linoleum, placing one in each pocket of his trousers so that the jingle of coins wouldn't betray him. He was almost out of the door when his mother called him back.

"Don't wear those again today love," she said, "I've shortened a pair of Fergus's that are much better. Here, there's no patches in these, and they look as good as new. Give me them old things and I'll see if there's anything I can save for Keiran."

She threw him a pair of Fergus's trousers that he'd grown out of. They looked almost brand new. It was her response to his complaint on that first day of school when wearing shabby clothes had seemed the worst of all his misfortunes. My God, what a bloody fool he'd been.

"Come on, get those off yourself and give them to me. I'm just sorry I couldn't have had the new ones ready sooner." She was smiling at him, expecting smiles in return. Getting a new pair of pants, pants that actually looked new, should have had him grinning all over his face.

Instead he stood there bewildered. She expected him to drop his pants right there and put on the new ones. But then what would he do with the half crowns?

"Hang on a minute," he said. "Wait there," and rushed into the front room.

Thank God the others weren't up yet. He hauled his pants down, clutching the half crowns in two sweaty palms, and almost jumped into the new trousers. Less than a minute later he was back in the kitchen, strutting about to please his mother and forcing the smile he knew was required.

"And what's got into you then?" she said. "Too grown up now to undress in front of your mother are you?" She looked at him with an expression of sad amusement. "Well, those new trousers certainly make you look the part."

She approached him and bent down to tug and smooth the cloth over his legs, examining her handy work, but he backed away, brushing her off in case she felt the coins in his pockets. She looked hurt, but what could he do?

"They're great mam, thanks. And they fit perfect. Gotta run. See you later. Bye." And then he was in the street wondering how many times, and in how many ways, he'd have to kick his family in the teeth.

His answer came at the end of Cack Alley.

"G'morning our Sean."

His grandmother was standing at the exit of the Alley in an attitude that could only mean she'd been waiting for him. He tried to turn his look of shock into one of surprise, but it took a visible effort and he knew that his gran was wise to the act.

"Hi gran, what are you doing here?"

"I'm waiting for you, aren't I?"

"For me, what for?" The act was strained to breaking point but he kept it up, and the look on his gran's face grew even darker.

"Yes, for you. I thought you might have something to say to me."

He tried to laugh as though this was some kind of game, but her expression showed she was in no mood for fun.

"Something to say to you gran - like what?"

"I think you know like what, and if you don't you're not the lad I took you for."

It was the first time he'd met the full force of her contempt. He'd laughed often enough at that expression of hers as she passed sentence on the likes of Tommy Aden and Tony Dennis for their thieving bloody ways, but now the tables were turned.

He faked a look of contrition. "Look Gran, if Ottie Ward's been talking to you about those Benson and Hedges, I can explain. You see.....

"SHUT UP!"

The words stopped dead in his throat. He'd never seen her this furious before. He realized now that all the abuse aimed at Tommy Aden and Tony Dennis had been played for laughs. This was what she was really like when faced with a thief - as hard and as sharp as a pickaxe.

"Shut up and listen to me! I don't know what else you've been up to, but you know damned well why I've collared you this morning. I thought you might have had the guts to own up while I'm giving you the chance, but maybe you haven't got it in you. Maybe you really are as bad as all that. But you think on, my lad - I'm giving you until tomorrow to come and see me, and if you don't I'll be seeing your mother and your father instead. And then God help you. Your dad's my eldest and he'll flay you alive when I tell him what you've been up to. Aye, and while I was feeding you and all, you lousy thieving bugger!"

And then she was off, turning her back and storming away as if she couldn't stand the sight of him.

Chapter 37: Sheer Bloody Madness

Told you didn't I! Now who's Chief Inspector Mong?

-Wotcheronabout?

-Told you it weren't one of us didn't I?

-One of us what, you spaz?

-One of us on the walk.

-What the hell are you rabbitting on about?

-The cops have figured it wasn't one of us on the walk so they're going to interview everyone else in the school, just like I said they should have done right from the start.

-What? Everyone? What's the point of that?

-Going to need an alibi isn't he, whoever did it, and if he hasn't got one.........

Dougie Dougan pulled on an imaginary rope and twisted his head sharply to the side. Sean could almost feel himself dropping through the trap.

The day passed in a blur. He'd been silent with Bill O'Rourke in the morning, silent in classes, and silent on the bus home. The police were closing in. They'd be interviewing him tomorrow, and what could he possibly tell them? And then there was his grandmother. If she went to his parents that would be the end of everything. His dad would punch the truth out of him - the Woodbines, Flint, the sponsored walk......the murder. Somehow he had to get the money back to her, to make her understand that it was a mistake, some crazy aberration, a prank, a dare, anything, but he had to get it back before she went to his dad with the story.

"So where's the B and H then Tarzan?"

Flint was at the usual spot in Cack Alley, waiting for him.

"I don't have them."

"What! Are you trying to be funny with me?"

A dog-end drooped from his lip. As he approached Sean he flicked the ash, exposing the glowing tip. He held with the cigarette out in front of him.

"I meant what I said Tarzan. I said specifically I wanted B and H, and I told you what would happen if you didn't bring them, didn't I? Now if I don't stub this ciggy in your face you're going to think I'm not serious aren't you, and we can't have that can we Tarzan? You've got to learn what's what, don't you?"

Sean flinched away from the outstretched hand. He had his back to the wall in every respect. His one chance was that Flint was bluffing. Maybe he was as scared as Sean of being found out. Maybe all this was a sick game.

"You won't do that Flint. If you stub that thing in my face I'll tell my mam you did it and she'll have you in court in no time. And if you mention Sandcaster, or the old woman, I'll tell them you've been bullying me all along. I'll tell them you forced me to come with you to Sancaster, and I'll tell them everything about the boats, the girl, the rifles, and about you throwing that ball."

Flint leans in closer. He says nothing. He grips Sean's shoulder with his left hand, holding the glowing cigarette in his right, as if taking aim. His face betrays nothing, no hint of intent, no sign of pleasure.

Sean twists his head sideways as the cigarette jabs for his left eye. There's a searing pain in his scalp and the stench of burned hair. Flint, furious at missing his eye, grinds the butt into his head.

"Jesus, you mad bastard! Let go of me. For Christ's sake Flint, I'm on fire!"

Sean struggles against the hand on his shoulder and shakes his head into Flint's face, convinced that his hair is in flames, terrified that he'll be scarred for life.

Flint digs his fingers into Sean's face, forcing his head up and slamming it back into the wall. An inch more travel and the force would have cracked his skull. Sean sags like a rag doll. Only Flint's hand around his jaw keeps him from folding to the floor.

"You don't get it do your Tarzan? For some wanky Grammar git you're not smart at all are you? I don't give a shit, understand? Jimmy Flint doesn't give a shit about you or anyone else, and Jimmy Flint doesn't give a toss whether he lives with his fucking parents or with a bunch of psychos in Wormwood Fucking Scrubs. Want me to prove it? See that old geezer coming down the path?" He nods towards an old man a hundred yards away, trudging slowly towards them.

No, Sean thinks, don't, not another one. Please don't do it again. You can't.....

But Flint isn't thinking about murder. He has other ideas.

"Oi, Grandad!" he roars, "This here's Tarzan, and I'm his mate. We killed the old woman in Sandcaster. What do you think of that then, eh?"

Sean leaps forward and clamps his hands around Flint's mouth. Flint brushes him aside.

"Smashed her head in we did, me and old Sean here. Sean McCaffery's his name, and I'm Jimmy Flint."

Sean jumps at Flint from behind, clawing for his mouth, but Flint bends double at the waist and heaves with his back, sending Sean flying over his shoulder. He's laughing now.

"That's right, Sean McCaffery and Jimmy Flint, Your Friendly Neighbourhood Murderers. Know anyone that needs doing in, just give us a call."

Sean looks up frantically at the old man. He's stopped in the path watching two kids fighting, one of them shouting his head off. He looks uncertain, ready to turn back.

"He's mad," shouts Sean. "He's a stupid mad bastard. Don't listen to him." And then in a desperate whisper to Flint, "Shut up, I've got half a quid for you if you keep quiet. For Christ's sake shut up!"

"He's got half a quid for me," roars Flint. "Says he'll give me half a quid if I do you in too. Bargain!"

"Don't listen to him," shouts Sean. "He's my brother. Schizo. Not right in the head. He needs his medicine."

The old man turns, heading back the way he came, looking over his shoulder every few steps.

Flint is laughing.

"Brothers!" he seems to find this hilarious. "You and me, brothers. Christ my old man would love that. He'd have to buy himself another belt."

But Sean isn't listening. He's still looking at the old man. How much did he hear? How much did he understand? Was he going for the police, or just backing away from trouble. Could he have seen their faces? Would he recognize them again? Flint doesn't care one way or the other.

"Alright then Bruv, where's me half quid?"

"I'll give it you Flinty, but for Christ's sake keep your mouth shut. You can't want to go to jail can you?"

Flint reaches down and drags Sean off the floor. He pushes him back against the wall, but gently this time. Sean fumbles in his pocket for the two half crowns, and Flint takes them as if everything belonging to Sean is rightfully his. He leans forward, arms on either side of Sean's chest, hands against the wall. He's horribly close.

"Want to go to jail? Depends doesn't it. Depends on who you're put with. Get stuck with someone who can beat the shit out of you and it's not so great. But that's the same wherever you are isn't it? Now if I got stuck with you, we could have a right old time couldn't we? All kinds of fun."

He brings his face closer to Sean's, so close that Sean gags on Flint's breath.

"Yeah, that could be a proper lark couldn't it? I reckon old Flinty could teach a lad like you a trick or two. I bet a lad like you hasn't had much experience in things, especially in that poxy school of yours. I bet them Brothers haven't taught you half of what I could teach you."

Flints open mouth is just inches from Sean's. He tries to shrug his face away, but Flint shifts his hands, placing one on either side of Sean's head, keeping his face forward. Sean can sense Flint's excitement as the breath on his face quickens.

"Now that would be a right caper wouldn't it?" says Flint. "Yeah, I reckon it's time old Flint took a hand in your education."

He lets one hand fall and grabs Sean briefly by the crotch before trapping him again, face to face.

"Bet you thought that was for stirring your tea with, eh? Well, your old mate Flinty's going to show you different. You meet me here same time tomorrow. You and me are going to have some real fun, Flinty promises. But remember, if you don't show........Well I reckon I'll be seeing you in the cells, won't I?"

He brings his forehead against Sean's, their noses touching, and Sean, sickened beyond bearing, squeezes beneath the restraining arms. Then he's off, running towards home, determined that whatever Flint wants next, he'll never, ever get. Never!

The laughter behind him tells a different story.

That evening, Sean lies in bed, eyes wide in the darkness, his fifth night since the murder spent in the hopeless search for a way out of this bloody mess.

He has nothing to offer the Head. The poster boy is a mystery. No one is claiming responsibility. Sean has hung on the edge of every clique, spying like an arse-licking prefect for something to carry to the Brothers. Nothing. And if he couldn't give the Head a name, what then? He flinches under the bed sheets as he recalls the cane ripping into Halligan's arse. Not for a moment does he imagine what the Head really has in store for him.

And then there's the Police. They'd compare his face with the indentikit picture and recognize him immediately. It's the type of thing they're trained for. What could he tell them? He has no alibi. What lies can he come up with that would satisfy a professional investigator? He's heard the upper years talking about their

346

interviews with the Inspector. He'd wanted details. Why hadn't they gone on the walk? What had they done instead? Who had they been with? At what time? Who could corroborate their alibis? How could these people be contacted if it became necessary to check on the story?

What was Sean going to say? That he'd done nothing and seen no-one? That for eight hours on a Saturday he'd ceased to exist? That despite his need for food and shelter he'd been nowhere and eaten nothing in the presence of any other person who could vouch for him? The idea was ridiculous.

And then there was Flint. Even if he escaped the Head; even if he managed to come up with some story for the police, there'd still be Flint, waiting for him in Cack Alley. Waiting with some intent that made Sean sick to his stomach. He remembers him standing in the prow of the rowboat with that horrible thing extended, laughing outside the funhouse through a mouthful of pink spit, and last night, those putrid lips so close into his face.

Whatever Flint wants, Sean won't do it. Can't and won't. Flint will have to make do with Sean's dead body.

Unless........Unless Sean strikes first!

The idea snaps his eyes wider in the darkness. He's imagined it so many times, but what if he really were to kill Flint? The thought sends his heart racing. With Flint dead everything would be simple. And let's face it, he'd be doing the world a favour. Think about it - what if someone had known Ian Brady the way Sean knows Flint? What if they'd killed him before he murdered those little kids? Wouldn't it have been the right thing to do?

It made sense. Sean could kill Flint and no one would ever know it. The chance of getting away with it was far greater than the chance of getting away with the old woman's murder. In fact, killing

Flint might be the only way to avoid conviction for a murder Sean hadn't committed.

No one knows of their relationship. No one would ever guess that a fifteen year old Protestant delinquent from Borstal Billy's would have any interest in a thirteen year old Catholic Grammar School boy from Meadowlands. Considering all the other potential suspects in a town like Duggin, a boy from Meadowlands would be the last person the police would suspect. Meadowlands boys weren't murderers.

But how would he do it? What could he use?

He pictures their meeting in Cack Alley the next day, Flint's hands on his throat again, or pressing on the bones of his face to force him against the wall. His own hands would be on Flint's arms, trying to loosen his grip. But what if one hand were to drop to his pocket? What if one hand were to take a knife and ram it into Flint's heart? He trembles with the excitement of possibility. He could do this! He could do it and get away with it in the seclusion of Cack Alley. Do it and do the world a service.

Flint would never suspect what Sean had in mind. He would have no reason to keep his distance. He wanted to get close. And if it came to that Sean would tear his fucking heart out.

Next morning he pockets a knife from the cutlery drawer and goes out to face the most decisive day of his life.

Chapter 38: Queer Behaviour

He met Bill O'Rourke at the usual spot by the DIC. They fell into step without saying a word. It had been like this every day since the weekend, Sean lost in his thoughts and Bill seemingly content to leave him there. But today Bill cast side-long glances at his friend as they made their way to the bus stop, his face more than usually dour.

"Our turn for the cops today, then?" he said. The statement turned itself into a question, an upward inflection in the deadpan voice. It was obvious he wanted a response. Sean grunted, saying nothing.

"What are you going to tell them?"

"Same as you – I didn't do it."

Sean spoke more harshly than he'd intended, but Bill's question had grated on raw nerves. What the hell was he going to tell them? What could he tell them?

"I mean, what are you going to tell them about where you were?"

"Same as you, I'll tell them where I was."

"I was at my aunt Josie's most of the day, what about you? I thought you were supposed to be going on the walk."

Sean didn't like the edge in Bill's voice.

"Yeah, I was supposed to be going on the walk but I didn't, so I'll tell them that I wasn't at bleeding Sandcaster, and I wasn't at your bleeding aunt Josie's, and I was minding my own bleeding business like you ought to be doing because you're pissing me off. Now shut up and let me think."

The rest of the walk, and the trip to school, were spent in silence, Sean struggling to invent a plausible Saturday in which he'd done innocent things with innocent people - the uncomplicated Saturday he'd enjoyed every other weekend of his life without ever appreciating it. But how could he invent something so believably mundane? How could someone complicit in murder – someone who was planning to kill the maniac who'd done it - relate the experiences of innocence?

He strode away from Bill as they passed through the school gates, turning his back on him deliberately. He wandered the schoolyard, fidgeting with the knife in his pocket as he listened in on conversations. In the few days since the murder, the initial shock of it had worn off, and tragedy had morphed into comedy.

-Reckon it was one of us that did it then?

-What, the posters?

-No, they were done by Brother Michael, what do you think, idiot!

-You mean the murder?

-No, the My Lai massacre, Knob-Head.

-I reckon it was suicide.

-Bollocks.

-I'm not kidding. Did you see the kipper on the old biddy's husband?

-Face like he'd just followed through on a fart.

-Yeah. Looking at that every day'd send anyone over the edge.

-I reckon she saw that ball coming and jumped right for it.

-Bobby Charlton special. Diving header. Thunk! Game over.

-But someone had to throw it first though, right?

-And you reckon it was a Meadowlander?

-The cops do.

-An organization renowned for its particular intelligence.

-Smithers wants to be a cop.

-Well there you go then.

-Seriously though, could it have been one of us?

-Not a chance. Nothing exciting ever happens around here.

-Be great if it was though wouldn't it? Imagine the headlines?

-Meadowlands Grammar Boy – Murderer!

-Ooooh, Mr. Hemingway, Ben would be proud of you.

-Alright then, you do better.

-OK.   What   about........Meadowlands   Boy   Graduates   to
Dartmoor.

-Makes a change from Oxbridge.

-Not much of one.

-I've got it ....Brainy Junior Brains Senior.

-Egghead Scrambles then Scrams.

-It was a Cracking Throw says Young Murderer.

-Wife had been Feeling Shattered all Day says Husband of
Victim.

-Thought I'd Make a Splash, boasts Ball-Tosser .

- Tosser – you've got that right, anyway.

Sean knelt down, pretending to tie a shoe lace as the world tilted
around him. He put both hands on the ground to steady himself,
breathing deeply as he tried to shake off the nausea.

"You alright?"

Kevin Purvis stood over him, the feminine voice unmistakable. A week ago he would have made some remark about him sneaking up from the rear, but that seemed a long time past, and anyway, it no longer seemed funny. He glanced up, and the world began to tilt again as the blood drained from his head.

"Not really. Not feeling too good."

"School make you sick does it? I'm not surprised. It makes me fucking sick too."

Sean was shocked into looking up again. It was as if the Queen had used the F-word in her Christmas Address. He recognized the expression on Purvis's face - the desperate look of someone hopelessly trapped. It was there for just an instant before it flared into rage.

"Bunch of bastards aren't they? Bunch of bloody fucking bastards. Never leave you alone do they? Can't ever leave you alone. Well fuck them McCaffery, fuck the whole fucking lot of them. And fuck you too!"

Sean flinched away as Purvis shifted, half expecting one of those immaculate shoes to swing into his face. But the footsteps retreated, and when he raised his head again Purvis was gone.

He got to his feet. What had all that been about? What was that look on his face? Did Purvis know something? He'd get him on his own at recess and ask him. That wouldn't be difficult. Purvis was always alone when he wasn't hanging around Campy's office with the other queers.

But Purvis didn't show up for class after Assembly, and he wasn't in the schoolyard at recess or lunch break. And then, after lunch, Brother Lundy came knocking at the door of 3X, and Purvis became the last thing on Sean's mind.

It was during Latin class, with Horse-Face Logan in one of his more waggish moods.

"What's the verb to admire, Halligan?" asked Horse-Face.

"I didn't know there was a special verb to admire Halligan," said Halligan, "but I suppose there ought to be."

Horse-Face let this go with a good-humoured snort into the nose bag.

"Very well, Halligan, decline "to admire" in the past perfect."

"As you wish sir, I absolutely decline to admire anything at all in the past perfect."

"You know precisely what I mean Halligan, and one more smart comment like that might see you declining once again to hold out your hand for the Head. And you know what that might mean for your buttocks."

Halligan flinched, the perky impertinence draining from his face. He laboured through the declension of Admiror, screwing it up as usual.

"That was imperfect, Halligan," said Horse-Face grinning with all thirty two teeth. The suckholes in the class rewarded him with a titter, and he was moved to even greater efforts. "You know Halligan, given the brain's gelatinous nature and its proximity to the nasal passages, the ancient Greeks concluded that its function was to produce mucus for the nose." He snickered before delivering the punch line. "In your case I suspect they may have been correct."

This was quite funny for Horse-Face, and Sean wondered where he'd stolen it. But the distraction from his anxieties was quenched the instant Brother Lundy strode into the room. Brother Lundy didn't apologise to Horse-Face for interrupting his lesson, but nodded him aside as if to suspend a silly game for more important matters.

353

"The detective is ready to start interviewing the students in this class," he announced. "Interviews will be conducted in alphabetical order. The students involved are Adams, Cauldwell, Charrington, Dougan, Dougherty, McCaffery........

Sean stopped listening after his name was listed. He was sixth, that was all he needed to know. If each interview took ten minutes, this might be the last hour he'd ever spend at Meadowlands. He looked around the class and realized how much he wanted to remain a part of all this - how much the learning of a dead language, even with an idiot like Horse-Face, actually meant to him. In just sixty minutes all this could be gone forever. He had an hour to invent an alternate version of his life, and how the hell was he going to do that? The police would have to believe that for eight hours on Saturday he had become the Invisible Man.

Brother Lundy's words snapped him back to attention.

"The boys I have named will remain in this classroom until they have been interviewed. And I caution these boys right now that there is to be no tomfoolery with the Inspector. We want to get this procedure over as quickly and as painlessly as possible. I will accompany each boy to the interview room and will remain in the room during the interview to assure that correct behaviour is observed by both parties."

Oh my God, Lundy was going to be there! How could he tells lies with Lundy there? Of all the Brothers he was the one who could always see through you. And what then? Would he shop him on the spot? This was going to be far worse than he had imagined.

But there was worse to come.

"All interviews will be conducted in the same way. You will sit opposite the detective after I give him your name. The detective will compare your appearance with that of the suspects in an indentikit

354

picture, and will then ask you a series of questions concerning your whereabouts and activities on the Saturday of the Sponsored Walk. You will also be asked to provide the names of persons with whom you associated on that day. You will provide this information and nothing else. Any boy making light of these proceedings, or making statements in jest that might lead to a furtherance of these procedures, will be dealt with in the most severe manner. Is that understood? Adams, you're first, come with me."

Sean did not join the chorus of Yes Brothers. In his mind he was already in the back of the Black Moria. The identikit picture! How could they not identify him from the identikit picture? The cop would take one look at the picture, one look at Sean, and the cuffs would be on. His sisters had seen the resemblance in a second. God knows why no one else had. But the cops were trained in these things. Even if the resemblance was vague, Sean would have to score a perfect ten in his alibi for Saturday to put the detective off the scent, and right now he was standing at zero.

It was over. After the interview, it was over.

What would they do? Would they cart him away there and then? Would they get his parents first? Would the police believe him about Flint? If he told them the absolute truth would they still lock him up? But it would be his word against Flint's, and his fingerprints were on the ball too, Flint had made sure of that. And why hadn't he told them about it sooner? Why hadn't he gone to the police the minute it had happened!

He clenched the knife in his pocket. Flint! That bastard. That lousy stinking bastard. I'll cut the bastard's stinking throat.......

And then his hand was out again as if the knife had scorched him. They'd search him! The first thing they'd do was search him. And what excuse could he have for carrying a knife? None! A knife

355

could only have one purpose when carried by a thirteen year old schoolboy who looked so much like the thug in the identikit picture. It would confirm his guilt.

How could he get rid of it? He wasn't allowed to leave the classroom until the interviews were over. He could sneak it into his desk, but the cops would search his desk first thing if they suspected him of being the murderer. And what if Horse-Face, or one of his classmates, saw him pulling a knife out of his blazer? How could he explain that?

He was stuck with it. He'd have to take it into the interview with him. If the cop asked him to empty his pockets he'd leave it there. If they searched him, he'd tell them what Flint had been making him do....and what he was about to make him do that evening. He'd tell them that threatening Flint with the knife was his only chance of saving himself from the filthy business that the psycho pervert had planned for him. Not that any of his excuses would make a damned bit of difference.

Adams came back into the room, grinning as if he'd just pulled off some schoolboy prank. Brother Lundy, coming in behind him, was his usual serious self, so it was clear that Adams hadn't done anything to step beyond the mark.

"Thank you Adams," said Brother Lundy. "Cauldwell, you're next, and if you cooperate in the same sensible manner as Adams we might get this over sooner than I had hoped."

Adams flushed as the slurping started, but a sweeping look from Brother Lundy stopped it dead.

Sean gazed at the clock above the blackboard. Five minutes. It had taken less than five minutes. Half the time he'd anticipated. That meant he had less than half an hour to invent an entire Saturday for himself in which he'd spent eight hours totally alone in a town where the opportunities for solitude were virtually non-existent. He couldn't think. All the creative energy that had made him one of Ben's favourite students had fizzled to nothing. He could only stare at the clock, watching helplessly as the seconds ticked away.

Cauldwell came back, then Charrington, then Dougan. He felt madly jealous at the sight of each smirking face. What wouldn't he give to be like that?

Dougherty! My God, it was Dougherty's turn! He was next. Five minutes. What could he do in just five minutes?

He brought his hand to his forehead, then let it fall to his chest, scratched both shoulders with his thumb, disguising the sign of the cross as he invoked the Father, Son and Holy Ghost in a silent whisper. He bowed his head.

Hail Mary, full of Grace, the Lord is with thee......

Oh Holy Mother, please get me out of this! I'm truly, truly, sorry for all my sins. Just help me.........please, please help me.....

Our Father who art in Heaven, hallowed be thy name.......

Please don't take it all away God. Please get me off somehow. Just get me off and I promise I'll never, ever, ever sin again. Please God.....please....please....please......

The door opened. Dougherty strutted back to his desk, waving two defiant fingers to the class out of the view of Brother Lundy and Horse-Face Logan.

It was time. Sean was next. He willed his legs to work but they wouldn't obey him. He tried to control his face, but the muscles failed, dragging his expression into a mask of dread. It was over. It was over before he even got there. The fact that he couldn't get to his feet marked his guilt.

He turned his head sideways towards the door where Brother Lundy was standing. His eyes met those of Bill O'Rourke sitting in the desk alongside. There was fear in Bill's face too. It was unmistakable. Fear and an unspoken plea. He turned away again, forcing himself to get up, lifting his body as if it weighed a thousand tons.

But then there was a general stir in the classroom. Everyone was getting up as well. The whole class was on its feet and Brother Lundy was speaking above the noise.

"To the Assembly Hall boys. The Head has called a special assembly. Move quickly please. The interviews will continue tomorrow. Come along now."

Sean stood at his desk as the boys milled around him, not daring to believe his prayers had been heard. He had one more day. What would have been his last five minutes of freedom had been stretched into an entire day! It was a luxury of time.

He put his hands into his pockets as he slouched towards the Assembly Hall. The knife - Christ, he'd forgotten about it already! What should he do with it? He could toss it into a waste container as he walked by, but then again, maybe this was why Sean had been spared. Maybe God was cutting a deal. Maybe he had to do what he'd convinced himself he should do.

He clutched the knife as he approached a garbage bin, hiding the blade in his sleeve, ready to drop it in as he walked by. But somehow his fingers wouldn't open. It was as if an invisible hand was clasped over his own.

He slipped the knife back into his pocket and entered the Assembly Hall with the other boys, all eager to find what all the fuss was about.

Chapter 39: The Poster Boy Unmasked

The entire school was assembled. The teachers looked grim: Ben Gibbs grimly sad, Fatty Gruntle grimly gleeful, so whatever was about to happen couldn't be good. Either the Poster Boy was in for it, as Sean fully expected, or someone had owned up to the cops, which Sean knew to be impossible.

The noise clicked to immediate silence as the Head appeared on the stage. For what seemed an eternity he cast a dark glance along the ranks of boys, looking, it seemed, into every face for a sign of guilt. As his eyes lingered over the boys of 3X, Sean looked down, pretending to scratch some dirt from his blazer.

"In the name of the Father..........."

Sean's right hand jerked to his forehead. Prayers, for God's sake! Why did there always have to be damned prayers!

After a Hail Mary and an Our Father the Head got down to business.

"This school is under attack."

Halligan ducked and made as if to cover his head, but then remembered the whipping he'd received just two weeks ago and thought better of it

"This school is under attack," repeated the Head, "and it is my job to defend it with all the power invested within me. We have a

359

traitor amongst us. We have amongst us one who seeks to subvert all the principles that we, as decent honest Christians, hold dear. We have amongst us a coward who attacks in secret and then hides away. A coward who lacks the courage to fight in the open. A coward who stabs in the back and then flees."

"In the Second World War, not too many years ago, the same type of traitor sought to bring contagion into the hearts of the British people. Through sly whisperings and rumour and propaganda, spies and conspirators attempted to break the spirits of your fathers and grandfathers. To sully their beliefs. To propagate lies that cast a smear on their way of life, and to promote a newer, supposedly better, regime under the leadership of Adolph Hitler. Well boys, we all know how those attempts met with failure. We all know that truth, and courage, and the Christian spirit triumphed over the evil that was put in its way. We all know that however and whenever it has been challenged, Right must always prevail. From the conversion of the Roman Empire, through the time when the Crusaders set out to spread the true Christian word of God, no one has claimed victory against Christ's standard."

"And so it is true in Meadowlands. Though we are attacked, still we prevail. The boy who has sought to undermine our authority, to besmirch our teachings, and to spread the poison of anarchy among us, has failed. He has failed because he is here in this Hall as I speak....... And I know who he is."

The silence gave way to a shuffling murmur as heads craned, each boy trying to see beyond his neighbours to where the culprit might be standing. The Head's eyes scanned all of them, resting nowhere, not ready yet for a direct accusation.

He continued.

"Yes, he's here. The skulking coward stands within your ranks. The imposter! The spy! The traitor! You do not know him because he likes to think himself cleverer than you. He laughs behind your backs, enjoying your ignorance. You do not know him because he's afraid of you. He is aware, deep down, that his propaganda cannot bear your scrutiny. He knows that you would ridicule him had he the courage to stand before you. You do not know him because his real home is in the gutter, and we choose to walk taller than where he creeps. No, you do not know him. But I do. I have known him for some time. Known him, and watched him, and waited for him to come to me. Yes, I've waited for him to redeem himself, to accept the offer of clemency that I laid before all of you at Monday's assembly. I offer that clemency again now for the last time. Step forward boy! Step forward and admit your guilt. Step forward and apologise to me, and to your school. Step forward and receive the punishment you deserve, and there might yet be a place for you among us."

All eyes were on the Head. Who would he call out? Or would someone take the chance and own up? God help him if he did – there'd be a thrashing like no thrashing ever before. Sean couldn't watch it happen. He knew what it felt like now. He felt sick in at the thought of it.

The Head's eyes were traveling among them again.

"Very well," he said, "it's not surprising that such a coward................

"IT WAS ME! IT WAS ME YOU BASTARDS! IT WAS ME!"

The silence is shattered as a boy erupts from the door of the chapel. He dashes forward from the back of the hall, a white blur

361

that streaks along the avenue between the two blocks of students. A blur with two dark patches, one above and one below. It halts before the stage. The boys on either side back away. Behind him the crowd closes in again as those further back strain for a better view. No one can really believe what is happening. The rising murmer becomes a babble of surprise as students, teachers and Brothers find their voices.

There, standing before the Head, is Kevin Purvis, stark naked.

The rolls of fat quiver on his pasty body as he screams out his confession. There's terror in his eyes, and deep sobs ripple through his podgy frame, as if he's facing something terrible that has finally run him to ground. Tears course down his face, but he looks ready to fight. His confession is laced with challenge. It rings with accusation as he sweeps a finger across the line of startled faces in the Brothers' Gallery.

"It was me!" he screams. "Yes, it was me, and I hate every last one of you ....you.......you......fucking filth!"

His finger pauses on Brother Campion. "Filth!'" he screams. "Filth! Filth! Filth!"

For the first time in the orderly progression of his career, the Head is faced with a situation for which he has no ready response. He can only follow the quivering finger of Kevin Purvis to the startled face of the Meadowlands Deputy Head. Every eye is drawn to the same focus, and Brother Campion, realizing what might happen next, is driven into panicked mobility. He lumbers forward, almost falling down the steps to the where the boys are gathered, arms out as if to wrap Purvis in a comforting embrace. Purvis goes hysterical.

"Get away from me! Stay away from me you filthy pig! I won't let you do it. I won't let you do it again. I won't! I can't!"

362

Brother Campion continues to move forward, his hands waving towards the boy's face as if to stop his mouth. Purvis retreats backwards into the wall of boys, who shrink from all that naked flesh, pushing him away as he falls against them.

"Keep him off me!" he screams. "I......I......can't stand it any more. I just can't stand it. I want to be expelled. I've got to be expelled."

And he breaks down into convulsive sobs as if to spew his heart from his mouth.

Chuck Bones approaches him gently from behind and wraps a towel around him. Purvis lashes out, startled and terrified, but Chuck holds him tight until he collapses back into the big gym teacher's arms. Chuck lifts him, a bloated, howling, heart-racked baby, and carries him from the hall. His retreating sobs are the only sound in a school shocked into absolute silence.

The Head can find nothing to say. His plan is in ruins. Purvis is from a respectable middle class family. Good Catholics! He was almost certain to enter the Seminary. And then there's Brother Campion........Every eye is on Brother Campion, down there among the boys.

Campion breaks the silence, speaking too fast.

"The boy is mad Brother Loredano. He has lost his reason. He doesn't know what he is saying."

He looks as if he's begging the Head for support. He carries on, making it worse.

"I've never touched the boy Brother. I've never touched any of the boys. I don't understand this."

There's a rumble from the students. Sardonic mockery. "Yeah Right!" shouts someone. The sweat drips off Campy's blubbery face.

"He must be expelled Brother. Any boy behaving like that must be expelled. Any boy producing such disgusting posters can't be taken seriously Brother. He must be expelled. You said so yourself."

"KEVIN PURVIS DID NOT PRODUCE THOSE POSTERS!"

Another shock of silence. All heads snap towards the Teachers' Gallery. Gladys Hardy has stepped forward. He has both hands on the rail, leaning forward, glaring down at Brother Campion. This isn't the mincing poofter of the arts class but a Gladys no one has seen before. The feminine lilt to his voice is edged with violence.

"Kevin Purvis did not produce those posters," he shouts again. And there's such an absolute certainty about him that the idea of Purvis having anything to do with the posters becomes ludicrous.

The Head, calculating ever since Brother Campion opened his stupid mouth, emerges from his paralysis. Gladys has just given him space for recovery.

"Thank you Mr. Hardy," he shouts, "I am perfectly aware that the unfortunate boy whose breakdown we have just witnessed is not the person responsible for these acts."

As attention turns to the Head, Old Campy scurries back to join the Brothers on the gallery. They give him plenty of room, those closest cringing away. The boys look between Gladys and the Head, an increasing rumble of excitement building in the Hall. Gladys has not returned to his place. They sense the beginning of a fight.

"Silence!" shouts the Head, and every mouth snaps shut. He waits, drawing every eye to his face, re-establishing his position of absolute authority. When he speaks again it is with a measured calm: slowly, emphatically, mastering the situation, every word categorical with his incontrovertible version of the truth.

"What we have just witnessed is the mental collapse of a boy subjected to almost intolerable pressures."

Sean and a few others steal glances at Campy and the alarm written across his face. But the Head keeps his eyes on the boys, drawing them back. There's a forced sadness in his voice.

"All boys of decent upbringing will have felt these pressures," he continues. "Honest and decent boys could not help but be affected by the poison atmosphere of rebellion fomented by the person responsible for the obscene displays that have been forced upon us since the beginning of term. And though what we have just witnessed is shocking to us all, it is not entirely surprising that a boy of such acute sensitivity should become unbalanced by the emergence of so vile a corruption among us. It is not the first time that such a thing has happened in schools. Mr. Hardy is right...... " he flicks a glance to where Gladys stands, still in his defiant posture. Gladys doesn't budge an inch.

"Mr. Hardy is right," repeats the Head. "These obscenities were not the work of Kevin Purvis. Purvis is a victim of these acts, as are all decent and responsible individuals from the same class and background. These actions come from the gutter. The boy responsible for them comes from the gutter. And I'll make absolutely certain that the gutter is where he returns once he is expelled from this school. Such an individual can have no place among us."

He allows the whispering tide to rise as the boys speculate on who it might be. Sean's guts heave with the tension of it.

"Oh yes, I know who this boy is," says the Head, and immediately the whispering stops. He allows himself the approximation of a smile.

"I have known the identity of this individual for some time. I have asked this individual, publicly, in your presence, to come forward and admit his guilt; to come forward and face his punishment, hoping that some semblance of decency, some residue of courage, some particle of honour might still attach to him. Had this individual done as I asked he might have been granted my leave to stay in this school. But this boy is a coward. A coward that skulks among us. An insidious vermin bearing plague. A disease that must be eradicated. The time has come to stamp it out."

The Head raises his arm in a sweeping gesture, out from his side, hand extended, finger pointing, arcing over the heads of boys whose breath stops as it hovers, releasing as it moves on...... slowly.......ever so slowly...... the gesture as theatrical and elaborate as his speech..... the finger moving on....... moving on.........until it stops.

Sean is struck by lightning. An invisible force cripples him. The boys around him fall back as if thrust away by the power of it. It freezes his bewildered face as every Brother, every teacher and every pupil turns to stare at him. He wants to shout NO! but his throat is choked. He manages only to shake his head, mouth open, desperate in his denial.

"Yes, McCaffery!" roars the Head. "McCaffery is responsible for all the perversities we've been enduring. McCaffery has brought disgrace to himself, to his family and to 3X. Yes, an X class boy has been responsible for these obscenities –these grotesque abuses of intellect. And an X-class boy has brought about the breakdown of his classmate - a good and decent classmate from a good and decent family. But there will be no more of it. There will be no more of this

366

filth. The time has come for that boy to face the consequences of his actions."

His arm drops to his side and lifts again brandishing a cane that comes down viciously on the table beside him.

"Out McCaffery!" he spits. "Separate yourself from the decent people around you and come out here now." The cane slams down again.

Sean hardly hears him. He's facing the swinging fists of his father. He's melding with the mindless rabble at the Secondary Modern. He's shuffling with the proletariat through the gates of the DIC. He's severed from every quality of intellect that he's always taken so much for granted.

"Out now!" shouts the Head, taking Sean's inaction for defiance. "You will do exactly as I say!"

But Sean can't move. There has to be some way out of this. But how can he deny it? Who will believe him? His mother? His father? His father might take on Harry Marshall, but he'd crumble in the face of middle class authority, especially with the Church behind it. His Gran! His Gran would believe him – she'd take on the Head – she'd take on anyone! But then her face swims before him as he last saw it. That look of disgust. My God, she'd think he was lying now too! And how could he tell her the whole truth? He'd have to own up about the money, and that would lead to Flint, and Flint would lead to Sandcaster, and then it wouldn't be just school.......Oh Christ!

"Out now McCaffery before I drag you out myself."

There's nothing he can do. He begins to move towards the stage.

"NO! STAY WHERE YOU ARE McCAFFERY."

367

Heads snap to the teachers' gallery, and to Gladys Hardy, still standing forward, hands still on the rail, still in that astounding attitude of defiance.

"Stay where you are McCaffery," he shouts again. "I know you're not responsible for those posters, and so does he."

He points an accusing finger right at the Head's face where a momentary astonishment gives way to a blazing fury. The Head has never been challenged like this, not by anyone, let alone a lefty teacher just out of college. He can't.... he won't... have this man challenging his authority. The stick twitches in his hand. He can hardly speak through the rage.

"Mr. Hardy, you will leave this assembly hall immediately! Now, Mr. Hardy. Immediately! You will leave immediately!"

Gladys stands his ground. "No I bloody well won't. Not for a vicious, lying, fascist bastard like you."

The boys are amazed. This can't be happening. Gladys, the limp-wristed poncing pooftah looks ready and able to smash the Head right in his ugly face. They're convinced that only the distance between them stops him from doing it.

The Head roars at him. "Get out Mr. Hardy. Get out now. You are no longer a member of this school!"

Fatty Gruntle comes waddling from his position in the line of teachers. "Do as the Headmaster says Mr. Hardy. How dare you speak to Brother Loredano like that." He lifts a hand as if to lay it on Gladys's arm and then drops it again as Gladys turns towards him. The look on Gladys' face freezes him in mid-step.

"Shut up Gruntle. Shut up and get back to your cronies, you creeping lump of useless fat. You know as well as I do that McCaffery had nothing to do with those posters. And you know he had nothing to do with what's been happening to Kevin Purvis. God help us! It's perfectly obvious what pushed that poor boy over the edge. Talk about perversion! Talk about obscenity! But any excuse to get rid of a Duggin boy suits you just fine doesn't it? Especially if it keeps the lid on the shit that goes on in this school. Christ, you and your type make me sick."

Gruntle looks as if he's been slapped across the face; just like so many of the boys he's slapped in the past. Gladys turns back to the Head as Gruntle flounders.

"Did you really believe I'd keep quiet while you made a victim of an innocent boy? Did you really think I'd stand by like that lot (sweeping a hand behind him at the row of teachers) while you made him a scapegoat just because his father works in a factory? Do you think a job in this cess-pit of a school is worth that much to me? Just look at you....you and your band of hypocrites. You talk about honour when you don't know the meaning of the word. You talk about courage when you're the most craven among this cringing collection of cowards (a finger sweeping across the Brothers' gallery). You harp on about decency while you beat and molest and carry out the foulest obscenties. And you have the brass balls to call yourself a Christian."

The Head, isolated on his stage, can neither command nor beat Gladys into obedience. The line of Brothers look on from the other side of the hall, Brother Michael bewildered, Brother Jerome outraged, Brother Campion still white with anxiety. All of them shocked into immobility. There's nothing in their experience to help them deal with this. Gladys sweeps his finger across them again.

"Just look at yourselves," he shouts. "There's not a true Christian among you. You're thugs, savages and narrow-minded bigots, the lot of you. And **you** are responsible for them," Gladys continues, bringing the finger back to the Head. "You let them get

369

away with it. You know damned well that your Deputy is no better than a filthy groping pedophile. No better, and probably a damned sight worse – a bloody rapist! You know he's been molesting boys for years, but you'd rather sacrifice more victims like Kevin Purvis than have the filthy bastard locked away where he can do no more harm. Good Christ man, you make me sick!"

Ben Gibbs comes forward and lays a gentle hand on Gladys's arm.

"Glenn.....please..." he says "the boys should not be hearing this."

Gladys shrugs him off. "I'm sorry Mr. Gibbs, but the boys do need to hear it. They need to know what goes on here. And they need to know that at least one of us is on their side. They need to know that we're not all like them (pointing at the Brothers) or like that (pointing at Fatty Gruntle)."

The Head uses Ben's intervention to recover some ground. He doesn't like Ben, but he knows the students respect him. If he can side with Ben maybe he can restore some order.

"Thank you Mr. Gibbs," he calls, his voice now clipped and commanding. "Please escort Mr. Hardy from the Hall. He is obviously very disturbed. I will not subject the boys to these insane comments -these completely unfounded accusations - and I won't tolerate this outrageous behaviour from my staff. Mr. Hardy no longer has a position at this school. Please ensure that he leaves the premises at once."

Ben hesitates. His arm continues to rest on Gladys's shoulder, but there's a subtle change in attitude. He knows the truth just as well as the young teacher who is showing the guts to expose it, and the Head's attempt to co-opt him stirs revulsion into revolt.

"I'm sorry Brother Loredano," he sighs, "I'm afraid it is not my place to interfere with Mr. Hardy."

The Head takes a moment to recover. Ben is one of the senior staff, the Head of English. His insubordination throws him off balance. This open defiance is potentially far more dangerous to him than the rantings of a juvenile art master. Everyone knows that Ben is no excitable fool. He must show him exactly where he stands. When he speaks again his voice is ice.

"I decide your place in this school Mr. Gibbs, let there be no mistake about that. I decide whether or not you have a place in this school. Now please escort Mr. Hardy from the hall."

Sean fixes his gaze on the two men, aware that his fate is tied up in the struggle between them; the one in a barely contained rage, the other, the best teacher he's ever had, placid, controlled, and looking deeply sad.

"I'm sorry Brother," Ben repeats. "I have no jurisdiction over Mr. Hardy........" He pauses again as if pondering a very difficult question, then continues as if coming to a decision. "....... And I happen to agree with Mr. Hardy that McCaffery is being victimized unfairly. I'm aware that this is neither the time nor place to challenge your opinions on the matter, but really you leave me no choice."

No matter the balding head, the flabby body, the shabby suit and knitted tie, at that moment, to Sean, Ben has the stature of a Achilles. And with Ben on his side maybe, just maybe........

But the Head crushes any faint hope. He looks hard at Ben and Gladys standing there shoulder to shoulder, and passes sentence.

"Mr. Gibbs, you will leave this assembly hall now. Mr. Hardy, you will do the same." He turns the cold stare on Sean. "And you McCaffery will go immediately to my office where I will provide you with a note to your parents explaining the reason for your expulsion. Now all three of you get out."

Sean begins to drag himself from his place, knowing with heartbreaking certainty that he'll never occupy that place again. Tears mist his vision as he moves towards the doors. He tries to hold them back but they spill onto his cheeks. Boys glance at him and look away.

"Stay where you are McCaffery," yells Gladys. "That bastard has nothing against you – he can't prove you did anything. He can't throw you out."

Sean pays no attention. He's lost in the imminent future. His parents will accept his guilt no matter what he says. They'll bow down to what they'll accept as a higher authority, and in doing that they'll confine him to their own rank for the rest of his life.

The Head ignores Gladys. He can rant all he wants. He's no longer a member of the school. His opinions are irrelevant. The Head's plan will proceed as intended. He'll deal with any complications later.

But Gladys doesn't budge. He's not the arts master any longer, he's Che Guevara. He's leaning over the rail now shouting at the boys.

"Don't let them get away with this," he yells. "Fight them. Fight back. I know what you're going through. I was a pupil at this school too. I know all about the beatings and the buggery. I know all about the humiliation. I know every filthy trick they get up to. I've seen it from both sides. Don't stand for it. Tell your parents what goes on here. Tell them what I've said. Tell the newspapers. Tell anyone that will listen."

The Head hadn't counted on this. Gladys is getting very, very dangerous. He tries to shout him down.

"Boys you are dismissed. Return to your classes. Return to your classes now. Mr. Hardy is an intruder in this school, and if he does not leave immediately he will be dealt with by the police. To your classes now immediately."

But the boys don't know what to do. They're held by the force of Gladys's presence, his incredible mutiny, the fascination of a teacher exhorting them to rebellion. A teacher! It's unbelievable. This is the experience of a lifetime, and no one wants to miss a second of it. Only Sean continues his slow passage to the exit, impeded now by boys who stand in his way, boys laying hands on him, urging him to stop.

"Can't you see that he's afraid of you boys?" yells Gladys. "Can't you see that he's trying to protect himself. Him and his gang of perverts. They have no right to do what they've been doing to you. They're using McCaffery as an example to scare you. To keep you quiet. Don't let them get away with it."

"To your classes boys," shouts the Head. "To your classes immediately. Brother Michael, make sure the boys leave in an orderly fashion."

Brother Michael steps forward and opens the exit door at the Brothers' Gallery. "Twos Please", he whispers hopelessly to the backs of six hundred heads.

"Look at him," continues Gladys. "Can't you see the lies written across his face? He knows that McCaffery is innocent. He hasn't one shred of evidence against him. I know this for a fact. Don't let McCaffery leave the hall. I need him to hear this. I need you all to hear this."

Sean has reached the last row of sixth formers. He's about to climb the stairs towards the forlorn figure of Brother Michael, but hands grab him and turn him round. He tries to shrug them off, but they hold him tight. The rumble of excitement in the hall dies into an expectant silence. Even the Head is quelled.

373

"I know that Brother Loredano is a liar," shouts Gladys. "I know he is using McCaffery as a scapegoat. I know that he'd rather wreck a boy's career than lose one iota of his control over you. And I know that any evidence he has against McCaffery is manufactured and false."

He looks Sean full in the face for a moment, and then turns to the Head.

"I KNOW THIS BECAUSE I MADE THOSE POSTERS MYSELF!"

CHAPTER 40: Bill O'Rourke

Sean saw and heard nothing as he walked towards Cack Alley. His feet steered their way automatically between the crowds on the pavement and the filth under foot. He still couldn't believe it. Always he would construct an alternate ending – the interview with the police, being carted off in the Black Moria to some juvenile detention center, watching Meadowlands and all his hopes disappear behind him. Or the Head's finger descending on him with no rescue from Gladys standing forward to challenge the Head and then to take the blame.

He replayed the scenes again and again. The Head standing there on stage, shell-shocked as Gladys shouted in his face: "Yes it was me you lousy bastard. Me! I've waited for years to tell you shits what I really think of you, and now you're going to listen."

And on and on Gladys ranted as Gruntle and the Brothers herded the boys out of earshot to get them away from the spectacle of their Head struck dumb by the violence, and the undeniable truth, of Gladys's accusations. And Sean standing there, not knowing what to do or where to go as the boys surged around him, babbling with excitement. Then Gruntle pushing him towards the Head's office, still insisting he was to blame for all this, hatred bubbling in that sweaty fat face.

He'd stood there beside the Head's door watching the boys file to their classrooms, all of them lit by wild excitement, grinning at him, raising fists in solidarity, some of them shouting YES! and ALRIGHT! as the brothers slapped and goaded them on their way. And then the teachers hustling back to their Common Room, grim, silent and confused. Horse-Face Logan and Stooley had looked embarrassed and had pretended he wasn't there, whereas the Gruntle faction had glared at him with open animosity. And then had come Ben and Gladys at the tail-end, both of them slow and solemn. Ben had touched his shoulder as he passed. "It will be alright McCaffery'" he'd said and had moved on, taking a large chunk of Sean's heart with him. Gladys had tipped him a wink.

Last had come the Head, fury livid in his face, in the violence of his stride, in the swing of the cane slashing at his side. Sean had watched him approach with a sick dread, feeling certain he would lay into him there and then. He'd cringed as the black shadow loomed over him, but the Head didn't even look at him.

"Get back to your class," he spat, and the door of his office slammed behind him.

And that was that. All day he'd been so close to the brink, and now the day was almost over and there was still some hope that he'd find a way out of this mess. Saints had come to his rescue. Not the tawdry church icons with their candles and collection boxes, but real saints - men willing to stand their ground and tell the truth no matter the cost to themselves.

Yes, it had been a day of miracles.....and it wasn't over yet.

Bill O'Rourke trailed a half step behind Sean as they approached Cack Alley. He had been silent on the bus as the mob of boys had roared their support for Gladys and shrieked profanities about the Head. Just let the bastard try to cane them ever again, just let him try! Gladys had shown them the way. There'd be no more caning from that skull-faced twat. And as for Campy, let him try anything and they'd stuff the cane right up his arse. It had been a glorious, glorious afternoon.

Not one of them spared even half a thought for Kevin Purvis.

But Bill O'Rourke wasn't celebrating. He'd said nothing to Sean on the way to the bus stop, and had sat next to him on the bus without so much as a sidelong glance. Sean, lost in his own reflections hadn't noticed. He'd gone five paces into Cack Alley before the urgent ring in Bill's voice turned him around.

"Sean!"

Bill had the desperate look of someone about to tell a terrible truth. He launched himself into it head first.

"You're going to have to tell the coppers Sean! It's your turn first tomorrow and you're going to have to tell them, because if you don't, I'm going to tell them instead. I mean it Sean, I have to."

Sean turned as the enormous weight settled again on his shoulders. This wasn't deadpan Bill, the cynical side-kick. This was a Bill he hadn't seen before. This Bill looked scared half to death.

"What the hell are you talking about?"

He knew the answer. Of course he did. It was written across Bill's face in an accusation that could bear no denying.

"I'm not stupid, Sean. I've been watching you every day since the weekend. Every time anyone mentions the murder you go white as a sheet. And don't give me that crap about the wild-shites. I almost bought it on Monday, but now I know better. I thought that picture looked a bit like you the first time I saw it in the paper. And then I knew it was you when I saw the picture of that nasty looking bastard you've been hanging around with. I don't know what the hell you've been doing with a thug like that, but I'm telling you Sean, if he did it, if he killed that old woman, you've got to tell the cops. You have to or you're dead."

"You're mad O'Rourke. You've gone bleeding mental. I don't know what nasty looking bastard you're going on about. And I've got nothing to tell the cops."

"It's you who's mad Sean. I was watching you today when it was your turn for the interview. You looked like you were going to throw up. They'd see right through you if you went in looking like that. You'd be behind bars in no time. Your feet wouldn't touch the ground."

"So, I've been sick all week. So what? You'd have been sick too if the Head had been doing to you what he's been doing to me. You saw what he was up to today. I've had to put up with that for the last fortnight. All that stuff I told you about writing for the Brothers' magazine was a pack of lies. That bastard's been torturing me to find out who did those posters. And then he goes and blames it on me. You've got no idea what I've been going through O'Rourke."

Bill looked desperate now, pleading.

"For God's sake Sean don't you see? If you don't tell them up front, if you don't admit it before they drag it out of you, you're an accessory. That slimy shit will take you down with him. And if I don't tell them I know who did it, I'm an accessory too. I saw you with him last week. And it's his picture in the paper plain as day. And it has to be someone from Meadowlands who wasn't on the walk, the cops know that or they wouldn't be wasting time on the interviews. And when they put the finger on you, they'll come to me to find out what I know. They're bound to check on your friends, and it's not as if you've got many of them is it?"

378

"Well I've got one less now O'Rourke. And you know nothing. Nothing!"

Sean looked for something else to fling in Bill's face, but for the first time in their relationship he was at a loss for words.

"Tell them Sean! You're first up tomorrow when we start again. Go to them before they call for you. Tell them the truth. That way you stand a chance. If you don't, I'm going to have to drop you in it. Don't make me do that Sean. It's bad enough I haven't told my mam already, and she going to go bleeding nuts when she finds out."

"Your mam? Your fucking mam? What the hell are you talking about? You're worried about your fucking mam? Well why don't you just come down Cack Alley with me Billy-boy. Why don't you come and meet that nasty bastard you've been talking so big about? Why don't you come and see what he's got in store for me?"

Sean was almost screaming now, the days of lonely torment finding a vent at last. It was over! The secret was out. And the one person he might have chosen to share it with, the one person he might have trusted with the truth, was going to turn him in. Christ what an ending!

"Come on!" he yelled. "Flint'd be happy to meet you. He'd be happy to do to you what he did to Fearon. Come on, just tell him you're going to turn him in and see how far you get. Come and see what a nasty bastard he really is. Come on O'Rourke, what are you waiting for?"

Bill had nothing to say. The fear was stark naked in his face.

"Yeah, that's it Big Man. Why don't you go and see your aunt Josie instead. Like you did last time. Like you did when all this started, you fucking chicken. Go on O'Rourke, piss off! Just.........just.........piss off!"

379

And with tears of rage and frustration he turned back into the alley and sped towards his showdown with Flint.

CHAPTER 41: An End to Innocence

"Oy! Where do you think you're going then?"

The familiar snarl, the arm outstretched in front of his throat, stopped him dead.

"Don't you remember Tarzan, me and you have got business today haven't we?"

Flint grabbed Sean by the arm and dragged him off the path into the clearing behind the scrub. He didn't resist. The outburst against Bill, the realization now that it was all over, had worn him out. They were out of sight from anyone passing by, and somewhere behind his misery Sean felt again the sick fear of what was about to happen.

"Here we are then Tarzan," whispered Flint. He stepped behind Sean and wrapped an arm around his chest. Pressing his body close, he brought his mouth to Sean's ear and whispered again. "Lovely. I need you for a lovely little job." He laughed a filthy laugh.

"No!" shouted Sean. "I won't. You can't make me!" It was the frantic squeal of Kevin Purvis facing Brother Campion in the assembly hall.

Flint's fingers bit into his arm, crushing muscle against bone, until Sean shrieked in pain.

"TARZAN!" yelled Flint. "YOU'RE ANNOYING ME TARZAN! CAN'T YOU HEAR ME TARZAN! I'M TALKING TO YOU TARZAN!!!!!!" And his voice seemed to fill Duggin with a roaring accusation of murder.

"Stop it!" cried Sean. "Stop it. Don't call me that........I'm coming.......just.....just......stop it.........please! I'll do whatever you want."

He allowed himself to be thrown down and flipped onto his stomach as Flint straddled his back. He bit into the soil, filling himself with the smell and the taste of earth, steeling himself against what was coming. He could feel Flint's excitement against his buttocks and it turned him sick.

"Get your jacket off," said Flint, "I don't want you wearing that."

Sean wriggled in the grass, arms behind him, trying to free the jacket from his shoulders, feeling more and more helpless. Flint let him struggle, laughing softly, then pulled at his collar, yanking the jacket free.

"Now put this on," whispered Flint. "I fancy you in tart's gear." He laughed as he laid a black nylon stocking next to Sean's cheek......

This is beyond sick, thinks Sean. Anything is possible now. He makes spastic movements with the stocking towards his left leg, groping with his arm behind him, leg bent at the knee, foot in the air, Flint riding on his back.

"How can I get my leg in......" he pleads.

And then Flint is laughing like Sean has never heard him laugh before. He seems genuinely amused, his whole body convulsing. "Oh what a bleeding idiot," he roars. "What a frigging moron. Jesus Christ, you've got no fucking idea have you?"

382

He falls sideways off Sean's back, face to the sky, tears rolling down his cheeks as if he's having the time of his life. Sean hardly dares move, but twists his head sideways to see Flint shaking with hysterics. He catches Flint's eye, and for the first time since the day of the murder spies a glimmer of humanity.

"Not on your bleeding leg, you stupid twat. On your bleeding head. Like this!"

Flint brings another stocking out of his pocket and drags it down over his face. It smears his features. The ratty nose is spread wide. The fringe of hair is plastered in streaks of black and dirty grey against his forehead. Eyes become lidless and brutal. Lips are grotesque smudges surrounding a black hole as he laughs again. All the pointed ugliness of Flint becomes blurred into a mask that multiplies the cruelty of his face while hiding his identity. And Sean, who should be horrified by what this might mean, can only spit the soil from his mouth and breathe an enormous sigh of relief.

"Now you lie alongside of me and keep your eyes on the path. Understand TARZAN!"

Sean nods frantically. The stocking is sweaty against his face. It smells of woman. Old woman. Talcum powder and varicose veins. It smells, he thinks, of Flint's mother, and he gags against the air that carries her thighs into his mouth. He aches to rip it off and breathe the purifying stench of Duggin, but Flint has him in complete control. They lie together, shoulder to shoulder, waiting.

"Good boy," says Flint. "You play your cards right, do exactly as I tell you, and I promise you, you're in for a treat."

Sean's heart is thundering. He imagines the possibilities and recoils against every one of them. He won't do it. Whatever it is he won't do it. When Flint tells him to move he'll run, and then he'll run and run, and keep on running, out of Cack Alley, out of the

Entry, out of the cul-de-sac and out of Duggin to God knows where, but this is the end, he thinks, I can't stand any more of this. It's over now and I'm going to run.

There's a crunch on the gravel and Flint tenses. From their hiding place they see a man approach, middle-aged, lightly built, walking briskly as if late for opening time at the pub. He wears good shoes and his trousers are clean and pressed. In Duggin that means he has more money than most. Sean's heart beats so loudly he feels sure that the man must hear it. Flint lets him go by.

Why? What is he up to?

They wait.

Cack Alley is a lonely place at this time of day. Workers are still doing their shifts at the DIC, and their wives are spending the last hour before the factory buzzer in getting the kids fed and out of the way before the breadwinner comes home for his dinner. But someone will be along again eventually, and that someone is going to be shit out of luck.

"Hang on," says Flint "get ready."

This time the step is slower and heavier. Flint puts his hand on Sean's arm and grips him tight. He leans out ever so slightly from their hiding place, obstructing Sean's view. He laughs a soft, malicious laugh.

"Oooh, shall we?" he says. "What do you think Tarzan - shall we?"

The woman comes into view, and Flint's hand is on Sean's mouth before he can cry out. Just yards away, almost as if he could reach out and touch her, his grandmother treads the dirt of Cack Alley. He looks into her face, grim and set, and knows where she's going. It's over! In two minutes she'll be at Sean's door. In two minutes his mother will know that he's a thief. She'll know about the ten shillings, and the Woodbines, and that he kept silent while his brother got the hiding of his life. She'll know the person he really is.

"Only joking Tarzan. Only joking," Flint whispers. "Don't want to mess around with any old folk do we? No good at all that, eh?"

Sean struggles. He wants to run into his grandmother's arms. His last chance is slipping away with every step she takes toward his home. But Flint has one hand on his mouth and the other tight on his throat. He can only watch with bulging eyes as his grandmother moves into the distance.

"No you don't, Tarzan," Flint whispers. "You just stay where you are. You just do what Flinty tells you, or I'll do for you, and I'll do for your bleeding Granny too – understand?"

Sean nods, but there is a knot of determination twisting inside him. As soon as Flint gives him half a chance, he's off. He can't knife the bastard now that Bill O'Rourke knows their connection, but that's only one more reason to run.

Flint eases forward again as lighter footfalls sound on the path. A quiver of excitement ripples through him. "Now we're talking!" he whispers. "Oh yes Tarzan, now.... we...... .....are......talking!"

He flips over onto his side and looks back at Sean. He's grinning as he takes a broad bandage from his pocket. He wraps the ends of it around his wrists, leaving a section a foot long between his bunched fists. He turns back on his stomach, elbows digging into the earth, upright hands bound together by the band of cloth.

"This is your lucky day Tarzan," he whispers. "You just do as Flinty tells you, and in half a jiff you'll be like a pig in shit."

The smear of the stocking can't disguise the evil in Flint's expression. And there's a quality in his voice that Sean hasn't heard before. It's the calm intent of someone about to do something truly, truly terrible. This won't be a random act of violence. It won't be some barbaric reflex. This is going to be done in cold blood. Someone is about to be destroyed.

Sean raises his face from the grass and looks towards the path.

What he sees is not possible. This can't be happening......not here........not here in Cack Alley.... and for the love of God, please not now.

On this day of miracles, Paula Yates is walking straight into Flint's trap.

Chapter 42: On the Scaffold

Flint launches himself from the bushes as she moves past. He's behind her, arms arcing high above her head and then down. The bandage is pulled tight across her mouth before she can scream. He's dragging her down. Her arms claw at the air. She kicks at him as he pulls her backwards towards the bushes, where she knows, terrified, what is about to happen. She tears at the bandage, frantic. It slips between her teeth and she bites into it as it rips at the corners of her mouth. Blood stains her cheeks, and there's more blood as she reaches back and digs her nails into Flint's hands. They splinter as she struggles for her life. Her eyes are wild with panic.

"Grab her Tarzan! Grab the bitch and get her knickers off. You can have her when I'm done."

Sean is free to run now but he doesn't. Instead, he drags the stocking from his face and hurls himself at Flint.

"Bastard!" he screams as he hits him as hard as he can in the face.

"You fucking filthy bastard!" as he swings at Flint's head.

"Bastard! Bastard! Fucking Bastard!" as Flint falls to his knees, and the rock in Sean's hand, the rock he doesn't know he's holding, smashes down again and again and again.

Paula is screaming too as the blood-speckled gag slips from her mouth. Flint's arms are limp around her waist, his hands still tangled in the bandage. She kicks backwards, the heel of her shoe smashing against his ribs and face as he sinks to the ground.

"Get him off! Get him off me!" she yells, and Sean stamps on Flint's hands, pulling her away. She clutches at him as if to hide in his arms, as if he really is a match for Flint. He pushes her off, grabs her by the wrist and drags her back to the path.

"Run!" he screams. "For Christ's sake run!" And still clutching her wrist he pulls her along, out of Cack Alley, into the Entry and without thinking, acting for the first time in weeks without calculating the consequences, he drags her into his home.

Sean's mother and his gran are sitting at the table as they burst into the kitchen. His mother sees a blood-bespattered girl hysterical with fear. She throws open her arms and Paula falls screaming into the refuge.

And then it all comes out, a babbling, blubbering confession.

"Flint killed her, mum...... killed the old woman at Sandcaster. The sponsored walk...... I didn't go....... I took the money and I didn't go....... It was Flint's idea...... We went to Sandcaster and things got worse and worse....... and then he killed the old woman...... Jesus mum, I can't.....I didn't!..... Right at the end he went and killed the old woman...... it wasn't me....... I tried to stop him....... and the cigs...... it wasn't Fergus...... I had to take the cigs or Flint would tell....... tell everyone we killed her....... he didn't care...... kept calling me Tarzan...... what was I supposed to do?....... and he made me steal the money out your purse gran........ he didn't need it .... he thought it was funny...... kept tormenting me....... what was I supposed to do?....... and the old woman's dead....... I keep seeing her dead....... every night I see her dead....... he smiled at me...... the

388

old man smiled at me when I was so scared and Flint killed his wife........ killed her dead...... Christ!...... just like that he killed her dead........ and he kept calling me Tarzan....... kept making me do things........ like the cigs and the money......... and they tried to blame me at school......... just because of my dad......... just because of Duggin....... and I didn't do it......... I didn't do those posters....... and I didn't kill the old woman....... Flint........ Flint did it....... and then he wanted me to....to.....to.... with Paula...... to...... to....... the dirty........ filthy...... what was I supposed to do?........ I smashed his head in......... in Cack Alley........ I had to ....I smashed his head in with a brick......... But for Christ's sake what was I supposed to do?"

And Sean folds slowly to the floor crying his heart out.

His Gran steps over him, her face a slab.

"Look after that lass our Lizzie, and stay where you are," she says. She drags Sean to his feet. "You! You get to your room. I'll get this sorted."

And then she's gone.

In his nightmare Paula lies on the grass, her head tossing back and forth, her golden hair trailing in the dog shit as she screams. She's looking right into Sean's eyes, begging for help, her face twisted with agony and terror. He hammers at the thing on top of her, smashing it with a rock, slamming at its head again and again. But he can't stop the thing from doing it, and Paula keeps screaming and screaming and screaming........

The screaming wakes him, the pitch alternating high and low - an urgent mechanical howl. There's more than one of them, getting closer, compelling him to get up, to go to the window of his bedroom. It's early evening. His gran hasn't wasted any time.

The wailing intensifies, and through the fog of his nightmare he recognizes the sound just as two Panda cars screech around the corner into the cul-de-sac, their lights flashing. They skid to a halt in front of Flint's house and four policemen launch themselves from the cars, clearing the fence at a run and massing at the door. One cop pounds on the door with his truncheon, and the others stand ready at his back, truncheons drawn.

In the cul-de-sac, faces are pressed to windows, and doors open. Mrs. Farrell walks to her gate and plumps lardy arms on top of it, a brazen spectator. Others follow her lead. His gran is there too, out in the street at the foot of the lamp post. Sean can hear the neighbours shouting across at each other.

-What's going on then?
-Jimmy Flint I reckon.
-Bugger's been up to summat again.
-Aye, and summat big by the look of it.
-One little monkey that sod.
-Thieving?
-Likely. Thieving and worse I shouldn't wonder.
-Well I hope they lock him up.
-Aye, serve the bugger right.

Elsie Flint opens the door, gimlet face pinched in fury. Like the neighbours, she knows there can be only one reason for this. The police push her aside, ignoring the stream of filth from her mouth as they shoulder their way into the house. Sean hears screaming, the roar of voices and the splintering of wood. Jimmy Flint's bedroom window is thrown wide and he's out onto the porch above the open door. He crouches, leans forward to check there's no cop standing beneath, and then he's down.

"There he is!" yell the neighbours as he jumps the fence and sprints towards the head of the cul-de-sac. He's battered and bloody, but has lost none of his speed.

A third Panda car rounds the corner and slews sideways to a halt, blocking the road. Two cops are out in seconds. They move slowly towards Flint, arms wide. He turns and races back towards the Entry, but the cops are out of his house now, two of them blocking the path to Cack Alley, the other two mirroring those up the street, closing in on Flint from behind, the four of them closing a square with Flint in the middle.

Flint shuffles from side to side as they converge, teeth bared like a cornered animal. He lets them get close, and as arms reach to grab him he flings himself to the ground and rolls. The cops grasp at the air, and Flint is back on his feet, ready to run. But he's rolled the wrong way, putting himself between Cack Alley and the four cops that spring back from their bungling and stand shoulder to shoulder, blocking his escape.

Flint glances at the terraces on each side of him, and at the faces of his neighbours. Stone. The houses and the faces are stone.

Behind him, the two cops at the entrance to Cack Alley stand their ground. Flint backs up towards the Alley as the other cops advance. He moves left and right, darting forward now and then, trying to tempt one of the cops to open a gap. But they've got the measure of him now. He's a wily little bastard, and they won't make that mistake again. They advance slowly, matching pace with Flint's retreat.

Flint turns a last hopeless glance towards Cack Alley, and Sean, perched just above, sees his face for the first time. It's purple with bruises and smeared with blood. His mouth is open and the jaw hangs crookedly. He dribbles pink spit. His eyes are wild with pain and fear and a look of wretched desolation that goes straight to Sean's heart. For an instant he understands the whole terrible tragedy of Jimmy Flint.

But then the look is gone as Flint evades the grasping arms of Sean's gran and leaps for the lamp post, dragging himself upwards arm over arm to the cross bar. The six cops gather below, one speaking urgently into a crackling two-way radio. The Chief shouts up at Flint, tells him to come down, to give himself up. Tells him it's hopeless. The neighbours leave their gateposts and spill out onto the road, necks craned to the cross bar where Flint sits. At his bedroom window Sean is closest to him. He can look straight into his shattered face as he perches with the crossbar below his knees, hands holding onto the slender metal rod that supports the streetlight.

The cops are trying to move the crowd back, away from the base of the lamp post, but no one is budging. The neighbours want to know what it's all about. What he's done. What's going to happen next. A real drama is playing out that beats anything on Coronation Street, and they're not going to miss a second of it. It's only when Vinny Flint pushes his way through them that the jabbering falls silent.

The police give him space and he stands there looking up, squat and solid. Even now there's the stump of cigar in his mouth. He takes a last drag and crushes it under his heel. There's not a line of emotion on his face. His mouth, his eyes, everything about him, is set. Thick fingers move to the leather belt around his waist, thumbs resting on the heavy square buckle.

"Down! Now!" he shouts.

Flint doesn't move. His eyes are a million miles away.

"You! Down! Now!" shouts his father.

There's a gasp from the gawkers as Flint falls backwards, hands and knees swiveling on the crossbar as he turns upside down.

"Jesus, Mary and Joseph," whispers Mrs. Farely as Flint's shirt falls up under his arms. His naked back is a palette of multi-coloured stripes. Sick rainbows end in a square welter of purple, black and red. His ribs and belly are pock-marked with sores. Some are new and suppurating, others are scabbed over. A circle of them ring his navel like a decoration. The sores are round, an inch across.

The Chief moves forward towards Flint's father, but a thick forearm holds him back.

"I'll deal with this," says Vinny Flint. "You just stay out of it. I'll get the bastard down."

The Chief doesn't know what to do. He has no other plan until the Fire Brigade shows up with the ladder. Maybe it's best to let the father try. Maybe he really can get his son to come down. And when he does he'll make damned sure that Vinny Flint gets nowhere near him. Not now or ever again. And he vows that he'll be having a long session with Vinny Flint, personally and in private. He'll show Vinny Flint what a bloody good hiding from a grown man really feels like.

"DOWN!" yells Flint's father. "DOWN! NOW!!"

Flint hangs, just feet from Sean's bedroom window, and Sean yearns to reach out and drag him in to safety. It's over. Everything is over. All that's left is hopeless despair. Despair and a terrible dread as Sean realises that there is no reason in the world why Flint would give himself up.

It's as if Flint hears his thoughts. He looks directly into Sean's face. The twisted jaw moves in what might be an attempt at a smile. Is he happy it's over, or is this one final act of malice?

Flint's hands slip from the crossbar, and he lets himself fall.

Sean's gran rushes forward with her arms out as Flint plunges head first towards the pavement. She collides with Flint's father as he leaps backwards out of the way. Sean doesn't see the impact. He throws himself to the bedroom floor. But he can't escape. He's there on the pavement as Flint bursts. He's there and he feels it – a body spilling brains and blood, gristle and bone, life and spirit.

Sean had prayed for this to happen. Prayed that Flint be destroyed in the same way he'd killed the old woman. An eye for an eye. Well, it seems that God had been listening after all, and in His wisdom had granted Sean a ringside seat.

Sean retches until he's empty of everything and then collapses into the pool of his vomit.

Chapter 44: Epilogue

Seven days later. Seven days and the excitement hadn't dimmed in the slightest.

Gladys had written a letter of resignation and the Head had refused it. The Head wanted him fired... booted out... humiliated. He wanted to ensure that Gladys would never work as a teacher again.

The Board of Governors had met the day after Gladys had made his devastating confession, and the Head had demanded he be dismissed. The Governors questioned, probed and considered consequences. At all costs the school must avoid a scandal, and this whole affair stunk of just that. Imagine it – a bright boy from a good family suffers a nervous breakdown and denounces the deputy head as a rapist. A junior teacher, an Old Boy no less, exhorts the students to open rebellion. It was the type of thing The Sun and The News of the World would smear across their headlines like faeces. It would drag the school, the Brothers, and the Catholic Church through so much dirt they'd never appear clean again.

The Governors acted swiftly. Some had influence with the media, and there were a few Old Boys scattered among the higher echelons of the press. They would keep the lid on the story. An envoy was sent to the Purvis family's Parish Priest who visited the

Purvises immediately to provide spiritual succour and guidance. His counsel was clear and succinct – keep it quiet. The Purvises, by nature a modest and retiring family, wanted no word of their son's disgrace to travel beyond the confines of their household. They'd known for some time that Kevin was queer, and had burned with the shame of it. They were grateful that the school would not further expose his perversion. Kevin's time at Meadowlands was over. They'd worry about where to send him next after the psychiatrists at Rainhill Hospital had finished with him.

The Head had to leave. Both him and his deviant deputy. The Governors were resolute about that. It was impossible that either Brother could function in the environment created by Glenn Hardy's tirade. The day after the Governors met, the Head was transferred to a swanky new school in the Home Counties – just the place where his views and values would meet the least opposition. Brother Campion found himself on a plane to Boston Massachusetts to take up a vacant Headship in a sixth form college. There, he'd either temper his inclinations or adapt them. For both Brothers the change amounted to promotion. They left willingly without fuss, and, in the case of Old Campy, with a great deal of relief.

And Gladys Hardy was given the boot. No ifs, ands or buts about that. His teaching career, just a few months old, was over. Yet he seemed oddly content as he gathered his belongings from the Staff Common Room. He had been away for the week, and his sudden reappearance brought the conversational hum to an immediate silence. He looked around him and smiled. Horse-Face Logan and Old Stooley flushed with embarrassment and began to mark homework. Billy Gruntle stared with open hatred and began a self-righteous "What the hell do you think you're doing here....." speech, but Gladys pre-empted him.

"No need to get up Billy," he said with the same easy smile. "Just come to clear out my stuff. I wouldn't want you getting into my poster materials. You never know where it might lead you."

Billy, whose real name was Randolph, looked on the verge of a blue fit, which made Gladys smile even more.

"Best sit down until I've finished Billy," continued Gladys. "Take the weight off your feet or you might do yourself a mischief."

Only Ben Gibbs looked on with any expression of regret. Gladys had been a good student at Meadowlands and had returned as an excellent teacher. His loss was a terrible, stupid waste.

"Goodbye then," sang out Gladys to no one in particular as he headed for the door. "You lot be good......and keep your hands off those kids."

And then he was gone before Gruntle could force words through the spit that choked him.

"And good riddance!" shrilled Brother Jerome as the door shut. The cowardice fell flat against the airy impudence of Gladys's remarks, but it catalyzed a few other venomous outbursts.

Ben couldn't stand it. The whole thing was making him deeply sad. He left the Common Room in search of fresh air, and came across Gladys as he stood by the car park with his bags at his feet. Alone, and thinking himself unobserved, Gladys had lost his buoyancy and looked on the verge of tears.

Ben struck a match and lit a cigarette to announce his presence. Gladys didn't turn, so Ben said, "Do you need a lift anywhere Glenn? I'd be glad to drive you."

Ben thought Gladys was growing to cry, but he marshaled himself, smiled the impish Gladys smile and said, "No thanks Mr. Gibbs, Shirley will be here in the MG soon. I reckon I can cram all my stuff in that. I'd rather be leaving on the back of the Norton – roaring away into the sunset - but I have burdens to carry."

"Yes, we all have those," said Ben, and the two men stood in awkward silence, Ben drawing on his cigarette, Gladys staring towards the school gates.

"Terrible thing about McCaffery, don't you think?" said Ben. He had decided to see Gladys off, and be damned to what his colleagues might think, but he needed something to fill the void of waiting. Gladys looked relieved and grateful.

"Yes, it seems he's been put through the wringer over the past few weeks. Imagine living with all that bottled up inside you. I'm surprised he didn't end up in Rainhill with Purvis."

"Still time for that unfortunately," said Ben. "The effects of such things may not manifest themselves immediately. He may yet suffer for it years from now."

"Well at least he wasn't charged as an accessory. And it shouldn't affect his academic career."

"No, he comes out of it more a hero than anything else. Saved a young girl from a vicious rape and ended the monstrous activities of that other poor boy."

"Poor boy! Poor bloody savage you mean."

"Yes, a savage, but he wasn't born that way, was he? Savage children are the products of a savage environment? And I don't believe in Original Sin, no matter what the church may say about it. You know the father is being charged with assault? Apparently the boy's injuries were sustained over a considerable period."

"Is he expected to recover?"

"You know as much about that as I do. Massive head injuries and a broken back. If he does make any type of recovery he'll likely face murder charges in adult court and could spend the rest of his life in prison. The public appetite for vengeance will see to that."

"But McCaffery is definitely in the clear?"

"It would seem so. Apparently the police tried to take him into custody, but they were thwarted by McCaffery's grandmother. By all accounts she's some hybrid of Boadicea and a bulldog."

"And he will be back at Meadowlands?"

"Perhaps. I hope so. He's a bright boy, and now that Brother Loredano has gone he has less to fear from those whose job it is to support him. Brother Lundy is a good man, and as interim Head he'll likely smooth the way. Of course McCaffery will face major difficulties from the likes of Mr. Gruntle. Unfortunately, this whole incident has rid us of only two of our worst influences....... And, I have to say, it has cost us one really fine teacher we can ill afford to lose."

Gladys blushed and said nothing. Ben took an angry drag at his cigarette, threw the stub to the ground and crushed it under his shoe with uncharacteristic violence. He stood there in silence for a few seconds as if struggling with indecision, then almost shouted. "Why the hell did you do it man? You were getting along so well here, and were so good for the boys. Why would you throw it all away with such a stupid bloody prank? It makes no sense."

Gladys continued to stare into the distance. The brief pleasure in Ben's praise had disappeared. Instead, he looked offended, then disappointed, and there played on his face a reflection of Ben's previous indecision before he responded.

"You don't really believe I produced those posters do you?"

Ben was lighting another cigarette. It almost dropped from his lips.

"What? You mean that you didn't.......Then who the hell?...... Not McCaffery after all?...... It couldn't be....... And why.......?"

"No not McCaffery. And not Purvis either, though I'm hardy surprised he was driven to seek his own expulsion. Remember that I was a pupil here too. I know only too well how hard it is to be homosexual in a school like this – and to have the likes of Brother Campion groping in your underpants."

Ben looked as if he were seeing Gladys for the first time. "Homosexual.....you? I know the boys make fun, but....... but what about Shirley?

"Shirley? The Dyke on the Bike? Oh, she's a great sport is Shirley. She lays it on a bit thick, but I can just imagine the commotion if my real partner had been taking me home. Roger would have gone down a storm. But Shirley's always ready to provide cover for a fellow gay. Did you know that's what they call us these days - Gays? Ironic isn't it, when most of the world tries to remove all the gaiety from our lives? I've seen Purvis in so much misery I've almost wept for him. So many times I've wanted to help him out, but I always feared he might misinterpret my motives, especially after his experiences with Campion. So I failed him. I couldn't fail the boy who made the posters."

"You know who is responsible then?"

"Oh yes. I've known for some time. Right from the start really. The Abortion Bill poster was so typical of him, though he tried to hide the style. Typically brilliant. There are very few boys at this school capable of that level of draughtmanship, and only one I know with the imagination. The lad has a dazzling career in front of him provided it isn't nipped in the bud by an expulsion. Like most of the rougher kids he has nowhere else to go if that happens. Nowhere except the factory, that is. I couldn't let that happen. So I detained him one day after class and told him I knew that he was responsible for the posters. I also told him they were juvenile, offensive, brilliant - and fatal to the only chance he might ever have of nurturing his talent at a decent University. I told him to stop the madness at once, and on no account to own up, no matter what the Head might threaten. You and I know the Head wanted to sacrifice McCaffery, but I wasn't going to let that happen either. The only option was to take the blame myself. After all, who would not believe me if I owned up? Poor Purvis's was a surprise, but it didn't really alter things. And I thought, what the hell, why not rub their noses in it at the same time? I've often wanted to do that as both pupil and teacher, and I might as well be hung for a sheep as a lamb. Seeing their faces almost made it worthwhile."

Ben was silent, the unlit cigarette dangling from his fingers. He couldn't find the words to express himself.

"Good, here's Shirley," Gladys continued as the MG roared into the car park. "Daft really wasn't it Mr. Gibbs, me coming back to Meadowlands when I hated it so much as a pupil? I really didn't know what I expected to achieve."

Gladys picked up his bags and moved towards the waiting car. "Easy come, easy go, I suppose. Well, best of luck Mr. Gibbs, *nil satis carborundum* and all that."

Ben seemed to snap out of a daydream. "Wait, Glenn!" he called.

In the staff common room, Gruntle and the Stomachs had been drawn to the window by the sound of the MG. Gruntle was looking with disgust at bra-less, mini-skirted Shirley who he wanted to shag so very, very badly, and at Gladys who stooped over the open-top sports car to kiss her full on those full pneumatic lips.

401

"Well, let's hope that's the last we see of him.......and his bloody tart," he spat.

"A disgusting display," agreed Brother Jerome. "I hope none of the boys are witnessing that."

Some hope! Every boy with a window seat had called every other boy to get a good gander at Shirley's magnificent tits. The classrooms resounded with expressions of sexual longing. But there were sighs of regret too as they watched Gladys place his bags in the MG.

In the staff room Gruntle was about to turn away when a movement outside caught his eye. "Wait a minute," he snarled, "what's that traitor Gibbs doing? You don't think he's another one of those bloody fairies do you?"

Chuck Bones looked on with a sense of shame as Ben embraced Gladys before waving him farewell. The courage of his display imparted a little of itself to the young gym teacher.

"It would seem to me, Gruntle," said Chuck, making it absolutely clear at whom his disgust was directed, "that Mr.Gibbs is shaking Mr. Hardy's hand."

THE END

Acknowledgements

Thanks to all the friends who read various drafts of the manuscript and were friends enough to say unfriendly things: Donnie Baergen, Mary-Anne Kuzma and Maciej Kuzma. Thanks to the late Homer Hogan, a superb story-teller, who encouraged me to write and keep writing, and to his wife Dorothy and son Dan for sharing his enthusiasm. Special thanks to my brother George and Stevie Hale who were the most critical and, therefore, the most useful of reviewers. Special thanks also to the maddeningly creative Ken Foster for a great cover design.

The publication of this book is due in large part to the efforts of my wife, Monika, who urged me continually to brush the dust off the manuscript and just get it done. *Dzienkuje bardzo moja perelko: bardzo cie kocham.*

This book is dedicated to Ned who would have lamented both my grammar and ingratitude, and was everything a teacher should be.

About the Author

Stephen Hunt was born in Prescot in the UK where, as a ten year old in 1966, he sold his first collection of short stories to a school friend for two shillings. That was the last time he made good money as a writer. He has been short-listed three times for the Canadian Broadcasting Corporation's annual literary awards (travel, short story and creative non-fiction categories), three times for the Writers Union of Canada short prose contest, and was a winner in the 2015 Writers' Digest annual short story competition. *Sean McCaffery You Are Totally Screwed* is his first novel.

Steve is an adjunct professor at the Queen's University Department of Biology and CEO of Qubit Systems Inc., a biotech company that designs and manufactures equipment for teaching and research. He has published numerous scientific articles and is an author on six patents. When not writing, Steve enjoys playing squash (badly), hiking, canoeing, skiing, scuba diving, mountain biking and singing baritone with the Kingston Choral Society and Kingston Capital Men's Chorus. He lives in a log cabin in the countryside north of Kingston with his wife, two teenaged kids, great dog, horrible cat and ruinous horse.